The Trials Of Max Q

By Derek Ciccone

ISBN 978-0-9854287-0-9

Interior Layout by Cheryl Perez, www.yourepublished.com

This book is a work of fiction. The names, characters, places, and incidents are products of the author's imagination or have been used fictitiously and are not to be constructed as real. Any resemblance to persons, , living or dead, actual events, locales or organizations is entirely coincidental.

Chapter 1

Perfection is like the mechanical rabbit used to lure greyhounds at the dog races—tantalizing, but unobtainable. It seduces you into believing you can catch it, only to ruthlessly dart away at the last moment. As I peer into the perfect blue sky of a late July day in Saratoga, New York, it's a reminder of how I know this all too well.

The crowd is bubbling with anticipation for the next mad-dash of thoroughbreds at Saratoga Racecourse. I strain my neck to look for my friends, Mac and Ashley Cirillo. They left to place wagers on the upcoming race, what seems like twenty minutes ago, even if my watch tells me it has only been five. But having known Mac since college, I know the only sure bet is that he stopped off to purchase a beer and a plate of nachos.

No sign of Mac and Ashley, just another postcard-esque view of the Victorian grandstand. It's another packed house at America's oldest racetrack.

I sit at a picnic table in the general admission paddock area. I'm not far from where my family, the Lawsons, normally sit with the flamboyantly rich in the luxurious box seats at the finish line. The same seats the Lawsons of yesteryear once sat in, arm-in-arm with the Vanderbilts and Rockefellers. But from a social-class point of view, my seat is a galaxy away. I can't avoid the obvious symbolic separation from my old life.

The Lawson legal dynasty began when Thomas Lawson arrived in Boston Harbor from the mother country in the first half of the eighteenth century, eventually settling in what is now Greenwich, Connecticut. He set up a small law office on nearby Manhattan Island, and after years of chasing the horse and buggy version of ambulances, he grew to be one of the most powerful lawyers in the New World. He was so taken with the law (more precisely, its lucrative rewards) that he decided that all future Lawsons would follow his lead, coining the phrase "Lawsons are lawyers." To ensure his mission statement would be carried out, he linked each descendant's inheritance to their joining the family business.

Over the years, the mechanical rabbit the Lawsons chased became narrowly defined. The acquisition of unimaginable wealth was part of it, of course, but my family views true perfection as being *perceived* as perfect by those around them. Or what I like to refer to as the meaningless quest for the approval of others.

The thoroughbreds are led into the starting gate. One feisty colt is having second thoughts and puts up a fight, but eventually gives in—the rebel always seems to lose in the end. As bugles signal the race is about to commence, I spot the oversized white hat of Ashley Cirillo. She strolls through the thick crowd with her usual grin and the grace of an old-time movie star, the haughty Saratoga background fitting her like a Vera Wang dress.

Walking alongside Ashley is her husband, Mac. He is looking frat-boy scruffy, as if he didn't get the memo that states you aren't supposed to look and act the same at thirty-two as when you were twenty-two. They are an odder couple than Felix and Oscar ever were, their only noticeable commonality is the "in-love" smile they wear for each other.

"I love the smell of trust funds in the afternoon," Mac jokes upon reaching me, dramatically sniffing the air for effect.

I smile and grab one of his cheese-glazed nachos.

"So who'd we bet on?" I ask Ashley. I always follow her lead on such matters. Her success often exceeds that of the so-called experts, even though her technique of picking the horse with the "prettiest tail" has yet to become an accepted technique of professional handicappers.

"Mac bet on a three-to-one shot called Old Wino, not exactly going out on a limb," she begins.

"I couldn't resist, Jack, it reminded me of your grandmother," Mac states. He looks proud that he extracted a grin from me. Lately it's been a challenge.

"The combination of my family and your lifelong losing streak doesn't exactly scream winner," I reply, and then get to the all-important bet. "Which one has the pretty tail, Ash?"

"Actually, I'm going away from the plan this time, Jack."

Before I can question this dramatic change of course, Mac explains, "It's destiny, Jack—as big of a lock as you in the courtroom. The horse's name is Clotheshorse!"

For years Mac has playfully referred to Ashley as "the Clotheshorse" in response to her expensive addiction to shopping.

"It's fifty-to-one, Jack, but I don't know how it can lose," Ashley adds with enthusiasm.

We walk to an outside grill that's situated right next to the track, and is VIP only. I use my Lawson influence to get us in, so we can stand by the rail. It is one thing to watch the race, it's another to feel the horses thunder past you.

A ringing of bells halts our conversation. The gates burst open and the rumbling of hooves crackles through the thick summer air. Those in the grandstand rise out of their seats. "And they're off!" shouts the track announcer.

It feels like the earth is shaking as the horses bend around the first turn. "Old Wino shoots to the lead!" belts out the announcer.

Ashley excitedly urges Clotheshorse on, "C'mon baby, mama needs a new pair of shoes!"

"Mama has a whole closet of shoes she has never worn," Mac reminds her. He is trying to remain confident, but I can tell he's already sensing another bad ending.

I maintain my cool demeanor that has always served me well in the courtroom, but sometimes gives the perception of aloofness outside of it.

At the halfway point, Clotheshorse, the fifty-to-one shot, has done the unthinkable by overtaking Old Wino. Mac nervously chain-eats his nachos as we watch the horses head down the home stretch, while Ashley cheers on with a knowing grin.

It's Clotheshorse by a nose ... Old Wino makes his move on the rail ... Old Wino moves to the lead ... Here comes Clotheshorse ... It's too close to call...

That's when a seven-to-two shot named Bossy Cow makes a move on the outside. She is a dark brown filly with a white stripe down her nose. She passes with ease and cruises to a three-length victory.

Old Wino takes second, giving Mac slight bragging rights over Ashley, who watches Clotheshorse drop to fifth and out of the money. She curses herself for abandoning her system.

"Typical woman," Mac impugns the victorious filly. "Just when you're feeling good about things, she sneaks up behind you and ruins all the fun."

The comment leads to a group laugh—a nice moment between friends. One that's been lacking during the recent stage of my life, which officially is being called a "sabbatical," while the whisperers behind my back tend to prefer the term "mental breakdown."

I currently live with Mac and Ashley at their house on Otsego Lake in Cooperstown, a small village ninety miles northeast of Saratoga, and known for being the home of the Baseball Hall of Fame. That is where Mac works as the Assistant Director of Marketing, a step on the path to his dream job, which is to be the curator of the museum.

Ashley followed Mac to Cooperstown after graduation, and the city girl became so bored in rural upstate New York that she began doing errands for everyone she met to keep busy. This attempt at curing boredom developed into a profitable business she aptly named Ashley's Errands, making her the true breadwinner of the family. Mac often jokes that the errand business is just an excuse for Ashley to go on shopping sprees, even if they are for others.

We all met at Brown University, thirteen years ago. Mac chose Brown because the Ivy League education allowed him to pursue his dreams and escape the blue-collar town of Poughkeepsie. Ashley chose it because

Providence was near her Boston home and she considered it a "hip college town." I went to Brown because my aristocratic mother patterned her life after Jackie Kennedy, and if Brown was good enough for her son John Jr., then it certainly was good enough for Jack Lawson.

Having grown up at the corner of rich and delusional, I rarely interacted with real people. This changed when I met my college roommate, a sophomore named Mac Cirillo. He was nothing like anyone I had ever met before. He was funny, comfortable in his own skin, and wasn't overly concerned what others thought of him. He is known for being a little "out there" with his offbeat theories that he calls Macademia—combining his name with academia, because in his words, he is educating us. I more associate the term with macadamia nuts, which I think might be a better description of Mac. His belief that man never landed on the moon is the one he is most passionate about.

The big favor I did for Mac was introducing him to Ashley Armstrong, a gorgeous leggy blonde with grace, style, and pedigree. In other words, way too good for him. Ashley will be the first to admit she is girly, but if you call her high maintenance you'll have a fight on your hands. She can fish and talk trash with the boys as effortlessly as she can pick out a pair of designer shoes. Her father owns a private airline company called Armstrong Airlines, and Ashley is an accomplished pilot herself, giving lessons on the weekend. But most importantly, she has always been my biggest source of support—a support I've needed the last couple of years.

I consider them to be my real family. So when I took a leave of absence from my family's firm, Lawson Baird & Gentry, I ultimately migrated here. It's where Mac returned the favor by reintroducing me to a great love of mine—the law. It's the one great legacy of my family's incessant shove in that direction. But I don't love the "Lawson Law" of money, schmoozing wealthy clients, and making partner. The law I fell for was the one that represents justice, and speaks for those who can't speak for themselves. Which is what led me to stay in Cooperstown, and take the job as Chief Assistant District Attorney for Otsego County.

Chapter 2

Mac peers over his guide as if he's proofreading it. He isn't very good at betting, but he sure gives it his best effort. He scans the horses in the final race and a sly grin appears on his face.

I know the source of his amusement and don't allow him to milk the moment. "I know—my grandmother's horse is running in this one."

The name of the horse is Attorney@Lawson. It has received much buzz this first weekend of racing in Saratoga, and is an early favorite to take the prestigious Travers Stakes in August.

"What happened, Jack—your invitation get lost in the mail?" Mac asks.

"I wasn't so lucky. I was supposed to attend the traditional breakfast this morning."

"Why didn't you go, Jack? You haven't seen them in so long and the breakfast is fabulous," Ashley chimes in with her typical concern for me

"My grandmother did mention it's a time-honored tradition."

"Then why not go?" Ashley pushes.

"I told her I was an even more time-honored tradition to spend it with you guys."

Ashley flashes me an annoyed look. "I'm not one of those juries that your BS works on, Jack."

"I've just started getting things back together and I wasn't ready to face them," I come clean.

Ashley appears satisfied with my answer, and perhaps a little surprised by my candidness. I'm usually quite skilled at being evasive and mysterious when I want to be. And if that doesn't work, my courtroom oratory skills—or

BS-ing, as Ashley calls it—often come in handy.

Ashley takes my answer as an excuse to segue to the other part of my life that she harbors great concern for—my love life. Or more specifically, my lack of one.

"So how did your date with Jessica go?" she asks. I can tell she's wanted to ask me about it all day.

When I don't respond, Ashley slumps with disappointment. "What happened, Jack?"

The Jessica in question is an Assistant District Attorney in my office named Jessica Shepherdson, or Shep, as she goes by. Ashley has been backroom campaigning for her to be my running mate since last March. I think she might have an ulterior motive, since Jessica shares her passion for clothes and shopping. Although, Ashley's love stems from her pure joy of the sport, while Jessica's motive is more about getting the right outfit to move up the ladder of success.

"I'm just not ready to date right now," I proclaim.

"Jack Lawson, I can't believe you—you two are so right for each other! You would be like the super-cute lawyer couple," Ashley gives me one of her pep talks, but skillfully avoids the topic of Reyanne, which hangs over the moment.

Super-cute might be a stretch, but you can't imagine how much better a trust fund makes you look to people. I have light brown, wavy hair and a six-foot, slim body that's the ideal build for wearing a suit. On the downside, my skin is on the pale and pasty side, and the body, while thin, isn't exactly beach-toned.

"C'mon, Jack. She even went fishing with you. No girl does that unless she's totally into a guy," Ashley pleads.

Fishing on Otsego Lake in my Adirondack guide boat is a hobby I've picked up that's helped me gain some peace. And I admit that Shep going out of her comfort zone to join me was an impressive gesture. But I have to put an end to this.

"Thanks, guys—I know what you are trying to do, but we already had the talk."

"The talk?" Ashley inquires, looking confused.

"You know—I like you, but we work together and the timing is off, so it's best to maintain the status quo."

Mac shows me some support, sort of, "Besides, Ash, our friend Jack has now become a local celebrity by prosecuting that Andy Kass wacko. The laws of the universe state that once you become famous you must drop the current girlfriend and upgrade to models. So what would be the point in Jack dating someone he would have to dump anyway?"

Another dose of Macademia, followed by a sigh from Ashley. It's business as usual. Andy Kass is a local high school student who got a little perturbed at being picked on by his classmates. So the day after his graduation, Andy decided to combine his explosives fetish with a little bomb-making instruction from the Internet, to drop Otsego High School to the ground. Nobody was present at the time, so there were no casualties. But it has become a hot-button issue in Cooperstown, which normally only gets excited when the topic is whether or not Pete Rose should be included in the Baseball Hall of Fame. The debate has divided the Cirillo household.

"He's not a wacko," Ashley states passionately. "He was making a statement about an institution that mistreated him for years. Was it wrong? Of course. But he shouldn't go to jail. It wasn't Columbine—he didn't try to hurt anyone."

Mac rolls his eyes. "C'mon, Ash, the fact that nobody got hurt was sheer luck. I think it's a blessing we got this guy at a young age before that anger escalated. Sweep it under the rug and sooner or later he is swinging on the monkey bars at al-Qaeda camp."

"What do you think, Jack?" Ashley asks me, but she knows I can't talk about the case. I wouldn't get in the middle of their border-skirmish, anyway.

"What I think is that we're running out of time to place our bets on the last race," I change the subject, then force the issue by walking toward the nearest betting booth.

"Who you betting on, Jack?" Mac asks as he follows.

"Not Attorney@Lawson, even if he has the prettiest tail."

Chapter 3

As we make our way through the crowd, a low rumble begins in the grandstand area. It soon grows to a buzzing roar.

All eyes go to the striking woman who is strutting down the incline of stadium seats, toward an expensive box seat. The attention is not new for Laney Bang.

Her thick mane of blonde hair dances gracefully in the summer breeze and despite the July heat, she wears a long, black leather trench coat. She smiles, both at her admirers and those who think she is the devil, without playing favorites.

Upon arriving at her seat, she engages in a long production of unbuckling the strap around her waist and removing the coat. She reveals a Catholic schoolgirl outfit with micro plaid-skirt that leaves little to the imagination, along with black, knee-high boots. It leaves the crowd speechless.

"Now that's an entrance," Mac breaks the silence, still trying to catch his breath.

"Way to keep it classy, Saratoga," Ashley quips. "I guess I missed the sale on school uniforms at the whore store."

When Mac wisely doesn't respond, she asks, "What is she doing here anyway?"

"She's a horse owner—has one racing today that's Attorney@Lawson's main competition in this race," I intervene.

"The name of her horse is La Levrette," Mac adds with a sophomoric grin.

Since we all took French at Brown, I know that the name translates to "The Greyhound." I'm hoping the reason for the name was that the horse runs like a greyhound. But I know that la levrette is also the French term for a certain sexual position.

"She's disgusting!" Ashley confirms my fears.

At one time, not long ago, the idea of an adult-film actress entering the mainstream seemed farfetched. But Laney Bang has thrown out the rulebook. Her memoir is currently number one on the *New York Times* bestseller list and her cable talk show is challenging the giants of late night. Her films, the kind that once were hidden in brown paper bags, are often shown to large audiences in mainstream theaters. Rumors of movie roles with her clothes actually on, and of running for political office, no longer seem outside the realm of possibility.

The blonde sex symbol has always been a staple of Americana, as much as baseball and apple pie, but none of her predecessors reached the heights of controversy, or provoked national debate like Laney Bang. To some, she's the ultimate male fantasy and the darling of Madison Avenue, while others see her as a weapon of the devil, which needs to be disarmed. All anyone can agree on is that they've never seen anything like her before.

The horses are led to the starting gate. Laney Bang takes her seat and the crowd's attention reluctantly returns to the track.

Ashley remains focused on her, snipping, "And where do they come up with those names? Laney Bang sounds like some deadly plague that was rampant in the seventeenth century."

Realizing a wrong answer could have him sleeping on the couch, Mac retreats to his comfort zone, which is his vast baseball knowledge. "I think you get your porn name from taking a derivative of your first name, while the surname is based on occupation. You see the same thing in baseball. For example, Don Mattingly was always known as Donnie Baseball, and Ted Williams was Teddy Ballgame. Her real name is probably Elaine, so she went with Laney Bang."

Ashley gives him a "do I know you?" look.

For reasons only known to him, Mac thinks he's on a roll and continues, "That's not the only way. As we all learned from the classic film *Boogie Nights*, the traditional naming process is to take the name of your first pet and combine it with the name of the road you grew up on. I lived on Broad Street and our dog was named Rex, so I would be called Rex Broad."

This time Ashley smiles and plays along. "I would be Missy Carriage! How about you, Jack?"

I reflect on this for a moment, and as it usually does when the subject is my childhood, the memory turns negative. "We were never allowed to have a pet."

"Your sister is kind of a pit-bull, so maybe she could be considered a pet," Ashley offers.

"Then I would be Kerri Silvermine," I say. I shake my head, not believing I am having this conversation. "If we are going to place bets we better hurry."

"I'm going back to the original plan," Ashley states.

"I'll bet if La Levrette is anything like its owner, it will have a pretty tail," Mac adds with a grin.

Glare from Ashley.

Chapter 4

We walk briskly across the grounds, passing picnic areas and concession stands that entice with the aroma of grilling hamburgers.

A man cuts off our path. He is wearing formal dress and a large top hat that looks like something out of Lincoln's closet. He stands out as odd, since the majority of high society in their suits and fancy hats are located in the clubhouse, or the numerous luxury boxes added in recent years. This area is where the T-shirt picnic crowd hangs out.

“Mr. Jack Lawson?” he addresses me.

“Who would like to know?”

“Mr. Lawson, your company has been requested in a private suite to view the next race. And you’re welcome to bring your friends as guests.”

“And who is this request coming from?”

“Ms. Ethel Lawson, the owner of Attorney@Lawson.”

As I formulate my escape strategy, Ashley decides for me. “We’d love to! C’mon Jack, it’ll be fun.”

“That area is formal dress,” Mac cautions. “While my lovely wife is dressed to thrill, Mr. Lawson and I are dressed to grill, as in burgers.”

I glance at my colorful Hawaiian shirt, which hangs loosely off my lanky frame, and then look down to the shorts and sandals that emphasize the whiteness of my legs. For better or worse, I’ve come a long way from my prep school youth in which I never even owned a pair of jeans.

Mac isn’t auditioning for *GQ* magazine either. He wears what he always wears when he’s not in the office. He is an avid sports memorabilia collector and the latest rage is overpriced sports jerseys of historical athletes. Today’s model is a Mickey Mantle, circa 1956.

“Exceptions are made at Ms. Lawson’s discretion. But if you would be more comfortable, I could loan you a jacket and tie.”

We decline the formal wear, but agree to follow. We move into the clubhouse, and I feel like we’ve traveled back in time to an era of high society and glamour.

The clubhouse has been given a few uplifts over the years, but for the most part it has maintained its traditional look, and probably doesn’t look much different than it did on August 3, 1863 when Lizzie W became the first thoroughbred to cross the finish line.

We pass the Club Terrace on the second floor, before being whisked through the formal Turf Terrace dining room. We enter a forty-foot luxury suite. It has all the modern amenities—stadium seating, private bathrooms, an open-air observation deck, and a large spread of catered food.

The sight of yours truly stops all conversation, and I don't think it's because of my outfit. I can feel the stares. I recognize them—they are my family.

A tuxedo-clad waiter provides me with a copy of the track magazine called *Post Parade*. A young female waitress, also in a tuxedo, offers us flutes of champagne. I accept, take a swig like I'm doing a shot of gin, and then hesitantly venture into the hornet's nest.

My cantankerous grandmother approaches with the help of her ever-present cane, her face straining to transform her usual perma-pissed look into a pleasant smile. "Jack—it is so good to see you!" she exclaims, and gives me what is as close to a hug as she is capable of.

Via a complicated process of succession, Ethel is the current matriarch of the family, despite not having Lawson blood. She is the judge, jury, and executioner in determining who is to receive inheritance, and of equal importance, how large that inheritance will be. My sabbatical from the firm, publicly at least, has been handled with much more care and support than expected. I am an asset to LB&G and wanted back—hence this orchestrated pep rally. My excursion to the Otsego County DA's Office has been spun as a temporary civil service that I'm offering to mankind before I hop back on the money train.

"You look well, Jack. We've all been pulling for you in your rough time. But we knew you'd come through with flying colors—you're a Lawson, and Lawsons aren't quitters," Ethel states, pulling away from our quasi embrace. Her pep talks are usually more Patton inspired than Hallmark.

"You remember Mac and Ashley," I introduce my friends.

Ethel has always been fond of Ashley, never failing to remind me that she would have made a "suitable" Lawson wife. On the other hand, she has never had any use for Mac, but for my benefit, she provides him with a wrinkled smile and an admirable attempt at a warm greeting.

Ethel then guides me around the suite like I'm a show horse, reintroducing me to my own family. Uncle Thomas, Uncle Charles, nieces and nephews in miniature tuxes as if they are in a Lawson training course.

I don't have much to say. First of all, I don't particularly like most of them. Secondly, I am a little apprehensive about my current situation. But most of all, I'm what Reyanne used to term a "social moron." In the courtroom I resonate total confidence. While outside of my comfort zone, I tend to trip over myself and often retreat inward.

I can tell Mac is feeling equally out of place. He whispers in my ear, "I am so hopelessly middle class." He takes another glass of champagne, looking to take the edge off. In contrast, Ashley seems born to be in this company, which I suspect is adding to Mac's anxiety. I think he fears waking up one day to find she desires a more grandiose life that doesn't include him.

The dog and pony show continues. More uncles, aunts, nieces, nephews, and mistresses. All are staying on message with encouraging words and smiles.

The underlying reason behind the pomp and circumstance is that I have a certain natural talent. A trial lawyer is a specialized calling, and not easily replaceable. Most lawyers, Lawsons included, seldom speak in open court, and many go their entire careers without entering a courtroom. For many years, major law firms considered it to be somewhat disreputable to have a criminal lawyer among their partners. But with the explosion of corporate crime and an epidemic of indicted CEOs, I became a necessary—and very profitable—evil. Which made it that much sweeter (at least for me) when the ugly duckling of the Lawson family became the golden boy of LB&G. But thankfully, Reyanne saved me from that path.

I scan the room, and to no surprise my mother is nowhere to be found. She has been ostracized, although still getting paid handsomely. For the most part she's been written out of Lawson history. It doesn't bother my mother—if Jackie could leave Aristotle Onassis, then surely she could live without Andrew Lawson. The only thing my mother and father ever agreed on was their aristocratic view that they were chosen to be above the masses.

My father is both welcome and present. He's attempting to appear happily stunned by my appearance, but he isn't a good actor. I like that I was passed on his genes for height, but avoided his hairline.

"Jack, I hear nothing but good things of your work at the District Attorney's Office. We are proud of you," he regurgitates the company line.

"It's great to see you again," cheerfully states Mandy, Mindy, or whatever is the name of my father's twenty-something girlfriend. She wears an almost identical ensemble as Ashley—white sundress and oversized hat with her long blond hair stylishly streaming from the back—and greets me with a hug and loving kiss on the cheek, which I find odd since I've never met her before.

My father orders more champagne for Mindy/Mandy, as he is programmed to always be in control to the point of obsession. As a member of the chosen elite, he is above the randomness of life.

Our conversation takes on the shape of most conversations we've had since my youth, and we are quickly reminded that we have little to say to each other. We shake hands like the strangers we are and I move on to greet more people being forced to suck-up to me.

I am greeted by another twit cousin with a sense of entitlement, an uncle who looks like he dyed his hair with a black magic marker, and a few VIP guests of LB&G.

Suddenly before me is a recognizable figure. He stands about six-foot-three with a golden helmet of hair that outlines his sculpted face, highlighted by a jaw that looks to be carved from marble. He is dressed differently from the others, wearing the uniform of a polo player. A baggy red shirt with sleeves to the elbow, and a bright yellow stripe running diagonally from his left shoulder to his right hip. He wears white breeches tucked into dark brown English riding boots. If I had to describe him in one word it would be...perfect.

Chapter 5

"Jack, I would like to introduce you to the next governor of the state of New York—Drew Anderson," Ethel states with great pride.

A few people surrounding Anderson salute him with a light golf clap in his honor. He shrugs it off, as if such flattery has wounded his humble spirit.

"Ms. Lawson is being kind, as usual, but I haven't even decided yet if I'm going to run."

Those around him grin, knowing that Drew Anderson running for governor is one of the worst kept secrets of all time.

The Thor-like Adonis reaches out and shakes my hand with a vice-like grip. "We've met before," he informs Ethel, then returns his focus to me. "I want to congratulate you Jack, on all the fine work your office has done with S.A.F.E," he says like a skilled politician, making me feel like we are old friends.

S.A.F.E is an initiative that Anderson founded, working closely with my boss, Otsego County District Attorney Gifford Brown. It stands for Society Against Failing Ethics, an initiative that prioritizes the prosecution of smaller crimes deemed to lower society's values—things like prostitution and pot smoking. Or ideally, hookers who smoke pot.

Anderson moves his campaign to the next potential voter. "Good to see you again, Mac," he greets him with a glowing smile. They have actually worked together on numerous occasions. Anderson is the owner of Max-Q-Collectibles, a giant in the sports collectibles and memorabilia industry, which often works closely with the Baseball Hall of Fame.

He saves his most gushing introduction for Ashley. "This beautiful specimen must be related to you, Ethel."

Ashley giggles like a schoolgirl. "No, I'm Mac's wife. He is a big fan and talks about you all the time, Mr. Anderson."

"Call me Drew."

Mac doesn't look thrilled about the future governor flirting with his wife. "You are a lucky man, Mac," he says, before comfortably turning the attention to himself.

"I apologize for my appearance. I just played a match at the Saratoga Polo Club. But I promised Ethel that I wouldn't miss this exciting day for Attorney@Lawson."

"Did you win your match?" Ashley asks.

No answer is necessary. Of course he did. Everything he touches turns into gold. He is even nicknamed Max Q after the ultimate atmospheric force that is created during a space launch. It occurs when increasing speed and decreasing density both reach their maximum. And for the ship to pass successfully pass through Max Q, it needs to achieve ideal performance. In life on earth, the rare point where ideal performance and ultimate force intertwine is termed perfection. The experts say that maintaining perfection over a long period of time is virtually impossible. But Drew Anderson seems to be beating those odds.

He came into the national consciousness at twelve years old when *Sports Illustrated* did an article on how his father had been grooming him since he was in his mother's womb to be the next great quarterback. And despite some initial controversy concerning the tactics, his father looked like a prophet when Drew went on to win the prestigious Heisman Trophy at Florida State University.

Drew then shocked the world by shunning the multi-million dollars of professional football to join the military, which he called his "patriotic duty." He cemented his hero status when he rescued a downed pilot in Bosnia, and they were forced to survive a week in enemy territory with no food or water.

Upon returning to civilian life, his next challenge was the business world, where he rode the wave of the exploding sports collectibles industry, after witnessing how sought after—and lucrative—Drew Anderson memorabilia had become. The twelve-year-old kid from *Sports Illustrated* was now a sophisticated businessman on the cover of *Forbes*.

I've always been suspicious of things that appear too good to be true. And if anything in this world reeks of being too-good-to-be-true it's Drew Anderson.

Chapter 6

A silver haired man with leathery tanned skin appears next to Drew and pats him on the back like they're old chums.

"James Lansdale, I would like you to meet Jack Lawson," Drew introduces us, leading to an awkward handshake. Like I said, this is not my element.

"Thank you, Governor," he says in an accent derived from his native New Zealand. He is a billionaire media mogul, and I assume another one of LB&G's prized clients.

I know of Lansdale for a couple of reasons. One, is that he keeps his enormous yacht on Otsego Lake in Cooperstown, which he travels to and from by helicopter. Our office is forwarded the many complaints about the noise. There has been discussion of passing legislation to deal with the problem, but the county doesn't even have the budget for a police patrol of the lake, so I'm not sure who would enforce it.

The other is that he has made headlines with his morality crusading group called Smut Cleanser. On the group's website is a "Most Wanted" type listing of those people in violation of Lansdale's personal code of morals and ethics. Of course, Laney Bang is on top of the list, causing me an inner chuckle at the thought of the bitter rivals spending their day at the same venue.

"Jack is with the Otsego County DA's Office," Drew informs Lansdale.

It seems to jolt the memory of the seventy-five year old man. "So you are the prosecutor who never loses a case."

"That's him," says my biggest supporter, Ashley.

"Your office is doing fine work with S.A.F.E. With your help, they were able to shut down that raunchy strip club on Route-60. I think S.A.F.E. will become a model for other communities. Often, the money is put into law enforcement, but it neglects the prosecution stage, which is the only way to truly keep the smut off the street."

By the proud smile on my grandmother's face, I realize her support for my work likely has more to do with keeping Lansdale and Anderson happy, than my well-being. She always has an agenda.

The crowd begins to buzz. The race is about to begin and all Lawsons and assorted guests move to the suite's balcony, which provides a panoramic view of the racetrack.

Lansdale is monopolizing my grandmother's eager ear, discussing the numerous horses he keeps at his many estates—Saratoga, Florida, and New Zealand. But then, as if his radar had spotted an enemy MIG, his eyes lock on the woman in the front row. A dark cloud of irritation blocks out his sunny charm. "I can't believe they let that piece of trash in here! The standards are just not what they used to be."

Ethel also looks disgusted by the woman's presence, although to be fair, rainbows and puppies elicit the same scowl. "She is a nasty strain of profane that is polluting this country. I can't believe they are allowing her to have a signing for that trashy book of hers in Cooperstown tonight."

"She is such a bad influence," Ashley adds, in full agreement. "I took my thirteen year old niece to the mall last week. You should see what these girls are wearing, it's appalling."

Ashley receives strange looks. I'm not sure anyone in this room knows what the mall is.

"We'll be there to protest with our people," Lansdale growls. "And I'm sure Jack here and the District Attorney's Office will be doing a full investigation. So I'm confident she'll be arrested for the proliferation and trafficking of obscene material, and the books will be confiscated."

I never appreciate those trying to drag me into their agendas, and feel my law swagger coming on. "What she's doing is not illegal in the state of New York," I reply, triggering a deathly silence throughout the room. I'm surprised I said it out loud—I must have thought I was in a courtroom.

My honeymoon with Lansdale is over, his eyes filling with fire. But before he can respond, the sound of bugles signals the start of the race. As if preordained, Attorney@Lawson takes the lead.

But someone must have forgot to send the memo about the coronation to La Levrette, who catches Attorney@Lawson at the one-mile mark, before leaving him in the literal and figurative dust, and winning by seven lengths.

It's like a bomb went off in the room, causing a temporary paralysis. But they quickly locate their inner-Lawson and fire up the blame game—jockey, trainer, weather.

I watch as Laney Bang rises triumphantly, puts on her trench coat, and proudly saunters out of the arena. She disappears into the tunnel, and we decide to follow her lead and make a fast getaway. Lucky for us, my family is too engrossed in picking their new jockey to notice.

The only person to bid us adieu is Drew Anderson. He kisses Ashley on the cheek, to her husband's disapproving look. After shaking hands with Mac and me, Drew announces that he's in a rush because he has to be back in Manhattan tonight to attend a party with his wife. He then vanishes into a sea of angry Lawsons.

As we enter the parking lot, Ashley beams, "Drew Anderson is a really nice guy."

The comment agitates Mac. "I used to think so, but the more I see him the more I think he's a 'too cool for the room' phony."

Ashley looks to me to break the tie. She knows Mac and I share an innate ability to pick out a phony. Mac can do it because of his street smarts, while my knack comes from being surrounded by them since birth.

I nod. "I think Mac's right. I never trust these guys who seem too good to be true."

"He does seem too good to be true, haters, I'll give you that," Ashley makes peace. She then puts her arm around her husband and radiates a smile. "But he can't stack up to my guy, whose jealousy is duly noted and will be generously rewarded."

"Come join us at Touch 'Em All, Jack," a rejuvenated Mac offers, referring to our favorite watering hole. As with everything else in Cooperstown, the name has a baseball connection.

"C'mon, Jack, it will be fun," Ashley seconds.

"Thanks, but no thanks," I beg off.

Ashley looks disappointed, but doesn't push it.

"Honey, Jack will be too busy busting up the Laney Bang book signing," Mac says with a laugh, and receives a smile from his wife.

Actually I'm going to spend the night with my one remaining love—the law—preparing for my meeting with Andy Kass and his lawyer tomorrow morning.

Chapter 7

I wander aimlessly through the sea of vehicles jammed into the parking lot, and by sheer luck I locate my transportation. I pull a change of clothing out of my knapsack—black leather jacket, jeans, boots and helmet. A few minutes later I'm headed toward Cooperstown on my F-41.

I briefly get stuck in downtown Saratoga. The small town has enough trouble dealing with the traffic that's filing out of the racecourse, but the popular Hats Off Festival is being held this weekend, drawing even more tourists to the area. Once I escape the logjam, I speed onto the New York Thruway. *Lean right, lean left, try not to get yourself killed, Jack.* I bump over the rolling hills of upstate New York, the scenery shifting between forests and fields. I'm the first to admit the motorcycle was not my idea. It's all about Reyanne.

I lean sharply to the left and my elbow almost scrapes the asphalt. I feel the sharp breeze shooting against my neck and take the nimble machine to a higher gear. I hunch my weight forward on a straightaway, holding on for dear life, then plunge into a shadowy ravine. I feel the temperature dip as I'm swallowed up by the darkness being cast by towering pines. Within seconds, I return to the sharp daylight.

I promised Reyanne that I would "LLF" (live life to the fullest). Since she, for all intents and purposes, saved my life, the least I can do is try to try to keep my promise. I smile, thinking how she would always remind me that my over-analysis of the acronym—I was bothered that it didn't include the "to" and "the"—proved beyond a reasonable doubt that I was living life with a stick wedged up my ass.

My eyes moisten. I lift the visor on my helmet and look up at the flawless sky, which is my way of surrendering my fate to the jury of the universe. I have found that life is similar to a trial case—we put on the best case we can, but no matter how much control we think we have over the final decision, the outcome is decided by others. And sometimes those decisions are random and cruel.

It was a day eerily similar to today, twenty-two months ago, in what feels like a different lifetime. Fifty-eight people died, and numerous others were maimed or injured in what became known as the "New York Subway Bombing." I'm not ashamed to say that if given a choice to save all of them not including Reyanne, or just save her, I would choose the latter.

We went to breakfast that morning at a hole-in-the-wall diner in the Chelsea section of Manhattan where we lived. I owned a lavish Upper East Side apartment, but Reyanne would have no part of it. So I moved into her apartment, trading in my doorman and cleaning service for cockroaches.

I was obsessing over the fact that I was late for court. My priorities annoyed Reyanne, who quipped, "Stop being such a Lawson, Jack."

As usual, she got me to smile. "Hey, I'm just trying to LLTTF."

She shook her head. "Jack, it's my acronym and if I want it to be 'LLF' then it will be." But it was the next part I'll never forget. She turned as serious as I had ever seen her, and said the strangest thing, "Jack, if something ever splits us apart you have to promise me you truly *will* live life to the fullest." She kept pressing me until I agreed.

The image of her gracefully descending those steps of the subway station is burned into my brain. So is the one final look she gave me. I had no reason to believe it was going to be the last time I saw that amazing smile, but sometimes I get the feeling that maybe she did.

I met Reyanne in an Upper West Side sports bar called Nellie's. Mac was in town for a sports collectibles convention and Nellie's was known for three of his most favorite things—baseball, dark lager beer, and nachos. Everybody noticed when Reyanne walked in. It wasn't so much her physical attractiveness, but rather, something magnetic about her aura. Don't get me wrong, she was drop-dead gorgeous. She had this unruly, skater-boy haircut of bright red hair, a look that is impossible to pull off without natural beauty. And of course that smile, *oh* that smile.

I couldn't pull my stare from her, and when her spellbinding eyes busted me, I squirmed like a child caught in a lie. Mac encouraged me to go over and buy her a drink. If it were a courtroom I would have marched up to her and astonished myself by seamlessly slipping into witty banter. But since this was a bar, I gripped my beer bottle tightly, unable to distinguish the perspiration of the bottle from the nervous sweat on my hands. Reyanne told me later that she knew instantly I was either her soul mate or a serial killer, and figured either way it would be interesting. It turned out to be much more than interesting—that walk across the bar was the best decision I have ever made.

I returned to LB&G at the end of October, six weeks after her death, and attempted to pull myself up by the bootstraps like the Lawson family handbook dictates. But I no longer had any desire to be there. So I sold my apartment to help fund the leave of absence that I'm still on, and began aimlessly wandering the world. I eventually landed in Cooperstown. I thought my stay would be temporary, but time kept passing and I kept staying. Then I rediscovered my other love—the law—giving my life a purpose once again, and a reason to get up in the morning.

I force thoughts of the past from my mind. I rev the bike and zoom toward my uncertain future. Reyanne would be proud.

Chapter 8

A weathered sign informs me I've arrived in Cooperstown. It reads: *The Most Famous Small Town in America.*

Cooperstown nestles beside the shining Otsego Lake. It began as a Victorian resort community that was founded by the family of the famous author James Fennimore Cooper. It probably would have remained that way if a man named Abner Doubleday hadn't invented a game there in the nineteenth century called baseball. At least that's how the story goes.

The winters are bleak, featuring frigid temperatures and barren streets, but the spring and summer explode with the buzzing of tourists and trolleys.

The F-41 speeds onto Main Street—I'm just along for the ride. It's a classic Main Street USA, shaded with maples, while red geraniums cascade from every lamppost. I pass the Hall of Fame museum and numerous shops, one of which is Max-Q-Collectibles.

My progress is soon stopped. The traffic is backed up, turning Main Street into a parking lot. Crowding is always a problem in summertime Cooperstown, but it's even more congested than normal on this Sunday afternoon, and before long I understand why. Sitting on a patio in front of Cooperstown Books, still dressed in her provocative schoolgirl outfit, is Laney Bang. A line of people wraps around the small store, waiting patiently for her to sign her bestseller, *Big Bang Theories.* The book is an account of her rise to fame, and has generated much publicity due to her naming many of the rich and famous she's spent "quality time" with. It's flying off the shelves, despite many stores refusing to sell it.

I take advantage of my sleek piece of machinery to swerve around the many onlookers who are gawking at the buxom blonde, and shake my head at the absurdity of the whole thing. I pass historic-looking shops and restaurants, when suddenly a police cruiser pulls in front of me. The window rolls down, revealing mustached County Sheriff Roddy Opp, who is sporting a two-faced grin.

"You'd think the Chief Assistant District Attorney of Otsego County wouldn't be so quick to break the traffic laws," he remarks.

I plant my boots on the ground for balance and flip up the visor of my helmet. "Guarding a porn star, Roddy? They only give you the most dangerous assignments."

The police and DA's Office have a strained relationship. Stuff that goes back to before I got here. But professional courtesy still rules the day, and he lets me proceed. My original intent was to swing by my office at 197 Main to pick up a few folders on the Andy Kass case, but it's on the far west side of Main Street and traffic is too congested. It can wait—I have memorized most of the information, anyway.

I take a sharp right on Fair Street to escape the blockage. I pass a couple of Victorian homes, along with our favorite watering hole, Touch 'Em All. I make a left on Lake Avenue and sneak a peek at the picturesque Otsego Lake, which was dubbed Glimmerglass by James Fennimore Cooper.

Otsego Lake stretches for eight miles, with Cooperstown docked at its southern tip, and is surrounded by emerald hills that appear to be protecting it. Today it's dotted by brightly colored sailboats.

Lake Avenue morphs into Route-80, a rural road that traces the west side of the lake, and leads me to Mac and Ashley's residence. Their secluded home is built into the side of a hill, across the road from the lake. It's built on levels that hug the contour of the hill, giving it a unique style—much like its owners.

I park the F-41 next to the Ashley's Errands van in the musty three-car garage. My mountain-bike and Adirondack guide boat are hanging on the wall. I shut the garage door and begin to climb the steps. I pass the main house and continue up another level to my one-room apartment above the garage.

My room consists of bookshelves overflowing with law books, a past-its-prime television, and a futon. It's reminiscent of my dorm room at Brown.

A sliding glass door leads to a deck that hangs over a rocky ledge, and has a brilliant view of Otsego Lake. It's too inviting to pass up. I sit on the deck, sipping a beer and viewing an occasional boat glide by. I watch the sun drop behind the lush hills to the background music of crickets, and decide it's better than most of the stuff I've heard lately on radio.

As the lake becomes painted with darkness, I retreat inside with to work on the Andy Kass case. But thoughts of Reyanne keep flooding my mind. It's going to be another long night.

Chapter 9

My alarm jolts my eyes open. The 1980s pop song "Manic Monday" fills my room.

The alarm was a gift from Reyanne. It plays day of the week themed music. For example, tomorrow will be "Ruby Tuesday" by the Stones. Most of my Reyanne memories are either filled with unfathomable joy or the deep sorrow of loss. The alarm clock is just annoying. But I try to hold onto every piece of her that I can, even though I know she wouldn't approve.

I drag myself out of bed and step out onto the porch. I spot the Ashley's Errands van erratically backing out of the driveway.

"Have a great day, Jack!" she yells up to me.

I wave back and hold my breath, hoping she won't back into a fast-moving truck on Route-80.

"Take it easy on that Kass kid—he didn't mean anyone any harm."

I agree with Ashley, but there are a few complications. For starters, he did commit a crime of epic proportions, so to give him leniency will encourage every picked-on kid to take matters into their own hands. Secondly, the community wants to make an example of Andy.

I don't really care about the latter. If I ever start consulting lynch mobs on my cases, that'll be the day I walk out of the courtroom and never return. The bigger problem is Andy's delusion of grandeur, combined with the lack of strong counsel to guide him in the right direction. He wants the courtroom to be his pulpit to speak out for all the bullied kids in the world, and his public defender has given him the rope to hang himself.

The day is shaping up as a typical triple-H July day, so I toss on a pair of black biker shorts and a T-shirt, then strap my plastic bike helmet over my greasy hair.

Shep would normally pick me up in her flashy 7-Series BMW. Another notch in her meaningless pursuit of the approval of others that she could never afford on a county salary—supposedly she comes from a well-to-do Boston family. She treks in from Albany, which is a forty-five minute commute on a good day.

Our meeting with Kass is scheduled for ten. I wanted to arrange it for first thing in the morning before any of our co-workers arrived, but Shep hit me with the last minute information on Friday that she had an appointment of a personal nature this morning that couldn't be adjusted. So I have some extra time on my hands, which allows me to do a few errands around town in preparation for the meeting, including a trip to the bank.

My commute normally takes about twenty minutes with my full-suspension, lightweight aluminum mountain-bike, which is more my speed than the motorcycle. I soak in the soothing sounds of chirping birds and all of a sudden Monday morning isn't so Monday morning anymore.

I think of Andy Kass, trying to decide if my strategy for today's meeting is too radical. He's a tough nut to crack, and I need to scare him out of his comfort zone before he gets himself locked up for the next thirty years. So I feel I have no choice.

Our building is located right next to the old courthouse. It's a rare modern structure in Cooperstown that we share with numerous civic related agencies such as the Clean Water Agency and the Department of Transportation and Tourism.

I arrive just before ten, carrying my bike into our first floor office.

Nobody greets me, which isn't unusual—my co-workers view me as the big city pedigree who swooped into town to steal the job they were all destined for. But today I notice a heightened buzz of excitement in the office. *Because Andy Kass has arrived?* The six o'clock-news type stuff rarely happens in Otsego County.

Jana, who is one of two administrative secretaries for the office, informs me that Andy has indeed arrived. At LB&G I had six admins assigned just to me, and if I was working on a case for a high priority client, there were often more.

A group of ADAs are huddled, eating doughnuts, gossiping, and complaining, probably about me.

I move past the peanut gallery, but I'm close enough to catch the term "crime of the century." Since the Kass case is about the biggest crime seen in Otsego County, and I don't think it would qualify, this century or any other, I can only surmise they are referring to my outfit.

The one ADA not present is Shep. Even with her previous engagement I thought she'd beat me here—she might be the most punctual person I've ever met.

As if hearing my thoughts, she bursts through the front door, almost tripping over her expensive heels, looking out of both breath and sorts. She is sporting glasses today, a change of pace, but her hair is in its usual conservative bun. She's wearing a button down Oxford with pinstriped slacks, and carrying a navy blazer.

She's an impeccable dresser, in her typical obsessive way. Designer of course, because it's most important what others think. Shoes, bag, and nail polish are always a match. She definitely buys into the theory that you should dress for the job you want, not the one you have.

She originally came from the New York State Prosecutors' Training Institute in Albany. She made an immediate impression with her intelligence and ambition, and now is here full time. Or at least until a better offer comes along. I know somewhere inside her is someone who wants to be a great lawyer. At the moment she wants to be a great success, which is different.

I don't receive the good-morning smile from her that I've grown accustomed to. She has a great smile. Not the Julia Roberts megawatt type, but a more understated one that shows off a softer side that she tries so hard to cover up—it's like finding a rare treasure.

I motion her to my office, where we can speak about our upcoming meeting in peace. I casually lean my bike against a bookshelf and try to act as if I don't notice the awkwardness between us.

Without a word, Shep hands me a list of questions and goals she prepared for the Andy Kass meeting. I immediately crumple it and toss it toward the garbage can. I know this will irritate her, but sometimes you have to throw out the book and write your own script. They never taught Andy Kass in law school.

She glares at me with her big brown eyes. "Andy and his lawyer are here. Should I tell them you are too busy preparing for the Tour de France?"

"I'll just be a minute," I say and grab a change of clothing that is hanging in a small closet. I carefully maneuver through gossip central and down a musty stairwell to the shower, located in the men's bathroom on the basement level.

I finish in world-record time, dress in a dark suit, and expertly tie my tie. I run a comb through my wet hair. I've had the same parted-to-the-side hairstyle since the sixth grade, except for my time with Reyanne when I was forced into five different hairstyles in fourteen months.

I meet back up with Shep, who is making no secret about looking at her watch.

"Are you ready?" I ask.

"Are *you*?"

I grab my bag and we head down the hallway to the conference room where Andy Kass and his lawyer are waiting. From what I have seen so far, the lawyer tends to be more nervous than Andy.

"So what did you end up doing this weekend?" I try to make small talk with Shep.

"Not that it's any of your business, but a friend invited me out on his boat."

"Is that what this late Monday was about?"

"You made it clear that we should keep our relationship professional, so how about keeping up your end of the bargain."

Her icy stare ends the conversation. We pass the other ADAs, still munching and chatting, and I again catch the term "crime of the century."

"I'm guessing that they're talking about my outfit and not yours?" I say with an olive-branch smile.

Shep remains stoic. "My sources tell me that a woman was found dead at Drew Anderson's estate this morning. I think that's what has everyone buzzing. Rumor is that it might have been one of the cleaning staff who committed suicide, but nobody's really sure at this point."

The news catches me by surprise, but I play it off. "How come everybody has sources but me?" I ask, and then break into laughter.

"What's so funny?"

"I think the peanut gallery thinks Anderson might have something to do with the woman's death. A suicide wouldn't exactly qualify as a crime of the century."

"Anderson a killer? Doesn't sound likely."

"Plus, I know he wasn't in town last night."

"I thought you didn't have sources?"

"I don't. I ran into him at Saratoga yesterday. Said he was returning to Manhattan that night to attend a party with his wife."

Chapter 10

Andy Kass sits with Susan Pinnick, his assigned public defender. Showing either great nerve or great stupidity, he wears a T-shirt dedicated to his graduating class at Otsego High. I shake hands with Susan, but Andy remains seated in protest.

Andy is short with a portly build and a ruddy complexion. His eyes are of someone much older, but not necessarily wiser. His sense of humor is dry as the Sahara, leaving most people unsure as to when he is being serious.

"Jaaack," he greets me with a goofy grin, and saying my name in the long drawn-out style that has become his custom.

After the brief greeting, he returns to the same book he's been reading the last three times we've met. It's about the enslavement of workers in the diamond-mining business in Africa. The kid is not shallow, I'll give him that.

"Mr. Lawson, I think it is time to talk deal," Andy's lawyer begins the meeting, as I take a seat across from them at the conference table. "This game of chicken we're on is going to end with my client being made an example for the sins of others. If we just stick to the law and not public sentiment, I'm sure we can hammer out a deal that benefits all parties." She sounds rehearsed.

I'm more interested in what Andy is reading. "I see you're almost done with the book—is it good?"

Usually his replies are one-word answers, but not this time. "Good? Yes, Jack, it's fantastic that those with power treat human beings like sewage. It is really *good*."

"I meant is it an interesting read?"

"I don't particularly find human suffering at the hands of those with power interesting, but if you do, perhaps I can loan it to you when I'm done."

Shep gets things back on track. "Ms. Pinnick, this deal you talk of would require a few things. First of all, we need your client to fully cooperate with us. Second, he must be prepared for prison time. You do understand that complete leniency in this case would create open season for those who feel being picked on gives them the right to resort to violence."

"A property was destroyed. Nothing more, nothing less. This is a case of vandalism at the highest level. Not an act of terrorism. Some of these statutes with life sentences that Andy is being charged with are ridiculous. They need to be taken off the table for us to cooperate with any deal."

Andy looks up from his book, showing unexpected interest. "I will not accept any deal. This matter should be decided in a court of law. I told her this, but she won't listen. You're fired, Ms. Pinnick!"

Normally such a rift between lawyer and client would be heavily in our favor, but I don't have the time or patience for it. "I want to talk to Andy alone," I interrupt their bickering.

Susan refuses my request, but Andy reminds her that she's no longer his lawyer.

"Okay—five minutes" Susan says and reluctantly leaves the room, seemingly not taking her firing seriously. I get the feeling that it's not the first time it's happened.

"You too, Shep," I say.

When she grasps that I'm serious, her face turns angry. She stands, performs a half-pirouette and stomps toward the door. She slams the door on her way out.

Point taken.

It's just Andy Kass and me, one-on-one. Something I've craved for weeks. I'm going to get justice, whether Andy likes it or not.

We sit in a macho-staring contest for a minute, before his eyes return to his book. My impulse is to rip it out of his hand and throw it against the wall, but I've seen enough of his act to know that he'll shut down completely—like a turtle retreating into his shell. Especially since I think the book represents some sort of brotherhood of the downtrodden.

"So how did it feel?" I break the ice.

Andy glances up at me with a confused look, gauging my purpose for this alone time. It's a chess match.

"Wow, Jack, you are both a shrink and a lawyer. That's like having cancer and heart disease at the same time."

"So how did it feel?"

"I don't know what you're talking about."

"Sure you do. You went through months of planning to blow up that school, yet you haven't been able to talk about it. You're already screwed—the explosives match the ones found in your parents' garage, and we found piles of Internet printouts in your bedroom on how to make the exact type of bomb used in the explosion.

"You told a few classmates before graduation that something 'huge and explosive' was going to happen. I haven't heard one denial on your part, and your lawyer, besides having a difficult client, is begging me for a deal because she knows I have enough evidence to put you away for a long time. So tell me how it felt when that school fell to the ground. The place that tortured you five days a week for years. How did it feel, Andy!?"

He explodes with emotion., "It was perfect! Like the forces of the universe came together in unison. The most beautiful thing I've ever seen!"

I say nothing.

Andy's body is pulsating. "Are you happy now?"

I should be—confessions tend to be helpful in my line of work—but not in this case. "My girlfriend died in an explosion. I don't think they are beautiful at all."

Andy looks dismayed. It's the first time I've seen him drop his aloof facade. "I'm sorry, Jack. I didn't mean…"

I stand, cutting him off. "Now there's a term we can work with…*I'm sorry*. I think we're making progress, Andy."

"I said I was sorry about your girlfriend, not what happened to that school—stop putting words in my mouth."

"How come you didn't kill anyone?" I press on.

Andy remains silent, pulling the book closer to his face. He made sure nobody was present when it went down. I don't think it's a coincidence the night janitor had his tires slashed on his truck so he couldn't go to work that night.

"I have five witnesses who saw someone matching your description at the scene. Logic says they saw you setting up the explosives for your performance of Oklahoma City the sequel, but I think you were doing a final sweep to make sure nobody was in the building."

"So what if I did?"

"Andy, I wouldn't have had as big of a problem with those subway bombers if they got everyone out before igniting the explosives. It would still be off-the-charts wrong, but my job is to work with levels of wrong."

"What's your point?"

"Despite what most people in this community think, I know you didn't want to harm anyone. You're not the devil. In fact, you're quite the opposite. And if you apply yourself in the right way, you can become a leader for the downtrodden. God help us all, maybe one day you can even run for president."

"You have to be rich to be president, Jack. Where did you go to school, Naïve University?"

"All I'm trying to say is that the world will be a better place with Andy Kass fighting for the people who can't fight for themselves. But the only way for that to happen is for you to step up to the plate with a big fat 'I'm sorry,' and then we'll work out a deal that punishes what you did, and not what people want to hang you for. It's your choice, Andy, but if you go to jail, then who's going to fight for the diamond miners?"

He nervously fidgets, digesting my words. "I'm going to trial—it's my constitutional right, and there's nothing you can do to stop me."

It's the expected answer, but I feel I'm starting to wear him down. I reach into my bag and pull out a large mailing envelope. I hand it to him. He looks apprehensively at it. My eyes encourage him to open it and he follows my cue. "If so, then you're going to need this," I say.

He pulls out bricks of money, looking uncertain.

"It's ten thousand dollars. I want you to fire Susan for real this time. She has talent, but like most public defenders, is overworked, underpaid, and inexperienced. I included a list of defense attorneys who I think are good."

"I can't take this."

"You have no choice. I'm the best prosecutor in the area. I will crush you in court if you choose to go there. You don't only need money to be president, you need it to have a fair shake at justice."

Andy sits quietly, staring blankly at the money.

"I'm just doing what you do, Andy—helping those who can't help themselves."

Our staring contest resumes.

I'm still baffled by the "walk on water" confidence I have in situations like this, compared to my self-esteem-challenged non-law life. But I'm convinced it's the only way that justice will be achieved in this case.

Andy shoves the money back at me as if it's unstable uranium, which I knew he'd do. Or at least that's how it played out in my mind. Not sure what I would've done if he had actually taken it.

I give Andy a "suit yourself" shrug and shove the money back into my bag. I stand. "I enjoyed our conversation," I say and head for the door.

"You're different, Jack," he shouts to me.

"I'm not much different from you, Andy," I reply, and leave the room.

Chapter 11

I leave Andy Kass in the conference room. I nod to Susan Pinnick, who immediately goes to see if I harmed her client. I wonder if she's secretly hoping that I did. The once buzzing office is now a ghost town.

With the exception of Shep, all the ADAs were in court this morning, which is one of the reasons I scheduled Andy at this time. In case something went wrong, I wanted as few people present as possible. Or what they call in my profession, witnesses.

Jana approaches me with urgency in her step. She delivers me the message that Gifford Brown is demanding my presence in his office ASAP. She adds that she's never seen him quite so mad.

He couldn't know what I just did—could he? The only thing I can think of is that his paranoia caused him to bug the conference room.

I give two quick knocks on the heavy elm door and enter. Gifford terminates another cigarette. Smoking is banned in the offices at 197 Main, which is why his door is usually shut. By the look of things, there are at least ten extinguished cigarettes in the ashtray. A sign that I'm in trouble.

Gifford removes his coke-bottle glasses from his balding dome and cleans them with a baby-wipe. His nervous energy is really concerning me. He stands, making me feel small, blocking the sign that sits behind his desk, which reads, *Give 'em a fair trial & then hang 'em.* He is abnormally thin and six-foot-four. He played basketball for Syracuse University back in the '60s, which is hard to picture looking at him now.

"Where is Shepherdson?" he barks.

"Right here," she says, sliding into the room like a student late for class. She looks at me with bewilderment. Our earlier animosity has been brushed aside in favor of a bond of survival.

"Sit, both of you—and shut the door, Shepherdson."

We follow his orders. Gifford remains standing, looking down at us in his intimidating way.

"If this is about the Kass case I …" I nervously stutter.

"You're not even a brick in the foundation of my misery, Lawson," he snaps at me. He lights another cigarette and inhales deeply.

Gifford begins pacing—cigarette balancing seamlessly on his lips as if they are one—his long, thin legs making him appear to be more giraffe than human. "This morning a woman was found dead at the estate of Drew Anderson. Her name was Darby Kelleher."

"Was she the maid? I heard rumors she committed suicide," Shep says.

"You need better sources, Shepherdson. Darby Kelleher was actually an actress. You might know her better by her stage name—Laney Bang."

Shep and I gasp, but can't get any air. It feels like all the oxygen has been sucked out of the room.

"Oh, it gets better," he continues. "The police…*without consulting* the DA's Office got a warrant and arrested Drew Anderson for her murder."

Gifford looks like he wants to turn his cigarette around and jam it in his own eye. His color is normally not that of health, but he now looks like a corpse that's a few quarts low on embalming fluid.

"Problem is, we currently have no physical evidence, murder weapon, witnesses, or motive. To make matters worse, we're dealing with the arrest of an apple pie American hero, and with all due respect to the deceased, it's always an uphill battle when the victim is sleazier than the defendant."

"Why didn't they consult us—why the rush?" I ask. Andy Kass seems like a lifetime ago.

"We got Kobe-d," Shep mumbles under her breath. She's referring to a rape charge against basketball star Kobe Bryant in which the police acted on their own, without consulting the Eagle County DA's Office, putting them in a no-win position.

"No, we got rammed in the ass by a telephone pole is what happened," Gifford clarifies.

He then angrily tosses a pile of police reports onto his desk, along with the evidence reports. I pick up crime scene photos and can't believe I'm looking at the body of Laney Bang. Stabbed to death. It's surreal!

I suddenly comprehend why we're sitting here. And judging by the look on Shep's face, she has also figured it out. Nobody interested in a career would prosecute Drew Anderson with little or no evidence. And if we drop the case, we look like we are cowering to Anderson's celebrity, and possibly letting a murderer walk. Gifford is very interested in his career, which is why he's going to assign it to Shep and me.

I consider Gifford to be a good prosecutor who takes a particular pleasure in putting away the bad guys, but there's a warning label attached. The District Attorney is a political position, and by nature, politicians lose all ability to think for themselves. It becomes about votes and aligning oneself with the special interests that can deliver them. It's like going through life as a coached witness. And one special interest that Gifford has aligned himself with is Drew Anderson.

"My connection to Anderson is no secret," Gifford says, as if reading my mind. He extinguishes another cigarette, before plopping into his swivel chair. "He was the biggest contributor to my campaign last year. The S.A.F.E program is the biggest revenue generator in this office. And of course, I consider him a personal friend. That is why I'm going to remove myself from the case and assign it to you, Jack, with Shepherdson assisting."

Shep tries to bargain, "But my caseload is full. Wouldn't Flint or Garfield be better to assist Jack? I think they would—they have much more experience than I do, and I believe it's imperative to have experience on such a high profile case."

"I think the only thing that's *imperative* is that you put a sock in it and listen up. We don't have much time, Anderson will have his first court appearance this afternoon."

"How should we proceed with that?" I ask, beginning to accept reality.

"Shepherdson will handle it. Do your best—argue for no bail—but I can't see any judge refusing Anderson bail. While you're doing that, Jack and I will hold a press conference to try to get ahead of the story."

Gifford knows what he's doing. I'm the logical choice—an excellent lawyer with a reputation for being fair. I come from a background of being on the other side, as a defense attorney. But my biggest asset is I have no designs on his job. He believes I'm just passing through Otsego County, before moving on to bigger and better things.

Whether the case proceeds to trial or not, there will be a mammoth PR hit for arresting a demigod, and despite our office not being in the loop on the arrest, we will be branded for life—guilt by association. But luckily for Gifford, people with a dog don't have to bark. In this case, he owns two dogs—Shep and me.

Gifford removes a micro-cassette tape from an evidence bag and places it in a small recorder on the desk. "This morning at 6:05 a.m., a call was made to 911 by a woman claiming to be Laney Bang."

He presses play.

"My name is Laney Bang. I am at Drew Anderson's home in Cooperstown. Help...No...Drew...help!" the familiar voice screams in panic.

He plays it again. *"Help...No...Drew...Help!"*

"For this tape to mean anything it better say that Drew Anderson is the one harming her. But it doesn't. She could be calling Drew for help—who knows," I say.

"It ain't worth diddly-squat—and here comes a bigger problem...the Sheriff's Office considered the call a hoax, made it a low priority, and didn't show up until 7:30."

I cringe. This gave the murderer a ninety-minute head start on the clean up.

"And when they did decide to make an appearance, things went downhill from there." He points to the folder in my hands. "You can read the rest of the gory details in the police reports."

We have no time to lose, so I gather all the folders and stand. Shep remains seated, as if staging a sit-in to protest.

Gifford gets the last word, "My only stipulation is a swift investigation—this isn't any random case where we can go on investigating for months before making a decision on whether to prosecute. Each passing day, evidence will drown in the murky, shark infested waters of the media and blogosphere. Let the evidence write the story, not the background noise."

I nod, but my thoughts are already on the challenge before us.

Chapter 12

I read and re-read the police reports. I am in agreement with the police that Anderson displayed suspicious behavior upon their arrival. He wasn't honest with his initial statements and the alibi he provided was flimsy at best. This would make him the lead suspect. But they made a big conclusion jump to arrest him for murder at this stage. There is no murder weapon or an obvious motive.

And what the many reports—arrest report, fingerprint form, evidence report form, and the standard suicide evaluation form—don't mention, is that Drew Anderson is an American hero, whose name is synonymous with perfection. This will make a conviction an uphill battle, even with strong evidence.

Shep drives us to the medical examiner's office, which is located in the neighboring town of Oneonta. I sit in the passenger seat, shuffling through crime scene photos. There are long distance shots, medium distance shots, and close up shots of the body. They all show a gruesome murder.

"He couldn't have done it," Shep blurts out, seemingly out of nowhere.

"How can you say that? You haven't seen any evidence yet."

"I just know."

"Why, because of his carefully marketed image? If you're so sure, then who did it, counselor?"

"It doesn't matter who did it—we're not cops. Our job is to decide if the accused did it, or more specifically, if we can prove he did it."

"But if we can determine another possible suspect, it would move us toward dropping the charges."

"In that case, I think James Lansdale is behind it. She is at the top of the hit list on his website. And he lives in Saratoga, just over an hour away."

"One slight problem—you have to prove he was there."

"I didn't say he was the one who plunged the knife into her. He could have hired one of his 'smut-hunters' to do it. Unlike Anderson, he had a motive."

"Anderson had a lot to lose if he was having an affair with her, and word got out."

"He could have denied it, just like a whole bunch of other celebrities in her book. And with his reputation, his word would trump hers."

"My only point was that we need to have an open mind."

"Maybe if Laney Bang spent more time with her mind open instead of her legs, then she wouldn't have ended up dead. But now we're the ones who are going to end up paying for her reckless behavior."

"No matter what you think of her, she's the victim, and it's our job to deliver justice for her. And the only way to do that is to follow the law."

When I look at Shep, I am confident she will keep an open mind when it comes to the case. But her face tells me that she's already made up her mind when it comes to me.

Chapter 13

We pull into the small office of the medical examiner, tucked away in the rural backdrop of Oneonta. We enter, and follow the smell of formaldehyde to the small corner office of ME Gretchen Hewitt.

Gretchen has matted gray hair, and wears a loose lab coat that hides her plump waistline. We sit facing her desk, which is cluttered with containers of takeout Mexican food.

There's not a lot of homicide in this neck of the woods, but I did investigate a drowning on the lake a few months ago. During my visit, I became queasy and passed out, banging my head on the floor. So it was decided that all future meetings were to be held in Gretchen's office, away from the bodies.

"To what do I owe this pleasure?" Gretchen asks, but I'm certain she knows exactly why we're here.

"We just dropped by to see how business is going," I say.

"It's a dying business, but we manage," she displays her usual morbid sense of humor, before scooping a heaped spoonful of refried beans into her mouth.

She then provides a forewarning of the potential absurdity of this case, "I got a call from someone a few minutes ago who wanted to purchase the deceased's breast implants for a hundred thousand dollars. And there has been no formal press release yet about her murder."

I hope she's kidding, but quickly realize she's not.

She hands me her initial analysis, which I skim. "Did you find any evidence indicating that she recently engaged in sex?" I inquire.

"There were no items transferred, such as fluids, that might connect the victim to Drew Anderson. But I did find numerous vaginal lacerations consistent with someone who recently had rough sex, but not necessarily consistent with rape." Not missing a beat, she picks up a quesadilla with her hands and takes a crunchy bite. "And by recent, that could mean anytime in the last few days to a week."

"Since she has sex for a living with men who look like circus freaks, it would make sense," Shep says with attitude.

Gretchen smiles at me. "You don't have to be the medical examiner to know who in this room isn't getting any."

I can't stifle my laughter, which officially removes me from Shep's Christmas card list. She refocuses her anger on the initial blood report, asking, "Was there any blood found that doesn't belong to Laney Bang?"

"Sorry. She had AB Negative, which is extremely rare. In fact, it makes up less than 1% of the population. AB Negative is all that was found."

I look at photos of Laney Bang's naked body lying lifelessly on Gretchen's examination table. I feel a sudden dizziness coming on. Gretchen calmly cleans the food off her hands with a paper towel, and is able to take back the photo before I pass out.

"Maybe it's time for a career change, Jack."

I fight off my nausea, and resume examining the photo. "Tell me about the wounds?"

"Three hits—left lung, heart, right lung—dead instantly. It was surgical. Definitely not some sex game that got out of control," Gretchen says, almost showing admiration.

"So you are saying it's the work of a professional hit?" Shep follows up, likely in an attempt to revive her "Lansdale hired a hit-man" theory.

"I'm saying whoever killed her, meant to kill her. Who did it? That's your job."

"Anything you found that might make the job easier?" I ask.

Gretchen thinks for a moment, before saying, "The thing that struck me about it was that there was no fight. No scratches, nothing under her nails, no bruises. No evidence that her arms or wrists were tied. It's as if she trusted the person to come toward her with the knife."

"From the police reports, there was no evidence of a struggle at the crime scene—no furniture tipped over or ripped clothing," Shep interjects.

"Could she have been drugged?" I ask.

"Initial tests show that she had nothing in her system but dinner, but complete toxicology tests might take weeks to get back."

"It doesn't add up," I say. "It completely contradicts the 911 call where she claims to be in danger."

The phone call is the key piece of evidence so far. It tells us that Laney's state of mind was one of fear and urgency, and she had to be fully awake to make the call, which likely confirms she wasn't drugged. It rules out a sneak attack that she didn't see coming, and if it were a "professional hit," it strikes me as odd that the assassin would be so clumsy as to allow her to make a phone call.

On the other hand, if the call was made under duress, as part of a plan by Laney's attacker to set up Anderson to take the fall, then you'd think there would be some signs of struggle when he came toward her with a knife.

Our trip here has led to more questions than answers. I stand to leave, trying not to faint. But before we go, Gretchen reaches under her desk and pulls out a hardcover book. "I think you might find this an interesting read, Jack."

She hands it to me. On the cover is Laney Bang, looking a lot better than she did in the crime-scene photos. It's her bestselling memoir, Big Bang Theories.

When I open to the inside front cover, I'm surprised to find it autographed. "I didn't know you were a fan?"

"Best thing I've read since the *Da Vinci Code*. Got it signed by the author yesterday at Cooperstown Books. I could barely get near her with all the security—one day later I'm cutting her open…"

I wince at the irony.

Gretchen sadly shakes her head, and picks up where she left off, "I think you'll find it interesting, Jack. There's a lot more to her than meets the eye.

She wasn't about sex, she was about power, and I'll bet you'll find that is why she got killed." She pauses again, before adding, "If Laney Bang were a man she would've been hailed, her memory praised, but because she was a woman her name will be denigrated."

Shep looks disgusted. "For God's sake, she had sex on camera for money! Spare me the Gandhi comparison."

Gretchen chuckles. "Honey, I've been cutting dead people open for a living the past twenty-three years. There are a lot worse jobs than having sex."

I look at the book, and for some reason get the feeling it contains the answers I need.

Chapter 14

Shep and I backtrack down Route-80. We pass Sam's Boat Yard, the Cirillos' house, and eventually the famous Glimmerglass Opera House.

Anderson Estate is located on the north end of the lake with a direct view of the Otesaga Hotel. It sits on a hillside terrace at the foot of Mount Wellington, the property sloping down to the lake.

Drew Anderson and his wife split their time between Manhattan, where Max-Q-Collectibles is headquartered, and this estate in Cooperstown. This is a strategic area for his company, due to their important working relationship with the Hall of Fame.

As we drive up to the gatehouse, I notice a crowd assembled outside the entrance. It includes numerous trucks with satellites on their roofs, along with swarms of nattily attired television reporters talking in front of hand held cameras. The Otsego County Sheriff's Department unsuccessfully attempts to push them back. *They started the mess and now they can clean it up,* I think to myself.

Shep slows to a stop at the gatehouse. A black man with bright white hair comes to the window. The man's name is John Scurry, and from what I've heard, he has been working at the estate for years, long before Anderson moved in. He's one of those people who nobody has a bad word for.

He performs a methodical inspection of our DA badges in between sips of coffee. He looks shaken by the events, and is probably annoyed at the battalions of pushy media members he's had to deal with all day. He eventually returns our IDs and the electronic gates open. We proceed toward the crime scene.

"So this is what heaven looks like?" I comment, observing the estate grounds for the first time in the daylight. We follow the paved, one-lane road that winds through ten acres of manicured lawns. We pass an area of equestrian course to our left, which conjures up an image of Drew Anderson at the races yesterday, standing confidently in his polo uniform.

The stately limestone structure is a forty-room, neoclassic mansion built for the English aristocracy. The front entrance, which has appeared on the cover of many magazines, features seven grand columns that look like they were shipped over from Ancient Greece. Above the columns rests a large balcony with an elegant wrought iron railing.

It looks much different to me than it did the night I attended the charity dinner here for S.A.F.E. Today it's littered with police cars and yellow crime scene tape. Roger Beneke, a young, stout policeman waves us through, but not without incident. He yells to the closest officer, "Look, the DA's Office is here. Is DA short for dumb-asses or double agents? I always forget."

Shep and I are about to jump out of the car, kill Beneke, and then drag his corpse into court to indict it for obstruction of justice. But cooler heads prevail. At least for now.

We drop the Beemer at a circular driveway in front of the seven columns and are whisked inside by another young policeman—this one I don't know.

"Sheriff Opp wants to see you immediately," he says, which almost sets us off again. *He wants to see us? Au contraire, we want to see him.* We stroll through the front entrance, into a large room with a vaulted ceiling that has a cold, museum-like feel to it.

We follow the officer up a staircase that looks like a swirling diagram of DNA, and then through a billiard room that is an ode to Max-Q-Collectibles—framed jerseys of famous athletes lining the walls like paintings in an art gallery.

We pass an exquisite dining area that features large windows that look out at the front balcony. *Why not just push her over and claim she had too much to drink? Seems easier*, I think to myself.

We are taken down numerous corridors until we reach a yellow-tape factory, better known as the master bedroom.

Investigators are furiously taking photos. Bustling police officers move in and out of the room.

Roddy Opp looks up from an inspection of the floor.

I start, "What the hell were you thinking, Opp?"

"You obviously weren't," Shep adds.

Opp looks annoyed. He barrels toward us and physically pulls Shep and me into another bedroom. He shuts the thick wooden door and latches the lock.

"We did this by the book and any attempt by the DA's Office to say otherwise will be met with a strong response from our office," Opp asserts.

"Was coming to a call for help ninety minutes late by the book?" Shep fires back.

Opp is no rookie, he knows it doesn't look good. "Do you have any idea how many false alarms we received this weekend with Laney Bang in town? If we replied to all of them, with all the overtime, the county wouldn't be able to pay Gifford Brown's fat salary. Since it originated from a cell phone that was unidentifiable at the time of the call, we chose not to give it the highest priority."

"But you sure made it a priority when you decided to make a high-profile arrest without consulting the DA's Office," Shep retorts. "Not to mention that you have nothing but circumstantial evidence. Now we are stuck trying to clean up your mess."

She is actually spitting as she talks—I've never seen her so pissed.

"We did what we had to do. We aren't the enemy. Perhaps you should take a look at your own office."

"What's that supposed to mean?" Shep confronts him.

I hate to admit it, but we're going to need his cooperation, so I try to mediate, "What's done is done. There will be plenty of time for finger pointing when this is over. They had a call to make and they made it, and even though it doesn't always seem like it, we are on the same team. But now it's our turn to make a call, on whether to prosecute Anderson. And to do so, I'm going to need to know everything that went down here last night."

Opp looks smugly at Shep. "It's all in our report."

"I want it from you," I state.

He looks tired—the day is taking a toll on him and it's not yet lunchtime. "Roger Beneke took the call, and like I said, it wasn't a high priority. When he arrived he came across suspicious elements that changed his alert level."

"No staff were present, except Scurry at the gate, and the front door was open," I recall from the reports.

"As isolated incidents, neither of them met the standard to enter the home. But when combined with the 911 call, Officer Beneke had reasonable suspicion, and was correct in entering. He went in with intent to help, not arrest anyone, and loudly announced himself. Nobody answered."

"But he wasn't alone," I say.

Opp nods. "He found Drew Anderson standing in an upstairs hallway, looking out of sorts and sweating profusely. Beneke began asking him questions about the 911 call, and Anderson's answers raised further suspicion. Beneke drew his gun, pushed past Anderson, and began a sweep of the home. He found Laney Bang in Anderson's bed, dead, three stab wounds to the chest and enough blood to fill Otsego Lake."

"How did Anderson respond?" Shep asks, her tone calmer, following my lead.

"He lied—told Beneke that he just returned from jogging, which explains why he's dripping with sweat, and why the door was open. He claimed he had no idea who the woman in his bed was, or why she was dead."

"How did you know he was lying?" I ask.

"Because the Otsego County Sheriff's Office gave Ms. Bang an escort onto the grounds last night. Something about a business meeting." He rolls his eyes. "He knew exactly who she was. And I think we all know what her business was."

"I really hope you've got more than that," I say.

Opp holds up a plastic bag containing a cassette tape.

Chapter 15

"We have Anderson's denials and contradictions on tape," Opp says smugly

"Why isn't that in the evidence report?" I respond with anger.

"Our report isn't complete, but we thought it would help to have an initial report sent to our *good friends* in the DA's Office so they can get a head start before this becomes CNN-city."

As I seethe, Opp continues, "Beneke pushed Anderson about the escort the night before, and he miraculously recollected his meeting with the woman he initially had no knowledge of." Opp raises a sarcastic eyebrow. "According to Anderson, the meeting ran late so she slept over in one of the guestrooms. He went out for a morning jog and he returned to find her dead.

"Beneke wasn't sure what to do, so he sought my advice. When I arrived, I learned that the front guard hadn't seen Anderson leave for a jog, and he had sent the entire staff home the night before, which was unusual. We had probable cause, got the warrant, and made the arrest."

"What about his wife?" I ask.

"First person we inquired about—Murder-101. Maybe she caught her hubby screwing around with Laney Bang, so she thought he'd find her less attractive with three large holes in her chest. But she was in Manhattan and accounted for. Numerous witnesses put her at a party in the city until 11:00, and she was also spotted returning to their home, afterward. A neighbor claimed she was so inebriated from the party that he had to help her in, and doubted she could have made it to bed, much less a murder scene hours away. She was at work bright and early the next morning, probably with a nice hangover. She works in the public defender's office in the Bronx, where we contacted her."

"Don't you find it odd that Anderson had a dead body in his home, and likely knew the victim called 911, yet he left his front door open?" Shep wonders aloud.

"Maybe he was too preoccupied with getting rid of the murder weapon—we haven't found it yet—it's been my experience that those who have just committed murder tend to make large mistakes. But we'll find it, and when we do, this will be the easiest case you two have ever prosecuted."

"Were other people present this morning, or at the supposed meeting last night?" I ask.

"His personal assistant, Ryan Maxon, lives in one of the guesthouses on the property. We have it confirmed that he was not on the property at the time of the murder. The only people present were Drew Anderson and Laney Bang. If he wasn't a celebrity, we wouldn't be having this conversation."

"Could someone else have gotten in and out of here?" Shep asks. "This place has access by land, sea, and air. We passed a helipad on the way in."

"He has the best security system going. I should know—I'm the one who installed it," Opp remarks boastfully.

"Then I guess that makes you a suspect," Shep zings.

Opp holds up the tape once more. "Anderson confirmed on tape that he was the only one home, besides the victim. The guard, John Scurry, said in his statement that nobody came in or out during the time in question. John isn't exactly the lying type."

I reach to grab the tape, but Opp snaps it back. "When the evidence is officially registered we will turn it over to the DA's Office. We do things by the book in our office—not the politics that I'm sure you two are familiar with."

"If you have something to say then say it!" Shep comes back at him.

Opp obliges. "Off the record, Drew Anderson isn't the squeaky clean character he's made out to be, and he has a *very* good friend in your office. Last year we were involved in an investigation into Anderson's business practices with Max-Q-Collectibles and were ready to make an arrest. We cooperated fully with Gifford Brown, only to have him squash it out of the blue. You draw your own conclusion as to why. Your office gets huge funding from supporting the S.A.F.E program, and Anderson was one of the main reasons why Brown got re-elected. When he becomes governor, my guess is your beloved DA will go with him.

"We had probable cause—we made the arrest—end of story. Sorry if that put you two in a bad position, but the arrest is not disputable. Although, I'm sure there's someone in your office who will try."

Opp gives another pendulum swing of the bag containing the tape. As I watch it sway from side to side, I realize that the evidence is starting to swing toward Max Q.

Chapter 16

Jessica arrived at the historic building off of Main Street where the arraignment was to be held. She had made the walk numerous times over the last year, for what normally was a brief formality. But this time it had a different feel.

Once all parties were standing before Magistrate Engler, the case was announced—the State of New York versus Andrew Christian Anderson.

He entered through a side door, looking disturbingly out of place in an orange Otsego County Corrections issued jumpsuit, and handcuffed. Anderson joined his lawyers in front of the magistrate.

His fair-skinned lawyer had the stylish look of Park Avenue—blue tailored suit and diamond earrings. Her briefcase was leather and expensive, as were her shoes. She appeared to be the lawyer that Jessica dreamed of becoming, and just this morning the possibility seemed to be in her sight.

The woman's partner, standing in her shadow, had ruffled gray hair. His suit was also pricey, but he lacked the polish of the woman.

The magistrate looked over the charging documents, then spoke in a gritty voice, "Mr. Anderson, you are being charged with the murder of Darby Kelleher. The crime took place on the morning of July 24 at your estate in Cooperstown Village. Do you understand the charges against you?"

Before he could speak, the woman lawyer interrupted, "A rush to judgment has occurred in this case. We motion for the charges against my client to be dismissed."

The magistrate looked annoyed. "I was just about to inform Mr. Anderson of his right to counsel, but I see counsel is in place." She strummed through a stack of papers until she found what she was looking for. "Mr. Hal Metzer will be assisting, while lead counsel is Ms. Kerri Lawson of Lawson, Baird & Gentry."

Jessica was caught off guard. Without thinking, she turned toward her adversary and blurted, "As in Jack's sister?"

"Once again, I see that when the going gets tough my brother sends someone to do his dirty work for him. Typical Jack—always running away from responsibility," she responded.

The magistrate announced that she had no time for childish sniping, before proceeding, "By law, your client has the right to a preliminary hearing. You can make any requests for dismissal at that time. Before I get interrupted again—representing the Otsego County District Attorney's Office is Jessica Shepherdson. Now I need an answer from Mr. Anderson about those charges."

"I understand the charges against me," Drew Anderson spoke for the first time, in a low but confident tone.

"Good—let's get to bail. Ms. Shepherdson, you first."

Jessica's voice trembled, "The defendant brutally murdered a woman who willfully came to his residence..."

"I know the allegations, please tell me why I shouldn't grant him bail," the magistrate interrupted.

Jessica made eye contact with the gloating Kerri Lawson, whom she already found great distaste for. Jack's unflattering description seemed quite accurate, and possibly understated.

"The defendant has vast wealth, homes around the world, and is a trained pilot from his time in the military. He once survived on the land for a week in Bosnia with no food or water. Facing a life prison sentence, he has the motivation to flee. He is the definition of flight risk."

"Vast wealth is not necessarily connected to flight," the magistrate countered.

"My point was that he has the means and the ability to do so. Bail is rarely granted in capital cases and it is the state's position that it shouldn't be awarded in this case."

The magistrate tilted her head toward the defense. "Ms. Lawson?"

"My client is a luminary of this community. He is an American war-hero, and gives more time and money to charity than most small cities. The evidence against my client is weak and circumstantial. He has no reason to flee, because that would be the only indication of guilt the prosecution would have. He is not a flight risk."

"Bail denied," the magistrate barked. "The case will be assigned to Judge Patricia Schanz's part. All parties should contact her court for future court dates."

Chapter 17

Jessica left the room in a daze. She never believed for a moment that Anderson would be denied bail.

Kerri Lawson gave her a final smug look, not appearing overly concerned her client was headed back to a prison cell for the foreseeable future.

Outside, the media had dwindled to just a handful. This surprised Jessica, who had braced for their onslaught. As she watched Kerri Lawson enter a long stretch limo, Jessica couldn't help but think about the road that brought her to this defining moment.

She had fought her way out of Rome, New York, leaving behind the dysfunctional parents and the haters at school who despised the fact she wanted to better herself.

She worked four jobs to pay her way through Syracuse—undergrad and law—and then just as she had prayed each night as a child, her prince came to sweep her away to a better place. But Brad turned out to be more like her father than a prince—both men wanted to be anywhere but with their wife, and when they were home, frankly, they were a little scary. But she dusted herself off and resumed her climb to the top. The ADA program that sent her from Albany to Cooperstown was just a small step on that climb, or so she had thought.

It was in Cooperstown where she met Jack Lawson. For a brief moment in time it wasn't about where she was going—being around him made her savor the present moment. But Jack turned out to be nothing more than another mirage that steered her off course. A painful reminder that the only person she could rely on was herself, which was the reason she was late this morning. As she stood watching Kerri's limo pull away, she never felt so alone in her life.

That's when she came across a familiar face. Ira Montini of the local *Cooperstown Crier* newspaper. Ira had been on the crime beat since she arrived in Cooperstown, and she and Jack had gotten to know him well.

"Where did all the big boys go?" she asked.

"Thanks a lot."

"That's not what I meant, Ira."

"If you have your big moment and nobody is around to cover it, is it really your big moment? It's kind of like that tree falling in the forest stuff."

"I hope my big moment in life isn't jailing the messiah," she replied. She could eradicate world hunger and the first mention in her obituary would be that she was the one who tried to take down the great Drew Anderson.

"I think the mass exodus occurred because your cohorts are giving a press conference at the other end of Main. Once you sent Max Q back to prison there was no longer a story here. I think everyone expected Anderson to be free on bail."

"A lot of faith in me, huh?"

"Faith, maybe not, but Jack did leave you his mountain-bike to get over there. It's wall-to-wall cars on Main and he mentioned how slow you walk in those 'success heels' you're always wearing."

"Why did you stay behind?"

"I figured an unknown lawyer winning the first battle in the latest trial of the century was the story that history would smile upon, not some boring press conference shrouded in 'no comments'."

Jessica climbed on Jack's bike, smiling for the first time in days. "Thanks, Ira, I've got a boring press conference to get to. And for the faith," she yelled back. She peddled away, muscling through the thick crowds by displaying her DA badge. Nobody seemed to recognize her.

She passed TJ's Grill and an old-style brick bank, and then crossed the street. The Cooperstown streets buzzed with the hum of gossip. Reporters circling like sharks had replaced the usual throng of children in Little League uniforms clutching their fathers' hands.

She passed Doubleday Café, Cooperstown Books, where Laney Bang had been signing books less than twenty-four hours earlier, and the Max-Q-Collectibles shop. Lines were out the door. Murder must be good for business, she thought.

Arriving at 197 Main, she dropped the bike and pushed to get a good view of Gifford and Jack. They stood on the steps behind a podium displaying microphones with familiar names on them—NBC, CBS, ABC, CNN, FOX, and GNZ. Normally, Otsego County DA press conferences consisted of Ira Montini and a few other local reporters. Afterward, they would join Gifford and the crew at Touch 'Em All for a couple of beers. This was different ... much different.

Gifford began the press conference by distancing himself from the case, citing his relationship with Anderson. He stated that he had talked to the governor and attorney general of New York, and all were in agreement. He then introduced Jack, highlighting his 98% conviction rate.

She watched as Jack walked to the podium. His confident persona of the courtroom seemed to be missing, as it often was when Jessica would do stuff away from work with him, like their fishing trips. As painful as his words to her were the other night, watching him stumble all over himself as he attempted to deliver them was equally agonizing. It was a quirky dynamic about him that she found strange, but intriguing.

Once Jack found his sea legs, he made a brief statement about the case, overusing the words truth, evidence, and justice. He then engaged the media in the frivolous exercise of them asking him questions that he was unable to answer at this time.

Jessica was befuddled by the absence of questions about the two lead attorneys being siblings. And when a few questions pertained to whether Jack believed Anderson would get bail, it became obvious to her that word had yet to travel—a little strange in this era of instant news. She briefly smiled, thinking that something good finally came from the crappy cell phone service in Cooperstown. She could hear the muffled complaints about smartphones being rendered useless.

Before the press conference concluded, Gifford made one final statement. He announced that for the good of all parties involved, he and Jack had agreed a decision would be made on whether to prosecute by the following Tuesday.

Jessica muttered, “A week from tomorrow? What the…”

Eight days in this case would be like a minute, and putting a deadline on it made no sense—there was a big difference between “not go on for months,” as Gifford had requested, and “next Tuesday.”

By his astonished look, she could tell that Jack was thinking the same thing. That’s the thing about ambushes—the guy being ambushed is always the last to know.

This brought Jessica back to the core problem, which was the police not following the proper procedure of coming to the DA’s Office for a warrant request. They would have reviewed the facts and sent it back to the police, encouraging further investigation. And not just to find probable cause for arrest, but to gain enough evidence to prove it in court. Unfortunately, the police chose to act unilaterally, and now she and Jack were paying the price in front of a worldwide audience.

Jessica didn’t believe Anderson committed the murder, and wanted no part of being connected to the case in any manner, but she was steamed that she and Jack were getting sold up the river, and felt her competitive side awakening from its slumber.

Following the press conference, Jessica found Jack and Gifford meeting behind closed doors. She’d never seen Jack so mad. The normally calm, cool, and collected prosecutor was reiterating what she’d been muttering at the press conference, except he was using more colorful language.

She remembered Roddy Opp’s words at Anderson Estate about Gifford having an agenda to protect his friend, Anderson. She walked into the office and her entrance put a stop to their screaming match.

“What is it, Shepherdson?” Gifford asked with irritation.

“I just wanted to inform you that Anderson was denied bail.”

Gifford looked as if he’d never really considered the possibility.

Jack slumped down in his chair. He ran his fingers through his hair and grumbled, “Great. Anderson never should have been arrested in the first place, my own boss sandbags me with a bogus deadline, and now we’ve turned him into a martyred hostage.”

He sighed deeply, looking toward the ceiling as if it might have the answers. After a long pause, Jack seemed to summon the last ounce of energy to ask the ceiling, "Are there any more bombshells anybody would like to drop on me?"

"Yes, Jack," Jessica said. "Drew Anderson is being represented by your sister."

Chapter 18

I awake to Mick Jagger singing goodbye to Ruby Tuesday, and realizing that yesterday wasn't a bad dream. The only positive I can muster is that the case overshadowed the visions of Reyanne that normally haunt my nights, and I actually got some restful sleep. I almost forgot what it feels like.

I move out onto the deck to witness another prototypical summer day in upstate New York. The lake is rippling, the smell of pine is in the air, and there isn't a cloud in the sky. I watch Ashley backing her van into the driveway and then begin unloading piles of newspapers.

Upon noticing me, she shouts, "Hey, Superstar—you're on the cover of every newspaper in the county!" She holds up the *New York Times* and the *Washington Post* with the look of a proud parent.

Suddenly the enormity of this whole thing hits me. There have been huge cases before with the world watching—Lindbergh baby, Nuremberg, OJ. But never before has there been a famous person accused of killing another (in)famous person. This is unprecedented. Well, at least since society started frowning on men solving their differences with a good old fashioned duel like Hamilton and Burr. I also begin to grasp the social context. Drew Anderson and Laney Bang were opposing five-star generals in the ongoing cultural war.

My eyes wander to Otsego Lake, focusing on a lone sailboat. What seconds earlier seemed innocent now has my antenna up. I think of those paparazzi with the long camera lenses always trying to get a photo of some pop star on vacation, so they would conceivably go to great lengths to get a picture of the unknown lawyer who has the fate of Drew Anderson in his hands.

I shake off the paranoia and return my thoughts to Ashley. I can't help but smile at her. She will probably have a completed scrapbook for me by dinnertime. After a last glance at the sailboat, I stroll back into the house.

I click on the television. The arrest of Max Q is all that is being talked about. I start with the cable news. Legal "experts" are debating the precedent of brother and sister going up against each other as dueling lawyers.

"Legally there isn't a problem and there are numerous precedents—just not in this type of high profile case," says a dapper looking man, whose title is listed as CNN legal analyst.

I begin flipping channels. The perky host of *The Today Show* is interviewing a husband and wife who once went against each other in court. An older gentleman on FOX states, "If siblings could fight against each other in the Civil War, then I see no problem in a courtroom." By the look of this guy, he might have been an eyewitness.

I feel uncomfortable being center of the story, so I desperately surf channels, seeking an escape hatch. On GNZ, a bespectacled legal analyst is praising Shep's work in denying bail. I, on the other hand, am getting panned for placing a deadline on our investigation.

"It shows Jack Lawson's inexperience," grumbles the famed lawyer Barney Cook. "He is giving into public pressure for a deadline. He should admit he made a mistake and take his time in deciding whether to prosecute Anderson."

"They might have won the battle with the bail, but they are losing the war. Kerri Lawson and Hal Metzer already got word out to the jury pool that the police screwed up, and now they're covering their rears. Jack Lawson is already swimming in a polluted jury pool," states a frizzy haired, female television-lawyer.

"In cases of *he said—she dead*, you need hard evidence—and my sources tell me the prosecution has none," retorts Cook. Again, more people with sources.

They claim I will need a miracle, but I just got a panel on a cable news network to agree on a subject, which has to rank just a notch below turning water into wine. I flip channels, determined to change the subject. I pass Sesame Street and I swear I hear Big Bird and Elmo discussing the case. I decide I've lost my mind and move on.

Finally my channel surfing rides a wave to *Good Morning America* where the female host is calmly interviewing Drew Anderson's wife, Marissa Torres-Anderson.

She is dressed in professional business attire and her long tresses of dark hair are tied in a ponytail. I am drawn to her flawless olive skin and magnetic green eyes, but what really stands out is her composure in such a troubling moment in her life. It matches her reputation. While I have never met her, I am aware of her work as a defense lawyer from my time in Manhattan.

"My husband is being set up for this crime," she states, not a hint of doubt in her voice.

"Who would be setting up your husband, and for what reason?"

"I can't get into the specifics, but after talking to his lawyer last night, I am confident she has evidence that Drew wasn't present at the time of the murder. As his wife, I didn't need proof of Drew's innocence, but as a lawyer, such evidence is always comforting."

"You mentioned your unbending belief in your husband, which leads me to my next question—the one that is on the tip of tongues across the world this morning. How can you not question his fidelity, when a woman like Laney Bang spent the night at your residence while you were back here in New York City?"

Marissa doesn't give an inch. "I was fully aware of his meeting with Ms. Bang last night, which was business related, although I am not authorized to go into the details of that meeting. But I can assure you it was not a scandalous affair, as the tabloids are reporting."

She is impressive, to say the least. And when I mentioned that she's a New York defense lawyer, I didn't mean she works for a place like LB&G with a swanky corner office and a view of the Manhattan skyline. She is a public defender in her native South Bronx, which means she doesn't deal with the easiest of characters. And in the case of public opinion (i.e. the jury pool), she just landed one hell of an opening argument on the national airwaves.

This isn't the first time she's fought an uphill battle against rumors and innuendo. When American hero Drew Anderson turned away a long line of Hollywood actresses and socialites in favor of a poor-born public defender without pedigree, the media tried to paint her as a "gold digger." But when she refused to marry him without an ironclad prenuptial agreement, she won over another jury. Marissa was probably too busy to be worried about such public opinion, having continued in her low paying/long hours job at the Bronx public defenders' office. But everything changed yesterday morning when her husband was arrested. Now the opening round of his trial is being fought in the all-important court of public opinion, and I get a sense she is fully aware of the fact.

I halfheartedly eat a bowl of cereal, pull on my biking outfit, and head out. As I pedal toward Main Street, I think to myself that an idyllic summer day like this in Cooperstown was probably the inspiration behind the invention of the sport of baseball. To find out for sure I head toward the Baseball Hall of Fame.

Chapter 19

I arrive at the Baseball Hall of Fame, a classic redbrick building that anchors the east end of Main Street. About 300,000 visitors a year visit the historic museum, which is filled with archived memorabilia of the national pastime.

I chain my bike outside and follow a shrubbery-lined walkway to the front entrance. I avoid the cover charge by displaying the "year round" pass Mac provided me, and stroll unnoticed into the museum. The thick summer crowd swallows me up. I hang a right by the gift shop and slip into the spacious Plaque Gallery—a cathedral-like room with walls lined with the bronzed plaques of the chosen few baseball immortals who have been inducted. The plaques are displayed in an atrium in which rays of sunlight shine down on them through a skylight, as if the baseball gods are showing their approval. For a baseball worshiper like Mac, this room is sacred.

At the front of the room is a life-size statue of Babe Ruth, arguably the greatest baseball player ever to have lived, and certainly the most famous. The Babe is standing in his trademark left-handed batting stance, gripping his heavy maple bat. Even in bronze he looks like he could hit a couple of home runs today. And more importantly for my purposes, he's the man I'm here to see.

I leave the gallery and take the elevator to the second floor, the location of Mac Cirillo's office.

As the Assistant Director of Marketing, he's in charge of the many programs the museum offers—tours, stories and activities for children, and author book signings, to name a few. But this time of year Mac and his team are like Santa and the elves the week before Christmas. So my visit will be brief.

"All we ask for is one weekend out of the year and you have to steal our thunder, Jack," Mac greets me with a chuckle, sitting behind his small desk.

I remain serious. "This is going to get worse before it gets better. So if you and Ashley want me to move out, just give me the word. I won't be offended."

"You aren't going anywhere. First of all, with the Max Q murder circus in town, and the induction ceremonies less than a week away, there isn't a place to stay within a hundred miles of here. And more importantly, Ashley is smitten that she's living with a celebrity, and she would kill me if I let you move out."

"I think I'm more infamous than famous at the moment. And after trying to put away Drew Anderson, my next trick will be to take down the Easter Bunny."

"Well Jack, the good news is that they're still making movies about Pontius Pilate."

"That's comforting."

Now it's Mac's turn to put the serious face on, his voice lowering to a whisper, "You saw it when we met Anderson the other day. It's blasphemy to say it around here, but the guy is a phony and we both know it. I don't know if he killed her, but he's not perfect like they say."

My gut feeling is that the more I look into Drew Anderson, the more I will find things that I won't like. But I'm going to need more than that to prosecute him.

Mac's smile returns, this time a mischievous one. "Why don't you go see a movie, it'll help you relieve some stress. *Pride of the Yankees* is playing in the Bullpen Theater."

That's the cue I came here for, and with a nod of appreciation toward my grinning friend, I'm on my way to meet my contact. I head back to the ground floor, passing numerous exhibits until I find myself at a small movie theater with an old-time looking marquee. The Bullpen Theater is dedicated to the hundreds of films that have been made about the sport of baseball, and original movie posters line the walls of its entrance—*The Natural, Field of Dreams, Cobb.* Today's showing is *Pride of the Yankees,* starring Gary Cooper as tragic Yankee legend Lou Gehrig.

I open the theater doors and locate George Herman sitting in the back row. He's hard to miss. As my eyes adjust to the dark, Cooper is delivering Gehrig's famous dying words, *Today—I consider myself the luckiest man in the world...* The small theater is almost full—summertime always brings out the tourists. And this is nothing compared to the induction ceremonies next weekend, when thirty thousand visitors are expected to invade Cooperstown.

George Herman is a Babe Ruth impersonator by day. He is hired for everything from business conventions to wedding receptions, and Mac often summons his services for Hall of Fame events. *Who better to give groups a tour of the Baseball Hall of Fame than the Babe himself?* Until I moved to Cooperstown, I would never have guessed in a million years that there was such a demand for an impersonator of a dead baseball player.

He's a dead ringer for Ruth, featuring the same pug nose, bowling ball head, booming voice, and a thick head of hair. Like Ruth, his torso is heavy, but his legs are like sticks. He has the same passion for the Babe that I do for the law. And his parents must have known something when they named him, because Babe Ruth's real name was George Herman Ruth.

It seems like everybody in the small community knows him, and most just refer to him as Babe. But what they don't know is that George also happens to be one of the best private investigators in upstate New York, his persona serving as a great cover. Nobody expects him, or sees him coming. Mac was one of the few to whom he confided his secret, and he introduced me to him when I took the job at the DA's Office.

We have a traditional investigator on staff, but I use my own funds to hire George. Even so, we are behind the eight ball in this case. I'm sure Kerri and LB&G have a whole team of investigators digging for dirt and witnesses, leaving no stone unturned.

"I've already started my investigation, kid," George informs me, before I can properly greet him. He calls everyone kid because the Babe called everyone kid. Although, I think Ruth did it because he couldn't remember names. George points to the screen, informing me that Ruth played himself in *Pride of the Yankees.*

"The sad thing is that during the filming the Babe was sick himself, and would be dead within three years from throat cancer," George educates in a booming whisper.

Normally I enjoy George's "Babe-isms," but I'm too busy obsessing on some of the strange looks we're receiving. Although, they're understandable. George is wearing a wool New York Yankees uniform in the summer and I'm still in my biking outfit. We look like we are the construction worker away from a Village People reunion.

I have to make this fast. "I need to know who else was in the house that night."

"Done, kid—already working on it."

"Also, why was Laney Bang there? They are trying to claim it was business related, but I'm not buying it. The answer to that question will lead us to a motive."

"The Babe has a *pretty good idea* what she was doing there," George responds in character, then swipes his hand into a bucket of greasy popcorn. He offers me some, but I decline.

"Basically, this case is top priority. Everything else, including Kass, is on the back burner for now."

George smiles. "Speaking of other cases, I've done some research on your girlfriend. Consider it free of charge."

"Girlfriend?"

"That pretty little ADA, Jessica Shepherdson."

"Shep? She's just my co-worker."

"That isn't what Mac and Ashley told me. But if you don't want to know what I found out it's your call."

He has me hooked. Angel on one shoulder—devil on the other. The devil wins again. "Okay, let's hear it."

"She's actually pretty boring, except I thought it was interesting that she was married to the son of the soon-to-be former governor for the state of New York. The marriage was annulled."

Shep was married? And to Brad Chapman. I knew him as a hotshot Manhattan prosecutor back when I played for the other team—defense—but he is much better known for his latest job, which is chief legal counsel for the current governor of New York—his father. And since his father seems to be attracted to scandal—the reason why Anderson likely would have beat him handily—he has spent much time in the news lately.

"She never mentioned anything about being married in her application, and there is no record of it—the DA's Office does a full background check prior to hire."

"Hence the term, annulled. But that's why you hire me—to dig below the surface. You, of all people, know the rich and powerful can erase their mistakes from the public record, kid."

Shep being married to the son of Anderson's opponent in the upcoming election is a major conflict of interest. And it surprises me that she hasn't used it to get off this case, which she appears to want no part of. She must really want to keep it a secret.

George is engrossed in the movie again. Lou is dying in black-and-white and his beloved wife, Eleanor, is trying to be strong as she watches the once sturdy love of her life wither away to nothing. George begins to cry, wiping away the tears with his big mitt of a hand.

"This is one of the great love stories of all time," he blubbers.

I pat him on the back. "I didn't know the Babe was such a big softy."

As tears drip down his bloated cheeks, I get up and leave the theater.

Chapter 20

I'm standing along Main Street, my eyes still adjusting to the bright July sun. But I can see well enough to notice that members of the media are everywhere, so I do my best to blend into the crowd.

"Jack—there you are! I've been looking all over for you," a voice blows my cover.

I look up to see Shep dashing toward me, which is preferable to a horde of reporters. I'm still trying to register the marriage tidbit George gave me—there's certainly a lot more to Shep than meets the eye.

She appears to have more pep in her step. Perhaps it was the compliments she received on the national news regarding her bail denial.

"I've scheduled a 10:30 meeting with your sister and Metzer at our offices. I think it's a good idea to feel them out, even if it doesn't accomplish anything tangible," she states upon arrival.

"Sounds like a plan, but first I want to grab a bacon, egg, and cheese at Touch 'Em All."

My craving angers Shep. "You spent the morning fooling around at a baseball museum, and now you want breakfast? You can't rely solely on your talent on this case, Jack; you are going to have to put in the time. We only have a week!"

"Nice to see you somewhat interested today. I thought you were going to call in sick for a couple months."

Just as the words leave my mouth, a camera flash goes off, startling us. I can already visualize the headlines: *Case Falling Apart—Prosecution Fighting on the Street!*

I start walking across Main Street. "What do you say we get that sandwich?"

This time she doesn't put up a fight. Our cease-fire lasts almost until we get to Touch 'Em All, when she asks, "What were you doing at the Hall of Fame, anyway?"

"Doing a little research," I reply vaguely. I feel the press following us, breathing down the back of my neck.

"Are you holding back on me, Jack? I thought we were partners. If we can't trust each other...."

I put a smile on for the cameras, and then lead Shep down the stairs to the below-ground entrance.

While Touch 'Em All is best known as a bar, they also make a particularly good breakfast sandwich. And more importantly for us, the owner, Augie, has an "only locals welcome" policy to deal with the overwhelming number of summer baseball tourists. We use it to our advantage to find refuge from the rabid media.

We walk into the dark bar. The room has a Cheers-like mahogany bar centered under a tin roof. It is connected to a hotel named The Carriage, established 1832. On one side of the bar is a huge mural of 19th-century Cooperstown Village, depicting horse drawn carriages traveling Main Street.

Like a clash of cultures, the other side is a typical modern sports bar—pool table, darts, and a large old-fashioned jukebox. The walls are littered with autographed photos of baseball greats. Ruth, Willie Mays, Hank Aaron, Ted Williams.

The place is a little bit Ashley, and a little bit Mac, which is part of its charm.

Our presence immediately shuts down the heated local gossip, most of it centered on the Max Q case. And while we don't receive a Norm Peterson greeting, the vibe isn't unfriendly. The locals respect our job, even if they aren't rooting for us.

Safe from outside forces, I decide it's time to resume our battle positions. "I admit that I met with my investigator, whom I hired with my own funds. But he's the best in the business and that's what we need. His rule is that only I know his identity. I'm not holding back on you, and as soon as he provides me with any information I will share it. Are you providing me with all the information I should know, Shep?"

"Of course—what's that supposed to mean?"

"Ever going to tell me you've been married?"

Her glare indicates that if I don't lower the volume I'm going to get an expensive heel in the groin area. "My personal life is none of your business. You made that quite clear the other night, Jack. Are you checking up on me?"

"It's only considered your personal life when it doesn't affect the case. When the press finds out that one of the lawyers prosecuting the potential future governor was once married to the son of the man he might be replacing, they are going to have a field day."

"It's nobody's business. Besides, if we choose to prosecute, we'll have so much bad PR that it'll just be another log on the fire. But if you don't want me on the case, make my day and drop me. I never asked for this!"

The words "One bacon egg and cheese," breaks up our scuffle. We take a seat at the bar next to Matt the local drunk, who, no surprise, is downing a pre-noon Jack and Coke.

I check the baseball-shaped clock on the wall. It's 10:26. We're going to be late for our meeting with Kerri—let her wait. Shep doesn't see it the same way, and practically drags me out of the place as I scarf down my sandwich.

Back in the sunlight, I head for my bike, while Shep chooses to walk.

"Get on, I'll give you a ride."

She declines out of spite.

"Come on, Shep, I don't want you to scuff your pretty shoes."

She shoots daggers at me with her eyes. But I can tell she's weighing her options, which are limited. "Fine," she grunts, then grudgingly follows me to the bike.

She sits behind me, holding on for dear life around my chest, restricting my ability to peddle. I notice a group of photographers staking us out. This one will be a photo of unity.

We arrive at 197 Main, unwittingly waking up the bored media. We practically run past them, ignoring their rapid-fire questions.

"You have one week, Jack—do you really have time for bike rides?" yells one reporter, to laughter.

I carry the bike inside the building. Our presence stops all conversation. Something we are becoming adept at.

Shep follows me into my office with instructions that Kerri is waiting in the conference room. But first I head for my shower. I have it down to a science and I'm back in my office dressed in a suit in less than five minutes.

I attempt to take a moment to gather myself, before entering the coliseum to face the lions. But I underestimate my control-obsessed sister, whose voice screeches through the phone intercom on my desk, "You can run, but you can't hide, Jack—now get your sorry-ass in here!"

I unhook the phone and put my feet up on my desk, wondering if a brother/sister relationship can be annulled.

Chapter 21

Shep and I sit at the conference table, facing Kerri and Hal Metzer. Sort of like a mixed doubles match of the legal world.

The national networks have praised Metzer's legal mind, and more importantly, his experience in the courtroom. Despite her highly touted pedigree, Kerri lacks courtroom experience. The more I think about it, the more I believe her presence is a ploy by LB&G to get under my skin and throw me off my game.

Kerri opens with predictable gusto. "So Jack, are we done with this charade?"

"Charade?"

"Let me define charade. Locking up my client, who has a spotless reputation, even though you have no evidence. Shall I go on?"

"Please do."

"Okay, let's start with motive. What did my client have to gain by killing that whore?"

I guess we won't have to hold our breath to see if the defense is going to use 'blame the victim' tactics.

"I'll tell you what his motive was," Shep interrupts. "He was having an affair with Laney Bang. She threatened to expose him, damaging his so-called spotless reputation, not to mention ruining his marriage."

I know Shep isn't a firm believer in Anderson's guilt, but I think my sister has sparked her competitive spirit.

I pick up where she leaves off. "Your defense would be much stronger if she hadn't made that 911 call, upon feeling threatened by your client. And he was obviously unaware that she made it. Because he had a ninety minute head start on the police, yet he didn't dispose of the body that was in his bed."

"The reason he wouldn't know about any 911 call was because he wasn't present at the time it was made. And she obviously was calling for his help, not accusing him of anything."

"That would be more believable if he didn't then lie to the police. Claimed he didn't even know who Laney Bang was or how she got into his house." I foresee numerous holes in my theory, but I think it's more important to look assertive at this early stage.

Metzer gets involved. "Any statements that Mr. Anderson made to police, not knowing he was considered the lead suspect, and without being informed of his right to an attorney, will be inadmissible."

I hold up the plastic bag containing the tape that Opp finally had sent to our office this morning. "I say we let the judge decide that. But I must say, it sounds real good on tape. I think a jury will be particularly interested in the part where your client admits he fabricated the first story about not knowing who she was, only to make up an even more laughable one about a business meeting. You know, one of those typical business meetings where a porn star spends the night."

For a microsecond—you had to be looking for it—Kerri and Hal look stunned. But like the pros that they are, they immediately recover and shoot dismissive looks at the tape. It's to our advantage that at this stage of the process, discovery has yet to occur. So they don't know exactly what evidence we have.

"My client panicked, which is a natural reaction to finding a dead body in his home after returning from a morning jog. If by some bizarre twist of fate this actually goes to a trial, I'm sure a jury would understand Drew's reaction," Kerri proclaims.

"Let's get back to motive," Hal follows up. "The only person I can think of that *did not* have a motive to kill her was Drew Anderson. Ms. Bang had more enemies than I can list here today. But let's review the most likely. She was involved in a messy multi-million dollar lawsuit with MaddoXXX Video, which contends that she broke her contract to start her own production company. Her book, *Big Bang Theories*, has publicly exposed her intimate affairs with numerous rich and powerful men, and women. It's no secret such revelations ripped apart many marriages, families, and careers.

But I would say the biggest motive belongs to one man, James Lansdale, who has created an organization called Smut Cleanser, and its website lists Laney Bang as its number one 'Most Wanted'."

Shep elbows me, not so subtly pointing out that she and Metzer were riding the same wavelength. I'm not so sure—I think this is just the first of many "theories" the defense will be floating. And if we ever advance to the trial stage, I expect their strategy will be to dish up a smorgasbord of semi-plausible suspects, diverting the jury into believing that the prosecution failed to prove the case beyond the reasonable doubt burden. It worked for OJ Simpson at his murder trial.

"I might add that Mr. Lansdale lives locally and has been to Anderson Estate on numerous occasions. Of course this wasn't a theory that was even considered by the police, yet it makes much more sense than this crazy affair idea you are trying to sell," Kerri adds.

"Anderson Estate has access by land, air, and sea. It could easily have been penetrated by someone looking to harm Laney Bang," Hal tosses in as if he is discussing war strategy.

Once again, the defense and my partner seem to be sharing the same brain.

"Anderson Estate has one of the best security systems in the world," I try to fight back.

"Yes, Jack—a security system put in by Sheriff Opp. A man that has an obvious grudge against my client, and if need be, I can show evidence to prove it."

"What was the real reason Laney Bang spent the night at Drew Anderson's house, Kerri?" I ask.

"And try to do better than the excuses your client provided during his initial questioning," Shep throws in, I suspect only because she despises my sister.

"It was a business meeting," Kerri utters defensively.

"Was Laney getting into the collectibles business or was Drew going into adult entertainment? I ask

Kerri looks at me like I'm the snot-nosed little brother she thinks I am. "My client, at no time, had any type of intimate or sexual relationship with the deceased. Any insinuation that there was one is going to land you with a slander suit, little brother. Have I made myself clear!?"

"You two have no evidence that our client had any relationship with the victim," Metzer adds.

I lean back in my chair and grin wryly. "Sounds like a business meeting to me."

"What about his alibi of jogging—surely you can do better than that?" Shep interjects.

Kerri responds with a crooked smile that I vividly remember from my childhood. It usually appeared right before one of our "Lucy pulls the football away from Charlie Brown" moments. I was normally on the losing end of that smile, so I'm concerned that Shep just walked into a trap.

"I almost forgot," Kerri says. Then in a seamless orchestration, Hal unzips an expensive leather brief case and pulls out a small stack of papers.

Kerri slides them across the table. "These are three signed affidavits from witnesses who are willing to testify my client was jogging around Otsego Lake, just as he said, at the time of the 911 call."

Shep performs a quick scan of the affidavits, but won't go down without a fight. "I'm sure you know that the chance of accurately identifying a moving target at daybreak is slim, so these statements are suspect at best."

"*Suspect* is what you don't have," Kerri fires back. "At least not the right one. What we have here is a police department that not only failed to properly respond to a 911 call, but also failed to interview witnesses that backed up my client's alibi. They only saw this event through the prism of the grudge they hold against him. So now there are two victims—Laney Bang *and* Drew Anderson."

She is the ultimate front-runner—piling it on when she is winning. For some reason George Washington pops into my mind. The man spent the whole Revolutionary War retreating, yet still came out the hero. We need to follow George's example.

"Drop the charges and let's get to the business of finding who killed this woman," Hal Metzer gives his final word, as he tucks the deadly affidavits back in his briefcase.

I stand. "Thank you both for coming. Like I said in the press conference, our investigation will extend until next week. At that time we will make a decision on whether to formally file charges."

George Washington would be proud.

I reach my hand out and we all begin a handshake ritual. "Enjoy your fifteen minutes of fame," Kerri says—she always has to have the last word—before they turn and leave.

Shep slumps back into her chair. "That was embarrassing. Can it be any more obvious that they arrested the wrong guy? We should just go drop the charges and get it over with before we become fodder for the late night talk show hosts."

Everything they said about lack of motive, evidence, and witnesses to his alibi was correct, but my gut feeling is telling me that Drew Anderson did kill Laney Bang. Although, my job as prosecutor is to prove it, and right now I can't.

I get up without a word and head for my office.

"Where are you going?" she asks curiously.

"I'm going to my office to catch up on my reading."

"At a time like this, Jack, how can you even think…"

I enter my office and shut my door. I pull Laney's book out of my backpack. The cover displays a naked— except for strategically placed fig leaves—Laney Bang, stretched out like Jesus Christ on a wooden cross with an explosion of planets in the background. I'm not sure exactly what statement she was trying to make, but there's no doubt that she was making one. My initial impression of her is that every action she made was calculated, and I'm guessing that the last night of her life was no different.

I open to the first page. "C'mon, Laney—give me some answers. Who killed you?" I mutter to myself. I'm surprised to find a poem entitled "Baby Doll."

Sweet dreams they say, and don't let the bedbugs bite.
Whoever said it never endured my night
Lay still Darby and pray for it to go away
I feel the nightmare closing in and I want to speed to day

The nightmare begins with a creak of my door
Please not tonight. Please no more.
I pray even harder, but then I hear the call
My nightmare begins again—hello Baby Doll

I don't dwell on why my fate is so unkind
I know one day I'll leave it all behind
The nightmare creeps closer and it's worse if I fight
I'll leave Baby Doll behind, just not this night

I wasn't expecting poetry, but so far Laney Bang has been anything but predictable.

There's a knock on my door.

"Go away," I say and turn to the next page.

"Jack, open up—it's Shep."

"Go away!"

"Jack, we have to evacuate. There's been a bomb threat—they said if we don't release Drew Anderson, the building will be blown up."

Chapter 22

My alarm is blaring the Simon and Garfunkel classic "Wednesday

Morning 3 A.M." I lay in a daze, immersed in a dream of Reyanne.

A banging noise on the sliding-glass door jolts me awake. Then another. *Bam. Bam. Bam.* I remember the bomb threat from the day before and I'm instantly alert and on my feet.

I realize these are not shots from an AK-47, my window is being pelted by small rocks.

I slide open the door and step out into the hazy morning. A small pebble glances sharply off my left shoulder.

"Agh!" I scream out.

"Jack—I'm so sorry—I didn't see you there!" shouts Ashley, who for some reason is throwing rocks at her own house.

"What are you doing?"

"I was just trying to get your attention, Jack—I'm sorry, did I wake you?"

It's hard to stay mad at Ashley. "No, I was already up," I lie. "What's going on?"

"I was going to offer you a ride to work."

This doesn't strike me as an emergency of rock throwing proportions. Besides, the ride always clears my head. "Thanks for the offer, Ash, but I'm going to bike in today."

I contemplate other motives she might have for me in the name of Jack Lawson's best interests. Perhaps she plans to whisk me away for an early morning "stress relieving" skydiving trip. Or maybe she met a woman that she decided was beyond a reasonable doubt the one for me, and has set up a romantic breakfast for us.

Ashley remains steadfast. "Jack, I think it would be a *really good* idea for you to ride with me this morning."

I have never won one of these struggles with her, so I give in. "Just give me a minute to change," I say.

Ashley smiles at her victory.

I return to my room and flip on the television. Gifford Brown appears on the screen in a taped interview from yesterday. He's discussing the bomb threat that turned out to be a hoax. He reveals that the Otsego County DA's Office has received over a hundred death threats since the news of Drew Anderson's arrest. Most are just kooks looking to stir up trouble. But some threats, like yesterday's from a known group of fanatics, must be taken seriously. Their belief is that Drew Anderson was either innocent, or had performed a great deed for mankind by eliminating the devil. Basically, the same misguided nonsense that led to Reyanne being taken away from this world.

I throw on a pair of jeans and T-shirt that salutes my alma mater, the Brown Bears. I add a black and gold New Orleans Saints baseball cap that I bought when I went to visit Reyanne's family in Louisiana—an offbeat but tight-knit group that believed in pursuing dreams more than the almighty dollar—and round off my disguise with a pair of dark sunglasses. Just another tourist in Cooperstown.

I head back past the television where I catch a clip of Kerri. She is hitting home the same points she made in our office yesterday, and they are just as powerful.

I click off the television and head off to join Ashley.

I hop in the van and she jets out onto Route-80, driving toward Cooperstown Village. "What's going on?" I ask.

She nods her head toward the back, indicating for me to take a look. I get the feeling that this is not an impromptu skydive or blind date.

Behind the curtain, wearing his wool, pinstriped New York Yankees uniform, is George Herman…private investigator extraordinaire.

"I thought this would be a good place to meet, kid. Tough to get any privacy the last few days."

Ashley looks back with the smile of a Cheshire cat, proud of pulling off such a covert operation.

"I'm just going to do my normal schedule, while you two talk," she informs.

I nod and shut the curtain. I duck under hanging dry-cleaning, and try to avoid stepping on the many bags of groceries and other items marked for

Ashley's clients. I find my way to a bench that lines one side of the vehicle and take a seat next to George

Before he begins firing information my way, I ask, "George, would you mind if I brought someone else into this conversation? I promised her that she would be present when we discussed information pertaining to this case."

He is hesitant to bring in a third party, but agrees to make an exception in this instance.

I instruct Ashley to stop in front of 197 Main Street to pick up Shep. She agrees with a smile, loving the spy-movie she's playing the female lead in. I check my phone and notice a warning that says my voice mail is full—looks like one of my friends in the DA's Office gave out my number to the media, and I make a mental note to get a new phone, and possibly new co-workers. I call Shep's number.

"You want me to do what? We have a million things to do today, Jack. I don't have time to go on some joy ride!"

"Just meet us out front in five minutes, and don't tell anyone where you're going," I state firmly and hang up before she can respond. If she doesn't show, she can't say I don't trust her again.

I peer out the tinted rear window. We can see out, but the caravan of media following us—who seemed to have popped up from nowhere—can't see in. If Ashley keeps on the move, we'll have privacy. An ingenious idea.

We stop in front of 197 Main and are now surrounded like General Custer at the Battle of Little Big Horn.

Out of the chaos appears Shep, running awkwardly in her high-heeled shoes. She pushes her way to the passenger door, fighting through the crowd that's blocking her way. It looks like a crowd rushing the stage at a rock concert.

Ashley swings the door open and whisks Shep into the van. I can already visualize the headlines: *Assistant District Attorney Kidnapped in Broad Daylight!*

Ashley hits the accelerator, and the crowd parts. Nobody is willing to die for the cause.

"What's this all about?" Shep asks, as the van moves down the crowded Main Street. We are boxed in—a slow trolley in front of us and a funeral-like procession of media on our heels.

"Go back and find out," Ashley says with a smile.

Chapter 23

Shep looks at me, demanding answers with her eyes. I agree this could use some explanation, so I let her in on George's alter ego.

She thinks I'm kidding. Like most in Cooperstown, she only knows George as the lovable impersonator. Once she understands that I'm serious, her look turns annoyed. I can guess her thoughts—Kerri has an army of elite investigators working on this case and we have a Babe Ruth impersonator! But being underestimated has always been George's secret weapon.

While she appears skeptical, I have scored points for extending the trust branch. She sits down beside us, ready to listen, which is her way of saying thanks.

George starts right in with his businesslike approach. His serious tone is much different from that of his jovial Babe character.

"For a little background, Laney Bang arrived in Cooperstown on Sunday morning. Her first act was checking into the Otesaga Hotel with a fellow adult film actress who goes by the name Amber Jazz.

"Laney was brought by a limo service to Saratoga, where she watched her horse win the final race of the day. The second item on her itinerary was a book signing at Cooperstown Books that began at five o'clock that evening. Then the third and final act, was a scheduled meeting at Anderson Estate at nine o'clock."

"What was the purpose of the meeting?" I ask, still convinced it was just an excuse for Laney and Anderson to partake in a different type of business.

"From her perspective, she wanted Lansdale's group to back off. As much as the publicity helped initially, whether it be good or bad, eventually the loss of sponsors from her show, or stores not selling her book, would take its toll on the Laney Bang brand. She wanted to stop the decline before it started, and kept the negotiations secret so that she didn't hurt any of her anti-establishment street cred."

"But business deals are two-sided, what would Anderson or Lansdale's group get out of it?" Shep asks.

"Anderson is about to run for governor of New York. Whatever you think of her, Laney Bang had become an enormously powerful voice who could swing a large block of voters. And Lansdale probably wanted Anderson to win the governorship more than Anderson did. They were discussing a public truce, in which Anderson would have appeared on her talk show."

"It's good strategy," I say, thinking aloud. "He would appeal to those who never thought to vote for Drew Anderson. He might offend his closest followers, but they'll vote for him anyway. Not only will Bang's show get big ratings when he appears, but Max Q will also give her some mainstream credibility. She has gotten this far being the rebel, but ultimately the rebel always loses to the establishment. She was going to make an attempt to get her establishment membership card."

The van jolts to a sudden stop.

"I'm at CVS Pharmacy, guys. I have to pick up some prescriptions for a couple of my clients. Our next stop will be old Mrs. Johnson's farm in Milford," Ashley yells back to us.

A mob of reporters greet Ashley as she leaves the van and heads into the pharmacy. She strolls past their confused looks like a movie star working the red carpet at a movie premiere.

After the brief distraction, George continues, "The third person present at the meeting was Anderson's personal assistant, Ryan Maxon. The fourth was Laney's travel companion, Amber Jazz. And the fifth person at the meeting was James Lansdale.

"He arrived with Anderson at approximately eight p.m.—they had dined together at a Saratoga restaurant after leaving the racetrack. At 8:30, Anderson sent the house-staff home, citing an important and confidential meeting that was going to take place that evening.

"Laney Bang was supposed to wrap up her book signing by 7:30, but because of high turnout, it lasted an extra hour. The local police agreed to give her an escort to her meeting at Anderson Estate, due to concerns for her safety."

I remember Anderson telling me at the racetrack that he was returning to Manhattan that night to attend a party with his wife. Perhaps he wanted anyone and everyone thrown off the scent, but Drew Anderson not telling the truth is starting to become a trend.

"Roger Beneke was the police officer who escorted her," George goes on. "First, they dropped by the Otesaga Hotel to pick up Amber Jazz, before proceeding to Anderson Estate, where they were let in about 9:15 by the guard manning the front gate, John Scurry—the only estate employee still present."

"Beneke is the same officer who was the first one on the scene," I make a note of what I now see as an interesting coincidence.

"I have no idea what took place in this meeting," George admits, "but I do know that at eleven o'clock, Ryan Maxon and Amber Jazz left together. They took a motorboat across Otsego Lake to the hotel, where they made quite a spectacle of themselves at the patio bar. Drinking, dancing on tables, and generally all over each other. When their display became too graphic, they were asked to leave the bar area. They retreated to her room where they kept the neighboring rooms up all night with their antics—multiple complaints were filed with the front desk."

"What about Lansdale?" Shep asks.

"At 1:15, a helicopter arrived for Lansdale. It first took him to his home in Saratoga, where they made a brief stopover, and then on to New York

City."

Shep's mind is at work. "Maybe that's what he wanted people to think, but instead, Lansdale remained in Saratoga, so he could be in striking range the next morning to do some smut hunting."

"The thought did cross my mind, but we have confirmation he landed in Manhattan at the West 30th Street helipad at three o'clock, and security video shows him checking in to the Four Seasons Hotel—where he stays when he's in Manhattan—just before 3:30 a.m. And he was present at a meeting in Midtown at eight the next morning."

George provides us with a printout of the flight log. The helicopter left the West 30th Street helipad in Manhattan at midnight to pick up Lansdale—the trip took eighty minutes—then followed the path that George outlined, arriving back in Manhattan at three.

But there's a twist. The helicopter made another trip the next morning. Leaving Manhattan at 5:45 and flying to Lansdale's yacht. It returned to Manhattan, arriving at 8:21.

"If Lansdale was at a meeting in the city, then what was this flight about?" I ask.

"I also found it strange. But from what I've learned, Lansdale likes to keep his girlfriends overnight on his yacht and then fly them into Manhattan the next morning. According to my sources, and from checking past log records, it's nothing out of the ordinary."

George hands us a copy of a pilot's license. "I checked with the pilot, who was sworn to secrecy on the identity of the girlfriend, citing confidentiality agreement with Lansdale. But he did let it slip that the trip was to pick her up. He also revealed that Lansdale is especially protective of this one, since she's going through marital problems—as in she has a husband. The helicopter went directly to the yacht, then immediately returned, so it's hard to see how it could be connected to the murder, the time-line just doesn't seem to fit. But I'll dig deeper."

I look at the fresh-faced pilot—he looks to be about sixteen years old, even if the license says he's twenty-five. His name is Anthony Forge.

I hand the log and pilot license back to George, the meeting still tugging on my mind. "I just can't believe that Lansdale would be willing to risk his group's support to go into business with Laney Bang. That would totally crumble his credibility. And I met the guy at Saratoga—he's a true believer in what he's selling. "

"Don't underestimate how important it would be to have his friend as the governor, and possibly in the White House down the line," George turns into a political analyst before our eyes. "Can you imagine if President Max Q got the opportunity to reconfigure the Supreme Court? Endless possibilities in shaping the social fabric of America, which is what Lansdale's group really wants. He could sell that to his followers."

"Makes sense," Shep agrees.

"So between Lansdale leaving at 1:15, and Laney's call for help approximately five hours later, did anyone else come onto the property?" I ask.

"Nothing I can confirm, but I'll continue to work on it, kid."

I think what he'll find is that Laney Bang and Drew Anderson were alone on the estate for the next five hours. If she willingly agreed to stay, she obviously didn't feel threatened. I remember what the medical examiner said about the trust Laney Bang felt toward her attacker.

"Yesterday, we received affidavits from the defense, stating that Anderson was jogging at the time of the 911 call," I change gears.

"I checked with John Scurry. He didn't see Anderson leave, but he said that's not uncommon. The gate is there for vehicles, but there are numerous acres with access to the road. So there's no way to prove that he didn't."

"What about the cops?" Shep asks. "Beneke escorted her to the property the night before, so he knew she was there. And Sheriff Opp has been rumored to have an ax to grind with Anderson—not to mention a specific knowledge of the security systems at Anderson Estate."

The van begins to bounce over a gravel driveway. I was so wrapped up in the discussion that I didn't notice that Ashley had returned to the van and set out for her next destination. Through the tinted window, I view the procession of vehicles that are following us to Mrs. Johnson's farm, despite the numerous *No Trespassing* signs that feature a picture of a shotgun. After an abrupt stop—thankfully she's much smoother behind the controls of a plane—Ashley collects the items for Mrs. Johnson from the back of the van. I briefly consider how funny it would be for the three of us to carry them in with her.

"Opp was overseeing a security meeting for the upcoming Hall of Fame ceremonies at the time, so he is ruled out. Beneke was on duty, but that's all I really know at this point," George remarks.

"Anderson is the only one who could have done it," I assert. "Something happened in those five hours to give him a motive. Nobody rises to the top without collecting some skeletons in their closet. Perhaps Laney Bang threatened to use some of those old bones against him and it got her killed."

"We still have no evidence, no motive, and can't disprove his alibi," Shep isn't buying it.

Ashley returns and aggressively backs the van out of the driveway. The media vehicles behind us panic into reverse, causing a humorous domino effect.

"Next stop will be a dry cleaning drop off in Oneonta," Ashley announces, sounding like a train conductor.

"Anything else that can help us?" I ask George.

"I got Drew Anderson's cell phone records. He called his New York City residence twice. There was a twenty-second call at eleven o'clock, so I assume he left a message on voice mail. Called the same number again at 11:36 and spoke for almost ten minutes—probably talking to his wife.

"According to the police, she returned home from a party just after eleven. Was so intoxicated that a neighbor had to help her inside," I add.

"I'm curious if he told her he was having a slumber party with a porn star?" Shep wonders aloud.

"Regardless of the crux of the conversation, a husband calling his wife is not out of the ordinary," I add.

"No, but his other call might be. At 6:19 a.m. he called Ryan Maxon's cell phone," George says, unable to hold back a big grin.

Chapter 24

Shep looks at me—then at the motorcycle—before announcing, "I'm not getting on that thing!"

"Suit yourself—I'll go interview Maxon alone."

"How about I call someone at the office to drop off my car?"

"I don't want anyone at the office to know where we are. I don't trust any of them." Including our boss.

I straddle the bike and rev the engine. I toss her the only helmet. "You take it, you'd have a lot more to lose from a head injury."

The gesture evokes a brief smile and she cautiously climbs on behind me.

With the Maxon revelation, the dry cleaning in Oneonta was put on hold. We returned to the Cirillos' house, where George worked the phones. He confirmed that Maxon left the hotel by boat at approximately 6:30, or not too long after he received the call from his boss. He couldn't confirm whether Amber Jazz was with him, but doubted it, as his source informed him that you'd remember it if you saw her. George and Ashley then took off in opposite directions to confuse the media. So our ride to Anderson Estate is unimpeded.

Manning the gate once again is John Scurry.

"We're here to see Ryan Maxon," I politely announce, displaying my DA badge.

"Surprised you haven't arrested him—you've arrested everybody else around here," he replies, as surly as John gets.

I don't explain the fact that the DA's Office doesn't arrest people, or remind him that only one person has been arrested. But it's quite obvious we're not going to win any popularity contests at Anderson Estate, on Main Street Cooperstown, or in any national poll.

"Where can I find him?" I ask, this time forcefully.

"As far as I know, Mr. Maxon has not left the guesthouse since you arrested Mr. Anderson."

Again, we don't arrest people, but I let it go and drive the bike onto the grounds of the estate. A few wrong turns later, we find the guesthouse. Guesthouse being a relative term—a twenty-room mansion is a more appropriate description

A disheveled looking man opens the door, wearing a ratty bathrobe and three day facial growth.

"Can I help you?" he asks in a detached voice.

"My name is Jessica Shepherdson and this is Jack Lawson—we are from the Otsego County District Attorney's Office."

"I know who you are, I asked if I could help you."

"We have a few questions for you," I say.

Maxon looks like he's contemplating making our lives difficult, but can't summon enough energy to fight. He turns and slowly walks back into the house and plops into a leather recliner.

Shep and I follow him in, closing the door behind us. We take a seat on a couch, facing him. The living room area is littered with empty beer bottles. I also notice a pile of DVD cases are stacked next to the recliner. I read a couple of the titles—*Kitty Kitty Bang Bang* and *Citizen Bang.* He is watching Laney Bang movies. I'm not sure what to make of that.

"Having a little party here?" I ask.

He smiles slightly, but not a happy smile. "Alcohol and porn. America's real national pastimes."

"We have record of a phone call Drew Anderson made to you at 6:19 in the morning on Monday," Shep gets right to the point.

"So what?"

"Fourteen minutes earlier, a distressed Laney Bang made a 911 call from Anderson Estate. She was murdered shortly thereafter."

"Was she really?" he asks with heavy sarcasm. He veers between laughter and tears. Ryan Maxon is a troubling sight.

"Why did Drew Anderson call you that morning?" Shep asks.

"If you did your homework, you would know that Drew calls me every morning, to go over the days agenda."

"But this was the only day he called you after a murder took place in his house," I contest.

Maxon looks unimpressed. "I still don't know where you're going with this."

"I'll tell you where we're headed. We have confirmed that you left the Otesaga Hotel minutes after your call with Anderson, to return here by boat. Unless you can prove otherwise, you are on a collision course with an accessory to murder charge," Shep states.

I don't know if she is being inspired by the praise she garnered from the bail hearing, the trust I showed her this morning, or annoyance at Maxon's stonewalling, but she is now completely engaged, and I suddenly feel like I have a teammate.

Maxon twists the cap off another beer, while shaking his head sadly at Shep. He's despondent. I recognize the look as my own when I first arrived in Cooperstown. It's the look of someone who has been to hell. But unlike myself, Maxon has yet to catch his return flight.

"What was discussed in that phone call?" I inquire.

Maxon casually sips his beer. "We were supposed to leave for Manhattan by eight, as we had a full day of meetings set up, but Drew informed me that something had come up. So he told me to push back the flight, while he took care of it."

"Would the thing he needed to take care of be the body of a murdered woman?" I ask.

"If he actually killed someone, which he didn't, I would have been over immediately to remove the body. Even when he gets cleared in this case, he will always have some baggage hanging over him. I would've advised him to get rid of the body, whether he did it or not."

"So you would encourage him to break the law?"

"I would do anything to protect Drew Anderson and his reputation. Are you really here to debate hypotheticals?"

He must be unaware that he's dealing with Lawyer Jack here, not his weakling alter-ego. "I don't think it's hypothetical at all. I believe it's exactly what you did. Anderson ordered you back here during that phone call, and since you are a professional lackey with no mind of your own, you discarded the murder weapon for him. But before you could get back for the body, the police arrived."

Maxon takes another sip of beer—his way of saying he won't dignify my wild theory with an answer.

"Where were you going in that boat?" Shep follows up.

"Since our flight was pushed back, I had unexpected time on my hands. So I did what I always do when I have time to kill in Cooperstown—I went fishing."

"Did you catch anything?" I ask.

"Not a murder weapon, if that's what you're implying."

Everybody seems to have all the right answers in this case. Maybe because they're telling the truth. But I'm convinced that there's something Ryan Maxon isn't telling us.

Shep gets us back on course. "Tell me about the meeting the night before."

"Sorry to ruin everyone's fantasies, but it was a professional business meeting. I won't go into specific business details of Max-Q-Collectibles, but I can say that it was cordial, we made progress, and agreed to meet again in the near future."

"But you can't say for sure what took place after you and Amber Jazz left?"

"I can't."

"Drew and Laney Bang appear to be more like adversaries than business partners. How did such a meeting come about?"

I'm expecting him to claim an inability to discuss Max-Q-Collectibles business, but a proud look comes over his face. "I brokered the deal. It took months of secretive negotiations, and up until the last minute, I wondered if it would ever come off."

"Was it normal for Drew to put his assistant in charge of arranging such a sensitive meeting?"

I can tell he doesn't appreciate my use of the term "assistant," as I think Ryan Maxon had a grander view of his employment status with Anderson.

"It was a unique situation."

"Why was that?"

"Because I had a personal relationship with both parties."

"You had a relationship with the victim?" I ask, trying to hide the astonishment in my voice.

"She was a close personal friend of mine. Does this surprise you?"

Shep and I look at each other. Yes it does.

"How long did you know her?" I ask.

"Laney Bang?"

"I believe that's who we're talking about."

"We met at a New Year's party in Las Vegas about a year-and-a-half ago." The words seem to trigger something and he abruptly breaks down. Tears well in his eyes and he wails, "I can't believe she's gone!"

Shep and I make eye contact once more, each knowing what the other is thinking. Sounds like Ryan Maxon had a major thing for Laney Bang, which makes him much more interesting to us.

"Do you normally watch your friends having sex?" Shep asks, pointing at the stack of Laney Bang videos.

Maxon emerges from his tears with a weird smile. "Laney was an artist. Watching these tapes is no different than watching Monet paint."

Shep cringes.

I visualize some poor sap trying to use that as an excuse on his wife or girlfriend.

Maxon's smile washes away, and for the first time he speaks with confidence, "Drew will get off. Even if you had a video of him killing her, you couldn't get a conviction. Everything always comes out aces for him."

"Do you resent him for that?" Shep asks.

"I live in this beautiful mansion. I'm paid handsomely, and have job security that others can only dream of. When Drew Anderson goes to the governor's office, I'm going with him. I spent the night in question with a woman most men would give up ten years of their life for just one night with. Do I resent him? Hell no—I worship him, and I'll do whatever I have to do to protect him. My tears are for Laney, not Drew."

I decide that we're done, even though I can tell Shep has an extensive list of follow-up questions in her head.

"Good day, Mr. Maxon. You were very helpful and we are sorry for your loss," I say, while simultaneously yanking Shep toward the door.

He slumps in his chair, offering no reply.

Shep and I are off to question the woman who men would give up ten years of their life for.

Chapter 25

The sunny day has unexpectedly turned gray and drizzly. Through the mist, I point out some of the lake's finer points to Shep: Whistling Turtle, Woody's Point, Over the Edge. Her fright has lessened slightly, and she is holding steady on the back of the F-41.

George calls my cell. I pull over and put him on speaker. He informs us that Amber Jazz has been holed up in the Otesaga Hotel since Laney's murder hit the news.

"Has anyone actually seen her?" I ask.

"Yeah, kid, the room service waiters," he replies with a chuckle. "When they brought a meal to her room, they didn't know they were the entrée."

I smile. "Anything else?"

"I checked out Anderson's morning jogs. From what I could gather, he takes the same path every day—regimented to the point of obsession. He leaves Anderson Estate at exactly six a.m. and heads east, passing Glimmerglass State Park. He picks up Route-31 on the east side of the lake and runs toward Cooperstown Village. He does a u-turn at the halfway point and retraces his steps. It's about a ten mile run altogether. We can try to find people along the way that contradict those affidavits."

I thank the Babe and roar toward Otesaga Hotel.

The historic hotel is famous for its stately columns, inviting porch, and deep verandas that overlook the shores of Otsego Lake. The Lawson family are big fans, which is another way to say it's steeped in old money and timeless elegance.

Mac and Ashley had their wedding reception in Otesaga's grand ballroom. Then a weekend of boating on the lake and golfing at the acclaimed Leatherstocking Golf Course, which sprawls gracefully behind the hotel.

Shep and I walk under the grand neo-Georgian columns and into the glitzy lobby. The Otesaga normally has an ironclad policy about giving out room numbers, but Ms. Jazz has built up enough ill will that we're shown to her fifth-floor suite without having to display a badge. I knock on the door and shout "room service," which receives a begrudging smile from Shep. The door eases open and Amber Jazz appears before us.

I'm awestruck by her height—easily over six-feet with help from her skyscraper heels. Her look is stereotypical. Dramatic high blonde hair and breasts that need their own zip code. But compared to Laney, she seems plastic, as if she were created to be the bionic woman of sex. Laney had the ability to morph from the sultry seductress to the innocent girl next door, while my first impression is that Amber is a cold seductress.

She invites us into a room that smells like a Grateful Dead concert. She is wearing a microscopic T-shirt that exposes her flat abs. It's tied with shoelaces around her midsection, creating a harness effect that appears to defy gravity in holding up her enormous chest. It reads *Pornstar* across the front, perhaps in case we were to mistake her for a neurosurgeon.

While the body matches the reputation, from the neck up Amber Jazz is a mess. She looks tired, haggard, and far beyond her supposed twenty-five years of age. I don't know if it's Laney's death, or the effects of a three-day drug binge, but today's version of Amber looks more like the lead singer of Mötley Crüe than the epitome of male fantasy.

"You're not room service, are you?" she finally catches on.

"My name is Jessica Shepherdson and this is Jack Lawson, we are from the Otsego County DA's Office," Shep announces, all business.

A concerned look latches on to her face when she notices my examination of a joint smoldering in an ashtray.

"I'm fucked," she exclaims in a smoky voice. I can tell this isn't her first encounter with law enforcement.

"Maybe not if you help us out."

Amber grins, once again in her element. She drops to her knees in front of my "happy zone" to begin her version of a negotiation tactic. "You won't regret this, sweetie," she purrs.

I look to Shep for help, but all I get back is a horrified look. "Not that," I say, voice cracking. "By help us out, I mean answer some questions about your friend Laney Bang."

Amber's steely eyes soften. She looks like she wants to cry, but no longer possesses the ability to do so.

Needing to escape the smoky haze, I suggest we talk on the balcony. Shep thanks my quick thinking with a subtle look, and wipes tears from her eyes—the smoke is unbearable.

Amber grabs a pack of cigarettes and half-full glass of what looks like champagne, and seductively saunters to the patio. Shep and I follow, happy to get out of the room. The view of the misty lake is a beautiful sight, the rain showers have stopped and a rainbow arches over Cooperstown.

Amber sips her drink with her collagen-enhanced lips, leaving a residue of red lipstick on the glass. "So, Jack Lawson, have you and your girlfriend here ever brought another woman into the bedroom?"

My face turns cranberry red. "Um, what? She's not my …"

Shep is in no mood. "Let's cut out the games. Either cooperate with us or the only threesome you will be involved with will be the number of people in your cell."

Amber rolls her cigarette over her bee-sting lips. "You don't get it much do you, Ms. Shepherdson?"

Shep looks like she's using every muscle in her body to fight off the urge to beat Amber to a pulp, so I take over the questioning. "Tell us what happened the night leading up to Laney's death."

Amber swigs the remaining contents of her glass, and then becomes even more fidgety, if that's possible. "I knew it wasn't a good idea—I told her not to go through with it. She was playing with the big boys, and the big boys don't play fair."

"Go through with what?" Shep beats me to the punch.

"Laney had been planning it for a long time. As long as I knew her, she was obsessed with him," Amber rambles, then tries to drink again from her glass. When she figures out it's empty, she tosses it with frustration onto the cement patio. The shattering of glass momentarily startles us.

"What had she been planning?" I ask in a calming voice, but it has little effect on the hysterical Amber.

"Don't you get it—she was going to blackmail him! That night was to be the night. That's why I went to the meeting, to try to make sure she was safe. Laney told me that she'd be okay!"

Shep and I trade glances. Sure, Amber Jazz isn't exactly what you picture when you look up credibility in the dictionary, but this is the first piece of information that slightly resembles a motive.

"If Laney had been planning this blackmail scheme for a long while, then she must have had previous meetings with Drew Anderson," I assert.

Amber snorts a condescending laugh. "Meetings? I'm not sure meetings is what I'd call them. But sure, meetings will work."

"Laney Bang and Drew Anderson were having an affair?" Shep asks, reading my mind.

"Affair is something bored rich people do in the suburbs, sweetheart," Amber says between drags on her cigarette.

"Then what are we talking about?"

Chapter 26

Amber puts out another cigarette on the glass table, no ashtray required. "I need a drink—somebody get me a drink!" she yells out. I expect servants to rush to her beck and call, but there are none.

Shep is aware that we're onto something and runs back into the room. She returns to the porch with a half full bottle of champagne. Amber Jazz begins drinking straight out of the bottle.

The alcohol seems to calm her, and she continues, "I told her to stay away from that snake, but she wouldn't listen. They would go to Laney's secret spot in the city, and they'd have to hose down the walls when they were finished. Then Anderson would go back to his wife, and telling people how to live their lives like he was the fuckin' Pope or something. At least Laney wasn't pretendin' to be something she ain't."

"Where is this secret spot in the city?" I ask.

She shrugs. "Hell if I know. Wouldn't be secret if anyone knew."

"So you didn't actually see Laney and Drew together."

"I said they went to her secret spot, but I didn't say that was the only spot."

"So you did witness them in action?"

"Witness them? I wasn't just a spectator..."

I am rendered speechless, so Shep takes over. "You didn't happen to make any films of these get-togethers, did you?"

Amber shakes her head. "Film is business, this was personal for Laney."

"I can tell she was important to you," Shep displays surprising tenderness.

The tactic seems to work, as Amber begins to open up. "I was only sixteen when I got in the business—lied, said I was eighteen. Laney took me under her wing, I was gonna be her protégé—the next Laney Bang!" she states proudly, before adding, "Laney was bigger than life. She was different from the rest of us."

"How different?" Shep asks.

"She gave a shit. Every time I got hooked on drugs or got the crap beat out of me by another asshole boyfriend, Laney would take me in and nurse me back to health. She wasn't like the rest of them in the industry, who would suck every ounce out of you, then spit you out."

I realize we don't have much time before Amber is in an alcohol-induced coma, so we better get to the point. I don't know how believable her claims are, but it's our job to gather all the information and then sort it out. "Tell me more about this relationship between Laney and Drew."

Another long swig of champagne. "She talked about him even before she met him. We watched him on some talk show one time—and she started ranting and raving about the guy, saying she hates people like him who act like they are all perfect when she's sure he's a real creep when the cameras are off."

"So when did they meet?" Shep asks.

"We were at a New Year's Eve party in Vegas about a year-and-a-half ago. Anyone who's anyone was there. Laney went because she heard Drew was going to be there, but I guess he'd returned to New York—something about his wife being sick. But Laney met this guy Ryan Maxon who was Drew's assistant. She totally played him into getting an intro to Drew.

"Soon after, Laney's career started taking off. Real mainstream movie roles, the talk show, and the book. Shit that none of us could ever dream of. We used to joke with her that Max Q must have been pulling strings for her.

She certainly was pulling his." She takes a moment to laugh at her witticism, then the steely look returns. "It pissed her off—said she wouldn't take anything from that asshole. She was definitely setting him up to take a big public fall."

"How was Laney going to blackmail Drew?" I change direction. We are losing her quick.

"She never gave no specifics or nothin', but I just knew it was the night of the meeting."

"What was Maxon's relationship with Laney? He claims they were close personal friends," Shep says.

"Not as close and personal as he woulda liked. Maxon was truly in love with Laney. Hell, half the world was in love with Laney. She did care for him though, and didn't want to hurt him. That's why she wanted me to get him out of there that night before the shit hit the fan."

Amber puts on a pair of oversized sunglasses as a few rays of sun escape through the storm clouds.

"He seemed to be a willing participant," Shep points out.

"He's a man isn't he, sweetheart? I've never met a man who could say no to me."

I take note of her tone. Sex to her is like the courtroom for me. The arena that brings out her swagger. It's the other aspects of life that we struggle with.

"What about the phone call he received from Drew the next morning? I assume you two were still together doing whatever you do," Shep says, no longer able to mask her disgust.

"Drew pushed their trip back, so Ryan decided to go fishing. I'm not a fishing kinda girl, so I stayed behind and hung out in the room. Haven't left since."

It backs up Maxon's story. I study Amber, searching for any signs that she's lying, but find none.

She rises to her feet in a drunk stumble and methodically un-harnesses her T-shirt. She completely removes it, exposing a chest that seemingly could walk away on its own. "Do you think *you* can resist me, Jack?"

I look away. It's like looking into the sun—enjoy the heat, but don't look directly at it.

Shep saves me. "Thank you for your help. We'll be in touch," she announces, and drags me toward the door.

In the parking lot, sitting on the motorcycle, I remark, "We've got our motive."

"C'mon, Jack—she was stoned out of her mind. And who would believe her, anyway?"

"She never met a man who couldn't resist, remember? We will just have to get an all male jury."

"Including you—next time you should wear a bib if you're going to drool. What do men see in a bimbo like that?"

I rev the motorcycle, pretending I didn't hear her. I'm not touching that one.

"Where are we going?" Shep inquires, shouting over the noise of the engine.

"There's only one person we haven't talked to yet from that meeting," I shout back.

"Lansdale."

"Yeah, the guy with the ironclad alibi."

"We'll see," Shep says with an excitement in her voice. I think she might be starting to enjoy this.

We hit Main Street, then maneuver to the east end, passing the Hall of Fame. Main Street eventually turns into Route-31, which follows the path of the lake on the east side.

Rays of sunshine have successfully fought off the dreary rain. We pass Lakeside Cottage on our left and something hits me. "If Anderson took his typical jogging route, starting at exactly six a.m., factoring in about a seven minute mile, this is about where he would be when he called Maxon," I shout out.

Shep doesn't hear me, seemingly distracted. "Jack, I forgot to call into the office. Gifford must be having a fit. Crime of the century and his two prosecutors are AWOL."

She reaches into the pocket of my jacket and pulls out my cell phone. It gives me a tingle as she does. *It must be the wind whipping in my face.*

I pull off to the side of the road. Shep removes her helmet, sending her now un-bunned hair flying in all directions. She punches the number into the phone, looks perplexed, and then tries it again. She shakes it like it isn't working, before trying one more time. Her face lights up.

"Jack, there is no cell phone reception here!"

Her words are like an anvil to my head. It jars my memory—from Lakeside Cottage extending all the way north past Glimmerglass State Park, almost to Route-53, is a dead spot for cell phone reception.

If Anderson was on his normal morning route, then he couldn't have made that call to Maxon at 6:19!

Chapter 27

We speed down the New York Thruway toward Saratoga, passing sporadic pockets of traffic. With the rain now completely vanished, the setting sun is a bright fireball, obscuring my vision. Shep grips hard around my chest, holding on for dear life. I glance back at her and smile, but she is clearly lost in thought.

With the wind whipping in our faces, we leave the Thruway at Exit-24. We move onto Route-87, which takes us to the upscale resort town of Saratoga.

The streets are filled with the usual festivities of summer. We pass art festivals, small boutiques and sidewalk cafes full of tanned people in golf shirts and khaki shorts. We ride by the Saratoga Polo Grounds, where Drew Anderson will be unable to compete this weekend due to unforeseen circumstances. Then pass the racetrack—the place where only three days ago Laney Bang celebrated the victory of her horse. And where Drew Anderson told me point-blank that he was going back to Manhattan that night.

We arrive at James Lansdale's horse-ranch, twelve miles north of Saratoga. His seventy-four acre "summer ranch" features numerous riding trails in a manicured, park-like setting. We enter on an unpaved driveway, kicking up dust, causing both Shep and me to cough. There is no guard or security to impede our progress, as I had expected.

The driveway appears endless. To our right, we pass a half-mile training track. On the left, is a large indoor arena for horse training, which sits next to a large barn. I'm not sure exactly where we're headed and I can feel Shep's grip growing tighter with anxiety.

But after passing a couple of well maintained hay fields, as well as extensive riding trails, we arrive at a ranch house about the size of the Pentagon. Numerous vehicles decorate the front entrance—two pickup trucks, one looking as if it came from a monster-truck show. An elegant Mercedes, a military-looking Humvee, two Jeeps, and a Lincoln Navigator.

"What is this guy, a rapper?" Shep asks with a rare show of humor.

"The rugged outdoorsman—at least that's the image he likes to portray," I comment, viewing the scene. As we approach the house, I notice Lansdale's large helicopter sitting like a shiny trophy on a helipad.

As we get closer to the expensive used car lot, Shep points at on e of the vehicles. "What are those, Jack?"

I notice the steel guards sitting prominently on the front grills. I've seen them before. "They're called roo-guards. They are popular in Australia—used to protect vehicles from kangaroos and other large animals."

"Not a bad idea. I hit a deer on the Taconic Parkway last year and the bodywork was like two-grand. Where'd you learn about roo-guards?"

"I wrote a brief about them for an international law class, concerning a controversial law that banned them. It was passed due to a large number of children being injured or killed in low-speed accidents."

We head toward the front door. Just as we do, we are approached by a young man with a tanned, square jaw. He wears blue overalls over a tight long sleeve shirt that magnifies a gym-sculpted physique. His chest area is splattered with sweat stains from the humid summer day.

"May I help you?" he asks. I notice a twinge of an accent similar to Lansdale's.

"I am Jessica Shepherdson and this is Jack Lawson, we are from the Otsego County District Attorney's Office," Shep announces, and we flash our badges.

The man smiles back at her and I notice her knees slightly bend. "I'll bet you're looking for James Lansdale," he replies politely.

"This is his home, isn't it?" I say.

"Yes it is, but he's not here. He's in New York City on business."

Our faces drop. "Do you know when he'll be back?" Shep asks.

"Sorry, ma'am, I just work here," he says, nods, and walks off toward a rugged-looking Jeep.

"Now that is a man I'd give up ten years of my life for," Shep says, practically glowing.

The man fires up the Jeep and drives off into the distance, bouncing over the terrain with the setting sun in the background. It's like a living postcard.

"I should have called first to make sure he was home, we were just on such a roll today," I scold myself for the wasted trip.

"I like the accent," Shep states, still mesmerized.

We travel back to Cooperstown. The sun sinks behind the thick forest and the day turns to darkness, just like our investigation.

Chapter 28

It's been a long day and we can use a drink. We also crave some privacy from our new best friends in the media.

I park the F-41 on Main Street and we walk to Touch 'Em All. A hush comes over the crowd. I look around, expecting to see the president and first lady walking in, but then catch on that we are the cause of the silence. I'm happy to see Mac and Ashley at a table waving us over. George Herman also sits with them, looking different out of his Babe-gear.

I feel all eyes on us. People that a couple days ago we were sipping beers and playing pool with, now look at us like we're strangers.

Mac breaks the tension. He grabs a cocktail napkin and a pen, then rushes at us. "Can I please get your autographs!?"

A roar of laughter travels throughout the bar. I feel a sense of normalcy for the first time since this mess started.

Shep and I sit down and Augie brings us two beers each. "On the house, guys—I figured you'd need more than one."

"Thanks," we reply in unison and take big gulps from the frosty mugs.

Augie lowers his voice. "And between you and me, I think Anderson is a pompous ass, and if he killed that girl I hope you put him away for a long time. I'm not saying what she did for a living was right, but she didn't deserve to die."

"I'm not even sure we are going to prosecute, we are still looking at the evidence," I say, but the vote of confidence makes me feel good.

"Well, stall as long as you want. The tourism bucks from the media alone is putting enough money in the county to rebuild that school that was blown to bits," Augie adds, before returning behind the bar.

A television above the bar steals my focus. It's replaying a clip of this morning's antics. I watch Shep running awkwardly toward Ashley's van. Then after some pushing and a lot of yelling, the door flies open and Shep is whisked off like your normal everyday kidnapping.

The bar crowd recognizes the van and begins chanting loudly, *Ashley! Ashley! Ashley!* She stands and performs a graceful curtsey toward her adoring fans.

Never one to stick a toe in to check the waters, Mac dives right in on the touchiest of subjects. One that is being debated across the country. "I don't know if Anderson killed her, but he was definitely doing her."

"Honey, you know Jack can't talk about this," Ashley admonishes.

"I know he can't, but I can."

"It's the thoughtlessness that counts," I add with a smile.

"I don't get it. His wife is beautiful, smart, and they always appear so in love. Why would a guy risk that for a predator like Laney Bang?" Ashley asks, truly perplexed.

Just as Mac is about to respond, and likely get himself suspended from his bedroom, George steps in, "But, kid, you don't think Anderson killed her, do you?"

As far as I know, we are the only ones who have knowledge of his involvement in the case, and what his moonlighting gig is, so he can talk about it all he wants. In fact, it adds to his cover.

"Guys like that usually don't do their own dirty work," Mac responds.

"I think James Lansdale did it," an eavesdropping Augie shouts from the bar, and gets a smile from Shep.

"Not even a suspect," Mac counters.

"C'mon, Mac, the guy puts her on the website as number one on his hit list. The news just reported that he was at Anderson's house the night before."

"That's unconfirmed," Mac contends.

"You think it's a coincidence?" Augie asks.

"Lansdale is less likely to do the dirty work than Anderson. The only thing he does himself is walk up and down the steps of his private jet."

Pictures of Shep and me are displayed on the television. The first one is the two of us on the bike, riding toward the office to meet with Kerri. Another shot is of Shep holding on to me as we ride away. A stiff-looking anchor appears on the screen and announces in his best Ron Burgundy voice, "Drew Anderson's fate is in the hands of Chief District Attorney of Otsego County, Jack Lawson, and Assistant District Attorney, Jessica Shepherdson. Who are these two unknowns who have rocketed from obscurity to the national consciousness? Our panel will try to answer that question tonight."

"Jack Lawson is blue-blood pedigree, as part of the Lawson legal dynasty. But reports are starting to surface that he left the family firm due to what a few sources have described as mental health issues," states one esteemed panel member.

"Jessica Shepherdson is much more of a mystery. There isn't much out there about her. But in a high-profile case like this, no one will be able to exist under the radar for long," chimes another.

Then the announcer says, "I think the important question America wants to know about these young lawyers is, are rumors true of a romance between them, and how will their sometimes explosive relationship affect the case? We will discuss that when we return from this commercial break."

As they go to commercial, more photos fill the screen. One is of the two of us arguing yesterday morning outside the Hall of Fame. If I remember correctly, the topic was trust. We look like a couple having a lovers' quarrel. Another is of us on my motorcycle arriving at Anderson's for our meeting with Maxon. All eyes in the bar shoot toward us.

Reyanne taught me that the time when people expect you to be the most vulnerable is when you need to stand up the tallest. I turn to Shep. "Let's get out of here."

"But Jack everyone will think…"

I grab her quivering hand, stand tall, and with all eyes on us, we walk out of Touch 'Em All. Cameras are waiting for us outside the bar. I ignore them and get on the F-41. Shep climbs on behind me. I fire up the engine and leave the media in the dust. I drive her to 197 Main, where her car remains in the parking lot from this morning.

"Shep, don't let them get to you. It's what they want."

"It's not just that, Jack. It's this whole thing—it's overwhelming."

I don't want to tell her that it will only get worse when they get word of her marriage to Chapman. I'm baffled as to why it hasn't been found out already. But it's not the time or place for that discussion, so I go with a pep talk.

"I know this will sound clichéd, but we need to take it one day at a time.

Think how much progress we've made since this morning. We learned that Maxon, Anderson, and Lansdale were all at a meeting at the crime scene. We learned of the phone call from Anderson to Maxon. We learned that Laney might have been blackmailing Anderson, which is a potential motive. And best of all, we confirmed that Anderson likely lied about jogging, based on the dead spot in the cell phone service. That is one hell of a day, Shep."

"Problem is, Jack, that Lansdale, Maxon and Amber Jazz all have alibis. Amber backed up Maxon's story about the call. We can't prove that Drew was in that area on his jog—maybe he took a different route. We still have no physical evidence or murder weapon, and our motive comes from a drugged out porn actress. On top of that, Kerri has witnesses willing to testify that they saw him jogging at the time of the murder."

She's right, but I don't think it will help my pep talk, so I keep that to myself. I do take note again that she appears distraught that our case isn't heading toward a trial, much less a conviction. A few days ago, she would have been secretly thrilled to see this thing go away.

We have to get out of here quick, before the press shows up and gets a picture of us alone in a dark parking lot. *DA's Secret Love Nest!*

"What's on the agenda for tomorrow?" Shep asks, as she gets into her BMW.

"We are going to New York to see your friend Lansdale."

She sits tall behind the wheel. The fear appears to fade away into the cool night. "I'll pick you up," she says with conviction.

Chapter 29

I wearily return to my apartment and lay exhausted on my futon. My body feels drained, but at the same time the pieces of the puzzle are zooming around my head like the Daytona-500. Sleep is a long way off.

I reach to my nightstand and pick up my copy of *Big Bang Theories*. I open to the first chapter entitled *My First Movie*—this time it's narrative, not poetry. I figure this will be the closest thing I get to actual sex in a long while.

For some reason, I believe the book contains a clue that will lead me in the right direction. "Talk to me Laney," I say to myself.

Hello new life! At least that's what I thought when I moved out on my own after turning eighteen, but I found that it was eerily similar to the old one.

I first saw Mr. Perfect when I literally ran into him in the hallway of the complex where we both lived. He looked like he had jumped off the cover of one of those romance novels with the intent of writing a happy ending to my cautionary tale. But truth was, he barely noticed me.

I didn't receive the leers of men in those days. I had never even worn make-up at that time—forbidden by my strict parents—and my twig-like body had been nicknamed "Kansas" by my high school classmates because of my "flatlands"— the famous Laney Bang curves had yet to be attached.

Mr. Perfect didn't have any problem getting the attention of the opposite sex—the intimidating ones with their big-hair and showy cars, and who wore the tiniest of bikinis over their flawless bodies at the swimming pool. I didn't fit in with most of the girls, so I spent most of my time alone, hoping Mr. Perfect would look my way. I often fantasized that he'd see me across the room and walk by all the other beautiful girls to me. I would look smugly at their envy-filled faces as we rode off into the sunset. He would provide me a new life and I'd leave Baby Doll behind.

While I didn't catch his eye, I did befriend his roommate. We'll call him Friend because that's what he was to me. Friend didn't have the looks or status of Mr. Perfect, but he sure liked me a lot more, and turned out to be the most loyal man I've ever met. But Friend couldn't give me a new life; whisk me off into a fantasy like I thought Mr. Perfect would.

Friend took me as his date to Mr. Perfect's birthday bash. After the party, we returned to their place. That is when Mr. Perfect suddenly noticed me. In fact, so much so that he began ignoring his date, who looked like she appeared right off the cover of Cosmo. Looking back, I think he just wanted to put Friend in his place and prove once more that he could do whatever he wanted, whenever he so chose. But all I could see was the fantasy.

Miss Cosmo stormed out over the attention he was showing me. Now it was just the three of us. Mr. Perfect went to a small refrigerator and took out a bottle of Bacardi. This was the first time I drank alcohol, and the last. Friend became really drunk, brooding over the fact that Mr. Perfect and I were heavily flirting with each other, which we weren't being real subtle about. He soon passed out on the bed.

It didn't take long for Mr. Perfect to make his move. He was a lion and I was his prey. It was inevitable. I started to push him away, not wanting this to happen with Friend present, but the fantasy was too powerful. Before I could blink an eye, our lips were locked and our clothing was off. We climbed to the top bunk—my stairway to heaven—and he officially turned me into a woman. Goodbye Baby Doll—hello new life!

I left before Friend woke, not wanting to face him, but that didn't stifle my joy in the least. The next day, I couldn't wait to see Mr. Perfect again. I was floating on air, knowing that Friend had already left for the day and we could pick up where we left off. My new life awaited and I didn't want to put it off another second.

Even the knock on the door seemed wrong. Mr. Perfect didn't answer his door. Instead, it was a guy I'd seen hanging out with him. He blocked my path, informing me that Mr. Perfect didn't ever want to see me again. I can still feel how cold his voice was. I tried to force my way in, but I couldn't fight past him; he weighed an easy three hundred. "You know the rules—if you know what's good for you, you'll turn around and never come back here."

Full of shame, I walked back to my place. Once inside, I heard laughter from the TV room. I remembered my roommate mentioning something about having some friends over to watch the latest Jim Carey movie. Feeling humiliated, I had wanted to be alone, but for whatever reason I was drawn to the laughter.

When I stuck my head inside the door, a hush came over the group. All I could hear were the screams and moans—definitely not a comedy. Onscreen, were two naked bodies engaged in passionate sex. Sometimes moments are so surreal that they don't register right away—this was one of those moments. But when it did, I felt like I had been gut-punched. The two people on the tape were Mr. Perfect and me!

I was glad it was dark, so I didn't have to see the derisive expressions, nor could they see my humiliation. Who had filmed us? How could this have happened?

I wanted to run out of the room, but my feet felt cemented to the floor. It got worse. Mr. Perfect, obviously aware of the camera, played to it, winking, and even made a hand gesture to indicate that I was "just okay." At one point, he was mocking me while I was in the throes of passion.

Finally, I bolted from the room, feeling like my skin was on fire. Unbeknownst to myself, my new life had begun. It was just a lot different than I pictured it to be. The first seeds of Laney Bang had been planted.

My therapist believes Mr. Perfect is an amalgam of the many men in my life whom I put on a pedestal, and trusted in the deepest way, only to have them shatter that trust and taunt me in my dreams. And that Friend is a combination of the few loyal people who stood by me, and looked over Darby, as Laney climbed the ladder to fame. Basically, she believes I made up what I just told you as a way to summarize the pain from my youth, and rationalize becoming this character called Laney Bang.

Perhaps, but that doesn't change the fact that it still feels real in my nightmares.

Chapter 30

I awake to David Bowie singing "Thursday's Child." Thursday is not exactly the pick of the litter when it comes to day-of-the-week songs.

The book is lying open beside me. I expected a provocative tell-all of dirty secrets. Sure, the main topic was sex, and granted, it was only one chapter, but what I read was a heartfelt tale of betrayal.

If we take Amber Jazz at her word—I picture Shep having a good laugh at that one—we can conclude that the likely motivation behind Laney's murder was her attempted blackmail of Drew Anderson. But my impression of Laney Bang, so far, is that there is always another layer below the surface. So to tell the whole story, we will need to dig deeper.

I am fascinated by this Mr. Perfect character in the memoir, especially after Amber told us that Laney "hated" guys who hid their dirty laundry behind a pristine public image.

Come to think of it, most of the men she exposed later in the book—which soaked up all the attention from the press when the book was released—fit this category, as does Drew Anderson, which is likely why she had plotted his demise.

My thoughts are interrupted by three quick honks of a car horn.

"Jack? Are you in there, Jack? Are you ready?" I hear a voice shouting at me with annoyance. Definitely not the sweet tones of Ashley. I shake the cobwebs and remember our trip to New York today. My tardiness is threatening to derail Shep's itinerary and she isn't happy about it.

I stumble to the porch. It looks as if a heavy downpour could commence at any moment. I see Shep in a bright white pantsuit with white heels, looking like the Angel of Anal Retentiveness.

I negotiate for five minutes to get ready. Shep looks at the slim, gold watch on her wrist and sighs. "Hurry up, Jack."

I quickly shower and barely make my five-minute deadline. I fix my canary colored tie, and moments later I'm strapping myself into the passenger seat of Shep's Beemer.

She doesn't look amused. "You said you wanted to be on the road by seven, so we'd miss the heavy traffic."

Add lack of punctuality to my growing list of faults. I look at my watch—it's only 7:15, but I don't have the energy to fight. The streets are already crowded as we drive through Cooperstown Village. Mostly reporters who've descended upon our tranquil town. The unhurried pace of Cooperstown has quickened.

My mind is on food. We pass Carmen Esposito's Italian Ices, which always hits the spot on a hot summer afternoon. Then the Victorian looking Stagecoach Coffee Shop, which has the best strawberry smoothies in town. A group of tourists wander under the striped awning of Danny's Market, where I do my food shopping. I give in to my hunger and call in a bacon egg and cheese order. Five minutes later, and after numerous dirty looks from Shep, we pick up my sandwich from Touch 'Em All and head toward the New York Thruway.

We're traveling to the big bad city with hopes of capitalizing on the previous day's momentum. Shep seems troubled this morning. And I get the feeling it goes beyond my tardiness.

"Is everything okay?" I ask

"Yes, why wouldn't it be?" she snaps, before changing the subject. "I called to confirm with Lansdale's office this morning. I know it will take away the element of surprise, but I didn't want to waste the trip if he was out of town on business."

"Good thinking."

She looks like normal Shep—punctual, prepared with the day's agenda, conservative dress for success, and hands safely on the wheel at "ten and two" as if she came directly from drivers-ed class. But something is lingering below the surface.

She rambles on, "We will meet him at his Midtown office at eleven-thirty. He said he would give us an hour. I'm not sure if we will have time for lunch, so I packed a cooler with sandwiches and bottled water."

"Tell me what's bothering you. Is it those reports about us being a couple?"

"Nothing, Jack."

"C'mon, Shep—I thought we are supposed to trust one another."

She surprisingly relents. She reaches into her briefcase and pulls out a pile of papers and hands them to me. "I printed them from my email."

I begin to read the emails and I'm horrified. A death threat is one thing, but detailing the way they plan to do it, is another. I keep reading, one deranged paragraph after another.

"Have you told Gifford—maybe he can get the FBI involved? We need to get you protection."

"You said not to discuss the case with anyone in the office."

"This is different."

"One threat claims they can get to me anywhere, anytime and actually work with members of the FBI, CIA, and Secret Service," she tells me, her voice cracking.

"So what do you want to do about it?"

"I want to stop talking about it. I'll deal with it."

I take her tone as a sign to drop it. I reach in my bag and pull out *Big Bang Theories*. I open to my bookmark and begin to read the next chapter called *Epiphanies Don't Wear Clothes*.

When Shep grasps what I'm doing, her look turns to irritation. "I can't believe you're reading that trash."

"The last book you read was How to Get Rich by the classic author Donald Trump, so I'm not sure you're qualified to be a book critic."

"Sounds like you are just trying to get your jollies," she shoots back.

"You should always talk to the victim, Shep, and this is the only way she is talking these days."

Shep rolls her eyes and returns her concentration to the long road ahead.

Chapter 31

As if the heavens disapprove, the sky suddenly opens up and rain begins to pour down, but I read on.

Following the embarrassment of my first movie, I packed up my stuff, and made another attempt at a new life, ending up in Atlanta. I thought about returning home, but one thing I learned is to never go back. Just keep looking forward.

I got a job at the local movie theater—made minimum wage taking tickets, working the snack bar, and being an usher, but the fringe benefit of the job was getting free movie viewings. I loved escaping into my mind and sinking deep into a fantasy.

The Peachtree-7, which was the name of the theater, is where I met a beautiful girl around my age named Jade, and she asked me to be her roommate. The movie theater was Jade's second job—the one to fool her parents—she had another job that paid much better than the Peachtree. She worked as an exotic dancer at a club called Vixens out in Marietta. She would come home with fancy cars, the best new clothes, and would take expensive vacations with her sugar-daddy boyfriend of the month. The Bahamas, Greece, Italy...

Jade was always trying to get me to work with her at Vixens, knowing I was struggling to get by each month. I always declined. I think I had about enough public humiliation to last me the rest of my life. Taking off my clothes in front of a bunch of horny guys? I didn't think so. Besides, I didn't know how I could compete with the bodies of girls like Jade.

One night, Jade convinced me to come by and watch her dance. No pressure, just watch. Jade was up on a stage dancing around a steel pole in seductive style. I noticed how she had the crowd in the palm of her hand. Not to mention the wads of green cash sticking out from the waistband of her g-string. It was intoxicating.

Following her performance, she introduced me to the club owner, Tyler Maddox. He had long rocker hair and a goatee, and I was amazed by how young he was. It also impressed me how kind and supportive he was to the girls. Not the greasy, cigar-chomping sleazeball I expected.

By the end of our meeting, I had agreed to work at Vixens. Not as a dancer, the thought still was unfathomable, but as a barmaid. Triple my current salary and I didn't have to take off my clothes. Tyler called it an offer I couldn't refuse, and he was right.

One night, a regular customer, who many said was the richest man in Georgia not named Ted Turner, requested that I give him a lap dance. I tried to explain that I just served drinks and wasn't a dancer. He wouldn't take no for an answer and began shouting to the whole club, "I will give Darby five-thousand dollars for one dance. If she says no, I will leave and go home heartbroken. But if she agrees, drinks for the rest of the night are on me!"

The crowd went crazy! I didn't know what he saw in me compared to the other girls, maybe it was the challenge of my innocence. I felt like the crowd practically pushed me to Mr. Money Bags. I started slow and nervous, but I had watched the girls enough to know what I was doing, and I used my gymnast background to my advantage. Strippers aren't exactly going to put Ginger Rogers to shame, anyway. The whole place was focused on me—I felt alive—and I realized that I could become this character, like in the movies, and lift myself out of my life.

Over the next few months, I became the club's most popular girl. Tyler paid for my now famous surgical enhancements. He said if he could combine my innocence with the look of the classic blonde bombshell, we would rule the world. I became completely immersed in the character, and started going by the name Laney.

Tyler convinced me to take our success onto the road. He partnered with a fraternity at the University of Georgia for us to work their party. So on a humid night, typical of summers in the south, I packed with Tyler and a couple other girls, including Jade, into the back of a van and headed to the nearby college-town of Athens.

That's where I came across a Mr. Perfect type. A dance wouldn't be enough for him—he wanted to take me back to his room for more. I could tell from his eyes that he thought it was his God-given right to get whatever he wanted. When I turned down his advances, he offered me money—when I told him I don't do that, he started to get physical with me.

I had been separated from Tyler and the other girls, and felt completely vulnerable. But luckily, a young man who had been watching the festivities from the corner most of the night, came to my rescue. His name was Sean, and it was uncanny how much he reminded me of Friend. He told Mr. Perfect to get his hands off of me. Mr. Perfect didn't like being told no, and a showdown appeared imminent. But luckily the commotion attracted too much of a crowd for him to do anything to Sean.

I don't know what got into me, but I felt the need to reward Sean for his bravery, and wanted him to be noticed. I took him by the hand and led him to a table in the middle of the floor. The crowd circled around us, pushing forward. As if it were destiny, I seemed to have an out-of body experience. It started as a lap dance, but Darby was no longer in control or calling the shots. Lost in my Laney character, I removed the boy's clothing and led him on top of me on the table. As we kissed passionately, the crowd began chanting his name. "Sean! Sean! Sean!"

Sean came out of his shell, in more ways than one, and began to give back what he was getting. I writhed and moaned on the table, the sounds drowned out by the raucous crowd that chanted wildly. It was like nobody was in the room and the whole world was in the room at the same time—a level of intoxication that defied reality. Sean didn't let the crowd down and we lost ourselves in each other. As fate would have it, Tyler captured the whole episode on video—history has always been the most infamous book ever written and we were writing our own dirty chapter.

When we finished the shocking display, fraternity members actually came up to Sean and poured beer over his head like athletes do with champagne when they win a championship. A grinning Tyler brought me a towel for my sweaty body, and enthusiastically told me that he had never seen anyone capture a room like that before, and he had no doubt that I'd be the biggest star in the world one day. I was only half-listening—I was too busy watching the Mr. Perfect-type quietly exiting the room with his shoulders drooped. I smiled, but the scar remained.

Always the entrepreneur, Tyler owned the rights to our escapades that night and marketed the amateur movie. When the film hit stores, it became one of the top selling adult films of the year. What later became known as "dorm porn," took off on college campuses throughout the land. Our van was traded in for a tour bus, and we traveled to colleges throughout America like rock stars. Some said I was corrupting the youth of America, but I figure if you're old enough to go to war, then you're old enough to score. For better or worse, the legend of Laney Bang was now a train barreling down the tracks that nobody could stop, especially myself. Not that I wanted to. The faster the train sped, the happier I was. Darby and Baby Doll were left behind and I wasn't looking back.

"Are you *enjoying* yourself?" Shep awakens me.

I say nothing, remaining fixated on Laney's words.

"Guys are gross," she says with a shake of the head.

Chapter 32

"So did you enjoy your reading?" Shep asks me again, after we park the car in an overpriced Manhattan garage.

I detect a trap. "It's an interesting read. Kind of an erotic-thriller version of *My Fair Lady*. A rag to riches story. Triumph and tragedy."

"I'm sure it's a classic. What did you learn—that she was a greedy tramp who got herself killed?"

"I told you, it's important to get to know the victim."

"And now I'm sure you know her quite intimately."

She looks at her watch. "Eleven-fifteen, we can still make it," she says with urgency.

After hailing a cab, I cause her further despair when I change our plans. I instruct the driver to drop us on 18th Avenue in Gramercy Park.

"Are you going to let me in on what's going on, Jack? We had an eleven-thirty meeting with Lansdale—you know, the guy with the website that had the victim on a hit list. The guy who happened to be present the night before she was killed."

I don't want Lansdale to be overly comfortable, so I'm not worried about missing our appointment. What I am worried about is the rain that is pounding down. I open an umbrella and attempt to hold it over both our heads. Shep raises her own umbrella in defiance.

Our dueling umbrellas don't allow us to stand side by side, so I take the lead in trudging single-file up 18th Avenue.

"Where are we going, Jack?" Shep demands again, as she splashes through puddles in her pricey heels.

"You'll see," I say, adding to her annoyance. Silence grows between us.

Just as I begin to get used to the refreshing background noise of gridlocked traffic, Shep ends her speaking boycott. She points to a large modern skyscraper. "I interned there one summer in college. The top floor is Evans, Kramer, Gordon & Associates."

I'm well aware of who they are—one of the top law firms in Manhattan. They are known throughout the industry as EKG, which is ironic because the firm is known as being heartless.

"I was going to be back on top there one day as a partner. Now I'll be lucky to not be a punch-line."

I look up at the top floor that houses EKG, feeling small. I look back at Shep. I can see the fire in her eyes, but also an underlying hurt.

"I don't know exactly what you are looking for, but I know you're not going to find it on the top floor of a skyscraper."

"This isn't going to be another of your self-righteous lectures, is it?"

"Whatever mechanical rabbit you're chasing, it sure hasn't brought you happiness."

"I have no idea what a rabbit has to do with this, but better chasing that than a ghost."

She hits my weak spot. "Leave Reyanne out of this! At least I didn't marry someone because I thought they could take me up the ladder of success."

"That's not why I married him, and what would you know about the ladder of success? You were born choking on a big fat silver spoon. Or was it gold?"

This part I don't understand. Shep claims to come from a well-to-do family outside of Boston, and her car sure didn't come from her Otsego County salary. So either she's a hypocrite or there is something off here.

But she's right on one point—my job is built on not prejudging, yet I'm currently the worst offender.

"Because I fell in love with the idea of a new life. I could get rid of the old Jessica and start over," Shep says.

"And the question was?"

"Then why did I marry him? It's what you wanted to ask me."

I expect her to reattach her force field, but instead she opens up.

"My former in-laws were the rich ones from Boston. My family was a domestic disaster from Rome, New York. My father's three big hobbies were drinking, gambling, and leaving. My mother didn't care about me, except to put me down whenever she could. I put myself through college and law school, working up to four jobs at a time. Brad was the knight in shining armor who was going to take me away. It wasn't ever about the money, it was about a new life, getting to start over from scratch."

Shep pulls on her watch and announces, "Totally fake. My car is the one thing I got from my marriage, after selling my engagement ring. I wear knock-offs of Louis Vuitton. I got my purse and diamond earrings at the Sloan-Kettering thrift shop. Why do you think I never let anyone from the office see my closet-size apartment in Albany?"

She doesn't go into the details of the marriage, and how it ended in an annulment. I don't push. It hits me that Shep and Laney Bang had more in common than I thought—both looking for that new life to erase their past. On the downside, they both tended to sway from the truth to achieve this new life.

We walk past stout trees that date back centuries, until we arrive at a five-story townhouse that sits between 17th and 18th Street.

"The owner is Laney Bang," I inform.

Shep's mouth gapes open.

I continue, "It's supposedly a house for runaway girls called DK House, but when our investigator began digging, he found that the hidden owner, deep under layers of shell corporations, was none other than Laney Bang."

"Purposely hidden—as in the 'secret spot' in New York, just as Amber claimed."

"Exactly—the police missed it, but our investigator didn't."

"Another home run for the Babe!" she exclaims with an actual smile. I think she had been holding that new life stuff in for a long time and feels reinvigorated.

The location is low profile. Gramercy Park was once a collection of 19th-century homes surrounded by a private park. In recent years it has become an urban mixture of commercial high-rises and trendy apartment buildings, but it's still a lot more Lawson than Bang. And the last place you'd expect to find the world's biggest attention queen. Which was probably her plan.

The townhouse was built in 1892 from brick and carved limestone. Only a glass atrium on the roof reeks of glamour. No awning or doorman. I had expected shooting fountains and neon signs. But it seems to never be the obvious when it comes to Laney Bang.

We walk up the brick steps to the front entrance. Shep jiggles the door handle, and in doing so, makes a discovery. "Jack, the door is unlocked."

Before I can protest, she enters the home and I follow. I immediately begin to second-guess our decision, visualizing Kerri getting the case tossed out on an illegal search. But it's too late.

"Hello—is anybody in here?" I yell out. With every step, I become even more cognizant of what a bad idea this is.

"Hello … hello," Shep shouts, her voice echoing.

Nobody is home, but obviously somebody had been here—why else would the door be unlocked? My first thought is that Kerri's investigators must have beaten us to it, but LB&G only hires the best, and the sloppy work of leaving the front door open doesn't match their sophistication. I next wonder about Amber and Maxon, who might have felt they had some loose ends to tie up after talking to us yesterday.

Shep and I do a sweep of the downstairs. I expected a cheesy motif with mirrors on the roof and stripper poles in the living room. Instead, it's a place my family would be proud of—elegant dining room with a grand crystal chandelier. A comfortable living room with leather couches, glass tables, and a baby grand piano. Picassos and Monets line the walls like a miniature art gallery.

We move upstairs and split up. I wander in to what looks like a young girl's bedroom—as pink as cotton candy and a bed full of stuffed animals. It is the exact opposite of Amber's depiction of a tawdry hideout for Laney's trysts with married men. In fact, it's as if Laney had created this "secret site" to escape her Laney Bang character. And I don't think it's a coincidence it was hidden under the guise of a home for troubled girls—Darby was the troubled girl.

When I'm done playing amateur psychologist, I seek out Shep. I find her in a professional looking office going through Laney's files and computer.

Shep informs me that she hasn't had any luck with the computer, and jokes that it's so clean that it doesn't even contain any porn. At least I think she's joking. It's hard to tell sometimes with her.

While the computer is a dead end, the file cabinet does bear some fruit. I learn that Laney might be as anal retentive as Shep—all of her files are listed in alphabetical order with meticulously labeled subsections. So it didn't take Shep long to find a file marked *Anderson, Drew*. It was her largest file.

"She definitely has been tracking Anderson for some time," she says and hands me numerous folders

There is no proof of a blackmail scheme, but it does contain assorted information related to Anderson, ranging all the way back to his college football days. All the contents could be easily explained away as a businesswoman doing her due diligence on a man she was contemplating entering into a partnership with.

I instruct Shep to call Gifford and get a warrant for the townhouse. Maybe the science guys can find a Drew Anderson fingerprint, or other DNA related items, that would help confirm what Amber told us. And they can haul the computer and files to our offices in Cooperstown, where we can do a full analysis.

I browse through the file cabinet. As I sort through the folders, something strange hits me. "Do you find it odd that she has an extensive file on Anderson, but nothing on James Lansdale? He would be involved in this supposed business venture, and he was the one who was trying to destroy her."

"Maybe if we would have kept our schedule, we could have asked him. Now can we go talk to him before it's too late?"

"Not just yet. There's one more place we need to go first."

Chapter 33

It's a quarter past two. We are almost three hours late, and now James Lansdale is making us wait.

After we left Laney's townhouse, we made an unannounced visit to MaddoXXX Video, which is located in a swanky palace on Madison Avenue. My intent was to meet with its founder and CEO, Tyler Maddox—the guy who discovered Laney Bang in an Atlanta area strip club. That little discovery made Tyler Maddox and his company into the benchmark for success in the multi-billion dollar adult entertainment industry. Most interesting to me is that MaddoXXX Video was embroiled in a bitter lawsuit with Laney Bang at the time of her death.

Upon walking into the modern high-rise building, the first thing that struck me was how normal it looked. An office filled with cubicles and bustling men in suits. It could have easily been the corporate offices of a typical Fortune-500 company.

The well-groomed Tyler Maddox looked as if he just appeared off the cover of *GQ*. Gone was the long hair and goatee that Laney described in her book. He downplayed the lawsuit—the dispute was over whether Laney broke her contract with Maddox when she left to start a competing production company. He claimed their personal relationship was as good as ever. To make his point, he showed us a photo of his family with Laney after his daughter's dance recital in suburban Westport, Connecticut, just a week before the murder. With genuine emotion in his voice, he described how hard it was for him to explain her death to his children, as she was their godmother. The picture he painted was so mainstream suburban that I almost nodded off.

Tyler also explained how Laney was one of the few girls in the business that he'd seen beat the dark temptations. Numerous tales of how she took in the weary, tired, and poor like some sort of Lady Liberty of porn.

Relevant to our investigation, he tossed cold water on Amber's blackmail theory—aka our motive. "I would take what Amber Jazz says with a grain of salt," he told us.

"Because of the drug use?" Shep followed up.

"That has always been a problem with Amber. But a bigger problem is that she had an insane jealousy of Laney. She wanted to be the number one star in the world and thought Laney was standing in her way. Amber could be vindictive."

The rest of the questioning was uneventful, until Shep decided to pick a fight. She challenged Maddox as to whether he felt remorse for the lives he harmed by the so-called "dorm porn." Did he ever lose sleep over the kid who thought he was going to have a night of college fun and then either got kicked out of school or branded for life, and couldn't get a job because of one bad decision? "You basically lit the crack pipe and put it in front of these kids. Film is forever, Mr. Maddox," she fired away.

Maddox made a spirited counter that their monitored parties were much safer than the drunken and reckless sex that took place in the dormitories, or the typical college parties that often resulted in deadly drinking and driving. "If you're old enough to make a decision on who should be the president, then surely you are mature enough to make *this* decision. I sleep well at night."

They both stood and I really think she wanted to get in a fistfight with him. After her recent admission about her background, I view her in a different light, and understand why she's such a fighter. I got her out of there as expeditiously as I could, before she did something to harm her career. Besides, Lansdale had waited long enough and we needed to save some of that vim and vigor for him.

Sitting across from Lansdale's desk, I look at Shep and she smiles nervously back at me. We are the most united we've been since the case started. I view the room, finding it similar to the office of Tyler Maddox, including the breathtaking view of the Manhattan skyline. I see the irony of the porn producer and the anti-porn crusader ending up in similar palaces.

James Lansdale arrogantly marches in and announces, "You're late."

"Sorry, our helicopter got stuck in traffic," I sass back at him. I don't think he killed Laney Bang, but I certainly don't like him.

"Don't waste my time, Mr. Lawson," he responds in his usual condescending tone, taking a peek at his watch to further his point.

"Where were you between the hours of two and six-thirty a.m. this past Monday morning?" I ask.

"If you haven't already checked the flight records, then you are as incompetent as the media claims. Do you want me to bore you with details about the rest of my journey—what time I was seen checking in to the Four Seasons and such?"

"That won't be necessary."

"How did you feel when you heard of Laney Bang's unexpected death?"

Shep asks.

"It wasn't unexpected," Lansdale says flatly.

"It wasn't?" I ask, intrigued.

"She lived a life of sin, so it's logical that such a harsh judgment was cast on her. She also made a lot of enemies."

"Including yourself. I believe that Ms. Bang was number one most wanted on your Smut Cleanser website."

Lansdale shoots me an angry look. "That wasn't to be taken literally."

"Isn't it possible that someone who's a little less grounded than yourself may have gotten the wrong idea from the website, and believed he or she was doing God's work by eliminating Ms. Bang?"

"On the record, Mr. Lawson, the website in no way promotes violence, calls for the death or injury of anyone, or provides any incentive to those who might take it upon themselves to misinterpret our intent. The only thing the website asks is a boycott of these people's products or services." Lansdale now flaunts a smile. "But off the record, I would like to shake the hand of the person who did it."

"If you were to shake the hand of the man who killed Laney Bang, would it be Drew Anderson's hand that you shake?" I ask.

"I won't even dignify your question with an answer. The idea that Drew killed that piece of trash is absurd. He is a good and decent family man who has done nothing but heal people, not harm them."

"Absurd?" I ask with a puzzled look. "They found a woman murdered in his house, and nobody else was present at the time of the death. It really sounds *absurd* to you that he might have killed her?"

"You have no evidence, and lack a motive. And from my discussion with his lawyer, it seems he has witnesses to his alibi."

"What did you discuss in the meeting that night?" Shep asks.

"I'm not at liberty to divulge specifics, but the general mission statement, from our side, was that Drew sought to tap into her platform to enhance his campaign. In turn, she wanted my group to back off the sponsor boycott of her show."

“And you went along?” I ask with skepticism.

“I didn’t agree with any type of business relationship with Laney Bang, but Drew is a good friend, and when he puts his mind to it he can be very persuasive. And no, it didn’t escape my thoughts that if he became governor it would be quite a coup for myself, along with the long-term interests of those I represent. Sometimes you have to lose the battle to win the war.”

“Did you consider the meeting a success?” I ask.

“The end result obviously was quite a positive.”

I want to toss him out his window down onto Madison Avenue. And just because he’s pissing me off, I ask him about the helicopter trip the next morning to pick up his married “girlfriend.”

He looks like he wants to crush me like a bug. Shep doesn’t look thrilled that I brought up the subject, and in doing so, turned the interview personal.

Lansdale stands, signaling the end of the questioning.

“Due to your tardiness, I am late for a lunch engagement,” he announces. “You have no evidence against Drew, and you will be laughed out of court. But if you are foolish enough to attempt to prosecute him, I will use every ounce of my money and influence to ensure his full exoneration.”

He heads toward the door, but then stops like he forgot his keys. He turns to us with a look of regret. He takes a deep breath, and says, “I apologize for my rude behavior. I don’t know what got into me. It has been quite a stressful week.”

I eye him closely, trying to understand this sudden metamorphosis.

“Just so there are no hard feelings, please join me for lunch—you can continue your questions there.”

Shep is about to decline—something about it being inappropriate to dine with those under investigation by the DA’s Office—but I see an opportunity. I speak for both of us. “We’d love to.”

Chapter 34

A limo meets us at the front of the building, and we are taken to Carmazzi's, an Italian restaurant on the Upper East Side. Lansdale jokes that he prefers kangaroo meat, but his guest enjoys Italian.

Carmazzi's is small in size, but large in history and celebrity. It's a favorite of my family, and is one of the few things we agree on.

We enter under the red and green colored awning that depicts the map of Italy. To the left is an old-style bar that's an original from the opening night in 1928. To our right are circular wooden tables that sit under autographed pictures of numerous celebrities, including Sinatra, Bogart, and Babe Ruth—the real one—all photographed while dining here.

My senses flood with the rich aroma coming from the kitchen as we are escorted to a private VIP room reserved for special friends and guests of the Carmazzi family. When we arrive, I immediately lose my appetite. James Lansdale's lunch guest is none other than my grandmother.

Before I can flee the scene, Ethel stands with help of her cane. "Hello, Jackson," she says, using my full name, which is usually a sign she means business.

I was named after Andrew Jackson, which is strange, since he was the hero of poor and working class Americans. Although, I'm guessing the Lawsons admire anyone whose face is on a piece of currency. But since Jackson is only on the twenty, I see that their low expectations for me went back to the day I was born.

"And this must be the lovely Jessica that I see so often with you on television," she makes a rare attempt at charm. She extends her bony, wrinkled hand to Shep, who actually looks impressed. She'll learn.

"This is a great surprise," Ethel says. If by surprise, she means plotted, orchestrated, or contrived, then I agree.

We sit and engage in awkward small talk, but I can feel the storm on the horizon. A waitress approaches. Lansdale orders veal parm, I choose penne with vodka sauce, while my grandmother and Shep get matching salads.

"Jackson, we are worried about you and Kerri facing off in such an arena. We feel that no good can come of it, and the potential damage to the family outweighs any kudos that might come to either of you from this case," Ethel begins her agenda.

I look at Shep as if to say, "I told you so."

My law persona takes over. "Maybe Kerri should step down as Anderson's lawyer. Besides, he needs a real trial lawyer. I will smoke her in court and everybody at this table knows it."

Ethel looks distressed. I offer her bread, knowing her teeth won't survive the crust. She declines.

"Jackson, the family has talked it over and we feel you should step down."

"Funny, I wasn't invited to that meeting. And last I checked, I work for the Otsego County District Attorney's Office, not Lawson, Baird & Gentry."

Ethel never shies away from a battle. She looks frail, but fair warning to those who underestimate her, she will fight to the death. It's one of the few things I respect about her. "Blood is a constant. You will always be a Lawson first!"

"Maybe so, but it won't stop me from prosecuting you on an obstruction of justice charge."

Shep almost chokes on a piece of bread and washes it down with a gulp of water. But before things escalate, our squabble is interrupted by the mayor of New York, who stops by our table for a quick meet-and-greet with the rich and richer—suddenly Ethel and Lansdale are charm school valedictorians. Shep has a "we're seriously in over our head" look. *The mayor of New York is on their side!* She might be right on this one.

After a brief photo-op, the mayor leaves, clearing the way for Ethel to resume her attack. "For goodness sake, Jackson, I'm not asking you to do something illegal. All I'm saying is that this case is a conflict of interest that puts the family in an uncomfortable position."

"There is precedent to say it's not a conflict," I contend.

"Why not let this smart and talented girl take over? I have heard all about her on television and she did a marvelous job at the initial appearance. And she has no conflicts, so she'll be able to make more clearheaded decisions."

Shep is beaming from the compliments. But I'm steamed, which Ethel uses to bait me like a small-mouth bass. I respond, "And by clear-headed, I'm assuming you mean she will see things your way?"

"Jackson, you have always had a chip on your shoulder and felt second best when it comes to your siblings. I'm afraid that you are using this situation to try to prove a point. And I, along with the rest of your family, care very much about you. We have supported you and provided you space in your time of loss. So all I'm asking is that for once, you return the favor and support the family."

Lunch is served, allowing my anger to simmer. We all put our happy faces on for the waitress, before slipping the gloves back on. "Thank you for your concern, grandmother, but I'll be staying on the case."

"Your grandmother is just trying to help you. If you know what's good for you, you'll walk away," Lansdale butts in.

*If it walks like a threat...*I say nothing, which states loud and clear that I'm not budging.

"Go make a fool of yourself, be my guest," Lansdale says with a dismissive wave.

"So help me, if you embarrass this family any more than you already have," Ethel pauses for dramatic effect, and then points a crooked finger at me. "Consider yourself warned!"

"Go to trial against me and you'll go down hard. Consider yourselves warned," I come right back.

Ethel scoffs, "I don't know why you are being so stubborn, Jackson. You have no evidence or motive, and Drew has witnesses to his alibi. You will have no choice but to drop the charges."

I'm sure that someone spoon-fed that company line to Ethel. Despite marrying into a legal dynasty, she really doesn't know much about the nuances of the law, other than it pays well.

Ethel is on a roll, "That Bang woman was nothing but a glorified prostitute. Bringing an innocent man down certainly isn't going to bring

Reyanne back, if that's what this is about."

She has officially crossed the line. "Do not bring her into this."

"We're all sorry for your loss, but we have our limits. It's not as though you were going to marry an actress, and not even a working one at that. She just wasn't Lawson material."

I stand. "Thank you for lunch, we'll be leaving now."

Ethel doesn't even look at me. "Stop being so dramatic—sit down and finish your meal."

I pick up my plate of penne and I'm about to toss it on the floor and announce that I'm done. But that's the reaction they're looking for. No matter how badly I'm burning inside, I maintain my cool. I set the plate back down on the table and calmly walk out of the restaurant without a word.

I stand on the curb, visibly upset, the rain soaking through my suit. Shep finds me there. "Let's head back home—it's been a long day, Jack."

A yellow cab splashes to a stop and we pile into the back.

"No—I have one more thing to check out while we're here."

Chapter 35

We exit the cab into a puddle on 161st Street, across from the Grand Concourse Shopping Plaza in the Bronx.

"Are you going to fill me in on where we are going?" Shep asks again. Her empathy toward me outside Carmazzi's has turned to impatience.

"We're going to talk to Anderson's wife," I say.

Sigh. "She was seen at a party in the city, Jack. She's not a suspect."

"I know, but maybe we'll learn something."

Deeper sigh. "Even if she knows something, do I have to remind you that a wife has spousal privileges from having to testify against her husband?"

I tramp through sidewalk puddles and up the staircase of the Bronx County Criminal Courthouse. Shep reluctantly follows me up the stairs to the third floor, and we sneak into a cramped courtroom. We take a seat in the last row of the gallery, just in time for Marissa Torres-Anderson to deliver her final summation.

As a defense attorney in Manhattan, I always did my homework on potential opponents. And the name Marissa Torres-Anderson came up as one of the best. Usually going up against a public defender was like a match between the varsity and the JV. And even if the public defender had talent, there was such a vast difference in resources that it was a losing battle for them. I never faced Marissa, but there were many cautionary tales from my colleagues of how she beat the varsity on a regular basis.

This is the first time I've seen her in person. I can't take my eyes off her as she moves gracefully around the courtroom like she owns it. It's not her physical beauty that attracts me, although it is undeniable, but the powerful aura of confidence that surrounds her every move. I immediately flashback to that night in Nellie's when Reyanne walked in. I never thought I'd witness such a powerful force ever again.

Her wardrobe is on the flamboyant side for the legal world. A bright orange blazer over a tight-fitting blouse. Her skirt is mid-thigh and she saunters around the courtroom in a pair of strappy high-heels.

I can tell right away that her choice of clothing is bothering Shep. She has strong feelings about how a woman should dress in the workplace. Open toe shoes with no hose are a Shep no-no, so this ensemble must be driving her nuts.

Marissa is defending a client named Eusubio Rodriguez, who is charged with numerous counts of assault and battery, assault with a deadly weapon, and attempted murder. Eusubio is facing many years in prison, but won the public defender lottery.

She has the all-Latino jury as mesmerized as I am. In fact, the longer her summation goes the thicker her accent becomes, completely different from when I heard her speak on television. I figure by the time she closes she will need an interpreter for the English parts.

Shep doesn't seem as impressed; she looks at her watch, and predictably says, "Who wears an outfit like that into court? If that skirt gets any higher it will be referred to as her collar."

When Marissa finishes, I almost expect the jury to clap. She walks to her seat, leaving behind a vapor trail of charisma. The judge charges the jury on their deliberations and court is adjourned. I'm not sure the deliberations will be necessary.

We meet up with Marissa as she heads for the door. She looks at us like we stole her lunch money. "What an honor—it's not every day that you get to meet your husband's captors."

I barely notice the slight. "That was impressive," I beam, receiving a dirty look from Shep.

"It really isn't fair, I have the home field advantage," she replies, the accent suddenly gone. "It's all about perception in there."

"So you're saying you are dishonest?" Shep asks with attitude.

Marissa looks at me and asks, "Who's the intern?"

"My name is Jessica Shepherdson, and at least I don't need to hike my skirt to win a case."

Marissa just shakes her head and walks out of the courtroom. She heads to the stairs and begins to descend. We follow helplessly behind.

"You may be designer, Ms. Shepherdson, but here in the Bronx we are a lot more Señor Hoochie than Calvin Klein. I know my audience."

"We aren't interested in perception, we deal in reality," Shep retorts.

"If this were about *reality* then you would have let my husband go days ago. *Reality* is that you have nothing on him."

"You have no idea what we have," I counter.

Marissa stops in her tracks, halfway down the staircase. She looks back and flashes me a sly grin. "I hope you are a better lawyer than you are a poker player, Jack."

"We would like to ask you a few questions," Shep remains all business as we step off onto the busy first floor.

Marissa exchanges "hellos" with a few men in suits who are obviously lawyers. One tells her to keep her chin up, likely referring to her husband's predicament.

She smiles at me again. "Please tell me that you aren't just getting around to talking to his wife. The spouse is always the first to be questioned. You are either as inexperienced as they say you are on TV, or this visit is some sort of hope-and-prayer fishing expedition. Neither option screams a winner, Jack."

"Where were you when Laney Bang was murdered?" Shep asks. For someone who said this was a waste a time she sure has a lot of questions.

"First of all, I'm not exactly sure when she was murdered, so you will have to clarify. And if you two aren't sure when she was murdered, I suggest you go watch some CNN and get back to me. More importantly, I am late for a train. Thanks to your wrongful incarceration of my husband, I have to travel to Cooperstown to be with him. So I don't have time for your questions."

"We're headed that way, perhaps we can give you a ride." I offer, stepping out of the courthouse into the drizzling mist.

She shrugs. "If that's the case, then you two can interrogate me for the next few hours—I hate the train."

Shep pulls me to the side. She is irate, and admonishes me, using the term "totally inappropriate" over and over.

"You see totally inappropriate and I see a great opportunity to try to shed some light on a case that is in dire need of having some light shed on it."

She again disagrees, vehemently, but I choose not to listen.

"Our car is in Midtown, perhaps your car service can drop us there," I say to Marissa, trying to avoid Shep's menacing gaze.

Marissa looks at me and laughs. "Car service? Who do I look like—the Queen of England?" She begins to head down the courthouse steps and again we follow.

Marissa stops abruptly, halfway down, and looks as if she's just had some sort of epiphany. Perhaps she finally figured out that it's raining and she doesn't have an umbrella.

"It just hit me that the three of us actually have something in common."

"Outside of being lawyers, I truly doubt it," Shep snips.

"Sure we do—we all love screwing my husband. As much as I like to think I do it the best, I must admit that nobody has ever screwed him like you two."

She laughs as she briskly walks off.

I can't take my eyes off of her.

Chapter 36

We trail Marissa down a musty subway entrance and I'm overtaken by the humidity. The high security presence since the bombings, including bomb-sniffing dogs, brings back terrible memories—I haven't been on a subway since that day. But I don't have to think about it for long—the moment we set foot upon the platform, our train screeches to an air-braked stop. We board and find empty seats. Marissa sits opposite Shep and me.

"So, are you going to start those questions? I'm sure Miss Dress Code here has a whole list of them prepared."

"I don't think this is the proper venue," Shep snarls.

Marissa takes a look around. It's still her home field and she looks comfortable. "Well, if you two don't have any questions for me, then would you mind if I interview you?"

Shep crosses her arms and pulls them tightly to her chest, which means she's really pissed. "It's a free country."

Marissa scans the downtrodden passengers that surround us. "I'm guessing that most of these folks would disagree with you." She then turns her scrutiny to me. "I've studied your work, Jack—you're good. So I'm mystified that you're off to such a disastrous start to this case. I thought Drew might be up against some tough competition."

I don't take the bait, and reply, "Our strategy is to make the defense overconfident that we are going to drop the charges."

She smiles. "Bad start notwithstanding, I don't underestimate you—I think this move to Sticksville has strengthened you. If you had stayed in Manhattan you'd have turned into another soft, country club lawyer that LB&G is famous for. So what made you trade in the Rolls Royce for the beat-up Volkswagen?"

She is angling for my weak spot. But if she thinks she can engage me in a Reyanne conversation while actually riding in a subway car, then despite her claims to the contrary, she is underestimating me. I turn the subject back around, "I just played the hand that was dealt. You, on the other hand, are the one who chose to go against the grain?"

Before she can answer, we arrive at our stop and exit into a subterranean station. We ascend the stairs toward the rain-filled humidity of late July.

"If you mean keeping my low-paying job and not becoming a professional socialite," she says, as we reach the top of the stairwell, "my answer is that these people can't speak for themselves, so someone has to speak for them. To take that feeling of helplessness away. I hear everybody talk of a flawed system. The system isn't flawed; the problem is all the good lawyers run to the LB&G's of the world, chasing the almighty dollar. Nobody wants to play for the team in the low rent neighborhood, everybody wants to play for the Yankees. Well, if true justice is to happen somebody has to play for the Pirates."

"Behind every idealist is an incident that inspired them," I say, again thinking of Reyanne.

She nods, while maintaining her fast-paced walk. "My mother died when I was young. It was just my papa and me—he never remarried. He ran a bodega not far from the courthouse, and we lived in an apartment over it. One day it was decided that they needed more parking at Yankee Stadium, so people wouldn't have to park amongst us *undesirables* in the South Bronx. A parking garage was built on the spot of my father's store and we were supplanted. It wasn't about the store or apartment—we would find another place to live. But that place was our life and filled with the last memories of my mother. It was over twenty years ago, but when I think of it I still get that same pit in my stomach. That feeling of helplessness—when others control your destiny and can shatter your life on a whim. I vowed that I would control my destiny, and try to help others control theirs."

She has fire in her eyes as she recounts the tale. She subtly wipes a tear, acting as if the rain caused it, unintentionally showing a softer side.

When we arrive at the parking garage, Marissa has got her edge back. She runs her hand over the hood of the BMW in fake admiration. "Wow—can't get one of these playing for the low-rent team."

Shep's anger spills over. "You don't know me. You are the one with the million dollar husband."

"I always know my competition. And since you are trying to take away my husband, you are my biggest adversary."

"You're big on generalization and bluster, but low on facts—just like in the courtroom."

"You sure you want to test that one?"

Shep turns surprisingly quiet. She angrily turns the key in the ignition and drives onto the busy Manhattan street. Marissa has pierced her nerves like an elite sharpshooter.

As we move through the crowded city streets, Shep opens the questions. "Your husband called your residence at 11:36, the night before the murder. What was the purpose of that phone call?"

"Last minute details on where we were going to toss Laney Bang's body after we murdered her. Obviously we got our signals crossed—I said throw the body in the lake, but Drew insisted on leaving her in his bedroom."

"Do you find this funny?"

"The murder—no. This questioning and the bumbling by the authorities in this case—downright hilarious."

"What was the call concerning?" I repeat the question in a calm tone.

"He calls me every night that we're apart. He knows I try to be in bed no later than midnight, since I have to be in court early in the morning. I was impressed that he still called me that night, despite his important business meeting. If you two weren't so busy basking in your newfound fame, maybe you could have taken a moment to check the phone records between us to see the pattern."

"The call was ten minutes long—that's a long time to say goodnight. What else was discussed?" I ask.

"We discussed how boring Arleen Scott's party was and that he owed me for attending in his place. He also went into detail about his polo match and trip to the races on Sunday. But sorry, we didn't get into a jealous tiff over Laney Bang being there, if that's what you're hoping for."

"For such a boring party, you seemed to be having a good time," I mention.

"I take back what I said, Inspector Clouseau—you actually did do some research. My overindulgence of alcohol was more for survival than entertainment purposes. Not normally my thing, but then again, I don't usually attend Arleen Scott's parties."

"So you were okay with your husband's meeting?" Shep asks.

"Why wouldn't I be?"

"The Goddess of Sex spending the night alone in that house with your husband? The staff abruptly sent home? I'm not sure I would be so trusting."

"That's because you have trust issues, Ms. Shepherdson, as does my husband. But his issues are that he trusts people based on his naïve loyalty. He's appeased that freeloader, Maxon, for years. Lansdale is trying to ride his coattails right to the governor's office. And now he trusted this Bang woman. That's the only thing he is guilty of."

"Was your trust level altered when you found out he lied?" I ask.

"If you are referring to him panicking to the police, I wouldn't call that a lie. More like a normal reaction to an unthinkable situation."

"How about when he told me that he was going to join you at the party in Manhattan, yet in reality, he was chilling in Cooperstown with a porn star?"

She looks befuddled. "When would he have told you that? He gave no formal interview with the DA's Office."

"He told me at Saratoga Racecourse on Sunday afternoon, the day of the party."

She shakes her head, as if to pity my desperation. "I'm sure that will hold up in court, Jack. You two can keep trying to drive a wedge between us if you want, but if you attempt to put our relationship on trial, I guarantee you will lose. He'd do anything for me, and you'll soon learn that I'll do anything for him."

Shep pushes ahead, "So after you ended the conversation with your husband, did you go to bed by midnight, or did you make an impromptu trip to Cooperstown?"

Marissa laughs hard. "I say you call ahead to Roddy Opp and have me arrested when we get to Cooperstown. That would mean that Drew goes free. And even if you can somehow prove it possible that I was able to pull a superhero—travel to Cooperstown, kill Laney Bang, and set up my husband in a jealous rage over their alleged affair, then be back in court the next morning looking no worse for the wear—you are still going to face a big obstacle."

I play along. "Which is?"

"Being the diligent prosecutors that you are, I'm sure you've reviewed my pre-nuptial agreement."

Shep and I look at each other—we hadn't. Since she's not even on the radar of being a suspect we've done very little research on Marissa. But we don't want to add to our growing reputation of being morons.

"Of course we have," I say. "Go on."

"I only receive money if Drew dies what they term a normal death, while we are legally married—murdering him certainly wouldn't qualify. So while I would benefit financially from Drew having an unfortunate accident—it makes no sense to kill his alleged mistress and set him up to take the fall. If he goes to jail, not only do I kill the cash-cow, but Drew's a smart guy, and with endless hours in prison he'd eventually figure out what I'd done and would divorce me, meaning I'd get nothing. Even if I wanted Laney Bang dead, it wouldn't make sense to set up my husband, like somebody obviously did."

Shep keeps grilling her, "But you just told us that you aren't about the money. You play for the Pirates, remember?"

"I guess I've covered all my bases then, haven't I?" Marissa replies with a smug look.

Marissa appears bored with the process and sighs. "Please excuse my snark, but the bottom line is you aren't even in the ballpark of having enough evidence to bring this to trial. You're making decisions based on emotions, not facts. I don't blame you for trying to save face—the police put you in a terrible situation. I feel for you, but my loyalty is with my husband."

I have one last question for her, a little bit off the path. "What did you think of Laney Bang?"

She thinks about it for a moment, then replies, "On many levels I admired her. She did whatever was needed to claw to the top. She took control of her destiny, which isn't easy for a woman in a male dominated world. If you don't, then you'll never have a sense of security. David used a slingshot—Laney Bang used her body. I found her very Machiavellian."

As we continue along the tree-lined New York State Thruway, the concrete jungle of the city is left behind. The conversation turns informal; Marissa and I debate the law in heated terms. Case law, constitutional law, judges we like or dislike, and gossip about my former Manhattan colleagues. Shep remains quiet, obviously not pleased that I have ventured beyond the rules of proper etiquette. She also hasn't taken a liking to the fact that I've taken a liking to Marissa.

We drop Marissa at Anderson Estate and she sarcastically blows us kisses as we pull away. Shep drops me at the Cirillos' without a word. She begins to drive away before I'm even fully out of the car.

We didn't make any grand discoveries on our trip to the city. In fact, we created more questions than we answered. But there is one question in which the answer is becoming clear to me—Drew Anderson was the only one who could have killed Laney Bang. The problem is that the evidence is not backing me up, and with time not on my side, I must come to grips with the fact that the likely murderer will probably be set free.

Later in the evening, I settle in and turn on the television. Marissa is holding a press conference on the grounds of Anderson Estate. It's the Marissa from the courtroom—confident, charismatic, and empathetic. I remain paralyzed by her aura, even though she's tearing any case we might have to shreds. She warned me she'd do anything for her husband and she's doing just that.

Chapter 37

I awake Friday to my alarm clock blaring The Cure song, "Friday I'm in Love."

I rise off the futon as if empowered by the sharp ray of sunshine that's streaming into my room; yesterday's rain is a distant memory.

I have more hop in my step. And I know why. Spending yesterday afternoon with Marissa was in many ways like channeling Reyanne. The aura, the confidence, the way she could always get under my skin—it was uncanny.

I turn on the television, where Marissa's press conference from the night before is being analyzed. Like the experienced litigator she is, she's laying the foundation to both free her husband and revive his image. She is a big asset for him.

I switch channels to GNZ cable news. An anchor is holding up a copy of today's *New York Globe*. Shep and I are right smack-dab on the front page, along with our lunch-mates from yesterday, including the mayor of New

York. The headline is *Political Incorrectness.* I feel like I just walked in front of a right cross.

The consensus of the panel is that Shep and I are misusing taxpayers' money and should be fired. Although, one woman takes it a step further. Her belief is that we're so impressed with our newfound celebrity we are prolonging the investigation to feed our egos, and falsely imprisoning an *obviously innocent* Drew Anderson in the process. She is irate that we aren't the ones in prison.

On the other side of the spectrum, her fellow panelist is convinced that we're in cahoots with the mayor and Lansdale to drop the charges against an *obviously guilty* Anderson, in exchange for high-paying cabinet jobs. You just can't please everybody.

I begin my daily trek to the office. Usually it's a time for me to review the case, but today is different. The moment the front tire of my bike hits Route-80, the media pounces. They are shouting questions at me and following me in slow-moving vans, giving the impression that they are actually protecting me. I put on my headphones and ignore them the best I can.

Main Street is packed, which isn't out of the ordinary since it's the unofficial beginning of Induction Weekend for the Hall of Fame, but adding to the congestion is a "Free Max Q" rally in front of the courthouse.

I turn it into a positive, using them as interference to elude my friends from the press.

I haven't been in the office since Monday and receive awkward stares from my co-workers. I make eye contact with Shep, but she looks away and retreats into her office.

I do the same, but when I shut the door I find that I'm not alone. Jana is sitting at my desk.

"Welcome back, Jack—did you enjoy your vacation? I heard Manhattan is nice this time of year."

"Very funny—why are you in my office?"

"My computer is down. Gifford said the new website should be up today to filter all information about the Max Q case, so I'm checking on it. I've been getting about four hundred calls a day, ninety percent of them nonsense."

I act like I'm up on this, even though I'm completely out of the loop. "Good, I'm glad they got that running."

"Judge Schanz called about rescheduling a pretrial hearing for Andy Kass. I guess he changed lawyers and needs more time."

I completely forgot about Kass—a case that only a week ago was dominating my schedule.

"Gifford wants you in his office at ten o'clock, not ten-o-one," she informs, and then points to the large pile of boxes behind my desk. "These arrived this morning from the search of Laney Bang's townhouse."

"Thanks, anything else?"

"Jessica looked upset when she came in this morning. I figure it's your doing—should I have flowers sent to her?"

"Since the media has us carrying on some torrid affair, I don't think that would be the best idea."

"No offense, Jack, but you don't strike me as a torrid kinda guy. Would you like me to get you extra copies of that *New York Globe* with your pretty face on the cover—maybe for friends and relatives?"

"I'll pass," I say and Jana leaves with a smirk on her face.

I check my voice mail, and the first one makes me wince. "I apologize for my behavior yesterday," Ethel says, "I was out of line. I can only hope you can forgive an old woman who sometimes loses her sense."

I am not buying the nicety-nice for one second. In fact, I'm convinced the picture in the *Globe* was a setup, which means I have the Lawsons scared. Plan-A was for Ethel and Lansdale to intimidate me out of prosecuting. When that failed they went to Plan-B—to discredit me. And by doing so, they are also taking the spotlight off their client, and the murder allegation that hangs over him. They know exactly what they're doing.

I sift through the boxes taken from Laney's townhouse. The most intriguing thing I find is a notebook of handwritten poetry that expands on the Baby Doll poem. I never met Laney Bang, but I find her to be a fascinating character full of contradictions. And hopefully as we learn more about her, she will push us in the right direction—to prosecute or not to prosecute?

Jana knocks on my door and pops her head in. "Jack, I got a couple of visitors for you."

"Not now," I say, my eyes never leaving the book of poetry.

Jana sends them in anyway.

Stepping into my office is a Japanese woman named Aso Aoki. Her husband, Kazahiro, accompanies her. I recognize them immediately. They own a village store on Route-31 and are well known throughout the community.

"What can I do for you?" I ask the Aokis, as I show them to seats facing my desk.

Aso does the talking, as her husband speaks little English, "I see on news Drew Anderson claim he jog morning that woman murdered. He jog every day when he in Cooperstown and every day he come to store and buy bottled water. He come in exactly between 6:30 and 6:35 every time. We joke with him that he like clockwork. He tell us he take exact route every day—say he believe in discipline from his day in military. He say he never break pattern. On day woman murdered, he no come in store."

I sit back and rub my chin. This is information I can use. When combined with the cell phone dead spot, it looks as if Drew Anderson changed his routine that morning. *To return to kill Laney Bang?*

I go over the morning in detail with the Aokis for twenty minutes before I get another knock from Jana.

"Gifford says you are late and you need to get your ass into his office now."

I look at my watch and plead, "I still have a few minutes until ten."

"You know Gifford—he considers five minutes early to be late."

I thank the Aokis and head for the office of the Otsego County District Attorney.

Chapter 38

Gifford looks at me with condemnation. "You actually found your way to the office, Lawson—did that GPS I sent you help at all?"

Glad to see everyone took their wise-ass pills today. I don't have a chance to respond before he is standing in the frame of his doorway, shouting, "Shepherdson—get the hell in here!"

Shep enters without looking at me. We both take a seat and try not to overdose on secondhand smoke.

Gifford begins pacing. "So this is going well, Lawson. First off, I haven't seen you in days or been able to contact you. That is going to stop or your employment is going to stop—understand?"

As if he could find someone else willing to commit career suicide, I think to myself.

He picks up the *New York Globe* and shoves it in my direction. "But thank goodness I can keep track of you two in the paper."

He reaches into his desk drawer, pulls out a cigarette, and lights up. Then begins pacing and puffing again. I go over CPR steps in my head in case he keels over.

"So let's review. I have protestors marching on Main Street. I have my prosecutors hobnobbing at glitzy restaurants. We've had to evacuate this office numerous times because of bomb threats. But you are too busy with your touchy-feely." He fires a copy of *the Inquisitor* tabloid our way with a picture of Shep and me on my motorcycle with headline *Puckering Prosecutors—get the real scoop on the steamy love affair between Max Q prosecutors!*

Shep is outraged. "That's total bullshit!"

"Get over yourself—you could do a lot worse than me. And come to think of it, you have," I shoot back.

Gifford calmly puts out his cigarette, and instructs, "Follow me—we're going to discuss the case in a place we can get some privacy."

His Cadillac sedan is waiting for us at the back entrance. We drive down Route-80 in the direction of the Cirillo house. We stop at Sam's Boat Rentals and a small motorboat is already waiting for us.

"I'm not getting in that thing," Shep declares.

"You can swim if you'd like, but this meeting is mandatory, Shepherdson."

After Shep gives in, Gifford captains the boat out onto Glimmerglass. It's a good idea—allowing us to get away from the circus, and discuss the case without fear that our conversation will end up in the wrong ears. But then I remember who we're up against, and wonder if we should check the boat for listening devices.

The lake is crowded with boats on this splendid summer morning, but we find a private spot and drop anchor. As is his style, Gifford gets right down to business. "I am sensing a distrust toward me on your part, and I want to set the record straight."

We're all ears.

"I'm sure our friends at the Sheriff's Office have brought up the investigation of Max-Q-Collectibles last year, attempting to question my motives, which they used as their sorry excuse for arresting Anderson without consulting us.

"The case centered on a known forger named Tony Rivotti. Not that anyone believed that was his real name. When it came to forgery, he was a child prodigy—we projected his age to be around sixteen. It was rumored that when Max-Q-Collectibles ran into some financial trouble, Rivotti was secretly brought in. He would forge autographs on memorabilia—the signatures were of such quality that they could pass the strictest verification tests—allowing the items to be sold for a much higher price."

Gifford loosens his tie and lights another cigarette. "An investigation ensued, and the Sheriff's Office believed an arrest should have been made. I didn't feel they had enough hard evidence, so I sent the case back to them with instructions to continue the investigation. Soon after, Rivotti disappeared and hasn't been seen since. Opp and his team believe I gave my friend Anderson time to hide Rivotti, and effectively kill the case against him. This is not true."

He sucks more nicotine into his lungs, and continues, "The other issue is the deadline. I was wrong to not consult with you before making the announcement. But the fact is, we have a brief window to make a decision in this case. After one week, any shot at justice will have been lost to the best PR that money can buy. By announcing the deadline, we look confident—if you haven't noticed, the defense is out to make you look inept and overmatched—and are seen to be providing a fair and speedy trial, which counterbalances their strategy of painting Anderson as a martyr. Although, Shepherdson didn't help that by doing such a great job at the bail hearing."

He pauses, and actually elicits a smile from Shep.

"I have been honest with you from the beginning about my relationship with Anderson," Gifford states unequivocally. "But I will support you completely if you decide to prosecute, and I will toast you when you win."

Shep and I nod our support, even if we remain skeptical.

He peers at me. "Now that we got that out of the way, I turn this over to you, counselor—what's the verdict?"

Chapter 39

"Anderson killed her," I proclaim.

Shep sighs.

"Sounds like you have a different take, Shepherdson," Gifford says, turning toward her.

"I concede Anderson's involvement is not out of the question, which is in direct contrast to my original thinking. But we just don't have the evidence to prosecute."

"We'll get it," I state emphatically.

Shep rolls her eyes. "Why are you so obsessed with getting him?"

"I speak for Laney Bang, the victim, and I take that responsibility seriously. If you haven't forgotten, it's *our job.*"

"I'm the only one here who is actually thinking of the law. You are on a crusade to get the guy because you think he's a phony who reminds you of your family."

"Don't twist this," I say, angered. "This isn't about bringing down Drew Anderson; it's about getting justice for a woman who was brutally murdered."

"She was a terrible role model who lived dangerously and got herself killed. How many little girls now believe the way to the top is not by hard work, but by prostituting yourself? Frankly, the world is probably a better place without her—yet I don't let my personal opinion or emotions get in the way. Our job is about evidence and we don't have any!"

"People like Drew Anderson are nothing but bullies. They hide behind reputations and social class. No matter what her career choice was, I respect Laney Bang for having the gumption to stand up to the bullies."

Gifford gets us back on track, "Lawson, you take the side of prosecute. Shepherdson, you argue for drop the charges, and I'll be the referee."

I begin the mock trial, "Laney Bang was having a long-term affair with Drew Anderson. Her motivation for the relationship was to blackmail him, which in turn, was his motive for killing her."

"Can this be corroborated?" Gifford asks.

"Yes, by a drugged out adult film actress with an ax to grind," Shep interrupts. "And I use the term actress loosely."

"Do you have any physical evidence of this affair—pictures? Hotel receipts? If she were blackmailing him, you would think she'd be storing data. She did everything else on film."

"I'm going to have a second interview with Amber Jazz, I think she knows more than she's telling us," I say.

"Having met Amber Jazz, I think it is quite possible she once had this information, but it's likely that she snorted it up her nose," Shep piles on.

Gifford remains placid. "Blackmail works both ways. In other words, if you're trying to sell me that it was Anderson's motive for murder, you're going to have to prove Laney Bang's motive for blackmailing him."

"It's about revenge with her," I answer with confidence.

"Revenge for what? If I were you, I would always work the money angle first," Gifford preaches his golden rule of crime—it's not about money, it's about the amount of money.

"I have a witness who confirms that it's revenge," I declare.

Shep looks frustrated "Who?"

"Laney Bang herself, in her book. Her life was changed by a collection of men she refers to as Mr. Perfect, whom she put on a pedestal, only to have her trust betrayed. Look at the men she exposed in her book, they all fit that same description. And who more fits the bill than Drew Anderson? This is why she relentlessly pursued him, using Anderson's assistant Ryan Maxon to get to him. This launched a series of events that eventually ended in her murder."

"You have to be kidding, Jack. That is what you seriously want to go to court with? You should be a screen-writer, not a lawyer!"

Gifford interrupts our squabble, "I want to hear from Shepherdson,"

She continues to use facts. In contrast, she comes across as rational. "What most intrigued the medical examiner was that there were no marks on her body or signs of a struggle. If Jack's story were true, then she would have been apprehensive, due to the blackmail attempt. If he approached her, even if the knife was concealed, she would have been on-guard and the ME would have been able to see that in her analysis."

Gifford interjects. "The thing that doesn't add up is that she was trusting toward her killer, yet she made a call to 911. Those two events are in conflict with each other."

"We know he is lying about jogging," I use my only evidence. "Dead spot in cell phone area, and the testimony of the Aokis confirms that he broke his usual pattern."

"The defense has witnesses that say he didn't. It will be our word against theirs. And who do you think the jury will believe?"

"I'll take my chances," I state with all the confidence I can muster. Lawsons are not just lawyers—they are also stubborn.

Gifford finishes another cigarette and flicks it into the lake, which I'm sure is against some littering law. He sits back and takes a large breath of morning air with what's left of his lungs. "You both know George Herman, right?"

The reference staggers me. But I quickly realize that Gifford has no idea he is my investigator, or connected to this case. We nod.

"Then I'm sure you both have heard his dissertation on why Babe Ruth really did 'call the shot' at Wrigley Field in the 1932 World Series. Thousands of eyewitnesses in the crowd claimed Ruth *didn't* do it. But they lacked credibility, since they both had an adversarial relationship with Ruth, and also were consuming large amounts of alcohol. The Cubs pitcher, Charlie Root, also said Ruth *didn't* do it. But he had an agenda—not wanting the indignity of being the pitcher that Ruth 'called the shot' off of."

Gifford lights another cigarette and continues, "But the part that got me is that Lou Gehrig, who was in the on-deck circle at the time—perhaps the closest witness—was steadfast that Ruth *did* 'call the shot'. Gehrig was an American hero with a reputation for complete honesty. Plus, he was no fan of Ruth, which balanced his conflict of interest—that he was Ruth's teammate. The Gehrig testimony convinced this juror that he *did* 'call the shot,' even though the evidence was stronger on the other side. Basically, Gehrig's believability outweighed the evidence.

"In our case, Drew Anderson is Lou Gehrig. Even if the evidence is on your side, Jack, which it isn't, you will have a hard time having people not believe whatever he says."

"Then we will have to knock him down a peg. There is no bigger sin in people's eyes than a false hero. He lied to the police and I'm sure he has more Tony Rivottis in his closet."

"The statements made to the police, even if admissible, are easily construed as the understandable panic of someone who just found a dead body in his house," Shep says. "All we have is circumstantial evidence and innuendo."

"You say circumstantial and innuendo, while I say it's simple Lizzie Borden," I retort, to strange looks.

"Lizzie Borden? What the hell are you talking about?" Shep asks.

"You know—Lizzie Borden grabbed an ax, gave her parents forty whacks…"

Gifford steps in, "That could use some explanation, Jack—you think Lizzie Borden killed her now? I'm pretty sure she's been dead for over eighty years."

"Lizzie Borden was a young woman whose father and stepmother were found chopped to death in their Fall River, Massachusetts home back in 1892. Nobody in the community could believe a polished and educated young woman with such a good disposition could commit such a heinous crime. But there was one indisputable fact. Lizzie Borden was the only person who could have reasonably committed the crime. In this case, Drew Anderson is the only one who could have done it."

"Maybe so, but a creative lawyer will have a sympathetic jury believing wild theories of terrorist scuba divers arriving from under Otsego Lake and then disappearing into the night. It's classic confirmation bias. They want their hero to be innocent, and if the defense throws enough wild theories against the wall, eventually reasonable doubt will stick," Gifford states.

He must have heard enough because he starts the boat motor and begins the journey back to shore.

"Jack, unless you come up with something resembling substantial evidence in the next few days—I don't see prosecuting Drew Anderson as a remote possibility," he adds, as the boat chops over the lake.

"I thought it was my call?"

Gifford shrugs. "It's totally your call, Jack, and don't take my thoughts as anything more than an honest review of the evidence. But there are built-in safety systems like grand juries and preliminary hearings to guard against overzealous prosecutors."

I say nothing, maintaining my stare at the hills.

"My only other piece of advice is that the next time I see you two on the cover of a newspaper, it better be for winning a case."

We both nod.

"And one more thing, Jack," Gifford gets the last word.

"What's that?"

"Lizzie Borden was acquitted."

Chapter 40

George Herman took a deep breath of country air as he watched the Baseball Hall of Fame induction ceremonies at Clark Center in Cooperstown. This was his version of heaven.

He didn't wear his Babe uniform out of respect. You don't play piano in front of Mozart or paint in front of Picasso—and in George Herman's mind, you don't put on the Babe's uniform in his house. George wore an ill-fitting tan suit with open butterfly collar that was a replica of the one Ruth wore at the initial ceremony in 1939.

He thought back to when he was a kid, growing up in the neighboring town of Milford. His father would take him to the ceremonies—they never missed one—to see all the greats take their rightful place in history. They would arrive early, staking out a claim on the lawn. George's father and grandfather would hand down the mythical tales of the great Babe Ruth, and even joked of how young George looked so much like the Babe. Little did they know what a huge role that resemblance would play in his life.

George was approached by a vendor with a tray of drinks strapped around his neck. Being a local icon had its benefits.

"Mr. Herman, a man just purchased a beer for you and asked me to bring it to you," the teenage vendor said.

"That was nice of him—did you get his name?" George asked upon accepting the plastic cup of foamy beer, and thinking it would hit the spot on the sultry summer day.

"No, he didn't say, but he said he wanted you to have this," the boy handed George a folded piece of paper. He opened the note and read.

> *We both know that Max Q isn't as perfect as they say. If you want answers go to the place of true perfection.*

When he looked up, the vendor had disappeared into the crowd. Suddenly his day wasn't so heavenly—someone knew he was working for the prosecution! But how? He would trust Jack and the Cirillos with his life, but was now having regrets about letting Jack talk him into bringing that ADA Jessica Shepherdson into the loop.

George knew he had no choice but to follow the lead, even if he were walking into a trap. He hopped onto a shuttle bus that took him to the parking area, where he promptly found his 1940 Lincoln convertible. It was a gift given to Ruth by a sponsor, and it even had a faded inscription to the Babe on the front dashboard. George had bought it at an auction a few years back for a sum as hefty as Ruth himself. It was his prized possession, along with a 1937 Packard, which was modeled after the one Ruth used to travel between Manhattan watering holes. Between the impersonation and investigation businesses, he had done well over the years, but he lived modestly, which allowed him to splurge on Babe memorabilia.

He put on his derby hat and headed toward the destination. He knew exactly where to go, and he was sure that the author of the note was counting on it.

He drove northwest of Cooperstown for about sixty miles with the summer wind belting him in the face. He arrived at a genteel town with shady trees and plush lawns called Oneida. He maneuvered through small-town streets until he found 170 Kenwood Avenue.

The redbrick mansion had been converted into a museum that archived the history of a group founded by John Humphrey Noyes in 1848 called "The Perfectionists." He was sure that is what the message meant by "true perfection."

They lasted for about thirty years, numbering three hundred at their peak, with the majority living in this mansion. Eventually, public criticism forced Noyes and his followers to move to Canada. But the house was still used for tours led by descendants of the original Oneida society. George Herman loved history, but even he thought this one was a little weird.

George wasn't completely sure what to do, so he took the tour. It included photographs, letters, and historical documents. He didn't know exactly what he was looking for, but figured the message writer would let him know when he found it. He checked the other people on the tour—there were only four, including himself—for some sort of clue about the Max Q case. None came.

When George exhausted all possibilities, he returned to his car, shaking his head. Maybe this wasn't the place.

Tucked underneath his windshield wiper was a note, similar to the first one. He gathered it off the windshield and read.

You know that Max Q did it—the question is
HOWE he did it. Take a tour to find out.

George got in his car and sped out of Oneida. This clue was much easier to decipher. Howe Caverns was the oldest and most commercialized tourist attraction in central New York. An underground labyrinth of caves that were discovered in 1842 by a farmer named Lester Howe.

George bought a ticket like the rest of the tourists and waited in line for the elevator that would take him over a hundred and fifty feet below the surface and into the caves. As he waited, he took notes of the others on the tour. A couple of traditional cookie-cutter families with young children. A twenty-something who was traveling solo. George pegged him as a typical kid looking to lose the tour to go smoke pot in the many cave tunnels, as so many kids had done in the past.

The man who really stood out like a sore thumb was a thick-haired

Italian-looking man who reminded George of a character from *The Sopranos*. A fear jumped into his head that this might not be about information, but rather…no reason to think such thoughts.

The musty caves were just as George remembered—70% humidity and fifty-degree temperature. It didn't matter if it was summer or winter outside, the caves always remained a constant temperature.

When nothing out of the ordinary occurred on the tour, George concluded that he was being played—the defense was just playing mind games, sending him on a wild goose chase. They probably had information that he might be working for the prosecution, and wanted to confirm it. George left the caves, kicking himself for playing into their hands. He jumped on Interstate-88 and headed back toward Cooperstown.

The traffic was thick in the opposite direction from those exiting the Hall of Fame ceremony, adding to his misery. He got off the highway and drove through the empty back roads he knew so well. His gas gauge moved closer to empty, so George pulled into a small country gas station. The sky had turned dark, and he didn't want to risk being stranded in the middle of nowhere at night.

He purchased sixty dollars worth of gas and a two-day-old hot dog. He filled the tank and continued his journey back to Cooperstown.

George was about a half-mile from the gas station when he felt the cold knife against his neck. He glanced in his rear-view mirror and saw the man in the backseat wearing a ski mask. He must have slipped into the car when he purchased the gas. George cursed himself for making a rookie mistake.

"We are coming up to a farm on your right with a long driveway. I want you to pull into it," the man instructed, trying to disguise his voice.

George followed orders, feeling the blade tighten on his neck. He knew that trying to be a hero is usually what got people killed in these situations.

The driveway had large cornstalks on both sides, higher than the car.

"Stop the car," the man demanded and George hit the brakes.

The man forcibly walked George into the cornstalks, where he blindfolded him and tied his hands behind his back. The attacker then shoved George to the soggy ground.

He vowed that if this was it, he would die with dignity, rather than beg for his life. He'd lived a full life and had few regrets.

"Since your boy Lawson ain't worth a shit, I thought I'd help you out," the man stated coldly.

George felt an object being shoved into the pocket of his suit jacket, followed by the sounds of the man rushing away.

The blindfold came off easily and George was able to catch a glimpse of his attacker as he fled. It was the kid he pegged as a pot-smoker. While he couldn't see his face, the giveaway was the tattoo on his arm. It consisted of the letters J and M on the arms of a cross.

Then he heard an engine roar, followed by the screech of tires. *Oh no—not my car! The Babe's car!!*

George freed his hands, then reached into his pocket and pulled out a plastic case.

Chapter 41

It's Monday morning—one day before our deadline—and I'm still humming "Monday Monday" by the Mamas and the Papas, which my alarm clock drilled into my head this morning.

Kerri and Hal Metzer enter the conference room. I flash an insincere smile at my sister. "If you never leave, how can I ever miss you?"

She feigns a laugh. "You are almost as funny as your case."

Hal Metzer grows impatient. He unbuckles his leather briefcase and pulls out a pile of papers. "We are happy to see that you have finally come to your senses. This whole episode has been an exercise in futility, and proceeding would be a colossal mistake."

"Before we get to that, I thought we might watch a little film," I say, still smiling. I point to Shep and she places a DVD into the laptop computer that rests on the conference table. The video was provided to us by George Herman.

It begins with Laney Bang sitting on a bed, dressed stylishly in her birthday suit. It's not just any bed; it's the one she died in. We watch as her co-star enters the screen—Drew Anderson. I look at Kerri and Hal, but can't detect any response.

Max Q approaches Laney like a man on a mission and climbs aboard the "SS Every Man's Fantasy."

We stare in amazement at what follows. I imagine it is much like how farmers reacted to seeing the cotton gin for the first time, doing the work of fifty men. It was hard to fathom it could be done that well. But not exactly enhancing the reputation of the wholesome, All-American boy who would risk his life to help an old lady across the street. I notice a slight squirm from Kerri. Her vacant look is priceless. But I can't take satisfaction in her misery, all I can do is feel bad for Marissa.

The show must go on—Laney rolls on top of Max Q, reversing positions. They grind in rhythm until in the heat of the moment, Laney shouts out, "You're with a real woman now—not that cold wife of yours!"

Anderson turns visibly angry. He uses his superior strength to roll back on top of her. He grabs her around the throat and shouts, *"I told you if you ever said anything about Marissa again I'll kill you!"*

The lack of oxygen is turning Laney purple. I sneak a peak at Kerri and Hal, who seem to have turned the same color.

Shep ejects the DVD—we've made our point. I then let her do the honors. "We are going to formally prosecute your client, adding first degree murder."

She looks at me fondly—she's already apologized fifteen times for her doubts.

"First-degree?" Metzer scoffs. "Nothing on that video indicates forethought."

"Whether that video was from last month or an hour before Laney was murdered, the bottom line is that Anderson left for his jog and had time to think about what he was about to do. And what he did was return with the intent to kill—it wasn't murder with passion, or depraved indifference."

Metzer dismissively waves his hand at me. "It's a moot point. The video will be ruled inadmissible, then you're out of luck, because you got nothing."

Kerri comes to her client's defense. "Drew is a good man and doesn't deserve this witch hunt. You have no evidence he killed her, and all this tape will do is publicly embarrass him. Jack, if this is about that chip on your shoulder when it comes to me, then I will step down. But please don't punish an innocent man. Don't make this personal."

While the narcissism is predictable, I am struck by the conviction in her voice. Although, I shouldn't be totally surprised, since Anderson represents everything she's been taught to believe in. In a way, he's her dream guy.

But this isn't about Kerri or me—it's about evidence. "Your client and the victim were having an ongoing affair. It was a relationship sought by Laney Bang with intent to blackmail your client, which turned out to be his motive for killing her." I point at the video that sits in the open tray of the laptop. "I guess he came through on his threat."

I'm weak on the details, especially the part about where she put up no resistance and how that conflicted with the 911 call. But it should be more than enough to get an indictment, and it could be a year before we actually go to trial, so we'll have time to compile all the evidence we'll need. And if that doesn't work, it seems as if Laney might have a guardian angel working on her side to provide us with information.

Kerri is indignant. "Your blackmail motive is weak. And there were other people present that night who had more motive to kill her. You're a good storyteller, Jack, but you're still lacking evidence."

"That tape will be inadmissible," Hal adds, in case we didn't hear him the first time.

"I can prove it, and I will," I say, remaining in law-swagger mode.

Kerri latches her briefcase and stands to leave. "You couldn't get a jury to convict Drew Anderson if you had a video of him killing her," she shouts at me on her way out.

I smile again. "Maybe I do."

Chapter 42

Shep and I have no time to soak in our victory. We have scheduled a noon press conference. We know that Kerri will have all guns blazing in her spin-doctored response, so it's important for us to file our charges as speedily as possible. I want no part of playing the media game, but Kerri was right when she spoke of the difficulty we'll face in finding a jury willing to convict Drew Anderson. Avoiding the press is not an option for us. We can't let the defense control the story.

Shep leaves to prepare the charge sheet for the press conference. I draw the short straw and have to inform Gifford Brown of our decision to proceed to trial. He takes the news in stride, pledging support.

The office is empty—all the ADAs are either scheduled for court or at lunch. I return to my office and mentally prepare. I wonder who our video-providing angel is, and whether or not it's a good thing. She's no angel, but my money is on Amber Jazz.

Right after the noon whistle goes off, Shep and I stand outside our offices in front of a lightning storm of flashbulbs. I get right to the point and read the charge sheet.

"State of New York, County of Otsego against Andrew Christian Anderson. Jack Lawson Chief District Attorney of Otsego County, in the name and by the authority of the People of the State of New York, informs the court that Andrew Christian Anderson has been charged with one count of first degree murder in the unlawful death of Darby Kelleher, alias Laney Bang."

The press gasps upon hearing the words "first degree murder." Nobody in their right mind believed we could charge Max Q in the first place, but if we did, the "experts" let it be known that it was a crime of passion.

When I finish reading, I make a strong comment about our belief in Anderson's guilt, and how we will prove the charges beyond a reasonable doubt. I then take a few questions.

"Do you honestly believe there is a jury that will convict Drew

Anderson?" asks a man from CNN, sounding like my sister.

"I think you underestimate the citizens of Otsego County. When you take preconceived notions about the defendant out of the equation, it is an open and shut case. We believe that when the jury hears the evidence, the myth of Drew Anderson will be just that—a myth."

A reporter from the New York Globe shouts out, "Jack—there was a search of a New York townhouse this past Thursday, owned by the victim. Did evidence found there change your earlier opinion, and lead to this charge?"

"I had no earlier opinion. We viewed the accumulation of evidence and our conclusion was, and is, that Drew Anderson murdered Laney Bang with malice and forethought."

I give our local guy Montini the last question. "How do you react to the critics that say you are just seeking fame, and that the evidence simply isn't there to continue with this case?"

I hand the question to Shep, who says, "Sorry, Ira, we don't have time for your question. We're late for our lunch in New York with the mayor."

With that, we abruptly leave the podium to laughter. She smiles at me—it went just as we planned it.

Chapter 43

We retreat to 197 Main, where Jana informs me that I have visitors in my office.

Shep and I enter to find a woman with the brightest orange tan I've ever seen. She is wearing tight yellow stretch pants with palm trees prints, and a pink T-shirt that matches her glossy lipstick.

A man with a military-looking crew cut sits beside her, wearing a more conservative outfit of plain T-shirt and jeans

"Can I help you?" I ask in an unsure voice.

"My name is Marcie Kelleher and this is my husband Steve," the woman belts out in a shrill southern accent. "We are Darby's parents."

I'm momentarily stupefied. I never really thought of Laney Bang having parents or a family.

Marcie stands and wraps me in a hug. "We drove up here from Pensacola to take Darby back home. Steve and I are so grateful that you're gonna send Drew Anderson to jail," she states enthusiastically. "Even if we are Florida State fans."

Steve remains seated with his head in his hands, appearing distraught.

I don't have the heart to tell her that convicting Drew Anderson is a long shot. "Where are you staying? Perhaps I can talk to the county about helping you pay for your travel."

"We've been staying at Darby's place in the city."

So that's why the front door was unlocked. It seems as if the townhouse wasn't as hidden as I thought.

Marcie remains talkative, "It's hard to believe she's gone. Seems like just yesterday she was this rambunctious little girl getting into all she wasn't s'posed to on the military base." She smiles at the fond reminiscence. "Darby always wanted to be a star and I'm so glad she reached that, even if she left us too early."

My eyes wander to her husband, who doesn't look like he's found the same solace. His head is still buried in his hands and tears are streaming down his face. Marcie speaks for him, "Steve has been in the military for thirty years. So he's seen his share of death, but when it's your own daughter…" She lets the words hover over the room.

I've never worked a murder so this is all new to me. They say to bury a child is the hardest thing someone would have to do in this life. I can't imagine anything being more devastating than losing Reyanne, but I can't argue with the notion.

But I also have a job to do, and see another opportunity to learn more about the victim. "Was it hard for you to accept what she…did for a living?"

"At first it was, it's not exactly what you hope when you bring 'em home from the hospital, specially in the tight knit military world. I won't lie to you, Jack, and tell you there wasn't a real hard period where we weren't on speaking terms with Darby. But eventually you realize how short life is."

The term "short life" registers throughout the room. Even Shep, who is no fan of the deceased, has let her guard down and looks to be affected. Marcie gathers herself and continues, "But you learn to accept the choices of your children, even if you don't agree with 'em. I'm so glad we made peace before she passed—I feel so bad for the girls …"

"The girls?" I inquire.

"Darby had two sisters who disowned her for what she did. I kept telling 'em that one day they'd regret it. And now it's too late."

As if awakened by his wife's words, Steve removes his hands to reveal a face that is red with anger. He looks me in the eye and speaks for the first time, "I hope you put that bastard away for life. I can't believe he killed my Baby Doll!"

I immediately know. I make intense eye contact with Steve to let him know that I do. He looks away like a coward.

My tone shifts dramatically. "You need to get out of here right now. And do not ever step foot in this office again!"

Marcie looks unnerved. I don't know if she grasps what's just happened, but I have an idea that she was aware of what was going on in that house and never said anything about it. It's why Laney left the minute she turned eighteen, looking for a new life, and leaving Baby Doll behind.

"What was that about?" Shep asks after our visitors have left.

"Just a reminder about the importance of locking your doors. Especially at night."

Chapter 44

The man sat at the corner table sipping on his second bottle of Foster's. He scanned the room and listened to the heated chatter. *Anderson did it. Anderson didn't do it. Who else could have done it? Anyone but Drew Anderson—he's Max Q for God sake!*

He didn't care who killed Laney Bang. He just knew he had a mission to complete—a mission for *her*. She dictated the rules and he would do anything to win her back, no matter the cost.

He was eavesdropping on a guy who sat at a nearby table. He was the only one in the place who wasn't talking about the case. The man nicknamed him Mr. Baseball because he went on and on about the dreadfully boring Hall of Fame inductions from last weekend. Next to Mr. Baseball sat a woman named Ashley. The man was baffled as to what this classic beauty was doing with such an Average Joe.

They were soon joined by the stars of tonight's theatrics. Jack Lawson and Jessica Shepherdson.

Not only would the thin Lawson be no match for the man physically, but he seemed to have misplaced the confidence he had displayed at today's press conference. He would be easy prey.

The man's eyes turned to Jessica. He would be getting a much closer look at her later in the evening, and was looking forward to it. She had a fire in her eyes that he had witnessed the last time they'd come together, which made her dangerous. But then again, he was always attracted to danger.

After another hour of debate and banter, the two lawyers said their goodbyes and departed Touch 'Em All. The man followed at a safe distance. Main Street was abuzz with tourists and on the muggy night, making it easier to blend into the crowd.

His pickup truck was in the parking lot of the Lake Front Motel. He hurried to his vehicle and drove to Main Street.

Things were going as planned. Jessica was leading Lawson back to her car at the DA's Office. There, they got into a BMW and drove up Route-80.

He followed closely behind. He knew it would be easy—his car was built for this.

With brute force, the front grill of his pickup smashed into the trunk of the BMW. Then rammed the swerving car once more. She began to speed up, but he easily caught her and pounded the back bumper again. He was enjoying himself, but knew it was time to finish the job.

He put on a ski mask and gloves, without missing a beat in the chase. He then sped into the oncoming lane, pulling even with the BMW. He was able to get a good look into Jessica's eyes, and saw the same resolute determination as he had last time.

The man looked to the side of the road, noticing a five-foot embankment. He made a sharp right turn into the driver's side door. Doors banged hard and the BMW moved toward the edge. He braked, dropped behind the car, and gave it a swift kick in the rear, sending it down the slope to a metal-crunching stop at the bottom. It flipped onto its side, tipped back onto four wheels, then collided with a large oak tree.

A loud thud echoed over the lake. The man pulled his truck to the side of the road and reached into the glove compartment for his machete. He worked his way down the embankment to the mangled BMW that was fizzing steam from the punctured radiator.

He opened Jessica's battered door and dragged her out onto the ground by her hair. She cringed in pain and her pretty face was already bruising, but he was relieved he hadn't seriously hurt her. She took a good licking, but nothing debilitating.

He forced her onto her hands and knees. With knife to her neck, he whispered into her ear, "Good to see you again, Jessica."

Then purposely loud enough for Lawson to hear, he said, "Listen to me good. Drew Anderson is innocent. So you and your boyfriend back off this investigation. Do you understand!?"

She said nothing.

"Did you hear me?" he pushed the knife blade harder into her neck, coming perilously close to breaking the skin. He had always wanted to be an actor, and now he was getting his chance.

"Yes"

"I know that you two love the publicity, but if you don't back off, the next headlines will be for your funeral!"

He could feel the pulse in her neck vibrate against the blade.

Predictably, Lawson came lunging at him. The running start made the punch even worse. His face rippled and he crumpled to the ground.

"Jack!" Jessica screamed out and hurried to her injured partner.

The man returned to his truck. He paused for a moment, allowing Lawson to get a good look at its powerful grill. It was part of the message. A message he delivered for *her.*

Chapter 45

The case against Max Q is moving rapidly. Tuesday morning was a lawyers-only meeting before Judge Patricia Schanz. A woman in her fifties, sporting an unruly mop of hair streaked with gray. Her reputation is that she is pro-defendant—give the Miranda Warning with too much attitude and watch the charges get dropped—but it really didn't matter, as her courtroom would just be a short rest stop in a long trial process.

We agreed for a preliminary hearing to be held on Thursday—a prompt hearing to determine whether there is a "probable cause" to believe the defendant committed the crime. Most defendants waive it and move directly to a grand jury proceeding, but Kerri chooses to have the hearing.

For myself, I think the court proceeding will be a great break from the barrage of scrutiny in this case. I'll get a chance to do some actual lawyering. Take a vacation to my comfort zone.

On the other hand, Kerri is not suffering from any camera-shyness. One person's torture chamber is another person's reason to get up in the morning. She's been doing the media circuit like she's on a press junket promoting a blockbuster movie. But maybe that's exactly what this case is—a big budget film with some law thrown in for effect.

I'm intrigued by her attraction to the spotlight, especially since the Lawsons have spent centuries working behind the scenes, and preaching the importance of doing so.

Shep and I have been more concerned with the "accident" and what it means to our case, than preparing for a rubber-stamp hearing. We both got a good look at the grill of the pickup truck that had the roo-guard on it—one of Lansdale's goons was behind the accident. And surprise-surprise, he reported a pickup truck stolen from his property the day of the accident.

Shep picks me up in a black Lincoln Navigator with bulletproof glass, which is on loan to the Otsego County DA's Office from the state of New York. The state granted our office a budget for the case that is much greater than normal, but LB&G has an unlimited budget, and now we have to use a chunk of the budget on security. I have a guard stationed around the clock at my residence, while Shep's getting the same treatment at her apartment. This is Gifford's call, not ours.

I trade glances with Shep, who returns an unsure smile. Her face is rapidly clearing up, and with help from make-up, it's hard to tell that the accident was only a few days ago. It's her bruised sternum that's giving her the biggest problem. It hurts every time she laughs. The good news is that doesn't happen often.

"You look nice," I say. She's dressed in her pinstriped suit. It's the one she wore at her successful initial appearance. I think it might be a superstition thing. Mac once told me the story of a Hall of Fame inducted ballplayer who wore the same underwear for months during his career because he thought changing would jinx a hitting streak he was on.

Becoming more media savvy by the day, I wear my best charcoal colored Armani suit that I usually save for the funeral of a relative that I couldn't stand.

"Thanks, so do you."

"What's the verdict on your car?"

"Totaled."

"Ouch—at least you're okay."

"I guess."

We continue down the country road on the hazy summer morning. There's not even a hint of a cool breeze coming from the lake. We pass the spot where we were forced off the road.

After some silence, I address the attack, "I think the video scared Lansdale. They were convinced that the charges would be dropped at an early stage with an abject apology from us. But the tape means we are likely going to trial, and even if he doesn't get convicted, the tape, if played in open court, will harm Anderson's reputation, and he can kiss Albany goodbye. Anderson and his supporters are scared to death of going to trial, so they went for a mistrial the old fashion way, by threatening the prosecutors."

Shep doesn't necessarily agree, which might be a sign that things are getting back to normal, and she provides her own theories.

"Remember what Gifford always says," I tell her.

"I can't believe you're quoting Gifford Brown," she sighs. "It's always about the amount of money."

"What's the other thing?"

"Don't ignore the obvious, because there is usually a good reason why it's the obvious."

"Exactly. And the obvious is that Drew Anderson was the one who Laney was blackmailing. He was the one she was with on that tape when he threatened her. He was the one she was obsessing about for years. And he was the only one in the house when she was killed."

Lansdale might be working on Drew's behalf to end the trial, but they are up against a worthy opponent in Laney Bang. It appears that she had set up a contingency plan in case of her demise. Someone, whether it be Amber, Maxon, or some unknown party, is providing us evidence to keep the trial going. And Shep and I are caught in the perilous middle.

The courthouse appears in the distance and the butterflies in my stomach turn to pterodactyls. And this is only the preliminary hearing.

We receive a police escort to an area in front of the courthouse, which is blocked off with wooden barriers. Security hovers around us as we get out of the SUV.

We make the slow walk to the courthouse steps like we're the ones on trial. In a way, we are. The prizefight of the century is about to begin and Jack Lawson and Jessica Shepherdson are entering the ring as heavy underdogs, even with the soon-to-be infamous video on their side.

We keep looking forward, acting as if we don't hear the whirlwind of questions and comments being shouted at us. Lansdale's group is marching as close to the courthouse as security will allow, holding picket signs like union workers on strike.

Before entering, I take one last look at the craziness around us. I picture Reyanne looking down and laughing at me. Her mission statement was always to remove me from my comfort zone, which she said was the only way I would ever be challenged to grow. And now I find myself in the epicenter of a great storm. You win, Rey.

Standing in the entrance portico of the old courthouse, I look to the ceiling and whisper, "LLF."

Chapter 46

The Otsego County courthouse fits neatly into the Cooperstown landscape with its Victorian Gothic style. It's no spring chicken—built in 1880, and despite the face-lift it received in the 1980s, I always feel I should be wearing a powdered wig upon entering.

We proceed up a creaky staircase to the second floor, and enter the St. Anne's Courtroom. With its timber trusses and large stained glass windows, it reminds me of an old church. The high vaulted ceiling causes the courtroom to act like an echo chamber.

We move past the packed gallery and place our briefcases on a wooden table that faces the altar of Judge Schanz. To our left sits Kerri, her co-conspirator Hal Metzer, and the star of the show, Drew Anderson.

Anderson is wearing a navy suit and happy yellow tie. He sits expressionless, his only movement occurs when Kerri reaches over to whisper in his ear. My focus switches to the beautiful woman in the front row with dark curly hair and dressed in a light blue sundress. Marissa Torres-Anderson.

Like her husband, she looks stoically ahead. Her body language doesn't match the cocky, ball-busting persona she displayed in our first meeting. I feel instantly bad for her, as I'm sure word has reached her about the video. My eyes return to her husband and I feel a rush of anger. Not just for Laney Bang, but for what he has done to Marissa.

Next to Marissa sits Drew Anderson's other staunch supporter, James Lansdale. He is dressed in a navy sport coat and khakis—blue seems to be the official color of Team Anderson. He keeps checking the expensive watch like he is late for his tee-time. He occasionally grabs Marissa's hand in an attempt at support. I notice that Shep is fixated on Lansdale. A good Beemer is hard to replace.

Shep and I have our own support today. Ashley gives me a toothy grin, along with an excited wave from the gallery. Mac just coolly gives us a thumbs-up sign like this is some sort of everyday occurrence for him.

Kerri stands and opens her briefcase. She takes out a pile of paperwork, which I know is an attempt to intimidate us. *Look, Jack—more surprise witnesses.* Her designer look provides the outward appearance of sophistication, but at her core is a street fighter who'll do whatever it takes, not only to win, but to embarrass her opponent in the process.

"What's wrong, Jack? Can't say hello to your big sister," she directs toward me as she takes a seat.

"My apologies, I was thrown off by your early arrival. I figured that you'd use the time to mix in a couple more network appearances."

"Early bird gets the worm."

"But it's still eating worms."

"Well, maybe you can find me a few more to munch on when I wipe the floor with you."

And this is only the preliminary hearing. Our "pleasantries" are interrupted by the court clerk announcing the Honorable Patricia Schanz.

She orders us to be seated, before getting right to the reason for our gathering. "This is the preliminary hearing in the case of the State of New York versus Andrew Christian Anderson. The charges are one count of murder in the first-degree of Darby Kelleher."

It's really strange to hear the stunning charge read in open court with Max Q sitting just feet from us. I take a deep breath and call our first witness, Roger Beneke.

I walk in front of the table and begin what I believe should be a smooth questioning. "Good morning, Officer."

"Good morning," he responds in a shaky voice. The whole world will be over-analyzing his every word—who wouldn't be nervous?

"Please state your name for the court,"

"I am Officer Roger Beneke of the Otsego County Sheriff's Office," he states, and spells his name for the recorder.

"Officer Beneke—what were you doing on the morning of July 24?"

"I was patrolling the north end of Otsego Lake as was my normal beat."

"While on patrol, you received a call pertaining to a potential incident involving Laney Bang, is that correct?"

"I did—I received a call from Deputy Sue Kirkland in the Sheriff's Office. She reported that a woman claiming to be Laney Bang had placed a call to 911 at 6:05 a.m."

"And what location did the caller give?"

"Anderson Estate in Cooperstown."

Not that anyone needs a refresher course, but I note for the record that Laney Bang is an alternate name for Darby Kelleher and that Anderson Estate is the defendant's home. I then come to the first pothole I need to navigate around.

"Officer Beneke, why is it important that the name given by the caller to 911 was Laney Bang?"

Beneke takes a deep breath and releases. "Laney Bang was a well-known celebrity who was in town for a publicity appearance. All weekend long, the Sheriff's Office received numerous calls in which the caller falsely identified herself as Laney Bang. We couldn't possibly send an officer every time we received a call."

"So that is why you didn't respond until 7:30?"

Beneke tilts his head down, showing subtle regret. "Thinking it was a hoax, I didn't plan on responding at all, which was a logistical office policy that weekend. But the more I thought about it, the more the call bugged me. So since my schedule was light that morning, I decided to take a trip up Anderson Estate and check it out."

"What exactly bugged you about this call, compared to other false alarms?"

"Nothing specific. Just gut instinct of a police officer, I guess."

"What did you see when you arrived at Anderson Estate at 7:30," I ask, glad to move past the response-time issue.

"Everything seemed normal when I approached the gate. John Scurry, the long time gate attendant, was there. We spoke of the weather, and I explained that I received a call, and it was my duty to check it out no matter how ridiculous it sounded. I proceeded to the main house."

"Did everything still appear normal?"

"When I had previously been to Anderson Estate, there was always a bunch of workers present, performing typical tasks such as mowing grass and general landscaping. But I didn't observe any staff that day. I thought it was strange, but I wasn't alarmed."

"Then you arrived at the house—still appear normal?"

"I found the front door open. I called at least three times and received no response. By itself, it wouldn't have raised my suspicions, but when combined with the 911 call, it put me on high alert. I drew my gun and entered the house."

"What did you find?"

"At first, nothing. I identified myself and called to see if anyone was present, but received no response. I moved to the second floor and that is where I confronted Mr. Anderson."

"Please describe Mr. Anderson's appearance that morning."

"He was in a T-shirt and shorts. He was sweating profusely. I told him of the 911 call and he responded that no such woman was there. He appeared nervous, and his eyes were jitterbugging, much different from the self-contained man I'd met on occasion."

"So you grew alarmed?"

"Yes, I pushed past Mr. Anderson and began a search for Ms. Bang."

"And what did you find?"

"I entered the first door on the right, which was the master bedroom. The victim was lying face up, naked, on the bed with multiple knife wounds to her chest. I took her pulse, hoping she might still be alive, but she was clearly dead."

Beneke looks physically upset as he recalls the bloody discovery. The standing-room-only gallery buzzes, despite this being common knowledge.

I pause for effect, then ask, "What did you do next, Officer Beneke?"

"I secured the area and called for back-up. Then I questioned Mr. Anderson."

"Did you consider him a suspect at that time?"

"Honestly, I wasn't sure what to think. I was just buying time until back-up arrived. This was my first time at a murder scene. Mr. Anderson was receptive to talking, but still appeared to be dazed and confused."

"When he talked, did he tell you the truth, the whole truth, and nothing but the truth?"

"No, he told me that he had no idea how she got there."

I catch a glimpse of Marissa, who's still looking ahead with a stone face. I feel for her, but move on.

"And how did you know this wasn't true?"

"Because I was in charge of security for Ms. Bang the night before at her book signing. When it ended, she asked me if I would be able to drop her off at Mr. Anderson's house for what she termed a business meeting. And I obliged."

"So you escorted Laney Bang to Drew Anderson's home on the evening of July 23?"

"That is correct."

Another murmur from the gallery—the police escort had only been known to us.

"What about those who say this is your word against Mr. Anderson's?"

"I have it on tape—that would tell them all they need to know."

I pause to savor the small victory, and sneak a glance at Kerri. She looks to be bubbling with confidence, which concerns me. "No further questions."

Chapter 47

Kerri approaches the witness like a tornado. Beneke looks worried. He probably should be.

"You mentioned that the no-respond policy of the Sheriff's Office was related to being overrun with Laney Bang pranks and hoaxes. Please tell us how many Laney Bang requests you received while you were on duty the morning of July 24?"

"The call center was in charge of filtering them, so I really don't know."

"I asked you how many *you* received. I imagine it must have been a large number, being that you couldn't find the time to check it out for approximately an hour and a half."

"That was actually the only one I personally received, but like I said, the call center dealt with most of them."

"In that case, I'm assuming you had plenty of non-Laney Bang calls during that time."

Beneke squirms in his seat. "As I mentioned earlier, my schedule was light."

"According to your logbook, you had no calls—not one—during that time. No Laney Bang hoaxes, no domestic disputes, not even a request to rescue a cat from a tree."

Kerri introduces his logbook as further proof of such.

"For the life of me, I can't figure out what you were doing while Laney Bang was being murdered," she says, sounding perplexed.

Beneke looks embarrassed, and tilts his head downward. "I was sleeping."

Kerri looks aghast. "Sleeping!?"

"My schedule was usually light during the morning shift, so I would often take a nap up at Glimmerglass State Park."

"Can anyone vouch that you were at Glimmerglass State Park between the last entry in your log book at 5:45 a.m. and arriving at Anderson Estate at 7:30?"

He looks taken aback by the question. "Not that I know of. I didn't go out of my way to let people know I was sleeping on the job."

Kerri flashes a superior look and moves on. "In your earlier testimony, you mentioned that you were the lead security for Laney Bang on her publicity appearance at Cooperstown Books, and escorted her to Anderson Estate that night."

"Yes, that is true," Beneke replies, sounding proud.

"Was it part of your security guidelines to make illicit advances upon Ms. Bang? Then when she rejected your proposition, you responded with inflammatory and threatening language."

Kerri declares numerous signed affidavits as evidence, from witnesses at Cooperstown Books, who allegedly witnessed Beneke's advances and the specific remarks that followed.

"Objection, Your Honor," both Shep and I scream out and the judge calls a sidebar. I question the relevance of Kerri putting the police on trial, but the judge disagrees with me. Not surprising.

Kerri clicks her heels back to the defense table, and picks up more notes. "Let's move on to when you *finally* showed up at 7:30 at Anderson Estate. You said you didn't find anything, to use your words, alarming."

"Correct"

"So let me get this straight—you didn't find this to be an important call, and when you arrived you don't find anything alarming. But the fact that Mr. Anderson's door was open totally changed your thinking?"

"As I testified previously, it was the combination of things. No staff, the 911 call, and the open door."

"When you entered the house, you stated that you still found nothing out of the ordinary, yet you continued up the stairs?"

"It was a judgment call, I made it, and I stand by it," Beneke makes a brief comeback.

Kerri hits him with a smug grin and I know his momentum will be brief.

"Isn't it true, Officer Beneke, that you had more reason to know there was a dead body in that room than my client? You have no alibi, you reacted angrily to her rejection of your advances, and since you took her there the night before, you knew that she was present. Nobody can substantiate your whereabouts at the time of her death, and you failed to show up at the crime scene for eighty minutes. Then you arrest my client without reasonable cause. Was this the knee-jerk reaction of an inexperienced policeman, or a well thought out plan?"

"Objection! Objection!" I shout and stomp my foot as if it might help.

But Judge Schanz is already reprimanding my sister. Kerri looks amazed that implying a police officer might be a murder suspect without any basis of fact would be frowned upon. She claims she was just making a point that others had just as much motive and opportunity to commit the crime as her client, including Officer Beneke. She apologizes to the court and assures Judge Schanz that it won't happen again. But I see a foreshadowing of the defense's strategy.

"When you interviewed my client after finding the body, was he aware that he was your top suspect in the case? Did you inform him of his right to seek counsel?"

"We had no suspect at the time. Mr. Anderson could have easily been a victim who survived the attack. I had made no judgments at that point."

"Did you inform him of his right to counsel?"

"No."

"Officer Beneke, you taped this interview with my client. Did he know he was being taped?"

"If you have nothing to hide then no reason to worry about being taped." Beneke is starting to lose his cool.

"Answer the question," Judge Schanz states with authority.

"No, he didn't."

"Do you always tape interviews with suspects?"

"If possible, yes. I had a bad experience with someone making false allegations against me. It protects me from such acts."

"Would you be talking about a sexual harassment complaint brought against you by a female co-worker in the Sheriff's Office three years ago?"

"The case was dropped, it was baseless," Beneke states angrily.

Shep and I want to pound our heads against the table. The worst thing your witness can do is surprise you. Since the complaint was dropped and sealed, we had no knowledge of it. But obviously Kerri's investigators found it. We object, but the damage is done.

"Please get some help for your anger toward women, Officer Beneke," Kerri gets in a final lick.

"Objection."

"Sustained."

"Withdrawn."

Smirk from Kerri to me.

Chapter 48

The preliminary hearing has turned messier than expected. They're normally about an hour or two long without any questioning from the defense. The old joke is a grand jury will indict a ham sandwich, but at this point, even getting to a grand jury is not a slam-dunk for us.

I call Sheriff Roddy Opp to the stand, hoping he performs better than Beneke. *How could he not?*

Opp looks professional, wearing a suit, and I think he even groomed his mustache. Unlike Beneke, he appears confident. In fact, he looks like he is reveling in the spotlight. Opp initially put us in a bad spot in this case with the premature arrest, and he hasn't helped with his off-the-cuff press conferences, attempting to force our hand into prosecuting Anderson. I'm the first to admit that I don't like the guy, but I need him to come through for us.

Opp handles my questions like a seasoned pro, and makes no apologies for the arrest. I then hold my breath as I hand him off to Kerri.

As she begins hammering him for being in charge of a department that she is now calling the "Keystone Cops," I should probably take some solace in the police getting some deserved payback. But all I can see are Drew Anderson's hands wrapped around Laney's neck. And his henchman (via Lansdale) with that knife to Shep's neck. Then I picture him walking away a free man. If he does, I hope Marissa puts her hands around his neck, but so far she doesn't appear to be wavering in her support.

Kerri turns up the heat—using the jogging witness affidavits to prove an alibi, and also delving into the Tony Rivotti forging incident in an attempt to show that Opp and his department had a vendetta against her client.

Judge Schanz declares the Rivotti line of questioning to be not relevant in regards to this hearing, but it gets me wondering about Kerri's strategy. Why is she pulling out all the stops at the preliminary hearing?

The obvious answer is that when it comes to this case, the PR battle is just as important as what occurs in the courtroom. Kerri could be putting on a mini trial for public consumption, and perhaps she's angling to force us to use important evidence like the video at this time, to dull its effects for when the trial begins. She knows a worldwide audience is watching this hearing, and she's controlling the conversation. And since it usually takes about a year for a capital case to go to trial, the discussion between now and the first juror being seated will be of incompetent police and possible other suspects.

During a particularly heated exchange about the security system Opp installed at Anderson Estate, Shep whispers to me, "Wow, she's really going for the jugular."

For the first time, I realize that Kerri might be going beyond controlling the conversation. As crazy as it sounds, she actually thinks she can win this thing at the preliminary hearing stage. And why not take advantage of having the best ally at her disposal—the great advocate for defendant's rights, Judge Patricia Schanz? Why not end it right here before any more damage occurs to Anderson's image?

As I conceptualize the potential public humiliation awaiting us—I can already hear the jeering from the "experts" if we can't even meet the minuscule standard of "probable cause"—my attention is captured by rumblings that are coming from the defense table. Anderson and his lawyers are huddled, and seem to be in the midst of a serious argument.

I can't make out their muffled words, but there seems to be a serious disagreement. I use the commotion as an excuse to glance at Marissa, who also looks concerned.

Mac and Ashley look to me to explain the confusion. I shrug my shoulders—I have no clue what is going on.

Kerri is now shaking her head in disbelief and won't even look at

Anderson. "Your Honor, may I approach?" she asks.

Shep and I follow to the bench, not sure what to think.

"Your Honor, my client would like to stop this preliminary hearing at this time," Kerri states..

Shep and I swap puzzled glances. We both know they had us on the ropes, and had a legitimate shot at pulling an upset.

"He also is wants to waive his indictment by grand jury and consent that the court information submitted by the DA's Office is to replace indictment," Kerri adds.

Now Judge Schanz is confused. "Please explain, Ms. Lawson, why you were willing to come into this hearing guns blazing, but now want to pull the plug?"

"My client is adamant that if he doesn't prove his innocence in a court of law, he will be branded unfairly for the rest of his life."

I'm always skeptical of Kerri, so I search my mind for an ulterior motive.

"I take it you don't have a problem with this, Mr. Lawson," Judge Schanz addresses me.

"No…um…no," I stutter.

We return to our tables and Judge Schanz asks for the court to rise.

"Mr. Anderson, are you aware of the request to drop the remainder of this hearing and waive right to a grand jury indictment? In doing so, you will move to having your fate decided by a jury trial?"

"Yes I do, Your Honor. I believe it is the only way to regain my reputation. Living without that isn't much different than being in prison."

"You have been in prison for ten days, you might feel a lot differently after ten years."

"I plan to win my trial. I have a great life and career. But above all, I have a wife that I love with all my soul, and we plan to start a family as soon as I'm acquitted. I have great confidence that the truth will prevail and that I will be vindicated."

Judge Schanz doesn't look overly impressed by the self-serving speech.

But the general population will be. I can't believe we just gave Anderson a soapbox to declare his innocence. Now we're the heartless bastards who are preventing him from starting a family.

The judge reluctantly agrees to the waiver. To make it official, Anderson signs a written waiver in open court with his attorney present. When the paperwork is complete, the case is bound for the part of Judge Antonio Figliomini. The courtroom is deathly silent, except for the banging of the gavel that adjourns the proceedings.

Drew Anderson is taken away. As he's removed from the courtroom, he shares a glance with Marissa that angers me once more. The man had everything any of us could dream of wanting, but he had to have more.

Shep and I leave the courtroom in the same whirlwind we entered. A police officer clears our way past the waiting press. "No comment, no comment," we reply to their questions, still dazed from what just happened.

"They're up to something," I whisper to Shep.

"What they're up to is kicking our ass," she replies.

"Look at the bright side. We're going to trial without even having to go before the grand jury. We're going to court and we're going to win."

"Jack, can you please stop with the happy-happy nonsense," Shep gripes, but keeps her smile for the cameras. We've learned the hard way to become more media friendly.

"Hey, OJ Simpson was once a Heisman Trophy winner with a pristine public image," I say, trying to lift her spirits.

"One minor detail, Jack."

"Which is?"

"OJ got off."

Chapter 49

The Honorable Judge Antonio Figliomini reads the complaint to a resolute Drew Anderson. It is Monday, August 7, and we are in Judge Figliomini's courtroom for the latest arraignment of Drew Anderson.

When Figliomini finishes reading in his deep voice, he raises his head and stares at me. "Do the people accept the just read indictment as being factual, as you know it?"

I feel like the defendant. The so-called experts have been knocking each other over to get in line to bash me. We achieved our objective of getting to a trial, but nobody on our side would even hint that it was a victory. Gifford Brown referred to it as, "The operation was a success, but the patient died."

If the media had raised an eyebrow at my decisions so far, then what I'm about to say next will pluck the eyebrows completely off their faces. Still standing, and facing Figliomini, I utter, "Yes, Your Honor—and the people are seeking the death penalty."

The murmuring of the crowd turns to a buzz. Figliomini bangs his gavel and shouts, "Order!"

It's first-year-law-student-101 not to go after the death penalty in this case. Drew Anderson has more mitigating factors than we have evidence. Also, it can sometimes make the defendant look like the victim, while the prosecutors come off as cold and bloodthirsty. But I want to make a statement of how serious we feel about his guilt. We've learned that public perception is more important to the trial of Max Q than traditional items like evidence and motive.

Shep fought against my choice, but since she watched that video with Anderson's hands around Laney Bang's neck, she has acquired an open mind toward my out-of-the-box tactics.

Anderson enters his plea with the still-stunned gallery hanging on his every word. "I am innocent of all charges against me—I plead not guilty." His voice is confident.

Following Figliomini's order, everybody is seated. The whole courtroom is fixated on Anderson.

I make eye contact with Marissa, who is sitting behind her man. She looks striking, but the scathing look she greets me with is not so beautiful. I turn away—this isn't about the law anymore and my confidence wanes.

Figliomini begins to go over the other topics that will be covered at the arraignment. This isn't news to us, as we hashed it out this past Saturday in a lawyers-only meeting with the judge.

I awoke that morning to "Saturday (Night) is Alright for Fighting" by Elton John, blaring from my alarm clock, which was apropos. I dressed in khaki casual, but Shep came dressed to the nines, including a hat that was worthy of a royal wedding. She informed me that she had a date for later that day, and she and her new beau were going to Saratoga to watch the races. I had no right to be jealous, but man isn't always the most rational of creatures.

Figliomini was dressed for a trip to the Canadian border for a weekend of salmon fishing. Different from his courtroom persona, but still an intimidating presence. His thick jet-black hair is normally gelled back, but was pushed forward, covering his prominent widow's peak. He likes to think of himself as the "everyday man" who owns a farm and runs around town in his pickup truck. From an ideological standpoint, he is the polar opposite of Schanz, which in theory should benefit us. But a jury of his peers would be made up of the Andersons and Lansdales of the world, and there has been talk if Max Q ever made it to the White House that Figliomini might be a potential choice for the US Supreme Court. Where he stands could play a big role in the outcome.

With the plea still hanging over the courtroom, Figliomini instructs the bailiff to deliver copies of a gag order to Shep and me, along with the defense. To summarize, neither side will discuss the case outside the courtroom. He also reprimands the media for their performance so far, and warns against using his courtroom as a source of sensationalism. He then denies all motions made by the aforementioned media for cameras in the courtroom, along with the ones requesting to unseal documents of upcoming motion hearings.

Next up is to pick a trial date. Figliomini begins, "I've reviewed the defense's motion to fast-track this trial…

Kerri interrupts. She stands and makes a passionate plea for a speedy trial. She's grandstanding. She knows that a capital case usually goes to trial in minimum a year, and eight months is a minor miracle. She should know, it's usually because of all the endless paperwork and motions filed by high-powered defense attorneys like herself, and so far this case is no different.

Figliomini's face turns sour. "Sit down, Ms. Lawson—I have reviewed your reasoning and most of it I find to be self-serving rubbish…"

I can't hold back my smile.

Kerri persists. "My client is in danger in prison—someone has set him up for this crime and he is not safe. His trial must be…

Figliomini again cuts her off, "Sit down, Ms. Lawson!"

I have never seen my sister so desperate. I'm not sure what to make of it. *He's in danger?* I think Laney Bang was the one who was in danger … from her client.

The judge puts his reading glasses back on and starts again, "Having reviewed the facts, taking into the account the special circumstances and nature of this case, the trial date is set for Tuesday, September 5. Jury selection will begin that day."

If I were standing I would have fallen over. Shep looks at me in fright. It will take us months to interview possible witnesses and gather further evidence. The murder weapon would be a good start. *One month?*

I begin to argue, but Figliomini cuts me off.

"Mr. Lawson, for years prosecutors have screamed about defense attorneys using stall tactics. I will not pass up such a miraculous opportunity—a defense attorney eagerly requesting to go to trial. I have reviewed the facts of the case, and I see no undue harm being caused to either side by my decision."

I've been one of the chief complainers about the delay tactics of defense attorneys, especially the ones with unlimited budgets like LB&G.

"September 5—we'll be here," I proclaim, as if I have a choice.

Figliomini swiftly changes gears, moving to the bail hearing. The judge states that he has read the transcripts from the initial appearance and asks if either side has anything new to add.

Shep stands and restates our position, citing Roman Polanski and other high-profile celebrities who have fled the country instead of facing charges.

Not to be outdone, Kerri goes on a tangent that basically describes Anderson as the most perfect being to grace the earth, with the exception of those who have a religion created in their honor.

Figliomini takes a minute to absorb each side's argument, then barks, "Bail granted—it will be set at five million dollars."

Shep looks annoyed, but I think this might turn out to be a positive development for us.

In closing, Figliomini states, "I expect all motions from both sides by this Friday, the eleventh, and our next pretrial court date will be Wednesday, August 15." He bangs his gavel to conclude the proceedings.

Anderson triumphantly steps out onto the front steps of the courthouse like a conquering hero, a radiant Marissa by his side. The press is there to meet him.

He smiles confidently, politely dodges all questions by citing the judge's gag order, but does add that he has a deep belief in the court system and fully expects to be exonerated.

Shep and I watch the scene from a distance.

"We're screwed," she says dejectedly.

"We'll be fine—a short trial date favors us. They have the unlimited funds to drown us in motions and paperwork, and wear us down over the long haul. The defense just willingly gave up their most lethal weapon."

I can tell that Shep isn't buying. I really didn't even convince myself. We continue watching the jubilation surrounding Max Q. He descends the court steps, hand-in-hand with Marissa, while Kerri and Hal Metzer tag along.

"What now, boss?" Shep asks.

"Meet me at the office—we have no time to waste. We can't lose the motion on the admissibility of the video or we're finished."

Chapter 50

Over the course of the next week, Shep and I work twenty-hour days locked in our offices. Empty Chinese containers and pizza boxes become our new decorative motif. Shep is tireless, but I am annoyed by her obsession with detail, which causes her to constantly miss the bigger picture.

There is only one motion that we must win. Without the sex video to connect Anderson to Laney Bang's blackmail scheme, we have no case. The other motions, such as the admissibility of the police tape, are important, but secondary. I keep trying to get Shep to understand this.

She appears even more stressed than normal. At one point, noticing that her confidence is waning, I attempt to give her a boost. "You have the makings of a great lawyer. When we get in the courtroom trust your instincts and you'll be fine."

"Even though I make too many lists?"

"There is nothing wrong with being prepared, but remember—study too long and you study wrong … you know, paralysis by analysis."

"You're a poet and you don't know it," she says and strangely begins giggling. It's as if the dam broke and all her pent up emotions emptied through that one laugh.

"I've been reading poetry lately," I say.

This seems to really impress Shep, who declares, "I love poetry. I used to try to write it. I wrote some dandies about my parents and growing up in Rome, not to mention, my disaster of a marriage—they say a poem is best when the poet's heart bleeds onto the paper."

"I've actually been reading a dead poet named Laney Bang."

She exhales an exasperated sigh and returns to the motion she was meticulously working on. The conversation is over.

It is typical of our relationship. Begins with annoyance, then she pleasantly surprises me, but somehow we end up back at square one.

Chapter 51

All eyes are on the two naked bodies.

I glance at Drew Anderson, just as his onscreen alter-ego elicits another scream of pleasure from Laney Bang. He shows no emotion.

I tap Shep on the arm and whisper, "This is my favorite part."

"I told you if you ever said anything about Marissa again I'll kill you!"

Marissa isn't present in court today—not a coincidence, I'm sure—and I doubt she'd be impressed by her husband's passionate defense of her on film. After five long minutes, the lights are turned on. Everyone, with perhaps the exception of Max Q, is feeling inadequate.

It is August 15, and we're in court for the motion hearing—the most important one being the video we just witnessed. Even at this early stage, our case is hanging by a thread and a ruling against us will be a fatal blow. I feel like the law is on our side, but I can't shake the feeling that there are people who want this thing to go away ASAP.

The courtroom is empty, except for lawyers, judge, and defendant. The tape is not for public consumption at this stage. It's the first thing all parties have agreed on since the day of Drew Anderson's arrest.

After the general public and media are allowed to re-enter, Kerri begins her quest to rule the tape inadmissible. "The evidence offered on the tape is irrelevant, or, if marginally relevant, its probative value is substantially outweighed by its prejudicial effect, and the confusing of the issue for the jury."

I counter in English, "The prosecution contends that Mr. Anderson and Ms. Bang were having an affair, which we will prove is connected to an attempt by Ms. Bang to blackmail Mr. Anderson. The blackmail attempt is the motive behind her murder. Not only is the video proof of a relationship between the two, but it also shows the defendant threatening the life of the victim."

Kerri is impassioned. "A reasonable person would have stopped the act if they felt threatened—they were obviously role-playing. Sex by consenting adults is not a crime, and we think this video could falsely portray something more sinister going on, which will obstruct my client's right to a fair trial."

"Your Honor—if there were video of Lee Harvey Oswald in the book depository *role-playing* how he was going to kill the president, I believe it would be considered valuable evidence."

Figliomini reminds me that Oswald was never tried in a court of law, and therefore not relevant case law. He then puts the onus on Kerri to build a better case that the video should be inadmissible.

Up to the weekend, and then carried over into Monday, Kerri bores us with every psychologist who has ever done a study of the effects of television, film, and video games on society. They all agree that such a graphic video could cloud the jury's cognitive abilities, and provide an unfair advantage to the prosecution.

Two days later, we assemble in Judge Figliomini's courtroom to hear his ruling on all motions. But before he does, he lectures me about the leak of our witness list, which has caused quite a stir the past couple days. The judge knows I leaked it to Ira Montini—as do I—in defiance of his gag order. But he can't prove it, which has made him surlier than usual.

The reason the list garnered so much publicity had nothing to do with legal mumbo-jumbo like gag orders and leaks, it's because the list contained every A-list celebrity that Laney outed in her book. The media salivated at the thought of their favorite celebrities coming to town to add to the drama. The summer blockbuster of all blockbusters!

I probably should just take my medicine and keep my mouth shut, but I take the opposite path. I walk the fine line of not incriminating myself, yet defending the list. "Our witness list was created with intent to counteract the defense's 'semi-plausible OJ smorgasbord' strategy."

"Semi-plausible what?" Figliomini is losing his patience.

Shep looks horrified that I would tweak the judge with such important rulings pending, but I soldier on, "The defense is going to attempt to come up with a host of 'hey you never know' scenarios, throwing reasonable doubt against the wall until something luckily sticks, despite its lack of merit. It's what happened in the first OJ Simpson murder trial. We think those mentioned in Ms. Bang's book will be a focus of the defense's semi-plausible theories, so we felt it necessary to call them to refute such tactics."

"This is outrageous, Your Honor," Kerri bellows, as if she is above such tactics.

Figliomini is fuming. "Let me be straightforward, because I guess I haven't been able to make it clear to you two. My courtroom will not be a circus!"

Laughter ricochets throughout the room. Everyone knows this thing has passed the circus standard weeks ago. Figliomini bangs his gavel and glares at the gallery.

Without further ado, he delivers his rulings. The first one is technically a loss for the prosecution—ruling that the death penalty is excessive. It's expected and what I had hoped for. It was just posturing on my part. We will settle for life in prison.

The next ruling is that any mention of the Tony Rivotti investigation is irrelevant to the case and therefore inadmissible. He does leave it open to relevant new information that might be brought forward, but since I don't expect anyone to find Rivotti, it's a moot point.

The police tape is up next. While not as crucial to our case as the "sex tape," its admissibility is still important. It is not illegal to tape someone in

New York without his or her consent. But you can't do it when a suspect is in custody, unless you inform them that they are in custody and outline their Miranda Rights. It will come down to how narrow Figliomini's definition of custody is.

After Roger Beneke's performance, I am not feeling confident. But Figliomini rules that Anderson was not in custody during the initial meeting and the police reacted correctly. The tape is admissible.

A nice win, but our whole case is hanging on the video.

"I believe the majority of the video lacks relevance," the judge starts and I feel the air being sucked out of the courtroom. He also states that he has "serious questions" about how we received the tape, which we claimed had been anonymously delivered to our office. We didn't lie, but left out the part about George Herman, wild goose chases, and knives to necks.

"But the first five minutes that includes the alleged threats toward the victim, will be ruled admissible, and can be interpreted by a jury. This court is adjourned and will resume on September 5 for jury selection."

Gavel pound.

Shep and I look at each other and are almost too flabbergasted to be happy.

We exit the court, and any excitement we might have felt is tempered when we witness Drew Anderson once again holding court with an adoring media—smiles, laughing, and slapping backs. In the background a group of fans chant his name.

We know that today's victory was minor and it will take a miracle to find twelve people to agree to convict him.

Chapter 52

It's Tuesday September 5—the first day of the latest installment of the Trial of the Century.

I am working meticulously on my tie. *They can't start without me—can they?* But if you believe the reviews, it can be deduced that our case might actually have a much better shot without me.

Despite my nightly flogging over the airwaves and daily hate mail, my smile has returned. I attribute this to being able to block out the hoopla of the trial and concentrate on the law—my comfort zone.

The last few weeks, my office transformed into a fortress. Only occasionally did we venture out in my Adirondack guide boat on Otsego Lake, getting some much needed fresh air and change of scenery. Somewhere in the rummage of empty Chinese cartons and law books, our strategy developed. It was based on three simple parts: mortalize Max Q, give a few whacks of Lizzie Borden, and then make sense of the whole bloody affair.

The first is perhaps the most important. Right now, he is seen as superhuman. The Max Q brand name is synonymous with perfection. We have to change this perception. If we can't, then we won't be able to get him convicted for jaywalking, forget murder. The video will be our asset here—that's why its admissibility was imperative.

The second part of our case is to prove that he was, reasonably, the only person who could have committed the murder. Kerri and the defense will try to bring up every half-cocked possibility of anyone with even the slightest motive who was within a three-state radius, as she foreshadowed with her accusations toward Beneke. The only way to combat this is to show that Drew Anderson was the only person between 6:05 and 7:30 that fateful morning, who could have done the deed. Simple Lizzie Borden.

The final part of our case will be to make sense of the whole thing. Even if we're successful with the first two parts, a jury is still going to find it too surreal to pull the trigger on a guilty verdict. They will convince themselves that there must be some other explanation, even if they have to suspend their belief in reality to do so.

This is where the case against Lizzie Borden went wrong. Despite Lizzie's contradictory statements and the overwhelming evidence pointing in her direction, it just didn't make sense that this refined girl would commit such an act of savagery. It actually helped her that the murders were so violent—in 1892 it made sense that a woman would use poison to commit murder, but a brutish attack with an ax was unfathomable. In our case, we must show why these two wealthy, attractive people who had the world in the palms of their hands, would choose the nuclear option. Why would Laney go to such lengths to blackmail Drew? And what would make him respond with murder? It makes no sense, and remains a huge obstacle to a conviction.

I figure it isn't in my best interest to fight the first day of the Trial of the Century on an empty stomach. Mac and Ashley are long gone for the day, but sitting in all her glory at the breakfast table is Amber Jazz. Not an article of clothing in sight.

I decide to eat my cereal at the counter, which I deem safer. We have had to hide her out, and preparing her for testimony has become a full-time job for Shep. Amber wants no part of testifying, and is craving a daily fix, making her more of a flight risk than Max Q ever was. Keeping her clean has been no picnic either. We keep a female security guard with her during the day because we know a male wouldn't have a shot. We sometimes wonder about the woman, but we're just playing the odds.

"Why don't you come sit down—I don't bite," she says, as if she's seducing the plumber in one of her movies. I slurp down my corn flakes, not taking the bait. *I'll bet she does bite.*

I say my goodbyes from a safe distance, wondering how much longer we can keep her on the straight and narrow. Jury selection itself could take months.

"Are you sure, big boy?" she asks suggestively. She then stands and begins dancing like she is auditioning for the lunch-shift at Feel of Dreamz—even the strip clubs in Cooperstown have a baseball connection.

"I have to go get some justice for your friend," I say, trying not to look directly at her.

The mention of Laney jets Amber's persona from the tantalizing provocateur to a teary-eyed, somber child. Just another demon to add to her long list. "Your loss," she says and wipes a tear, before announcing to nobody in particular, "I need a drink *soooo* bad!"

This is our star witness.

A mob scene of television trucks and reporters are lined up six-deep. Even blanketed by security, the instability of the situation has me worried for my safety. I look at Shep and think of the night we were attacked by Lansdale's goon. She puts on her "tough guy" face, but I feel her trepidation.

The media is ready to pounce, and I can't blame them. In the case of the State of New York versus Drew Anderson they have hit the jackpot. American hero accused of killing scandalous sex-siren. Brother and sister rival attorneys. Murder, mystery, sex, and romance—it has it all.

Intriguing—yes. A new phenomenon—no. The first Trial of the Century occurred back in 1908 with the case of Harry Thaw, who murdered New York architect Stanford White in plain view at Madison Square Garden. As is often the case, it was over a woman. The case was filled with a frenzied press and merciless character assassination. White, the victim, was characterized as a serial philanderer and a pervert.

Another so-called Trial of the Century took place in 1921. Leopold and Loeb. The *Chicago Tribune* wrote concerning the case, "To safeguard American justice there needs to be a drastic restriction of pretrial publicity." The paper went on to call the trial, "an orgy of sensationalism" and "journalistic lynch law."

As Shep and I walk briskly toward the safe-haven of the courthouse, I'm reminded of the old adage that says the more things change, the more things stay the same. And I wonder what that writer would think if he were alive to see this spectacle.

A long caravan, looking like a cross between a presidential motorcade and a funeral procession, arrives in front of the courthouse. Out of the limo emerges Kerri, side-by-side with Drew Anderson. He is wearing a confident smile and a spiffy beige suit.

I grab Shep's arm and stop her progress. "Let them go first. It's like a boxing match, the champion always enters the arena last."

"And we're the champ?" Shep asks.

I look at her with disappointment.

"We're the champ!" she exclaims, this time with confidence.

I smile. "That's more like it, partner."

Chapter 53

I watch Max Q enter the courthouse. He looks at ease with the media, who are buzzing around him like gnats on a summer night. I've never liked bugs and have the urge to swat them away.

We take our usual places in the St. Anne's courtroom. Shep and I sit at the prosecution table, facing the judge's bench. To our left, Kerri is both scribbling furiously on a legal pad and biting her nails. A sign of nervousness that I remember from our childhood. She doesn't show weakness often, so I take note whenever she does.

I'm a little confused by her opening day jitters, as she hasn't met a camera she didn't like since this thing started. But today she looks like she has the weight of the world on her shoulders.

Drew Anderson doesn't appear to have any such anxiety. He turns to look at Marissa. She is dressed conservatively today with her dark curls neatly tied up. She mouths, "I love you" to her husband and he lights up.

James Lansdale comforts Marissa like a grandfather. He then gives Drew a supportive handshake.

I look for our support, but find none. Ashley and Mac were unable to make it. Gifford Brown gave me his support via telephone last night—he isn't going to be seen near the courtroom. But they won't be missing much. Everybody has been drooling over this September 5 trial date, but jury selection is about as exciting as watching grass grow. There's a reason they don't show voir dire examination on *Law & Order*.

But there are two people in the courtroom who find jury selection downright exhilarating. The attractive forty-something couple seated directly behind the defense table. Craig and Carla Robertson. The Robertsons are an industry famous husband and wife jury consultant team. Their job is to use their "intuitive gifts" to pick a sympathetic jury.

I think jury consultants are grossly overrated. Craig and Carla's fee is over a thousand dollars an hour plus travel expenses, so only the wealthy can afford their services. The system has always favored the wealthy, anyway. I will be impressed when Craig and Carla pick a jury that will get off the poor, minority kid with a rap sheet. Shep pushed for us to hire our own jury consultants, but I vetoed it.

Judge Figliomini enters in his black robe. He takes his perch on the raised bench and reveals a thick, bound document. "I have reviewed the defense's questionnaire for the jury. Does the prosecution have issue with the questionnaire?"

"Yes—it's too long," I respond. It is full of basic questions such as, how do you feel about the pornography industry? But also delves into psychological issues such as, what was your reaction when your first pet died? It is the creation of Craig and Carla, earning their thousand an hour.

Figliomini can't help a brief grin, knowing I'm right. "Any objections to the content of the questions, Mr. Lawson?"

"Not the ones I read, but honestly I could only hang in there for the first hundred pages. I was having flashbacks to reading *War and Peace* in high school."

"I'll take your poor attempt at humor as having no objections," Figliomini notes. I receive dirty looks from Craig and Carla for not properly honoring their masterpiece. It takes days for the prospective jurors to complete the tedious questionnaire, before we finally move to the actual selection of jurors.

Kerri is trying to eliminate prospective jurors who don't fit the profile designed by Craig and Carla, including those with loud and proud political views opposite from those of the man once thought a shoo-in to be the next governor. She also removes a couple of men who were arrested at a Vietnam protest during their youth. My guess is that Team Anderson believes they might be prejudiced against a man who served in the military.

I take a different strategy. I don't quibble with any of the jurors selected. In fact, I appear disinterested in the whole process.

As the fifth of twelve is selected, Shep leans to my ear and whispers. "What the hell is going on?"

"Don't worry, I know what I'm doing."

"The last juror listed his heroes as Drew Anderson and some conservative talk-show host. We have seven left, maybe it would be in our best interest to get someone on the jury who's not enrolled in the Drew Anderson fan club."

"I'm pulling a Joe Fallon."

Shep looks confused. "The guy from *Saturday Night Live?*"

"No, that's Jimmy, a comedian. This is Joseph, a legendary lawyer from the early 1900s. He believed in always taking the first jurors offered. When he accepted a jury right off, Fallon believed they were psychologically behind him. Because of this, when he objected during the trial, the jury felt he must have sound reasoning for doing so. Whatever jury we pick will already believe in Anderson's innocence from the outset. But when we begin to change their minds, they have to believe in us, or at least believe our reasoning is sound."

Shep gives me an "are you nuts!" look.

The defense agrees on the next potential juror. Shep reads back her answer on the questionnaire. "She answered that Laney was a sinner and her death was deserved."

I weigh what Shep tells me. Figliomini grows equally frustrated with my lack of response. "Mr. Lawson?"

"The prosecution has no problem with this juror," I say.

An angry look permeates the judge's face. "My chambers—right now!"

We enter the stately office behind the courtroom. Figliomini is steamed.

"Mr. Lawson, can you tell me what the hell you're trying to pull in there?"

"Pick a jury, I believe. Was I supposed to be doing something else?"

"In my business you hear a lot of rumors, and often where there's smoke there's fire. I keep hearing that there are those in the DA's Office who want this case to go away, and are just going through the motions. Nothing you've done here today has lessened my concern that this might be the case."

"You are supposed to be judged by a trial of your peers—these people that were selected actually might go to a Drew Anderson dinner party. They certainly are his peers," I say, enjoying the climb of his blood pressure.

"You are warned, Mr. Lawson."

"He's pulling a Fallon," Shep defends me without explanation.

"He's going to be pulling a contempt of court," Figliomini fires back.

"Your Honor, I have a 98% conviction rate. When you were the DA in this county, your conviction rate hovered around 79%. I'm a better prosecutor than you ever were. I don't tell you how to be a judge because I'm not qualified. So don't tell me how to prosecute my case, because you aren't qualified."

Up until 1819, in some remote places, trial by battle was used instead of trial by jury. We seem headed down that path.

Painful silence fills the chambers. Shep looks physically ill. I expect the contempt of court threats to begin again, but Figliomini smiles.

"That is more like it, Mr. Lawson. I hope you take that attitude back into the courtroom."

Days pass, including the anniversary of the Subway Bombing, in which everybody handles me like fine china. But the day doesn't affect me more than any other. To me, it's just another day further from the tragedy. I see life as a linear journey and not a circular loop like a Monopoly board. Ironically,

Reyanne taught me that.

On Wednesday September 13 a jury is in place in record time, eight women and four men. The jury fits the acquittal demographic. I hope Craig and Carla send me a cut of their commission for my help.

Figliomini again takes center stage. He addresses the jurors, who sit in a wooden box on the far left hand side of the courtroom under a large stained-glass window. He provides them a small sense of relief by choosing not to sequester them—at least until one of Lansdale's punks decides to run them off the road—then outlines a bunch of unenforceable instructions, such as no watching television or reading newspapers.

When Figliomini finishes his drill-sergeant routine, he looks at the jurors with his death stare. I can tell they either respect or fear him. Maybe a little of both. "Capiesce?"

They all enthusiastically nod.

"Good—we will take a fifteen minute break and begin with opening statements."

Chapter 54

"I just don't see what that accomplished, Jack," Shep says as we return to the courtroom.

"Kerri just forced the jury to take a tedious test. I'm going to show them porn. Who do you think they're gonna be liking more?"

"You're disgusting."

"You say disgusting—I say they will be remembering their college days. Who didn't like getting out of an exam and then watching porn in college?"

Shep looks at me like I'm from another dimension. She obviously didn't have Mac Cirillo as her college roommate.

I start my opening statement by laying out what the prosecution intends to prove and the elements of the crime. Basically the standard opening statement. But what I'm about to do next is anything but vanilla. I inform the jury that what they're about to see won't resemble *Masterpiece Theater*, and the lights are dimmed.

Drew shows no emotion. I look to Marissa and it hurts me that I have to do this to her. She stares straight ahead with a blank expression, just as I'm sure Kerri has instructed. They knew the tape was coming, but it still must be devastating to witness it in public.

Fortunately, it doesn't take long to get to the key phrase. *"I told you if you ever said anything about Marissa again I'll kill you!"*

The tape is turned off at that point. Marissa still hasn't moved a muscle. The lights come on and I view the jury. They look shell-shocked.

I stand up and Shep whispers sincerely, "Good luck."

I smile at her, and then approach the jury to continue my opening statement.

"There is going to be a lot of debate about my motives for showing you that video. I had one reason and it's the main theme of this trial—image versus reality. It is unfathomable to me, and I'm sure to you, that Drew Anderson could have committed murder. It's too bizarre. A man we watched graciously receive the Heisman Trophy, a man who gave up a lucrative career for the call of patriotism, and the same man who spends his off hours with sick children in cancer wards without telling a soul. We are asking you to believe that man murdered someone. And if that isn't hard enough to grasp, the woman he is accused of murdering stood for everything wrong in our society. It makes no sense…

"But I'm not asking you to convict the image of Drew Anderson, because it's as impeccable as everyone says. What I am asking you to do is to convict the real Drew Anderson. The one who is a stranger to us—the one who isn't perfect. The man you just watched grab the victim around the neck and threaten to kill her."

I get nothing but blank looks from the jury. Still not even a twitch from Marissa. If she's holding it all in, I don't want to be there when she erupts.

Time for some more Fallon. I stop in mid-pace and begin to laugh to myself. The whole courtroom is looking at me as if I'm having a mental breakdown. Maybe I am. Figliomini asks curiously, "Is something funny, Mr. Lawson?"

I toss my legal pad toward the prosecution table and it lands on the floor. Shep looks horrified. This wasn't in our endless practice sessions.

"This whole thing is funny, Your Honor," I say and turn back to the jury, still laughing to myself. They look unsure—murder trials usually aren't arenas of great laughter. "I'm trying to convince twelve intelligent people beyond a reasonable doubt that an American hero with a spotless reputation killed some glorified prostitute. Then on top of it, I don't have a murder weapon, and there are numerous people who had more motive to kill Laney Bang."

Shep looks too overwhelmed to act, or else she might shout, "Objection!" at our own opening argument. I can feel Figliomini's glare and expect another call to chambers, but he remains quiet. Like most people, he probably secretly enjoys watching a train wreck.

I move on, "And on top of that, this trial has already taken place. We are giving you all these rules about evidence and God-forbid don't watch television. But it's just a big sham."

"Mr. Lawson!" Figliomini admonishes.

"Sorry, Your Honor," I halfheartedly apologize, before turning back to the jurors. "Don't get me wrong, in most cases the system works better than people give it credit for. But not in a case like this. Because the minute the arrest of Drew Anderson was reported on July 24, the trial began in the public square. And all twelve of you have already made up your mind, and I don't blame you. Everybody in this country has already made up their mind. I've made up mine. Maybe you like the way Drew Anderson smiles. Maybe you resent women like Laney Bang. Whatever your reasoning, that's fine by me. Innocent or guilty isn't a right or wrong answer—it is something that comes from your heart."

I take pride in all the strange looks staring back at me. "I fully expect you to acquit Drew Anderson, but the law tells us that we have to go on anyway. So we are going to do our job and put on a show to make it official."

I take a mental temperature of the jury. Glazed looks still dominate. I'm not sure they've even heard a word I said since we played the video. It might not be a bad thing, since I'm not exactly making a good case to convict. But I smile.

"And when I'm done putting on this little three act play, you will go back and put on your own show called deliberations, before we all convene back here in this courtroom and you acquit Mr. Anderson. Sounds easy enough, except I foresee one problem along the way…"

I pause dramatically. I feel a shift in their body language, and that they're now hanging on my words, even if it's just for entertainment purposes. *I'm on their side.*

"The problem is, after I'm done with my case, it's not going to be *that easy* for you to acquit him. You all are honest people who will be nagged by your conscience to do the right thing. And when I'm done, you will be convinced that Drew Anderson is the only person that reasonably could have murdered Laney Bang."

Shep has a relieved look on her face. She wanted to believe I was going somewhere with this, despite the overwhelming evidence that I wasn't. The same thing I am asking from this jury.

I keep the insanity rolling, "In doing so, I'm not going to try to sell you on what a great person Laney Bang was and how tragic it is that she's gone. You're too smart for such foolery. I am not going to use her given name of Darby Kelleher and make her into a victim. Or tell a sob story about how a chain reaction of bad circumstance and betrayals took her down a path that eventually led her to entering the adult film industry, and all the perils that come with that. I'm not going to trot out her weeping parents or make excuses for her poor choices in behavior.

"She would do anything to get ahead—scratch, claw, sell her body—

whatever it took. What you witnessed on that video was a snapshot of an affair that was crafted deviously by Laney Bang to blackmail Drew Anderson. Witnesses will come before this court and testify to this, and will leave little doubt. If you feel Drew Anderson was justified to defend himself against this blackmail attempt by carrying out a premeditated plan to savagely kill her, then I support your decision to acquit him. But if you choose to follow the laws of the state of New York, you will agree to convict Drew Anderson of the murder of Laney Bang in the first degree…it will be your decision.

"The defense is going to give you a case of smoke and mirrors. They are going to tell you about other people in that house that night. James Lansdale, a man with a website dedicated to the downfall of Laney Bang and others like her. Amber Jazz, a woman who would do anything to replace Laney Bang as the industry's number one star. Ryan Maxon, Mr. Anderson's jealous assistant who had built up years of frustration playing second fiddle. And if that doesn't work, they'll move on to police officers with an ax to grind, celebrities looking for revenge after being exposed in her tell-all book, and high-ranking officials in the adult film industry whom she cost millions by breaking her contract.

"But when the smoke clears, Laney Bang will still be dead and Drew Anderson will be the only one who could have done it. Not the image of Drew Anderson, but the one based in reality who you just watched with your own eyes put his hands around the victim's neck and warn her … I'll kill you!"

As I walk back to the prosecution table, Shep plays the audio of Laney's 911 call. *My name is Laney Bang. I am at Drew Anderson's home in Cooperstown. Help…No…Drew…help.*

Chapter 55

As Kerri rises for her opening argument, I make eye contact with Marissa. She gives me a look to indicate that we're going to go down hard.

Kerri forces an uncomfortable smile at the jury and then begins, "I found it interesting that the prosecution showed you a film. Because most great films I've seen are based on fiction. And since the prosecution has decided to play games—I am going to follow their lead and play a game with you. The game we're going to play is called Fact or Fiction. I will throw out an element of this trial and then determine if it's fact or fiction. So let's begin: Fact or fiction—Drew had a long affair with Laney Bang?"

Kerri momentarily pauses. The jury looks confused, wondering if they should answer the rhetorical question.

"That is fiction. Drew made a one-time mistake. Laney Bang was a professional seductress whom he fell victim to. My client regrets what occurred. But that is a situation, as I'm sure you can understand, between him and his wife. They are working it out together, although it has been hard with such outrageous charges hanging over him. My client has a thirty-plus year track record of non-violence. Hopefully you give more credence to a life's work than one small, out-of-context snapshot shown to you by the prosecution for the sole purpose of defaming him."

Drew looks back at his wife and his love for her strikes me as being real. It makes the affair with Laney even more illogical.

"Fact or fiction—the prosecution will bring a witness to testify about a longstanding affair between Drew and the deceased? That is a fact. But what they won't tell you is that the witness is a drug abusing adult-film actress who has a history of not telling the truth. She also sought the removal of Laney Bang to secure fame. Unfortunately, she will get the attention she seeks at this trial."

Kerri continues to bounce around barking out "Fact or Fictions" like a weird game-show host.

"Fact or Fiction—the prosecution will have further evidence of blackmail besides the witness I just described? That is fiction. There will be no evidence beyond hearsay and innuendo."

Her opening is very argumentative, usually not allowed, but after my theatrics, the judge is allowing her a lot of latitude.

"Fact or fiction—Drew is caught on tape not being completely honest with the initial police investigation? That is a fact. But before you condemn him for this, please ask yourself one question. If you returned from a peaceful morning jog to find a dead body in your house and were confronted by a police officer—what would you do? I think panic is the normal response, and certainly not an admission of guilt as the prosecution will lead you to believe."

She looks at me for effect, then turns dramatically back to the jury. "And the most important question of all. Whether Drew was present on the estate at the time of the murder? This is fiction, and we will bring witnesses to state truthfully that they saw Drew performing his normal morning run at the time of the murder. And unlike the witnesses the prosecution will bring before you, they will be law abiding citizens from this community who have no agenda to push."

Kerri gives her most serious look. "My client is not perfect. He didn't create the image that he was—we did. Don't convict him based on the fact he wasn't able to remain on the lofty pedestal that we ourselves put him on. He is not a murderer, and nothing you will hear in this courtroom will make you believe he is. There was no blackmail, and therefore no motive, no murder weapon, no witnesses, no blood or DNA evidence. Just a regrettable decision by my client and a tragic death of a woman, with no evidence linking the two."

I watch Kerri closely. She really appears to be coming from the heart, which is a newsflash in itself—I didn't know she had one.

When she completes her opening argument, she takes her seat at the defense table and places a supportive hand on Anderson's shoulder. He nods his head in appreciation of the support. If they are faking it, then they are good actors. Gifford Brown told me once that the key to winning over juries is to be sincere, but then added, "And once you're able to fake sincerity, Lawson, you'll win every case."

Figliomini is less sentimental. "Is the prosecution ready to call their first witness?"

Chapter 56

Those craving glamour, sex, or mystery from the first witness will be disappointed. Gretchen Hewitt is the antithesis of those traits, and that is one of the main reasons she is our lead off witness.

Her purpose is to lay out the scene. Time of death, how Laney was killed, and so on. A bonus is that she is professional and credible. Normally I would lead off with the police, but for obvious reasons, I don't want Beneke and Opp to be our opening act.

Gretchen approaches the stand in cargo pants and a sweater-vest filled with cat hair. Most people, knowing their image would be broadcast worldwide, would have glammed-up. But not Gretchen, which is why she is the ideal first witness.

Her testimony is scientific and some would say boring. I would counter that it's a refreshing diversion from the tabloid sensationalism that's been dominating this case. We hit on two important points. The first is that her analysis shows a match between Laney's wounds and a knife owned by Drew Anderson. The other is that the type of wounds match a killing tactic taught by the Special Forces unit that Anderson was a member of. Score one for Shep's attention to detail during our research.

I set up a board that displays a diagram of the tactic, detailing how the knife would enter the victim. Gretchen testifies that the diagrams match the type of wounds suffered by the victim.

Kerri comes back swinging in her cross. She gets Gretchen to admit numerous other instruments could just as likely be the murder weapon. She also picks apart our knowledge of military tactics and provides the court with several other places where such tactics are taught.

When Kerri wraps up her questioning of the witness, the first real day of the trial ends. We are still far behind on the scoreboard of public opinion. The next morning the *New York Globe* runs the headline *Prosecution: We Expect an Acquittal*, twisting the words from my opening argument.

"The people call James Lansdale," I begin day two.

He walks to the stand, slightly hunched, but still fairly rugged and athletic looking for seventy-five.

I glance at Shep. It burns me, and further inspires me to nail this guy to the floor. Problem is, I need to make it clear that he couldn't have done it, since only his friend Max Q could have. So for the most part, I have to play nice.

Lansdale stares at me, his leathery face dripping arrogance. In some regards he is a terrible witness for us, in that he is loyal to Anderson, and will lend credibility to his defense. But he can help us in two areas—mortalization and Lizzie Borden.

"Good morning, Mr. Lansdale," I greet him.

"I guess that's in the eye of the beholder, counselor," he snarls back at me. He is breathing fire before I even ask a question. But I am confident. The courtroom is my turf.

"Mr. Lansdale, please explain your relationship with the defendant."

"Drew Anderson is a business partner and a confidante. He is someone I look up to and aspire to be more like. Most of all, he has been a loyal friend. I am blessed and honored to know him."

I take a brief glance at the jury and I can tell they are eating up every word, spoken with an easy-on-the-ears New Zealander accent.

"So your relationship with the defendant goes beyond just business?"

"Yes—Drew introduced me to the beautiful Otsego Lake. I dock my yacht there in the summer and I will often host Drew and his wife Marissa."

"What was your reaction when this friend of yours, whom you aspire to be like, became involved in an affair with a woman that your website had listed as its number one target?"

"It wasn't an affair."

"Then what would you call the relationship between the defendant and the victim?"

"Drew made a mistake. He is human—not God."

"Yes, Drew Anderson is far from perfect," I editorialize. Kerri objects, but I have made my point. Max Q is mortal.

I move on to Lansdale's organization. It's a tricky subject, mainly because I am trying to avoid areas that might make him appear to be a zealot—for instance, his desire to shake the hand of whoever killed her.

"Tell me about the organization you founded called Smut Cleanser."

Kerri objects on grounds of relevance, but is immediately overruled. Lansdale looks annoyed by her objection. I think he really wants to talk about his organization.

"Smut Cleanser is a non-profit organization dedicated to improving moral values, focusing on obscenity and pornography, and promoting clean-living lifestyles."

"And Laney Bang was an example of this smut?"

"A prime example."

"Does Smut Cleanser promote violence as a tactic to improve these moral values?"

"Objection."

"Overruled."

"Absolutely not!" Lansdale barks. "We do our work peacefully—organize boycotts and such. Any accusations to the contrary would be slanderous."

"But Smut Cleanser sponsors a website in which the deceased was listed as 'Most Wanted.' That doesn't seem like a peaceful term to me."

Lansdale takes a deep breath and blows it out to display his frustration.

"It's tongue in cheek. Nowhere on the website is violence condoned. In fact, quite the opposite."

Next up is the meeting the night prior to the murder. My interest begins when the party starts to break up. "At eleven o'clock, Ryan Maxon and Amber Jazz leave the meeting. So at this point, the only people present besides yourself, are Laney, Drew, and of course, the extensive staff?"

"No, the staff had been sent home."

"Drew Anderson sent them home?" I ask as if I'm bowled over by such a revelation.

Lansdale shakes his head at my theatrics. "The meeting was of a sensitive nature and we did not want the details to be leaked to the press. It wasn't the norm, but this wasn't your typical meeting. It was the prudent thing to do."

A glance at the jury tells me they think it's a logical explanation.

"So with the staff sent home, it's just the three of you remaining—until you leave by helicopter just after one o'clock."

"I had an early meeting the next morning and I was up way past the time a seventy-five year old man should be up," he says with a charismatic chuckle, showing a self-effacing sense of humor that is always popular with juries.

"And your arrival at 3:30 a.m. at the Four Seasons Hotel was witnessed by numerous employees, as well as being captured on security video," I add.

I have made my point—James Lansdale could not have committed this crime. Unlike Drew Anderson and Lizzie Borden, he has an irrefutable alibi.

"So when you left, Laney Bang and Drew Anderson were the only people remaining at Anderson Estate?"

"That is correct."

"No further questions, Your Honor."

Chapter 57

We reconvene on Monday, September 20. I made the decision to spend our weekend away from the case, feeling we were on the verge of burning out.

But any hope of some rest was dissolved when I ended up being stuck as Amber Jazz's designated babysitter. Mac had to work the weekend in preparation for his big Halloween event for the Hall of Fame. Ashley's September weekends have been consumed with flying-lessons. Shep went to Vermont with her new man.

That left Amber and me, along with a rent-a-cop that the powers that be in Otsego County believed would somehow protect us from a highly skilled assassin. Amber and I didn't exactly have much in common, but we eventually found a common bond in that we both had crappy parents. I vexed that mine were too busy to show up for the school play that I played the lead. Amber was still perturbed her parents didn't show up to the porn-version of the Oscars, where she won "Best Actress in a Group Scene." She was dead serious.

I was once again struck how her personality transformed in regards to sexuality. When she took it out of the equation, she was a mess. Crying, craving a drink or fix, and playing the victim. But the moment she transformed into Amber the sex siren, she oozed brash confidence.

Shep and I walk into the courtroom on Monday morning, heavily guarded by our security. "How was your weekend?" I ask.

"Good—real good," she gushes. "Vermont is so beautiful this time of year."

"Are you sure you should be out gallivanting during the trial? You know how the media scrutiny can be."

"Gallivanting? C'mon, Jack, it was your idea to get away for the weekend."

I nod. I hate when she's right.

"Speaking of which, how'd it go with the princess of porn?"

"Sex was great, but surprisingly the conversation lagged."

"You're disgusting. But I believe you actually have too much character to be with someone like that."

"Someone *like that* happened to win the Adult Film Oscar for Best Actress in a Group Scene," I say with a grin.

Shep laughs. "I stand corrected—she is both lovely and *talented*."

I get back to the case at hand. "We've made great progress. We have Maxon and Amber this week. Let's keep the momentum going."

"Momentum?" We have a jury stacked against us, no physical evidence, and a shaky motive that we still can't connect."

"The jury isn't stacked against us—they're against what they deem to be immoral behavior. The video identifies Drew Anderson as part of the problem, not the solution."

"If you say so, Jack."

As we walk into the courtroom a rare supporter greets us. He is a roundish teenager who is wearing a T-shirt saluting the animated, educational TV shorts *Schoolhouse Rock!*, baggy jeans, and a dated pair of Adidas sneakers.

"Jaaack," Andy Kass greets me with his usual stupid grin.

"What the hell are you doing here?" Shep barks back. She's not a fan.

"I thought you guys could use some support. I always have a soft spot for the underdog."

He turns to me. "For all your self-gloss about what a great lawyer you are, Jack, I sure haven't seen it yet. Lansdale practically took you over his knee and spanked your bottom on Friday. But I still support you, Jack. You'll come through."

"Andy, you do know I am prosecuting you, right? I'm not a friend."

"I don't come as a friend, Jack. I'm here as a supporter. I'm impressed that you're standing up for this outcast woman against the well-oiled machine of tyranny."

"By prosecuting you, I mean putting you in jail for a long time," I say, still baffled by his presence. Not to mention breaking his bail agreement and taking the risk of being sent back to jail.

"Thanks for the law lesson, Jack. I hear that my case is going to be given off to Will Flint because the Max Q case may drag on too long. I hope that's just a bad rumor. If I'm going to go down, I want to go down by the best."

This kid isn't hooked up right. "Well Andy, this is, um…"

"A major conflict of interest," Shep finishes my sentence. She grabs my arm to move on.

He chuckles. "Still a barrel of laughs aren't you, Jessica?"

With Shep's urging, we head toward the courtroom. Andy salutes me like I'm his commanding officer.

"Can't we get his bail revoked?" Shep asks.

"I agree that he's breaking his bail agreement, but he's not a flight risk, or a danger to anyone. And besides, he might be our only supporter."

Shep views the courtroom, realizing that I'm right about the lack of support. "You seem to have changed your view on him?"

"Sometimes when people grow on you, you see them in a different light."

She looks away, while nervously fiddling with the latch on her briefcase. It's pretty obvious that my statement expands beyond Andy.

We start today's proceedings with Cooperstown's finest. I've tried to keep them off the stand as long as possible, but I can't avoid them all together. Hopefully we've been able to build up enough goodwill in their absence. But as Roger Beneke once again takes the stand, I can almost hear the sound of the final nails being driven into our coffin.

I walk Officer Beneke through the basics—the call he received and why he gave it low priority. How his alertness level changed upon arriving at Anderson Estate, which led to him entering the residence and searching for the victim.

When I get to the part about pushing past a disheveled Drew Anderson and finding a dead Laney Bang, I get ready to present the jury with the gory crime scene photos. My thinking is that I can shock them into overlooking the numerous errors by the police.

As expected, an immediate objection from the defense results in a sidebar. Kerri argues that the shock-value of the pictures will outweigh their use, causing prejudice. Figliomini agrees and I'm overruled.

I move on to the important part that can't be objected to. I play the audiotape of a nervous Drew Anderson being questioned by Beneke. Kerri will play it off as a panic attack of a man who just found a dead body in his house, which is logical. But the tape is powerful. I look at the jury and while I don't think Max Q has been pushed off his pedestal, for the first time he's slightly rocking.

Kerri hammers Beneke again in her cross. Her main topics are: his threatening language toward Laney at the book signing, his decision to disregard the 911 call, which was either sinister or a sign of incompetence—neither is good for us—along with his hasty shift in priority once he arrived at the house that didn't seem to add up.

I redirect with one question I've held in my pocket to hopefully cushion our fall. "Officer Beneke, if you were such a threat to Ms. Bang, how come she felt comfortable enough to ask you for a ride to Anderson Estate that night?"

For once, Beneke does something to help our case—he says nothing. The only person who can answer that question is dead.

Chapter 58

After Kerri finishes beating up on the Otsego County police department, which has dragged into Tuesday, Shep and I go for a quick cheeseburger at Touch 'Em All. When we return, we call Ryan Maxon to the stand to begin the afternoon session. Another hostile witness for the prosecution.

Maxon has cleaned up from the drunken, distraught man that Shep and I interviewed back in July. He is clean-shaven today and wearing an LB&G purchased suit, along with a pair of horn-rimmed glasses. But money and a shower can only cover up so much—the dark circles under his eyes make it appear like he hasn't slept since the murder. I sense an inner turmoil, and I think the reason for his angst is that he is playing both sides.

Maxon is an important witness, but what intrigues me most about him is his relationship with Laney. I'm not sure if he was motivated by his feelings for her, or his jealousy of Drew, but I believe he was assisting Laney in her blackmail. At the same time, he was Drew's trusted confidante, who was called in a panic after Laney was murdered. That would mean Maxon knows everything about this case from both sides of the ledger.

Somehow I need to sew these angles together, all the while keeping Maxon safe from Kerri. I start with his unlikely relationship with a glitzy porn star.

I approach Maxon delicately. His body language reeks of victim and I feel if I raise my voice he might curl into the fetal position. "Mr. Maxon, you are employed by Drew Anderson, is that correct?"

"Yes it is," he says in a soft voice.

"Could you please tell the court what type of work you perform for Mr. Anderson?"

"Drew and I have known each other since college. For lack of a better word, I am his right-hand man. I assist him in managing his affairs."

"And by affairs, do you mean the one he was having with Laney Bang?" I can't help myself. It gets a few laughs from the gallery, but also an objection from Kerri and a strong warning from Figliomini.

I withdraw the question and move on, "Numerous times during this trial, we have discussed a meeting that took place at Anderson Estate on the night of July 23. Were you present at this meeting?"

"Yes I was."

"It seems unlikely to the average person that Drew Anderson would choose to conduct business with Laney Bang, and vice versa—they appeared to be rivals. Could you please explain to the court how such a meeting came about?"

"I set it up," he proudly proclaims. The first sign of life I've noticed from him.

"*You* set it up?" I ask, faking amazement. I'm tempted to question why Drew and Laney couldn't have arranged it during their lengthy time spent together in the bedroom, but I've already reached my wisecrack quota for the day with Figliomini.

"Would arranging such a high-level meeting be part of your normal job description?"

"I would normally assist, but I was the lead contact in this one."

"Why were you given such increased responsibility?"

"Because of my close relationship with Laney."

This wakes up the gallery. "Can you define close relationship?"

"I cared for her deeply. I didn't know her for long, but it seemed like I'd known her for years. She was one of those people you could tell anything to, and we instantly developed a close bond. With our different schedules, we didn't get to see each other often, but we spoke on the phone at least three times a week, sometimes into the wee hours." This is true—I have the phone records to prove it.

Normally it's like pulling teeth to get Maxon to expand beyond yes or no answers, but when it comes to Laney I can't shut him up. "What people don't understand is that Laney was not the person you saw on camera. That was a character that she played. Underneath, she was just a normal girl who wanted to feel safe and secure, just like the rest of us." He then adds, "I loved her. And I miss her every day."

The gallery buzzes. They have been waiting for soap opera moments.

But Maxon fans the flame. "You don't have to be romantically involved to love someone. I would describe our love as the type a brother and sister might have."

Kerri and I make eye contact, then break into laughter. "I wouldn't know much about that, perhaps you could enlighten me," I say. Within seconds, the whole gallery catches on and begins to laugh. I even catch Figliomini grinning.

When order is restored, I begin to work the blackmail angle. "You mentioned that you didn't know Laney long. When did you meet her?"

"I met Laney at a New Year's Eve party in Las Vegas, the year before last," Maxon says. In the middle of his statement he appears to become overwhelmed by emotion. He places his head in his hands and begins to sob.

We take a five-minute break to let Maxon get it back together. He is actually helping us more than I thought he would. He is making Laney seem human, and it doesn't hurt that it's coming from the man who supposedly is Drew Anderson's "right hand man."

When we restart his testimony, I try to insinuate that Laney attended that party in Las Vegas with the sole purpose of meeting up with Anderson, and in essence, putting her devious plan of blackmail into motion. But Kerri objects, and soon Figliomini puts me out of the speculation business.

"During any of your many phone conversations with Laney, did she mention a plan to blackmail Drew Anderson?" I ask.

"She didn't mention it, nor do I believe she had any intention to do so."

"Do you think Drew Anderson murdered your close friend … Laney Bang?"

"No."

Shep looks to be disgusted at my softball question, but I'm trying to protect Maxon from Kerri's smorgasbord, especially now that he just opened a can of worms by declaring his love for the victim.

"Since you cared deeply for Laney, maybe you became jealous when she started sleeping with your boss. You had access to the house, which gave you opportunity—maybe you killed her."

Kerri isn't dumb enough to object to this. I am doing her job.

"Of course not!" Maxon rebuffs.

I smile. "I know you didn't kill her. And I know this because you left with Amber Jazz at 11:00 p.m. for the Otesaga Hotel, and were still there at the time of Laney's 911 call. In fact, the two of you were so boisterous in your room that numerous complaints were filed."

Never a good sign when the highlight of the testimony is proving that your witness didn't commit the crime.

"Are you aware of the video I played during my opening arguments, in which the defendant and victim engaged in sex?"

"I am."

"Were you aware that Drew Anderson and Laney Bang were having an ongoing affair?"

"I don't know that they were. The video could have been a one shot deal."

"Fair enough. Then what was your reaction to your close friend being taped having sex with Drew Anderson?"

"What does that have to do with anything? It doesn't mean he killed her," Maxon states, his emotions still frayed.

"That wasn't my question—how did it make you feel?"

"Laney had sex with many men. It was her job—sex wasn't special to her. What we had was unique."

"Here's the thing about the video. I think Laney created it to blackmail your buddy Drew. You disagree. But you know who can break our tie—whoever the person was behind the camera."

Maxon shrugs, as I continue, "What I notice in the video is that Laney appears to know where the camera is, yet Drew appears unaware that he is being filmed."

Kerri objects. I offer to have the video replayed for the court to better explain my point. Figliomini informs me that the video is burned in everyone's retinas to point that it never needs to be replayed again.

"Could Laney have been the one to set up the camera? She was in the movie business and likely had picked up some knowledge about the tools of the trade along the way."

"I have no idea, I guess it's possible. But I doubt that she'd have the knowledge of the estate to be able to set up a hidden camera."

"How about Drew—could he have set it up?"

"I doubt that."

"And why is that?"

"For a couple of reasons. One, is that it would be too risky for him to make such a video—he would be putting his image in danger, and he would never risk losing Marissa."

"What's the other reason?"

"Drew is a techno-idiot. If it wasn't for me, his clocks would have been blinking 12:00 for the last ten years."

This gets a laugh from the gallery, and even a small smile from Drew.

"It sounds like you have some abilities when it comes to technology, and you also had expert knowledge of Anderson Estate, so I must ask you the question—did you make the video? Did you assist your close friend Laney in blackmailing Drew Anderson?"

"Of course not! I have been nothing but loyal to Drew, and I will continue to be when these trumped up charges are finally thrown out!"

"Let's talk about this loyalty to the defendant. He called you at 6:19, fourteen minutes after Laney Bang called 911. What was that call about?"

"He instructed me to move our travel plans back a couple hours."

"And what was his reason to do this?"

"He said he had something he needed to take care of."

"Something he needed to take care of," I repeat, letting the statement hang like a bad odor for the jury to get a good whiff of.

"It was my job to assist him, not to ask questions."

"Did you assist him in cleaning up a murder scene?"

"No! It was nothing out of the ordinary—Drew changed plans all the time."

"Oh, really. The man who this court has learned is so structured and regimented that he takes the same jogging route at the exact same time each morning, just whimsically changed his plans because something came up? Something certainly did come up. No further questions."

Kerri declines her cross-examination at this time, but will likely call

Maxon when the defense presents their case.

Maxon is shuddering like a wounded animal and glaring at me. I stare right back. He knows a lot more than he's telling us, and I want to let him know that I'm going to get to the bottom of it.

Chapter 59

I wake up to the twangy lyrics of Johnny Cash singing "Wednesday Car." It's ironic, since Shep and our security detail are already waiting outside for me in the car.

But the first order of business is to coax Amber into clothing that even Ethel Lawson would have found prudish. She wants no part of the outfit, or testifying, and getting her into the vehicle for the trip to court is going to be like conning a cat into its cage for a trip to the vet. But I pull off the miracle daily double in less than half an hour, hoping it's a good omen for her important testimony.

We arrive at the courthouse just in time to witness the ritual of Max Q's limo being greeted by adoring fans. We receive our usual razzing. It's not hard to figure who the home team is.

Before entering, Amber has to stop and nervously smoke a cigarette. She uncomfortably tugs on her outfit, not used to so much clothing. Security is heavy, and the guards seem to take extra pleasure in patting Amber down and thoroughly searching the oversized handbag she carries with her. I'm relieved they don't find any contraband in it.

Once inside the courthouse, Amber tells us in colorful language that she needs to relieve herself. We allow her to use the bathroom with a guard stationed outside.

Just as I look at my watch for the fifth time and again ask Shep, "What is taking so long?" Amber Jazz appears out of the bathroom. She no longer wears the outfit of a 1950s housewife. She is dressed in a black latex mini-dress, zipped up the front. It is choker style around her neck, but provides a Lake Michigan-size opening between neck and chest to show off her famous assets. The south end of the dress barely covers the minimum requirements, and her shoes are six-inch spiked sandals laced up to the knee. She looks like, well…Amber Jazz.

She smiles mischievously with a cigarette hanging off her painted lips. I'm struck by the transformation.

"Get back in there and put on the clothes we gave you! Do you understand what is at stake here?" Shep barks.

Amber grins. "No-can-do, honey. I ripped them up and flushed them down the toilet. Talk about a crime … those clothes."

Shep rips the lit cigarette out of Amber's mouth. I can tell she burned her hand, but she doesn't flinch.

"Let's go!" she says, angrily grabbing Amber by the arm and pulling her to the courtroom like she's her mother.

The courtroom is buzzing. By all accounts, the last week had been boring. People didn't come to see a silly little legal trial. They came to see the Greatest Show on Earth. Following Ryan Maxon's testimony, I put on numerous hotel staffers and guests from the Otesaga Hotel who were present on July 23 and 24. My goal was to once again prove Ryan Maxon had an airtight alibi, and more importantly, that Drew and Laney were the only ones on the estate at the time of the murder.

There were no fiery cross-exams from Kerri that have become the norm. She had no questions for the hotel staffers. For those in neighboring rooms who filed the noise complaints, Kerri's only question was if they actually saw Ryan Maxon and Amber Jazz in that room. The answer was no.

This process repeated over and over, and if you listened hard enough you could hear a yawn from the gallery

Next, I put on Mrs. Aoki. I wanted to prove that Drew never broke his regimented morning routine. I planned to back it up with the "dead cell phone" testimony. It would have been much more helpful testimony if the Aokis hadn't decided to sell their story to *The Inquisitor* tabloid for ten thousand dollars. Kerri hammered that point home. The jury's expression indicated that she did it quite well.

But today the room surges with excitement; the atmosphere is electric. Figliomini's arrival briefly settles the courtroom down. Shep stands and calls out the words that everyone's been waiting for, "The people call Amber Jazz."

She takes a slow, choreographed stroll to the stand, seemingly enjoying having all the eyes glued on her.

I have great confidence in Shep, who has been preparing Amber's testimony for a month. I wish I could say the same about Amber.

Shep doesn't even get to ask a question before we're at the sidebar. Kerri is objecting to Amber's choice of clothing, thinking it could sway the male jurors, and makes no secret that she believes this is an underhanded tactic orchestrated by me.

Figliomini is no fan of the clothing, or of his courtroom being used as a Vegas burlesque show. In rare acquiescence between lawyers, Shep and I agree with Kerri—we all want Amber to change clothing.

I momentarily think that everyone might be on the same page for the first time since the trial started, but no such luck. Figliomini asserts, "I've found with my teenage daughter that the more I fight her on the choice of clothing, the worse the situation becomes. If I ignore it, then it goes away. Also, I have no such confidence that Mr. Lawson or Ms. Shepherdson have any control whatsoever over their witnesses, so I think your conspiracy theory gives them too much credit. She wears whatever she has on, now let's move this along."

The Greatest Show on Earth resumes. Somebody cue the circus music.

Chapter 60

As we return to the prosecution table, I notice Mac and Ashley in the gallery. Ashley waves at me like an embarrassing mother at a Little League game.

Before Shep begins, I hand her a note. It reads: *For the first question—ask her how she got her name.* She looks strangely at me, but proceeds without questioning it.

She stands and begins what, at the very least, should be an entertaining examination. "Ms. Jazz, you have an interesting name—can you tell the court how you got it?"

Amber looks confident. "My father used to always use the phrase *and all that jazz*. When I made it big I wanted to remind that sorry excuse of a father that he couldn't ever hold me down again. I originally wanted to be called Andall That Jazz, but Tyler Maddox thought Amber Jazz would be better."

Shep looks at me and shrugs. I jot down notes as if there were some hidden meaning in the answer. I turn and smile at Mac—another theory of Macademia left in tatters. For the record, her real name is Courtney Hamilton and she grew up in Wichita, Kansas, before she got on a bus to LA on her sixteenth birthday. She was going to be famous, but I'm not sure she had this in mind when she bought that bus ticket.

Shep gets back to business. "Please describe your relationship with the victim."

"She was my mom," Amber replies. One real question and already she is off the script. *Good luck, Shep.*

Shep surprisingly goes with the flow. "As in the woman who gave birth to you?"

"She was the person who raised me, showed me how to survive in this world, picked me up when I was down and loved me when nobody else would. Laney Bang was my mom—it has nothing to do with giving birth."

On the whole, I find myself pleasantly surprised by Amber's oratory skills. After two questions, I had expected five F-bombs and an incoherent call for alcohol. But she sounds clear, concise, and yes, sober. I see a tear roll down her heavily made-up face. Add sympathetic to the witness résumé.

"Mothers and daughters often tell each other things that they wouldn't tell anyone else. Did you and your mom have these type of talks?"

"We told each other everything."

"In that case, did Laney tell you about the affair she was having with Drew Anderson?"

"Objection—speculation—leading!"

"Sustained."

"Did Laney tell you of an affair she had with Drew Anderson?" Shep reshapes the question to please the court.

"It wasn't like it was some dirty secret or something, if that's what you mean. Dirty, maybe, but not a secret."

"So it wasn't just a one time fling, as the defense contends?"

"It was an 'anytime they could get their hands on each other' thing."

This gets a rise from the gallery. I glance at Drew, and then Marissa. Both are emotionless. I can't tell if it's being well coached or they have ice in their veins.

We know Amber has a short shelf-life, so it's important to get her off the stand as swiftly as possible—connect an affair to our blackmail motive and then depart. So far so good.

Shep introduces travel itineraries into evidence. It details Laney and Drew having separate publicity engagements in the same city on the same day. On New Year's Day, he was in Phoenix to watch his alma mater, Florida State, play the Fiesta Bowl, while Laney was doing a promotional visit in Scottsdale. There are then about ten more coincidental trips between January and June.

"They also had dalliances closer to home, isn't that right?" Shep asks.

"They would usually go to Laney's secret place in the city. But they'd also hook up in hotels all over Manhattan."

"Hotels sound risky. Was Laney afraid of being spotted?"

"Laney could care less—she wasn't the one who was living a double life. He's the one who shoulda been worried."

"Yet he kept seeing her."

"He couldn't quit her—she was his drug. You can always tell when you got a guy hooked— they keep gettin' riskier and riskier."

When it comes to drugs, everyone in the courtroom would agree that Amber is an expert witness.

"Was Drew Anderson willing to take such a risk, as to have Laney at his house in Cooperstown?"

"All the time."

Shep feigns surprise. "So July 23 wasn't her first trip to Anderson Estate?"

"It was one of their favorite spots—he said his wife never liked coming to Cooperstown. Called it Sticksville. So it was safe. They spent many weekends up here last spring and summer."

I almost smile at what Amber just unknowingly did. The jury might take personally the slight on Cooperstown. I've only lived here for a short time, but it's impossible not to notice the civic pride and distaste for "city-types." Ironically, I learned this home court advantage tactic from Marissa.

Shep and Amber appear to have found a comfort zone. Although, I'm not sure how anyone wearing latex and six inch heels can find comfort on any level.

"Tell me, Amber, about the night of April 16 of this year?"

"Laney and I went to the Four Seasons hotel in the city to meet up with Drew."

"We found no record of this. Did you check in under your own names, or did you use aliases?"

"None of the above—the room belonged to a friend of Drew's, and I guess he gave him the key card or something."

"So on this occasion, you just didn't hear second hand about this affair like some of their other rendezvous. You actually witnessed it?"

Amber twinkles a sly smile. "I didn't witness it, honey—I was part of it!"

Gasps. Gavel. More gasps. Gavel.

When order is restored, Amber proudly explains the French import called the ménage à trois. "Drew loved to watch me and Laney with each other. But it wasn't about sex with him, it was about power."

"Explain these power tactics."

"He loved to degrade us and make us submissive to him. He was into all sorts of freaky stuff like spankings and tying us up. You know, bondage and stuff like that," Amber casually states like it's mainstream bedroom decorum.

I view the jury, the majority of them are cringing like they just ate a bad taco. Not sure which side that favors. But I think it's a good thing that we cut out some of the "even freakier" stuff that came up during our preparation.

"In regard to this event that took place on April 16 at the Four Seasons, can you tell me the name of Drew's friend who loaned him the room?"

"His friend James. He lived at the Four Seasons when he was in the city."

"What was James' full name?"

"James Lansdale."

I look to the seats behind the defense table where Lansdale normally sits, but he's missing today. Good move on his part. You don't become a billionaire by being stupid. Amber also clarifies that Lansdale wasn't present for the encounter, which thankfully removes a really disturbing image from my mind.

"Did Laney ever discuss Drew Anderson before they met?" Shep asks.

"All the time. She talked about how much she hated people who acted like they were perfect, when they were really the opposite. To Laney, Drew Anderson was the poster boy for these frauds."

I release a sigh of relief at every coherent answer. But she is getting more and more jumpy, and is now fervently playing with her hair. Our time is getting short.

"Did she ever act on this hatred?"

"Yes."

"How so?"

"She planned to blackmail him."

"By blackmail him—maybe try to ruin his marriage by having an affair?"

Amber laughs. "Laney only did things on a big scale, honey. She was going to go all the way. Expose him to the public. Ruin him. Put an end to that fake perfect image."

"So Laney pursued him?"

"For about a year. But the hard part was getting the intro. It's not like they ran in the same circles. Laney thought she had her chance at a New Year's party in Vegas a couple years back. Drew didn't show, but his assistant Ryan Maxon was there."

"This is the same Ryan Maxon you left the meeting with?"

She laughs her confident laugh. "I guess I always ended up with Laney's sloppy-seconds. Story of my life. Don't get me wrong, for some reason she liked that sap Maxon—she always had a thing for a good lap dog—but his main purpose was to get her to Drew."

"And it worked?"

"We wouldn't be here today if it didn't."

"And this pursuit came to a head last July 23 at Anderson Estate?"

"She never told me specifics, but I knew that's where the shit was gonna go down."

"And it looks like you were right, Amber," Shep makes a statement to the jury about Laney's competence, and Kerri jumps down her throat with a passionate objection.

A tear trickles down Amber's cheek. I wonder if it's premeditated. I'm convinced that hidden well underneath the drugged up bimbo persona is a conniving player, who like Maxon, knows a lot more than she's revealing—perhaps they are in concert with each other.

When Shep ends her questioning, Amber looks proud of herself, as if she just gave another satisfying performance in front of the camera.

Chapter 61

As she basks in her performance, Amber receives some troubling news. The defense lawyers now get their chance to grill her.

She looks to Shep and me for help. *Why does she think we spent all that time preparing her for Kerri's inevitable attacks?*

Amber instantly transforms into the cat that won't go into the cage. She begins playing furiously with her hair and adjusting the latex dress around her cleavage area. "I need a cigarette," she states with fear in her eyes.

Figliomini grants her wish and calls for a fifteen-minute recess. Giddy security guards escort Amber to a private courtyard in the back of the courthouse and fight over each other to light her cigarette.

She nervously inhales, before announcing, "I'm getting the fuck outta here!"

"You'll be fine—you did great," Shep again tries her best to comfort. "Remember, you are doing this for Laney … your mom," she lays it on thick.

Amber isn't buying it and tries to make a run for it. She doesn't get very far.

After her attempt to flee is thwarted, she is escorted back to the stand, this time exuding less bravado. Kerri immediately attacks like a barracuda.

"You were coached by Mr. Lawson and Ms. Shepherdson, correct?"

I never understand why this question throws witnesses off. Of course they were—it's expected. But I think they feel they are doing something wrong.

"No," Amber answers.

I want to bury my head—we went over this countless times in our sessions. Never start with a lie, and never tell an unnecessary lie. Only lie if you are in deep trouble—the Gifford Brown rule of honesty.

"You weren't … are you sure?" Kerri asks in an accusatory tone.

"Well … um … yes … no … yes"

"Yes? No? Which is it, Ms. Jazz?"

"Yes," she answers. She looks like she wants to crawl under the witness stand to escape.

Amber looks dishonest and the cross-exam hasn't really started yet.

"You seem to have a history of lying. I'm going to read a quote from an interview in *Hardcore Magazine*. 'All you have to do to be in porn is to be able to lie your ass off. Making the camera believe you are really excited to have some sweaty moron on top of you getting his jollies. Making some lonely guy at home believe I could really be with him. I lie for a living and I'm damn good at it.'"

I stand and shout, "Objection—is there a question in there, Your Honor?"

"Move it along, Ms. Lawson," Figliomini warns.

"Isn't your testimony here nothing but a lie and a publicity stunt?'

"No."

"In that same interview you were quoted as saying that of all the drugs you've partaken in, the one that gives you the biggest high is fame. You will do anything to be the biggest star in the world. And what bigger stage than this?"

I look at the jury and they're nodding heads. This is more what they expected. Kerri is making sense to them. Drew Anderson being involved in bizarre sex acts with adult movie stars doesn't make sense. Gifford was right—it might not come down to facts, but to making logical connections to confirm previous beliefs.

"No—Laney was my mom, and he killed her!" Amber stands and points at Anderson, who remains expressionless. I'm impressed that she has the fortitude to fight back.

"You talk about Laney Bang being your mom, but didn't you tell people in the industry on numerous occasions that she was the one holding you back. If you could get rid of her then you would be the biggest star in the world?"

Amber begins crying and this time I don't think it's an act. "I said that when I was totally messed on drugs. Laney was the one who got me through it. If it wasn't for her, I'd be dead. She nursed me back to health. If I wasn't on her side why would I agree to join her company and leave MaddoXXX Video?"

"Perhaps it was a case of keeping your friends close and your enemies closer."

"Objection," I yell.

Figliomini is already all over this one. "Sustained!"

"That night you described earlier at the Four Seasons—April 16—could you please describe the room you claim to have been in?"

"I don't know what you mean," Amber whimpers through tears.

"You were so specific on the details of what went on—I just want to get a description of the room to complete the image. The type of sheets? The smell? Pictures that might have been hanging on the wall? Describe the room."

Amber starts and stops three times. Then she completely shuts down. "I don't know."

"You don't know—why not?"

"I was too messed up to remember."

Shep massages her temples in frustration.

"And by that eloquent description of your state of mind, you mean that you'd been heavily sedated on drugs and alcohol for days?"

"Yes, but …"

"No further questions, Your Honor."

I decide not to redirect. In her emotional state, nothing good can come from it. Amber gets off the stand and bounces out of the courtroom. Literally. Shep and I try to console her, but she hits us with a stream of insults and bolts from the courthouse.

Chapter 62

On Friday morning, Ashley drove her van along Route-20 by the

Mohawk River.

She was to meet with a potential new client in the small town of Canajoharie. She had tried to call the number that was left for her, but got that annoying beeping sound. This wasn't unusual, since the potential client was a "new mover" and most likely didn't have a phone hooked up yet.

She continued to drive along the countryside on a splendid October morning, singing along to a catchy Taylor Swift song on the radio. Nothing could get her down on this day. It was a great day. She wasn't sure if it was her all-time happiest, but it was definitely up there. She couldn't wait to tell Mac the good news.

"We're going to have a baby!" she shouted to the empty van.

They had been trying to conceive since last winter. So much positive thinking and anticipation, followed by the emotional letdown.

When the home pregnancy test came up positive, the first person she thought of was her father. Donovan Armstrong raised Ashley alone after her mother died when she was only six years old. She still couldn't believe that they can put a man on the moon (at least most believe so) but haven't been able to develop a cure for an insidious disease like breast cancer. She could picture Grandpa Donovan with a little girl, and making all her troubles go away with just one hug, as he had done for her.

She pictured Mac more with a boy. She visualized father and son in his beloved Hall of Fame, the little one hanging on Mac's every word. *Hopefully he won't pick up the same crazy theories,* she thought with a laugh. Maybe they could team up against Daddy and roll their eyes at his wild theories. Most of all, she hoped the little one would inherit his father's joy for the daily grind of life. He knows who he is and what he loves. And, oh God, could he make her laugh. It sounds so simple, but so many miss it.

She was already going over potential names in her mind. If it was a boy, she thought Jack Donovan Cirillo would be fitting.

Jack was the big brother she never had, and she loved him unconditionally. He had always been such a glorious combination of blue skies and dark pain. So complex. In contrast to Mac's grounded self-satisfaction, Jack was a wandering brooder. She knew he wouldn't be sticking around forever, but she planned to enjoy him every minute while he was here.

She was so worried he would harm himself after Reyanne's death. The most horrible experience is to witness someone you love lose their will to live right in front of your eyes, while not being able to do anything about it. Her father never talked about the details of her mother's death, but his eyes told her that's what occurred.

All she could do was leave the porch light on, and then one day Jack showed up. She became his foundation of support, while Mac made him laugh, and the law did the rest. And now he was standing at the epicenter of the great storm and not even flinching. The next step was to get him and Jessica together. Ashley was convinced that Jessica was the one who would allow him to love again, and vice versa. You simply can't cuddle with a law book in front of a fire on a cold winter night.

After passing numerous Revolutionary War monuments along the countryside, Ashley arrived at a winding gravel driveway that was lined by cherry trees. It led to a rustic red farmhouse. Parked in the driveway was a truck from the phone company—just as she had suspected.

She was a few minutes early, and as she waited, her mind kept drifting back to their college days at Brown. Having a child is a special mark in time and it had put Ashley in a reminiscing mood.

She first met Jack Lawson at the John D. Rockefeller Jr. Library, or The Rock, as the students called it. He was her assigned tutor for a constitutional law course. She expected a typical jerk, since he came from some legal dynasty family. They were a dime-a-dozen at Brown. In the beginning, Jack was standoffish in their tutoring sessions, confirming her initial thoughts. But when she figured out his aloofness was the result of shyness, and in turn, he realized she wasn't like the other Theta girls on campus who suffered from eternal snobbery, they began to hit it off.

She invited Jack to a mixer party at her sorority. But the most important thing he did that night was to bring along his wardrobe-challenged friend

Mac Cirillo. The other girls turned their noses up at him, but Ashley knew right away that she'd met the man she would spend the rest of her life with.

She stepped out of the van, still smiling at the memories, and headed for the farmhouse. As she did, Ashley noticed the sculpted muscles of the telephone technician, who was heading back to his truck. Since he had his back to her, she took the opportunity to stare at his impressive derriere as he walked away. *The pregnancy hormones must already be rampaging,* she thought with a chuckle.

She arrived at the door and knocked. No answer. Knock again. Still no answer. She thought it was odd, since the telephone man just left the house. But you never knew with these farmhouses, perhaps they were out in the barn. Ashley decided to return to her van and call again. Maybe the phone was now hooked up and operational.

On her retreat, she looked up at the perfect blue sky. It triggered another memory. It was their last day of finals during their senior year at Brown. She had prepared a picnic basket and the three musketeers set up shop on the grassy quad outside of Mac and Jack's dorm. It was a quintessential May afternoon in Rhode Island.

It felt like it was yesterday. Mac was boring them with one of his Macademia theories, while Jack was complaining that his mother, instead of being thrilled that he was about to graduate with honors, told him that his college experience was a waste of time because he didn't rush Phi Kappa Psi—the Brown fraternity of John Kennedy Jr. At one point, Jack tried to shy off and go stick his nose in a law book, but Ashley made him stay. She thought it might be their last time together. Everyone makes great plans to remain in touch after graduation, but few actually keep the covenant. It's just the way life works, and college is usually the last act of idealism that can't be held onto, but nobody realizes it at the time.

She was expecting to spend a year in London after graduation. Jack was headed for Fordham Law School, while Mac was off to Cooperstown to pursue his dream job. Ashley took a picture in her mind, just in case it was the end. Being with her guys, Mac and Jack, eating bologna sandwiches on a blanket under a blue spring sky and having one of their usual quirky conversations. Hanging on as tightly to the moment for as long as they could. It was perfect—still is.

Ashley kept the smile on her face as she sat in the driver's seat of the van and called the number on the sheet. That is when she felt the knife on her neck.

Chapter 63

We take-off in a multi-engine Piper aircraft, just before eight o'clock on Friday night.

After I received Ashley's call about the attack, we arranged a meeting at a spot in Glimmerglass State Park, a rare place where I'm confident of privacy these days. She showed me the tickets—for a college football game between Florida State and the University of Miami—thinking I might be able to shed some light on their significance. Other than Florida State being Max Q's alma mater, I couldn't. But I knew from Ashley's description of the tattoo, that her attacker was the man who did the same to George Herman.

Ashley agreed to fly us to Tallahassee, where the game would take place at noon on Saturday. My cost was that I wasn't allowed to discuss with Mac the details of how she received the tickets. Ashley claimed to have a "special surprise" planned for him at Disney World—which we used as the cover story for the flight to Florida—and didn't want news of her attack to ruin it.

I sit beside Shep in rear seats of the plane, lost in a fog—my thoughts on Ashley's state of mind, and the nagging question of who's playing us. It's likely we're being set-up just like we were at Carmazzi's, and George was at Howe Caverns. But after our star witness was just ripped to shreds, I'm willing to take chances.

Mac is even chattier than normal, which is a mechanism he uses to mask his fear of flying. He is oblivious to his wife's distracted mood.

We land at Tallahassee Regional Airport just before midnight and go our separate ways. The plan is to meet back up on Sunday morning for the return trip.

Before leaving New York, Shep informed me that whenever the University of Miami invades Tallahassee to play Florida State, it's by far the biggest event of the year in northern Florida. We were unable to secure a hotel room, but a house along the Gulf was available for a weekend rental. It was off the beaten path, and likely over our budget, but the best we could do on short notice.

We drive directly from the airport to the beachfront house. It's thirty miles south of Tallahassee in a residential area called Panacea, located near Alligator Point.

After a day full of twisting emotions, we retire immediately to our rooms. The first problem I notice with the house is the air conditioning is broken. When I open the windows, seeking relief, all that does is attract the salt-water air, increasing the humidity level. But the lack of comfort is no match for my exhaustion and I drift into a deep sleep.

I get up early the next morning. But not as early as Shep. She's been out for a morning run, showered, and is already dressed. She wears a baggy, garnet and gold colored Florida State T-shirt, along with denim shorts that she had purchased during a crack-of-dawn trip to Target. She also purchased a similar outfit for myself, along with an FSU visor cap. She then wins my heart, having purchased a bacon egg and cheese sandwich from a local deli. It doesn't compare to Touch 'Em All, but it really hits the spot. We leave for Tallahassee on good terms.

When I think of Florida, my first thoughts are of flat swamplands, alligators, and palm trees. But Tallahassee is in the most northwest portion of the state and is often referred to as "the other Florida." We pass oak trees covered in Spanish moss that extend over the road, creating a shady canopy. The rolling hills of Tallahassee remind me of Cooperstown in the summer.

We park near the state capital building, which is walking distance from the campus. It's a superlative seventy-two-degree morning with a slight breeze. The crowds are thick, most everyone dressed in their FSU gear. Shep and I fit in easily—a smart move by her to pick up the T-shirts. Police are everywhere, making me slightly more comfortable.

It's only nine in the morning, and the kickoff isn't until noon, meaning that we have a few hours to kill. We stroll around the campus, passing old brick buildings that date back to the nineteenth century. We analyze each passerby within the large crowds, but soon grasp how hopeless this exercise is. We don't even know what we're looking for.

At one point, Shep receives a phone call from her boyfriend. She spends a half hour giggling into the phone like a schoolgirl, completely acting like I'm not there.

When she finishes, I try to pry. She declares that her personal life is none of my business, and once again reminds me of a certain talk that we had in which I made that abundantly clear.

But there is one part that does affect the case. "Does he know that you were once married?"

"Not that it's any of your business, but it hasn't come up. And besides, he's a mature grown up, so I can't imagine it would be an issue."

"Do you find it strange that the defense hasn't found out about it?"

"I knew you had an angle. I doubt they will—the Chapman family went to great lengths to make sure I never existed within their family."

"But aren't there records of your wedding? Newspaper clippings? Something that Kerri and her investigators might get their hands on."

"He married Jessica Hague, not Shepherdson. After the annulment I changed my name—we all wanted a new start. The Chapman lawyers were able to have all my college transcripts and all other important life documents changed to Shepherdson, which is why it was never an issue when I was hired."

I try to hide my astonishment. I want to trust her, but after all these months together, I'm still not even sure who she is.

"Don't look at me like that, Jack. You know as well as I do that powerful people can make things, and people, disappear when they want to."

"Like someone powerful enough to influence a high-profile trial."

Shep squints into the sun. "I'm just glad somebody is on our side, no matter who it is."

"If someone wants to help us out, I'm all for it. But it makes me uncomfortable not to be in control. I feel like there's a puppeteer pulling the strings."

"And in your scenario, we're the puppets?"

I nod my head. When I do, I feel like it's attached by strings.

Chapter 64

The stadium is surrounded by tailgate parties that scent the air with burning charcoal. Shep and I enter with a herd of other garnet and gold robots. The sun heats up and the cool morning transitions into a hot and muggy afternoon. We take our seats, which are on the aisle, about midway up the grandstand on the fifty-yard line.

"Whoever sent us here sure got us good seats," I acknowledge.

Shep doesn't respond. I notice her scanning the crowd, and like me, not knowing what she's looking for, but expecting to know it when she sees it.

As the clock strikes noon, an army of University of Miami football players explode from the tunnel and run onto the field to a chorus of booing and hissing. It's so loud I feel the structure shaking. They prance in their bright orange uniforms as if they enjoy the taunting.

"I hate Miami," Shep says.

The comment interrupts my scan of possible suspects. "Why do you hate Miami?"

"C'mon Jack. They used to beat out Syracuse every year for the conference championship—why don't you get your head out of a law book once in a while."

Learn something new everyday.

An explosion of energy greets the kickoff. Florida State receives possession of the ball and immediately their phenom freshman quarterback, Doug Leach, leads them on a drive. If the chatter around us is any indication, Leach is supposed to be the next Max Q.

A first quarter touchdown pass causes another aftershock of noisy jubilation. I view the crowd—still nothing. End of first quarter—still nothing. Miami matches the Florida State touchdown with one of their own. Jeers from the Florida State fans, but still nothing. I look at Shep and we both shrug.

My stomach begins to grumble. That bacon egg and cheese seems like ancient history. As if I'm giving off subliminal messages, a young vendor arrives at our seats.

"The gentleman over there said you look hungry, so he bought you these," he says and hands us each a hot dog.

"Ketchup? Mustard?" he offers, but we aren't listening.

"Who bought them for us?" Shep asks with urgency.

The vendor turns and points. "Right over…" His voice trails off and he shrugs. "Well, he was right over there. Do you want them or not?"

We grab the hot dogs. "What did he look like?" I ask hastily.

"Dude, there are like seventy thousand people here. I can't remember faces. He seemed pretty old—maybe like late-twenties."

Shep looks at the napkin that accompanies the hot dog. Written in block lettering with magic marker is the clue we've been waiting for—*If you want answers, go to Potbelly's and meet up with Prince Edward.*

I grab the vendor's arm as he tries to walk away, "What is Potbelly's?"

"You're not from around here, dude, are ya?"

I thought my Casper colored skin might be a giveaway that I'm not. "No—what is it?"

"Best bar on campus, located on College Ave," he answers, before a potential customer steals away his attention.

"Who is Prince Edward?" I ask before I lose him.

He shrugs. "Isn't that the dude from England with the big ears?"

We fight our way through the crowds and out of the stadium. We find a student with more facial hair than any twenty-year-old should ever have, playing an acoustic guitar. He seems to be the only person we've met not interested in football. He points us in the direction of College Avenue.

The outside of Potbelly's is surrounded by an eight thousand square foot concert area, making it hard to miss. We enter to the sounds of a rowdy crowd of students watching the game on a screen that looks like it was stolen from the local movie theater. A three hundred pound man tries to sell us T-shirts, but we politely decline and drop anchor at an empty table.

A young waiter approaches our table and Shep asks him, "Do you know who Prince Edward is?"

"Why, you guys looking for some T-shirts?"

"T-shirts?"

"Yeah, Prince Edward is PE Albertson. Used to play back in the Max Q days," he says and then lowers his voice to just over a whisper, "He's got a monopoly on the underground T-shirt market, but you didn't hear that from me."

He points to the large man we just passed. We thank him in waiter language—twenty bucks—and then approach the Prince of T-shirts.

The heat is taking its toll on the large man, sweat soaking through his shirt, and his neatly-trimmed afro is like a sponge of perspiration.

"Prince Edward?" I ask him.

"Who wants to know?"

"Cut the bull," Shep says and hands him the napkin.

If you want answers go to Potbelly's and meet up with Prince Edward.

He looks dismissively at it. I can tell by his blank look that he's never seen it before.

"So you didn't arrange this meeting … the tickets?" I ask.

He shrugs his enormous shoulders. “If you want T-shirts, I got T-shirts. If you want answers, I can’t help you.”

We’re stumped. We don’t know what else to say. “Are you Pótbelly?” Shep asks, trying to buy time. I hope he doesn’t take it as an insult and crush us.

“Is that any way to talk to a man on Atkins?” he says and flashes a charming smile that’s surrounded by a graying goatee. “Potbelly’s is a gold mine. If I was Potbelly, I sure wouldn’t be the night manager at a Chili’s, now would I?”

“Sounds like you do pretty well in the underground T-shirt market,” I retort.

PE smiles. “You can’t believe everything you hear.”

He unzips his duffel bag and pulls out a pile of shirts. I can tell he has no idea he’s talking to law-enforcement officials.

“I have a few good anti-FSU ones also, but you have to keep it down,” he says with a shush finger on his lips. “This is our best selling one.” It not so creatively combines FSU and suck into *FSUCK.*

“We don’t want to buy any shirts,” I announce.

His smile disappears. “What the hell is this about?”

“We are from Otsego County District Attorney’s Office in New York. We are prosecuting your old teammate, Drew Anderson,” Shep informs.

I brace for an angry response, but he smiles. His look says he knows why we are here, even if we don’t.

“So you knew Drew well?” I ask.

“Not only did I know Drew Anderson. But I also knew Darby Kelleher when she went to school here. You know—Laney Bang.”

Chapter 65

I admit we missed it. We never seriously sought any connection between the victim and the accused prior to that New Year's party when Maxon claimed to meet Laney. And we never came across anything that even hinted that Darby Kelleher spent a semester in college, much less the same one as Drew Anderson.

It was right in front of me on page one of her book—Mr. Perfect wasn't an amalgam of men who betrayed her, but a real incident between her and Drew Anderson from years ago. It changes everything.

"Not here—meet me at Chili's at eleven o'clock tonight," are PE's last words, before leaving as inconspicuously as a three hundred pound man can.

We have some down time before our meeting. I make the decision to remain at the festive Potbelly's, thinking we can use the diversion. As the game moves into the fourth quarter, the drunken crowd has graduated from boisterous to raucous.

Muscle-bound frat boys are swigging shots like they are water, while tanned coeds bounce around the room in skimpy outfits. At one point, an impromptu wet T-shirt contest breaks out in which they try to recruit Shep. When I prohibit her participation, I get booed—I'm getting used to it—and then they really hurt me when they chant, "Lose your daddy!" in Shep's direction.

I'm actually only a couple years older than her, although since I just found out that she really is Hague, and not Shep, who knows how old she really is. She goes on the warpath when I'm not completely transparent in any of my dealings with her, yet her whole life is wrapped in mystery.

When Florida State's last second field goal attempt sails wide, and Miami escapes with a one point win, the energy comes out of Potbelly's like someone popped a balloon. The locals mention that it is another example of something called the "Wide Right Curse." I've never really grasped the concept of sports curses. George Herman has tried explaining the "Curse of the Bambino" to me on multiple occasions, but I'm still confused why people would continue to watch if they thought some whimsical force of the universe preordained the outcome.

Shep and I follow the rest of the herd out of the bar, which has transformed into a morgue. We find a quiet coffee shop down the street, order a couple cups of java, and prepare for our meeting with PE Albertson.

"That is way different than my college experience," I mention.

"I know," Shep replies. "I worked four jobs and don't think I went to one party. Every day was like a battle for survival."

"Sounds like it turned out to be good preparation for later life."

"Nothing can prepare anyone for what we've been dealing with. How do you stay so calm?"

"Looks can be deceiving—I just hide it well. And when I get overly stressed, I think LLF."

"LLF?"

"Just something Reyanne used to say. An acronym for live life to the fullest. It puts things into perspective for me."

"What about the *to* and *the*?"

"That's what I always said," I reply with a smile.

Shep's jaw tightens with seriousness. "Jack, if I've never mentioned it before, I want you to know how sorry I am about you losing her. If I ever said anything in the heat of the moment…"

"Thanks. It gets a little better each day. Looking back isn't going to change anything."

"For what it's worth, I believe that sometimes someone is sent into our lives to save us from ourselves. When their job is done they have to move on."

"Like an angel?"

"Not metaphysical with wings. More like someone who directs us toward the people we need to be directed toward. Then the right person drops into our lives at just the right moment."

"Anybody like that ever come into your life?"

"Yes," she says, staring intensely at me for a brief second, but looks away.

We return to our coffees and talk until almost eleven. We then head out into the muggy night, eager to hear what PE Albertson has to tell us.

Chapter 66

The Miami victory has sobered Tallahassee, and Chili's is practically empty.

PE orders us to a booth with ripped upholstery in the back corner. He follows with a limp that he explains away as a souvenir from his FSU football days. "God damn Florida Gators, always playing dirty," he grumbles.

He sits facing us across a salsa-stained wooden table. He takes up most of his side of the booth, almost matching the combined width of Shep and me.

"I was Drew Anderson's left tackle. I protected his blindside and helped him win the Heisman Trophy. I was also his roommate at Byron Hall. Ryan Maxon, whom I'm sure you've met, was our suite-mate."

"How about Darby Kelleher?" I ask.

He raises a meaty finger to indicate he'll get to it.

"If Drew's sport was football, then his hobby was making films with as many girls on campus as he could. I think you know what type I'm talking about. The girls didn't know they were becoming movie stars, but I'm fairly sure most of them wouldn't have cared, regardless. Drew was like a god on this campus."

"Why didn't you do something about it?" Shep asks.

"Because I had no problem with it. Besides, if I did, they'd probably have kicked my ass out of here for bothering Drew."

"How did he conceal the camera?" I ask.

"We drilled a hole between our room and Maxon's. He was Drew's loyal lap dog who would keep things quiet, and be the one to fall on the sword for Drew if we were ever caught."

"But the night of the Darby Kelleher tape, Maxon couldn't have filmed it because he was passed out on the bottom bunk," I say.

PE looks at me curiously, as a round of iced teas arrive. Once our waiter has moved a safe distance away, he asks, "How'd you know that?"

"It was in her book—he's Friend and Anderson is Mr. Perfect. I figured they were just symbols. Laney laid out her obsession for revenge in print for the world to read," I answer, shaking my head with disbelief. Her words were as calculated as her actions.

Now Shep is the one who looks at me strangely. She can't believe reading Laney's book was actually beneficial.

PE shrugs. "Never read that puppy, but being there is usually better than the book. Maxon had a total thing for Darby. He was trying to use his relationship with Drew to impress her. But Drew was a cold-blooded shark. He would steal his buddy's girl just to prove he could, and not loose a minute of sleep over it."

"Sounds like there is no love lost between you two."

"Max-Q-Collectibles was my idea. I saw how the anti-Drew T-shirts would fly off the rack when we traveled to Gainesville or Miami. So Drew and I figured if they were gonna hate on him anyway, he might as well profit from it. He had too much on his plate, so he put me in charge of creating the business and I ran it from soup to nuts—creative director, designer, marketing, sales, distribution—and built it into a big time business that continued after we graduated.

"Drew came back from the military as an international star—college football had more of a regional audience—and at the same time the sports collectibles and memorabilia business took off. He suddenly didn't like sharing any profits, or credit, and cut me out. He also never paid me my share up to that point—I was naïve enough to buy his BS about putting all profits back into the product and that he'd settle with me down the line. I'm a loyal guy, so I believed my friend was going to be loyal to me—I didn't need no contract. Now he's living in a big house, while I'm selling T-shirts in the shadows like I'm some common drug dealer. Am I bitter? Hell yeah, but I think I have every right to be."

Shep and I nod, as our food arrives. I'm hoping that what PE tells us will deliver Anderson to the true "big house."

After a few bites of my cheeseburger, I ask, "With Maxon passed out, who filmed the tape of Drew and Darby that night?"

"It was a PE Albertson original," he states with a proud grin. "And when she came back the next day all in love, like they all did, I made it clear that it would be in her best interest not to pursue a relationship, and to keep her mouth glued shut."

"How did the video get out?"

"That's where I messed up. There was this cheerleader I was interested in named Tina. I tried to impress her by bragging that I was in Drew's inner circle and gave her the video to prove it. I didn't know she would give it to Laney's roommate, who would host a film festival for half the dorm. I broke the Drew Anderson cardinal rule by letting his not-so-perfect side get out. He's always been obsessed with his public reputation. And he never forgets—I was done at that moment, even if we worked together for years before he lowered the boom, I just didn't know it."

"Laney said she was horrified by the video—she accidentally walked in on the film festival, which sparked her quest for revenge."

"Yeah, she went ballistic. Began making threats and filing complaints with the university. I threatened her, trying to convince her to drop her claims. But that girl didn't take nothing from nobody—I kinda respected that. You should have seen the fire in her eyes. Man, she was different," PE concedes, sounding impressed.

With a look of confusion, Shep asks, "So there is an official complaint made with the university by Darby Kelleher against Drew Anderson? If this is on record, how the hell did we miss it?"

PE laughs at her naiveté. "I guarantee there is *absolutely no record* of such a complaint. Drew explained to the higher-ups that he filmed all his hookups in case one of them were to claim date rape to exploit his fame, and this particular tape got stolen. But there was never any official hearing because Darby dropped out of school. I doubt anything would've happened to him, anyway. Convicting Drew Anderson is no easy task."

"Tell me about it," I utter with a sigh. Just like the Chapman's annulled their relationship with Shep—stripped of any ties that bind, including her name—the same thing happened here with Darby Kelleher.

"What about the tape—could it be floating around somewhere out there?" Shep asks.

PE looks quizzically at her. "What is this, amateur hour? You will never find any evidence that Darby Kelleher ever stepped on this campus, much less a video."

"Laney wasn't giving up when she left school, she was retreating to plot her revenge." Very George Washington of her, I think.

"Revenge is a dish best served cold," PE imparts.

I wonder aloud about the source of our tickets. Ryan Maxon is sure moving up on the list of possibilities.

"I haven't seen any of these folks in over ten years." PE says and I believe him.

"Pack your bags, PE, you are coming back to New York with us to testify," I declare. I hope I don't have to risk my life by threatening him with a subpoena or an IRS audit that will expose his T-shirt business.

Thankfully, he doesn't put up a fight. If revenge is best served as a cold dish, then he is about to serve up a three-course meal of frozen dinners to his old friend, Max Q.

Chapter 67

Shep and I return to the rental house in Panacea. She remains excited that our guardian angel continues to supply us with helpful evidence. I don't want to throw cold water on it, but I think we're getting set up to take a fall.

We retire to our respective rooms. I watch a replay of the eleven o'clock news at one a.m. It's as if somebody died in Tallahassee. To toss some salt in the wound, quarterback Doug Leach tore a knee ligament on the second-to-last play of the game and will be out for the remainder of the season. I'm once again reminded of how quickly fortunes can change.

Unable to sleep, I lay frozen on my sweat-filled sheets. I can't help but imagine the look on Kerri's face when I introduce PE Albertson. I go through a mock testimony in my head. She will be able to make him look like he is a disgruntled former hanger-on with an ax to grind and a bank account to fill. But we have a second witness to back-up his testimony.

I look at the clock—3:52. I decide to end the torturous process. I pull on a pair of shorts and head to the beach, trying not to wake Shep, tiptoeing quietly passed her closed door.

I sit in the sand and stare out at the Gulf of Mexico. Silence fills the dark night, only interrupted by the light splash of waves hitting the sandy shore. Then a voice rises from the night. I look around, my paranoia getting the best of me. I turn to make sure it didn't come from behind. It's my turn to get a knife to the neck.

Nobody there.

I hear the voice again, this time a distant yelp. A female voice. I strain to get a better view. I see the silhouette of a woman breezily prancing in the moonlight. She is about fifty yards away, frolicking in the surf. The next sound I hear is a giggle.

Then like a beer commercial, the beautiful creature leaves the water and heads in my direction, wearing only a minuscule bikini. If she is coming to kill me I won't resist. When I enter her vision, a loud scream leaps from her lungs.

"Shep?" I ask, confused, fighting to see in the darkness.

"Oh my god, Jack—you scared the hell out of me!"

I can't stop looking at her. She looks like she leaped off the cover of a magazine. Her dark hair hangs down on her mist-covered shoulders.

"What are you doing out here?" I ask.

"I guess I could ask you the same question, Jack."

"Couldn't sleep."

A big smile comes over her face. "Me either. Gifford is going to have a cow that we ditched our security guards this weekend."

I don't reply.

"What is it, Jack?" she asks, confused by my stare.

"Do you go to the gym every day? You have one of those beer stomachs," I blurt out.

"I hope you mean a six-pack and not a beer-gut," she playfully scolds with a laugh. "Actually, before this case I used to go twice a day, but I can only go once since this trial started. I can't live without my kickboxing class." She pauses and giggles. "And don't you make fun of me for being so regimented!"

She lightly practices one of her kickboxing moves on me.

"I tried that Tae-Bo once, but I pulled a muscle in my hip and I couldn't walk for a week," I say with a smile.

"Let's go in the water—it's so refreshing, Jack!" she continues in her strange childlike state.

I decide against it. "I'm going back to bed—we have an early day tomorrow," I stutter.

"Suit yourself," she replies. She then lets me watch her as she strolls toward the Gulf, the moonlight highlighting every curve.

As she arrives at the water's edge, she turns back toward me. "We are going to bring Max Q down, Jack!"

I enjoy a private smile. It's good to see her let her hair down, both literally and figuratively. It's also really nice to see her more excited about trying to achieve justice than her climb up the ladder of success.

On Sunday morning, we meet Ashley and Mac at Tallahassee Regional Airport. We bring a large fifth wheel—PE Albertson.

"How did the big surprise go? I ask.

"Nothing special—we are just going to have a baby," Mac answers in an unsuccessful attempt to act nonchalant.

Hugs abound. Even PE Albertson, who just met them seconds ago, joins the love. The scene reminds me of a picnic we had at Brown when the three of us thought we were going our separate ways. Perfect moments can happen in such imperfect times.

Chapter 68

We arrive at work on Monday morning after a *really* long weekend. The calendar has flipped to October, and there is an autumn chill in the air, a big contrast from Florida.

We immediately are at a sidebar, where I'm trying to convince Figliomini to introduce PE Albertson to our witness list.

"We object to this!" Kerri loudly dissents.

When we retire to the judge's chambers, Kerri picks up right where she left off, "Your Honor, the prosecution is just trying to stall. There are only so many degenerates they can get to make false allegations against my client. If they have evidence my client killed Laney Bang—fine. But all they are doing is a character assassination without grounds."

Figliomini stares sternly at me. "Mr. Lawson?"

"Your Honor, Mr. Albertson came to us during our ongoing investigation. He will testify that Ms. Bang and Mr. Anderson met years ago … in college. His testimony will shed light on an event that led Laney to seek revenge on Anderson, and plan her blackmail scheme."

Figliomini looks skeptically at me.

I hand the judge copies of Darby Kelleher's grades from her first and only semester she attended Florida State. A 3.9—she never fails to surprise me. PE was right that there was no official record of her attending the school. But some quick thinking by Shep sparked a side-trip to Pensacola on Sunday morning, prior to meeting up with Mac and Ashley. More specifically, we went to the residence of Marcie and Steve Kelleher. A college doesn't send grades to the student, but rather, to the parents who pay the bill. I stayed in the car for obvious reasons, while Shep played nice with the Kellehers, and eventually found the report card in a box in the basement.

"I'll allow the witness," Figliomini renders.

"We will need time to prepare," Kerri grumbles.

"Three days—we will reconvene on Thursday, and Prince Edward Albertson will be on the stand."

Shep suggests that we use the time off to perform an intense mock trial to thoroughly prepare PE for the inevitable Kerri onslaught. Shep's "hair down" era appears over. But I think it's more important that he's relaxed. So I overrule Shep, and decide that PE and I will spend the three days on Otsego Lake.

"Do you fish?" I ask him.

"I'm from Mobile, Alabama," he responds.

I don't know what exactly that means, but I think it means he likes to fish.

He also introduces me to something called chili fries, for which I will be eternally grateful. I warn him that Kerri will try to paint him as a disgruntled, jealous ex-friend with his hand out. PE nods his gargantuan head. He seems to understand what he is in for, which is half the battle.

Prince Edward Albertson takes the stand on Thursday. He is at ease, generously flashing his charming smile. I can tell that he's wanted to tell this story for a long time.

I end the testimony by having him repeat a statement he made to us in

Florida. "Maxon loved her, but Drew was one cold dude. He would steal his buddy's girlfriend just because he could and not loose a wink of sleep over it."

Kerri takes over and predictably depicts Albertson as a washed up football player who is jealous of Drew's success, and is looking to make a quick buck. How come nobody else has come forward? If such a tape exists, wouldn't it have come out? Do you have any proof such a hearing happened with the university—and why is there no record of it?

I redirect. PE needs someone to corroborate his story, and who better than Laney herself.

Keri objects to my reading of *Big Bang Theories*, but is overruled.

I read her gripping tale about Mr. Perfect. The exact story PE Albertson just told the court about Drew Anderson. Kerri reminds the jury that I'm up to my old fiction tricks, and the idea that Drew is some unnamed character in a book is ludicrous. But when I view the jury, I notice some doubt creeping in regarding their golden boy. I think it's related to the third prong of our strategy, which is to make sense of this thing. The jury understands revenge, and if we were able to prove that is why Laney Bang came after Drew Anderson, then I think they will open their minds to the possibility that their hero could have committed this crime. An open mind is all I can ask for.

I glance at my watch. It's Friday at four o'clock—the week has flown by. It's also the ideal breaking point. We have established all three phases of our case as best we'll be able to, and I want the jury to spend the weekend mulling over our points before the defense begins their case.

I look over to the defense and they look away. Drew and Marissa remain stone cold. Finally, I look to the jury and confidently bellow, "The people rest."

This wakes up Figliomini, who announces that the defense will begin putting on their case first thing Monday morning.

Kerri stands and unnecessarily states, "The defense will be ready."

We return to 197 Main. Shep enters my office and surprises me with a huge bear hug. "We did it, Jack!"

I caution her that we are still a long shot to get a conviction.

Gifford Brown pops his head in the door and compliments us as only he can, "I'm just relieved that neither of you two tried to put a dried up, bloody glove on Anderson."

We laugh.

Gifford heads out to do whatever Gifford Brown does on a weekend, leaving just Shep and me.

"Would you like to go get a drink at Touch 'Em All to celebrate?" I ask her.

"I thought you said it would be premature. That the odds are heavily against us."

I smile. "I meant celebrate that the weekend is here."

Her grin fades and she subtly looks away. "Sorry, Jack. I can't."

"C'mon, Shep—you can go to the gym three times tomorrow and make up for missing tonight."

"I have um…I have a date tonight."

"Oh, well I don't want to keep you from that," I say with just enough annoyance for her to tell I'm feeling a little hurt.

When she departs, I barricade myself in my office. I'm still not sure why Shep's date bothers me so—I was the one who pushed her away. It's probably for the best.

I put in a couple of hours on the cases I've been brushing under the rug since July 24. The biggest of which is Andy Kass.

I leave the office at nine o'clock. Main Street is practically deserted. The summer tourist crowd is gone and the media can't leave fast enough when court breaks for the weekend.

I haven't been back to Touch 'Em All since we were driven off the road. As I walk in, my mind floods with the bad memory of that night.

The bar is as empty as I've ever seen it. Shep is on her date. The Cirillos have taken a weekend trip to Manhattan to shop for maternity wear—poor Mac. George Herman is at one of his Babe Ruth gigs, and Beneke and Opp are probably out butchering a crime scene somewhere.

I sit at the bar and Augie slides a frosty in front of me, on the house. "You've done yourself proud, Jack, no matter what happens," he tells me.

As I finish my third mug, a woman enters the bar. She wears a tan leather jacket over a form-fitting mock-turtleneck, with worn jeans and trendy boots. A large cross hangs gracefully around her neck.

I'm fixated on her, but not because of the obvious physical beauty. It is the aura of confidence that surrounds her. It's hard to explain, but easy to look at.

Chapter 69

"I'll have what he's having," Marissa says, while climbing atop a bar stool beside me.

There is an awkward moment of silence, before I break it, "This is totally unethical. You, of all people, should know better."

"This is just two lawyers having a beer."

"One of us needs to leave, and I was here first."

"You've been hanging around your uptight partner too long. Speaking of which, where is the ice queen tonight? She couldn't be on a date, could she?"

I don't respond.

Marissa reads my silence. "She *is* on a date! Wonders never cease."

I'm tired of her tweaking Shep at every opportunity. "She didn't do anything to you. It's not her fault your husband is a murderer."

I immediately regret my words, but Marissa appears unaffected. "Oh my god, Jack—you have a thing for her. You want to play with the ice-queen's icicles, don't you?"

"I don't have a…" I start, before catching myself. She can push my buttons and she knows it. “You should go.”

Marissa sips on her beer, a clear indication that she’s not going anywhere. “All I wanted to do was congratulate you on a great performance, lawyer to lawyer. They gave you nothing to work with, you had no evidence, and to say your witnesses lacked credibility, would be a great understatement. Not to mention, the cops put you in a bad spot to start with. You have no shot at a conviction, but you fought a valiant fight, Jack, and I respect that.”

She gets my competitive juices flowing, but I hold back. I feel more sorry for her than anything. I think she senses that and it further fuels her irritation.

“You landed a few good shots, I’ll give you that. The video was quite a coup and pulling the PE Albertson testimony out of your ass was impressive. But you’re using a pellet gun. You know as well as I do, when Drew takes the stand he is a nuclear weapon. Hey, it worked on me and I’m much more skeptical than that jury will ever be.”

While her blind faith toward her husband may be noble, if not delusional, it’s starting to annoy me. “Doesn’t it bother you that he cheated on you like he did? If he lied to you about that, what makes you think he isn’t lying to you about killing Laney?”

“What makes you think he lied to me?”

The answer is unexpected. “What?”

“Marriage is complicated, Jack. You just don’t throw the baby out with the bath water because someone made a mistake. It really is for better or worse. That kind of stuff doesn’t make your day, but if you truly love each other, you work it out.”

“So you would consider your husband making home movies with an adult film actress just a speed-bump on the road to eternal bliss?”

She shakes her head sadly at me as if I just don’t get it. “You have a lot of talent, but that’s the kind of stuff holding you back from being truly great.”

“I’m not following you.”

"A great lawyer has vision. Kind of like a quarterback in football. You have to see the whole field. You are going about this with tunnel vision."

"Still not following."

"Open yourself up to all possibilities. Why do you assume I'm a victim of my husband's infidelity? How do you know what Drew did wasn't in response to something I did in the marriage, and that is how he expressed his pain?

"Well…was it?"

"Nobody's perfect, and therefore no marriage is."

"That wasn't my question."

"All you need to know about our marriage, is that when Drew gets his freedom we will run into each other's arms and he will twirl me around like a scene from a movie. And even a cynical prosecutor like you won't be able to doubt our love. I just hope you're there to watch, Jack."

I'm tempted to debate her, but I bite my tongue. I can tell my refusal to fight her is pissing her off.

Marissa continues, "We both know that Drew isn't going to be convicted. So we have two choices. We can put our heads into the sand and pretend you prosecuted the right guy and the jury was ignorant by letting him walk. Or, we can find out who really killed this woman and why."

"Why would you care who killed her? You just told me that Drew was going to get off anyway."

"Someone is trying to frame my husband for murder. If they're willing to go to such lengths, his life will be in danger when he's acquitted. You're the only chance to catch this person before they harm him. Who else is going to do it, Jack—the ice princess? Gifford Brown? That inept police department?"

"That's an entertaining story, but unfortunately you aren't a very credible witness on this subject. I remember you telling me that you would do anything to get your husband off."

"The man whose star witness was a crack-head porn star is debating my credibility?"

"I'm sorry for what your husband did, but it's my job to review the evidence and present it to a court. The evidence tells me that Drew murdered Laney Bang, and you coming down here to try to sway me isn't going to work."

"Get your head out of of your ass, Jack! Key pieces of evidence just mysteriously fall into your lap? Including a video that a person would need intimate knowledge of Anderson Estate to be able to make. A witness with a connection to the incident at Florida State, or at least knowledge of it. How about you take your blinders off for a minute and tell me what the link is."

I say nothing, but I know who she's talking about. It's been bugging me since Florida. Ryan Maxon.

"I can't have this conversation," I say.

"A conversation is an exchange of ideas between two people—this is me talking to a wall."

Marissa stands to leave. Like a good lawyer, she's made her point and lingering can only diminish it. She begins to walk away.

She turns and shouts, "Drew is innocent," as if she is trying to convince herself.

I make a foolish decision. I get off my bar stool and catch up with her. "Let me walk you to your car."

She acts like she doesn't want to accept, but I've seen enough of her game to know she sees it as a great opportunity to plant more doubt about her husband's guilt. We walk out into a cool, moonlit October night. All it will take is one snap by a photographer and I'll have a lot of explaining to do.

"Sorry about that—I usually don't get so emotional. I guess you can take the girl out of the Bronx, but not the Bronx out of the girl," Marissa softens her tone.

She continues, "It's just that sometimes I fool myself into feeling safe. But ever since I was a little girl, the things I love were always ripped away from me. When I watched you in that courtroom, I visualized Drew being taken from me."

I remain quiet.

"What I would give to just feel that sense of safety. The feeling that things can't be taken away on a whim. Now that would be true perfection."

"Nothing is perfect, and nobody is guaranteed another breath. I've learned that the hard way."

"Call me an eternal optimist, but I've always believed you can reach perfection in this world. That feeling of ultimate safety and stability. And I thought I found it when I met Drew. But now it's being threatened again."

I try to avoid eye contact, just as I have all night. But I give in, and instantly realize that I've made a mistake. I see Reyanne everywhere.

I also understand how the things you cherish can be ripped away, and I agree, it would be perfect if they weren't.

I force myself to walk away.

Chapter 70

"So did you end up going out Friday night?" Shep asks me upon arriving at the courthouse Monday morning.

"Went to Touch 'Em All for a couple drinks and then home," I reply. I leave out the part about Marissa. I don't want to see Shep have a coronary on the courtroom steps.

"Aren't you going to ask me about my weekend?" Shep asks.

"I thought you didn't mix your private and professional lives?"

"Call me a changed woman. I didn't think we would be able to get a conviction, either, but we're going to do that."

I notice an extra pep in her voice. I hope the elation is due to the case, but I deduce that it's probably related to her boyfriend. I decline the details.

As we walk through security and past the daily cluster of media, it astounds me how I've become numb to it. It's amazing what you can get used to. "We have a long way to go," I say.

"Nothing we can't handle. We're the champ, remember?"

"We hit him with a few shots from our pellet guns, but when Anderson takes the stand he will be a nuclear weapon."

"What does that mean?"

"It's just a figure of speech."

She sighs. "What's with guys and war metaphors?"

We enter the courtroom. Marissa is in her usual spot, sitting confidently behind her husband in a body-hugging red sweater. She provides me a look that seems to be held over from our meeting on Friday. I am hypnotized. I pull away before Shep has a chance to pick up on it.

The first day of defense testimony has brought out all the big guns. As if to say this is the real trial and the prosecution case was just the dress rehearsal. James Lansdale is back, and my father has made his first appearance. The only one who acknowledges my existence is a hunched over woman with snow-white hair, pulling her wood cane close to her frail body. Ethel Lawson is still trying to have her cake and eat it too.

As is custom, the defense files a motion to throw out the charges based on lack of evidence presented in the prosecution case. As is also custom, Figliomini denies the motion.

Kerri is probably eager to get Maxon back on the stand to minimize any damage that PE Albertson may have done to her client—I know I would be. But she shows surprising restraint. She's aware that leading with him will give credence to Albertson's testimony. Starting with the jogging witnesses, with the intent to prove Anderson's alibi, is the prudent move.

The foundation of our case is that Drew is the only person who could have killed Laney Bang. If Kerri can prove an alibi, it'll cripple us. If she's successful, the jury will eventually give Shep and me a charity forty-five minute deliberation, followed by an overwhelming acquittal and a Mardi Gras style celebration on the courthouse steps by the Max Q supporters.

Each jogging witness puts Drew Anderson along his usual route within the usual time frame.

Shep does the honors on the cross-exam. The standard vanilla stuff. It was early in the morning and Anderson was a moving target for their early-morning eyes. *Are you sure it was him—are you really-really sure it was him—how did you do on your last vision test?*

She left out—were you paid off? We don't dispute that Drew went for a jog that morning. The fact we disagree on is whether or not he continued on his usual route.

The problem with the defense witnesses, from our perspective, is that they all ooze credibility. A sharp contrast to the sleazy boozers and hostile witnesses we put on the stand. At this point, I comprehend how much the Aokis selling of their story to a tabloid has hurts us. They could have provided a big shot of credibility.

Finally on Tuesday morning, Kerri recalls Ryan Maxon.

I watch him closely as he walks to the stand. He looks like a college professor in tweed jacket, khakis, and his horn-rimmed glasses. His thinning brown hair is neatly matted to his head. He remains the wild card in the case.

I notice Marissa glaring at him. While I have questioned Maxon's role, and wondered which team he is truly loyal to, Marissa insinuated that the part he played was much more sinister. She never came right out and said it, so I might be over-thinking her words, but I'm now open to all possibilities.

Kerri approaches Maxon. She tries to give the appearance of friendly restraint, but I can see that the back-alley bully dressed in Chanel is ready to pounce.

"Mr. Maxon, I would like to discuss the testimony this court heard from a man named Prince Edward Albertson. You know him, correct?"

Maxon seems uneasy, but the scripted questions allow some comfort level. "I knew him in college, but I haven't seen him in over ten years."

"Could you describe your relationship during those college years?"

"He was Drew's roommate. I lived in a connected suite. We were acquaintances, but I wouldn't call us friends. I believe he was jealous of my friendship with Drew."

"Objection—speculation," I shout out.

Kerri nods and revises, "How did Drew describe to you his feelings toward Mr. Albertson?"

"That he was a hanger-on. Someone always seeking the spotlight. Drew didn't trust him."

"So it doesn't surprise you that Mr. Albertson shows up again after all these years, and shines a bad light on Drew and yourself?"

"Not at all."

"Based again on what Drew told you, is Mr. Albertson the type of person who would seek out publicity for personal gain?"

"Yes he is."

Kerri looks at the legal pad she holds in her hand, and then looks back up at Maxon like these questions are off-the-cuff. "Mr. Albertson told this court about a video made between Drew and the victim back in college. Do you recall such an event?"

"I have no recollection of any video."

"A university investigation?"

"Not that I am aware of."

"Mr. Maxon—is it fair to say that you knew Drew Anderson as well as anyone, going back to your college years?"

"That is a fair statement."

"Based on this unique knowledge, did he even know Laney Bang, then known as Darby Kelleher, during that time?"

Maxon again chuckles.

If I were him I wouldn't be feeling so confident.

"Drew only had eyes for the most beautiful girls in the school, and at the time, believe it or not, Darby was more of a Plain Jane than the international sex symbol she became. Nobody really noticed Darby back then, and it's too bad because she was…" he pauses and the chuckle turns to sadness. He wipes away tears from under his glasses. "She was a great girl … I just can't believe she's gone."

Kerri pauses to give the impression she's concerned about Maxon's emotional state. When she determines the proper time has passed, she continues with a soft voice, "Mr. Maxon, I would like to clear something up. You told this court that you had met Laney Bang at a party in Las Vegas, but in actuality you were first introduced to her when you were in college. Could you explain this?"

Maxon again adjusts his glasses. "I have always considered Darby and Laney to be different people. Once Darby left college, I never saw her again. It was a different person I met at that New Year's party. They might have the same DNA, but from my perspective they were as different as night and day, except that they both had a big heart." More wiping of tears. "I should have made it clear, and I apologize if my answers were confusing to the court. But that was not my intent—I answered truthfully in my mind."

Kerri and Maxon are in a scripted groove. "During Mr. Albertson's testimony, the defense floated a theory that Laney Bang was blackmailing Drew, claiming this 'Mr. Perfect' character in her book was actually him. Being such a close confidante of hers—did your friend Laney ever mention this to you?"

"No."

"Did she ever mention any animosity toward Drew?"

"Never."

"Did she ever push you to meet Drew?"

"No."

"Did she push for the meeting the night of July 23?"

"No—the meeting was my idea."

"Had Laney Bang ever been to Anderson Estate prior to July 23?"

"Not to my knowledge."

"If she hadn't been there prior, then how was this video filmed? Wouldn't she have had to have been at Anderson Estate, as Amber Jazz had testified?"

"I didn't say she wasn't, but I don't believe it. It's one video, which proves she was there one time. That video could have been made the night of the meeting, after Amber and I left."

"Being in daily contact with Drew, wouldn't you suspect if he was having this ongoing affair, as Amber Jazz testified?"

"I knew of no affair."

Kerri begins to pace, her heels clicking the floor in a rhythmic fashion. I can feel the storm about to arrive.

Is that thunder I hear?

Chapter 71

Kerri pauses dramatically. She stares quizzically at her legal pad, appearing confounded. She looks up at Maxon, and then back to the pad. I have seen that look in her eye before. I hope Maxon has his health insurance paid up.

"Something doesn't make sense to me," Kerri says, shaking her pen as if it's helping her to think.

Maxon squirms in his seat, the tweed coat suddenly not fitting as well. I can tell this isn't in the script.

"Don't you find it interesting that Mr. Albertson just showed up during the prosecution's investigation? Totally out of the blue. It boggles the mind."

"Um…I guess."

"What I *really* find interesting is that night in college that he testified of, only three people would have been present—my client, who I doubt sought out Mr. Albertson. Laney Bang, who is deceased. And of course…yourself."

I see where this is going and vigorously object, but get no love from Figliomini.

"Come to think of it, Mr. Maxon, another piece of evidence mysteriously showed up out of the blue. The video of my client and Laney Bang. To create such a video, one would need both an intimate knowledge of Anderson Estate to be able to conceal a video camera, along with the technical ability to expertly operate the camera. Do I need to remind you that you, yourself, testified this to be accurate when asked by the prosecution.?"

"I didn't make that video!" Maxon replies defensively.

I object, and once again get shot down.

Kerri looks at her magical legal pad. "You also testified that to the best of your knowledge, Laney Bang had never been to Anderson Estate before, which would rule her out. And you testified that my client is too technology challenged to make a video. That leaves you, Mr. Maxon."

"I was with Amber Jazz at the Otesaga Hotel."

"But nobody actually saw you inside your room. Isn't it true that you played looping audio of you and Ms. Jazz at a high volume as a cover? Then you secretly returned to Anderson Estate and waited for my client to leave for his morning jog. After the deed was done, you stealthily returned to Otesaga in disguise, so that you could be seen leaving at 6:30, as if you had just emerged from your room for the first time."

"You think I killed Laney?"

You are finally catching on, Ryan.

"You have always hated living in the shadow of my client. And you've always been in love with Laney Bang, do you deny this?"

Maxon says nothing. The avalanche has begun and there's nothing I can do to stop it. The only person who can save Ryan Maxon is Ryan Maxon.

Kerri takes his silence as an admission, "You couldn't take it—could you!? Seeing them together, the love of your life with the man who always cast a shadow on you. It was too much for you to take!"

I could swear she just informed us that no such affair ever occurred. But maybe the thunder impaired my hearing.

"That's not true—I would never hurt Laney!"

"That explains her lack of apprehension when you approached her. You were her special friend—why would she suspect you were about to stab the life out of her?"

"No!"

"If you couldn't have her, nobody could. And you were going to let Drew pay for it. That's the real reason you went above and beyond the call of duty to set up that meeting, isn't it?"

"That's not true!" Maxon shouts through sobs

"Objection—badgering the witness!" I yell. Not my witness, but I give it one last shot.

"Overruled."

"I'll bet if we searched your belongings we would find that missing murder weapon. Wouldn't we, Mr. Maxon!?"

My objections continue to get shot down. Eventually I give up. I take my seat and watch the show. Like the rest of the gallery, I look on, mesmerized, as Kerri tears apart her own witness.

But then things turn interesting. Maxon's look transforms, almost like he put on a Halloween mask over his usual droopy look. It's the look of a man who has stared into the abyss. He now has nothing to lose, which makes him dangerous.

"Yes, I know where the murder weapon is!" Maxon screams out. The gallery rumbles. Shep and I look at each other with shock.

Maxon isn't done. "That phone call everybody is talking about at 6:19. Well, Drew had more to say than changing the flight. He ordered me back to the estate ASAP. When I arrived by boat, he handed me a plastic bag with a bloody knife and instructed me to dispose of it."

This time Kerri tries to object and Figliomini practically laughs in her face. Typical Lawson move—make a mess and then don't want to clean it up.

Maxon can't be stopped, his voice filled with betrayal, "He told me that a woman showed up and attacked Laney in a jealous rage. He claimed that she came after Laney with a knife and he was forced to act in order to save her, and ended up stabbing the woman in the scuffle. There was never any mention of anyone dying."

Maxon inhales a series of deep breaths. "It looks like Drew's pricey lawyer was going to set me up to take the fall. Loyal Ryan to the rescue. Lucky for me, I took real good care of that knife he gave me." He flashes a cryptic smile at Kerri as the stunned onlookers go silent.

Kerri looks devastated. *Could something ever blow up in your face more?* This will be a cautionary legal fable that will be handed down from generation to generation.

I study Drew and Marissa. They are a complete contrast. He is icy, looking almost unaffected. *Does anything bother this guy?* But Marissa is seething. I wonder if her Maxon insinuations at Touch 'Em All were because she knew he could hurt Drew. Nevertheless, I still feel a deep sadness for her.

When order is somewhat restored, the judge calls for an immediate recess and a full search for the alleged murder weapon. Maxon claims to have buried it on the construction sight of the new Andy Kass Memorial High School that is being built for Otsego County.

I rush by the maniacal press, shouting "no comments," and head to the safety of my office. I should be thrilled by the miraculous breakthrough in our case, but it has left me with a sick feeling. It was too easy, and seemed scripted. Since Shep and I were handed the case, we've been played like puppets—the video, the PE Albertson discovery, and now Ryan Maxon and the murder weapon. I have encountered a lot of bullshit in my life, so I know what it smells like.

All the major networks cut into prime-time programming to show hours of monotonous video of a backhoe digging up the construction sight. The sun hangs dramatically, as if it is cooperating with the search, but eventually relents and sinks to darkness. Hours pass, and if it weren't so sad it would be funny.

Just when the "great dig" begins to appear hopeless, something is found. Speculation and rumors spread like wildfire. An agonizing hour later, Sheriff Opp and an FBI agent named Hawkins hold a triumphant press conference. I think they might hurt themselves patting each other on the back. Opp dramatically holds up a plastic bag that contains a knife. I expect the self-promoter Opp to compare his finding to the discovery of Zinjanthropus at Olduvai Gorge and try to eloquently put it in its correct historical perspective. Hawkins downplays, mentioning lab tests that are required to link the knife to the murder, but everyone knows it's the murder weapon.

A quarter past midnight, Shep bursts into my office, exclaiming, "The tests just came back from the lab. Drew Anderson's prints are all over the knife. And so is Laney's blood. He is going down!"

I fake a smile. "That's great," I say, but my heart isn't in it.

Chapter 72

I walk into the movie theater in the Baseball Hall of Fame and slide into the seat next to George Herman.

The secluded movie theater is a relief from the media frenzy that has surrounded me since court broke yesterday afternoon. The loudmouth experts have spoken—the discovery takes our case from a long shot to a comfortable position in the driver's seat.

On the screen is the movie *Eight Men Out*. It's based on the story of the 1919 Chicago White Sox, who conspired with gamblers to rig the World Series. A conspiracy headed up by Arnold Rothstein or Meyer Wolfsheim, depending on whether you get your information from history books or *The Great Gatsby*.

A deep feeling inside is telling me that I might be involved right in the middle of a grand event being "rigged" in the 21st century.

"I looked into this Tony Rivotti character you asked me about and I got nothing," George informs in a booming whisper. The theater is empty, except for one older couple out of hearing range, even for George.

I nod my head, continuing to listen.

"The guy is like a ghost. No history, no pictures, not even a driver's license or a school photo. Stating the obvious, Tony Rivotti is most likely an alias. Talked to all the collectors who had come in contact with him during the height of his forging, but got mostly anecdotes that border on urban myth. Nobody at Max-Q-Collectibles knows anything, or won't admit it if they do. If he did work for them, he probably dealt directly with Anderson. I guess I could try to put together a composite sketch from those few who came in contact with him."

I was skeptical that the Tony Rivotti investigation would shed any light on this case, so the news doesn't faze me. It was a long shot. I tell George that the sketch won't be necessary, and let him move on to the main reason he summoned me to the movies this morning.

He reaches into his knapsack and pulls out a handful of glossy photos. "We got these from the security camera at the heliport on West 30th Street. It's the woman Lansdale had flown in from his yacht that morning."

I look at the shapely woman wearing a baseball cap and sunglasses, with a flowing mane of blonde hair streaming from the back of the cap. I don't know if she doesn't want to be seen because she's having a no make-up morning or because she's Lansdale's married girlfriend.

"Why doesn't he just get a private helipad on his building to avoid snoops like us looking into him?" I ask.

"No helipads allowed on buildings in Manhattan, kid. The one on West 30th Street is the closest to him when he stays at the Four Seasons, which is on East 57th Street."

So that's why my family didn't have choppers landing on top of the LB&G building. "Because of 9/11?"

"No, goes way back to the accident at the Pan Am building back in 1977."

He hands me more photos. "We also got shots of her moving down 30th Street and then up 12th Avenue. It's amazing how many private security cameras there are in New York City store windows. You could probably trace someone's whole day on film without putting up a camera yourself. Big Brother is here, kid."

"The woman checked out as Lansdale's girlfriend, mistress, or whatever you'd call it, right? Not some hit-woman he hired to get rid of Laney Bang, then hid out on his yacht?"

"Nothing new. Lansdale always had his 'girls' stay on the yacht, and the logbook confirms numerous similar flights over the past year—the neighbors jokingly call it the Lansdale Shuttle. But I still went to double-check with the pilot to see if I could get an ID on the pics."

"And?"

"He's vanished. Got a case of Rivotti disease."

It's interesting, but I don't know what it means. And honestly, all of this became background noise when Maxon dropped the bomb about the knife.

George observes me closely, looking concerned. "What's the matter, kid?"

"The way this whole thing is going down—it seems a little choreographed."

"I agree that it doesn't smell right, but you've done your job, kid. It's all you can do. You presented the evidence you were given. Ultimately the jury will decide Anderson's fate."

"I'd feel a little better if the evidence had been provided in a different manner."

"Lansdale and Anderson are both really powerful, so it makes sense that whoever gifted you the evidence would want to remain anonymous. Same deal with Maxon—he only gave up that murder weapon because he was forced into a corner. He didn't do it willingly."

"That, or Maxon killed her and is framing Anderson."

"He did seem to have a thing for her. I'll keep digging on Maxon, maybe something will come up," he says with a shrug.

I look at my watch—I have to be in court in fifteen minutes. "Got anything else for me?"

George pauses for a moment, as if not sure he should proceed, then says, "There have been a lot of leaks in this case, and sometimes it's hard to tell who plays for which team."

"Tell me about it."

"Just to be safe, I think I should do a scouting report on the home team. How well do you really know your teammates?"

I'm taken aback by the insinuation, but respect his instincts. George doesn't do frivolous. "I don't think that will be necessary. It's basically Shep and me, and I trust her."

"What do you know about her boyfriend?"

As I ponder this, I glance at the screen and watch Shoeless Joe Jackson hit the only home run of the Series. He got a bad rap in the scandal. I wish I could have represented him in his case. Then he would be enshrined here at the Hall of Fame like Mac tells me he should be.

I'm about to reply that Shep doesn't discuss her personal life, but catch myself, thinking how naïve it would sound. "No investigation is necessary," I declare, trying to sound confident.

George nods his pudgy face. "Just wanted to cover all our bases," he says, never lacking for baseball clichés.

I check my watch again, thank George for the info, and head to court.

Shep meets me on the court steps and looks perturbed. "Where were you?" she asks.

"I went to the movies. Then hit the showers at the office."

This is where she would normally chastise me, but we are on the verge of winning the law Super Bowl and even I can't dampen her spirits.

"Why the long face?" she asks. "If you haven't checked the scoreboard today—we're winning."

"Doesn't it bother you, Shep, how this whole thing went down? It's too scripted for my taste."

Shep shakes her head at my skepticism. She lowers her voice as we enter the courtroom, "Anderson is the only one who could have killed her. Simple Lizzie Borden, remember?"

I don't respond.

"You and Gifford Brown have always told me that the obvious is the obvious for a reason. Trust your instincts, Jack."

She smiles at me as court begins.

I'm a sucker for a great smile.

Chapter 73

The courtroom looks the same, but the mood is much different.

I view the Max Q supporters. They all have the same glazed-over look the Lawsons sported when Attorney@Lawson was overtaken at Saratoga, ironically, by Laney Bang's horse.

I look toward Marissa, but she avoids eye contact. I recall her words of the other night. *Open your eyes, Jack. Figure out who really did this. Somebody is setting up my husband.*

My eyes are now open, but I fear that I might be too late. I can't fight off the wild theories that fill my mind, and Ryan Maxon is at the forefront of those thoughts. Was he involved in manipulating the trial to set up Max Q? Perhaps, but I don't believe he'd ever kill the one he loved. Those who claim to kill in the name of love are obsessed, not in love. I'm convinced that Maxon truly loved Laney.

What's undeniable is that Maxon had a knife in his possession that contained both Drew Anderson's fingerprints and Laney Bang's blood. So if Maxon didn't kill her, and Drew is being framed, then there was someone else in the house that morning. My mind wanders to Amber Jazz.

"Mr. Lawson, are you with us today?" Figliomini wakes me from my daydream. *Crazy theories,* I tell myself. Drew Anderson is the only person who could have killed Laney.

I scramble to my feet and join the judge and the other lawyers in chambers. Kerri argues for a mistrial and is immediately shot down. When she seeks a continuance, Figliomini reminds her that she is the one who wanted to fast-track the trial, and denies her again. He does agree to allow a couple of experts to examine the fingerprints and blood found on the knife.

When we return to the courtroom, Kerri puts a plethora of witnesses on the stand who attack the competence and motives of Ryan Maxon. I know she doesn't like to lose, especially to me, but her anguish and despondency strikes me as unusual. She normally is a master of masking emotions.

I know that the only thing that will save Drew Anderson is for him to take that stand, declare his innocence, and fight off all of the accusations. The third prong of our case has always been our most vulnerable area—it just doesn't make sense that he would commit such a crime. After Maxon delivered the murder weapon, getting a conviction should be a fait accompli, but it's a credit to Anderson's stature that it is still in doubt.

My cross-exams consist of five words. "No questions for this witness." It makes us look strong. We have a knife with the victim's blood and the defendant's fingerprints. But when Drew takes the stand, all bets are off, murder weapon or no murder weapon.

A blur of witnesses come and go over the next two weeks. "Put Drew on the stand. C'mon Kerri, put him on the stand," I keep repeating to myself under my breath.

But she doesn't. "The defense rests," Kerri announces and I cringe.

Our summations are bland. Kerri focuses on the alibi of jogger witnesses. *He couldn't have done it.* She paints Ryan Maxon as the jealous assistant who is framing her client. *He had the access and motive to do so.* Most of all, she summarizes the highlights of the life résumé of Drew Anderson.

I want to call time-out to delay the inevitable. But I do my job. Drew Anderson is a mere mortal. Drew Anderson had an affair with Laney Bang and we have the video footage to prove it. Laney Bang was blackmailing him, seeking revenge for events that went back to their college days. Drew Anderson was the only person who could have committed the crime. And *oh by the way*, we have a knife that contains Laney Bang's blood and Drew Anderson's fingerprints.

They are the same points I've made throughout the trial—but this time I'm not quite as sure as I originally was. *Why didn't you put him on the stand, Kerri?*

After Figliomini sternly instructs the jury, they are herded like cattle to begin deliberations. They give the defense their forty-five-minute charity deliberation. As a tribute to the stature of Max Q, it lasts five hours.

I return to the courtroom full of gut-wrenching nerves. The jury foreman stands. Figliomini asks if the jury has reached a verdict. The foreman answers in the affirmative. You can feel the tension.

The jury foreman states that they agreed Drew Anderson has been a great role model who has given endless hours and dollars to charitable causes. He speaks of their admiration for his courageous service to his country. They conclude he is a loyal friend and loving husband. They even believe he was the victim of a blackmail plot. But in the end, they have no choice but to convict him of murdering Laney Bang.

"Guilty!" the foreman's voice echoes throughout the old courtroom. One word that rocks the foundation of a society obsessed with celebrity and hero-worship.

Marissa cries out and falls to the ground in a partial fainting spell. Lansdale helps her to her feet and attempts to comfort her, but she is inconsolable.

Gasps fill the courtroom. The unimaginable has just occurred.

Figliomini bangs the gavel and informs, "Mr. Anderson will be remanded to the Otsego County jail to await sentencing, which will occur two weeks from today.

I check my calendar. October 31. *Halloween—how fitting for this trial.*

Anderson looks strangely calm as he is led off to prison. But he can't take his eyes off Marissa, who in turn, can't stop wailing.

Shep turns to me, and is bewildered by my appearance.

"Jack, are you okay? You are white as a ghost."

My legs feel wobbly, so I sit. "I'm fine, just verdict-nerves."

She accepts my answer without much thought, and returns to her euphoria.

I sit motionless and ask myself, "Did I just send an innocent man to prison?"

Chapter 74

Following the conviction heard round the world, I have become known in what can only be described in complicated legal terms and jargon as "The Man!"

By dusk, Shep has already appeared as a guest on GNZ, CNN, and FOX, and is scheduled for *Good Morning America* tomorrow.

I have as much use for the media now as I did before. None. They're now my best friends, trying to latch onto a "winner." The feeling is not mutual.

One event I do feel obligated to attend is the party being thrown for us at Touch 'Em All. I fight my way through all my new "friends," who are staking out the entrance as if this is a Hollywood premiere, to find Shep waiting for me.

"Where have you been?" she asks, sounding irritated.

"I walked. I needed to clear my head."

"I don't understand you, Jack. Most people work their whole lives and never reach the pinnacle of their profession, yet you are acting like you're a prisoner of war."

"I'm a lawyer, not a press secretary."

"It's our obligation to talk about the case—it's part of our job."

"If Gifford wants a media-hound he should hire Kerri—I'm sure she will be out of a job soon. One thing my family is better at than the law is the blame game."

"You're impossible, Jack. We've been beaten down for months. Now you have a chance to take your bow and deliver some 'I told you so,' but you choose to be your usual brooding self."

We enter the bar and our squabble is ended by a loud "Congratulations!"

We wave in acknowledgment.

Gifford seems to be emceeing the event, while my co-workers, who for the most part can't stand me, look like they are being held at gunpoint. A bunch of county bigwigs are mingling, and even the defense's star witnesses, Opp and Beneke, are present.

Gifford comes through on his promise, and toasts us with champagne.

I need some sanity, so I ditch Shep. Actually, she runs off to work the room like she is running for office. Maybe she is.

I find the definition of sanity—Mac Cirillo. He and Ashley greet me with grins and hugs.

"What is wrong, Jack?" Ashley asks, reading my mood.

"It's nothing," I beg off with a shrug. I can't fool Ashley that easily, but she doesn't push it.

Augie wheels out a large cake to the center of the bar. It features a frosting photo of Shep and me. Besides the obvious disturbing thought of eating my own face, my desire for answers outweighs my craving for dessert. I turn and head for the door.

The minute I hit the cool autumn air, I begin to jog uncomfortably in my suit. About a minute into my run, I am wheezing and forced to stop for a moment. That's when I feel the headlights beaming onto my back.

It's the county-issued Lincoln Navigator with Shep behind the wheel. "Where the hell are you going, Jack?"

"Go back inside, Shep. Or go do another television interview."

I begin to run again. Shep trails slowly behind me in the SUV, shouting at me from her open window. "That's not fair, Jack."

I say nothing.

"I thought we're partners—we are supposed to be honest with each other."

I'm tempted to bring up her mystery boyfriend and identity change, but I choose to keep moving without a word.

Shep presses, "C'mon, Jack, get in."

I debate my options, and they are limited. So I cut my losses and climb in the passenger side. I have no time to lose in the name of pride.

"Where are you headed?" she asks.

"Take me home," I command like she's my cab driver.

"You stormed out of a party in your honor to go *home?"*

I begin to get out of the car.

"Okay, okay," she gives in. "Home it is."

We sit in silence during the ride, until Shep tries to break the ice with a smile, "If you desperately want to get home to catch the replay of my appearance on GNZ, you can stop worrying—I recorded it."

It doesn't work. For the remainder of the short trip neither of us utters a word. A concerned Shep drops me at the Cirillos', but before she leaves, she offers, "Can I do anything to help, Jack?"

"Yes, I need to find Amber Jazz," is all I say, before disappearing into the house.

Within minutes, I buzz out of the garage on the F-41, headed for Anderson Estate.

I roar up the driveway, avoiding the guardhouse by taking a wooded area to its right. I swerve around thick maple trees and proceed toward my answers.

I pass the dark limestone structure of the main house. Gone are the grand lights and lively chatter echoing off the lake that I remember from the charity dinner.

The house appears to be in the middle of a construction project. It strikes me that building onto a house he may never get to see again might make him the ultimate optimist. Or perhaps an innocent man believing in the system.

I continue about a quarter of a mile up the property to the guesthouse. The Sheriff's Office chose not to have Ryan Maxon arrested as a co-conspirator until they gather more evidence. Lesson learned.

I leave the bike and move toward the house. The door is open. I enter, calling out Maxon's name. No sign of him. I look under beds and in closets. The house is a mess and smells of beer and cigarettes.

From Maxon's bedroom on the second floor, a light catches my eye. It is coming from a window in the main house.

I run out of the guesthouse and dash toward the mansion, leaving my motorcycle behind.

I cut across the lawn in front of the house. I stomp through a small reflecting pool, ruining a favorite pair of dress shoes, and under the large white columns. Just like the morning Beneke arrived, the door is unlocked.

I ascend the staircase, my wet shoes squeaking. Upstairs, I find the light on in a large billiards room, but no sign of life.

I open the saloon-style door that leads to the balcony. Even at night, the view of Glimmerglass is breathtaking. My thoughts are momentarily captured by the lights of a small seaplane as it lands effortlessly on the water like a glider.

My eyes move to the fragile looking man sitting in a lawn chair. I know he feels my presence, but doesn't budge. He is contemplating something. I need for him to share those thoughts with me.

Chapter 75

"It's perfect," I greet Ryan Maxon.

Not a twitch of movement or an ounce of surprise. As if he expected my arrival.

"Excuse me?" he answers like I woke him from a daydream.

"Your palace coup, it worked to perfection. Now Drew is out of the way for good. So how does it feel to be king?"

"Things will never be the same without *her.* You should know that better than anyone," he says lifelessly.

Maxon reaches for something and I jump back. It hits me how bad an idea this is. He is a desperate man with nothing to lose, and I have no weapon of any kind.

He picks up a half empty bottle of Foster's.

"I guess we have a lot in common, Ryan—both of us losing the woman we love. Is that why you helped us so much with the trial? The video, the PE Albertson tip, and let's not forget that Oscar-worthy testimony you gave."

Maxon's distant gaze turns irritated. "I don't know what you're talking about. I wanted to help Drew—not hurt him. I didn't plant that video, and I certainly wasn't the one who sent you to Albertson. If you recall, his testimony wasn't favorable towards me."

"You sure didn't sound like someone who was protecting Drew when you were on the stand—in fact, you were the main reason he was convicted."

"Every question you asked me about the day Laney was murdered, I answered truthfully. The knife would have been our secret until the day I died, but your sister chose to attack me. If I didn't reveal the location of the knife, she would have planted it in my back and I'd be the one in prison. I really don't think it was Drew's decision to attack me."

"Burying a murder weapon will buy you a one-way ticket to prison, anyway, whether you eventually came forward or not," I try to leverage the truth out of him.

"I had no idea that was the murder weapon when he asked me to bury it. He told me he acted in self-defense, trying to save Laney from an attacker."

"But he didn't kill Laney, did he?"

He looks confused. "Then perhaps prosecuting him wasn't your best move." He finishes his beer and rolls the bottle off the balcony. It crashes onto the concrete below.

I need more from Maxon. No matter how sure I am that Drew is being set up, I can't explain away the knife that contained both his fingerprints and Laney's blood, especially if Maxon is telling the truth about Drew asking him to get rid of the weapon.

"Perhaps not, but that hide-the-knife story you concocted was his death knell."

"I never once said he killed her."

"Maybe you told the truth about what happened, maybe you didn't, but I know for sure that you lied about what went down in college. And you didn't initially tell the whole truth about what Drew asked you to do in that 6:19 phone call. You only revealed it when you were forced to save yourself."

He opens another bottle of beer and takes a swig. "Withholding information is not the same as lying. When asked directly, I answered honestly. I taped him with countless women over the years. I didn't testify to that either, does that mean I lied?"

"Have you heard of perjury or obstruction of justice?" I push. It would be an open and shut case for us, but I need Maxon to take down a bigger fish.

Maxon smirks, as if he knows something I don't. "Do what you please—I am already dead."

I believe him.

"We both know who killed Laney Bang," I say.

Maxon turns defensive. As much as I truly believe he could care less if he were to go to prison, I know that he will fight to the death to defend Laney's honor. "I told you, I would never ever…"

I cut him off. "I'm not talking about you. Amber Jazz is the one who killed her and you are covering it up."

Maxon's anger switches to hysterical laughter. Not the reaction I expected. "Are you serious?"

I spell out my theory about Amber. That Laney had recruited both Amber and Maxon to blackmail Anderson, but she saw an opportunity to rid herself of the one thing she thought was keeping her from being the biggest star in the world. I leave out the part that I think she conspired with Maxon—who equally wanted Drew out of the way—to fix the trial.

Maxon can't stop laughing. Within his laughter I detect the truth.

"So you are saying Amber didn't kill Laney?" I ask. I'm not as sure as I was a few minutes ago.

"All Amber truly cared about was drugs. And as long as Laney was around, she would always have the money to get her fix. Laney was a softy and would always take her back in, no matter how many times she fell off the wagon. There is no possible way that Amber would kill her meal ticket."

"She claimed fame was her biggest drug."

"Fame was simply an avenue to meet the people who could support her drug addiction."

Suddenly the long arm of the law reaches out and socks me in the noggin. I see the light about how wrong this meeting is. I have illegally entered a residence and didn't inform Maxon of his right to a lawyer. I decide to do this by the book from here on out.

"I need you to come down to my office for an official statement. You should call your lawyer."

"It won't be necessary," he says and stands. "Just give me a minute to change my clothes."

What can I do to stop him? I could get in more trouble for initiating this meeting than Maxon could by fleeing.

He takes a last look at the dark Glimmerglass, then walks back through the saloon door, down a corridor, and disappears into a bedroom. I follow him and stand outside the door.

Moments later, I hear a crash.

Chapter 76

I run into Maxon's room and he's nowhere to be found. I move to the window and notice that he used a scaffolding from the construction project to get to the ground.

Motion lights flash on as Maxon sprints across the lawn. One minute he's lifeless—now he looks as if he's training for the Olympics.

I race down the staircase, dash outside, and spot him in the distance. He is running toward the guesthouse. Suddenly I remember—my motorcycle!

I chase after him, slipping in my wet shoes. I reach the guesthouse, ready to collapse. The bike is still there—relief.

But it's fleeting. I hear the crackling of trees—Maxon has entered the woods behind the guesthouse. He is on his turf now.

I follow him into the woods. Branches snap back in my face, slowing me down, and I lose visual contact. When I come out the other side, Maxon is nowhere to be found. Then I hear the hum of a motor. I first think of my motorcycle, but it is coming from the area by the lake.

My eyes adjust enough to see him leaving via motorboat—the same way he came and went the night of the murder. I run to the edge of the lake and helplessly watch as the boat skims over Glimmerglass.

I search frantically for another boat, but they all lack motors. It's as if he planned this whole thing.

I have nothing else to do, so I yell at him, "Get back here, Maxon!" It's no use—I doubt my desperate shouts even reach him.

But as if he heard me, the boat stops. Maxon stands. He appears tiny, about a quarter-mile away from me. He walks to the edge of the boat. I now know what he's doing. "Ryan—no!" I yell.

But it is too late. Ryan Maxon launches himself into Otsego Lake.

I frantically search for a boat motor, but it's hopeless. There is no way I'd be able to reach him in time, anyway. I stand by the water and desperately shout for help. But there isn't another house for a mile.

I return to the guesthouse and call 911. It's now only a recovery mission. Soon the cavalry arrives. Opp, Beneke, Gifford Brown, and Shep are the notables.

"What the hell were you doing?" Gifford barks at me. A few hours ago he's toasting my brilliance, now I'm just another ass to kick.

I claim that I was seeking answers concerning perjury and obstruction. It sounds even less believable when I say it out loud, and Gifford unleashes another verbal barrage on me.

I take my deserved medicine, and then watch as Maxon is returned to shore in a body bag.

Gifford leaves to take out his anger out on an unsuspecting cigarette. Shep approaches. She hands me a police-issued poncho, as a light rain has begun to fall.

"You look cold, Jack."

I remain quiet, staring out at the dark lake.

"Are you going to tell me why you really came out here tonight?" she asks softly.

"Not now, Shep."

"I found out where Amber Jazz is."

This grabs my attention, but when I notice her grim expression, I know it isn't good.

"They found her in a seedy motel near Los Angeles—dead of an overdose. I guess she was out there to shoot one of her movies. No foul play is suspected, but I pushed for a full investigation, especially with the unique circumstances of her testimony."

There's no need. And knowing now what Maxon had planned for tonight, he had no motive to lie about Amber's possible involvement in Laney's murder. It wasn't her. I was wrong … again.

"Thanks," I say and dejectedly walk toward the lake. Shep turns her back on me in annoyance.

I sit down at the edge of the lake. I stare at the dark, misty water just as Maxon did, contemplating. I glance at the tall grass on my left, where land meets the water's edge. I notice a plastic case with writing on it. *To Jack Lawson,* it reads.

Chapter 77

Despite the fog hampering visibility, I can still make out the silver Mercedes SUV pulling out of the parking lot of the Otesaga Hotel.

My Maxon/Amber theory has been shot down, and not just because they are both dead. But I have a new theory based on the contents of the parting gift Maxon left me last night. It's one that I have an urge to discuss with Drew Anderson's lawyer this morning.

Dressed casually in a sweater and jeans, I pull my motorcycle in front of the entrance. I move to block the oncoming SUV.

Kerri slams her brakes, the vehicle skidding to a slip-sliding stop. Her look says she will enjoy dislodging a few of my favorite internal organs with her steel bumper, but she decides against it.

I leave the motorcycle on the side of the road and head for her vehicle. I expect her to peel out, once again pulling the football away. But she remains idling and unlocks the doors. I get in before she has second thoughts.

"What the hell are you doing, Jack? Trying to pull a Maxon?" she says, devoid of compassion. I can tell she's no fan of the man who wrecked her case. *Or did he?*

I clear boxes of legal documents off the passenger seat, along with the historic copy of today's *New York Globe*. A calm Drew Anderson is pictured during the reading of the verdict. The headline simply reads: *Max Q Guilty!*

The rear of the SUV is full of taped-up boxes. "You seem to be in a hurry to get out of town."

She hits the accelerator and we head up the wooded Route-31. "The trial's over, I'm returning to the city. Are you here to rub it in?"

"Drew Anderson didn't kill Laney Bang."

"No shit, Sherlock. But come to think of it, that would have been much more helpful information before you convinced a jury otherwise."

"We got a lot of help with our case."

"I hope Maxon is rotting in hell."

"Actually, sis, I think you are the one who gave us that help."

She laughs nervously. "And why would I do that, Jack?"

I take out my knapsack and remove the disk Maxon left for me. The Lawsons are always equipped with the best toys, so I insert it into the DVD player and it begins to play on the dashboard monitor.

Kerri skids the car to a stop in the middle of the road. It's another in the long line of Max Q sex tapes shot at Anderson Estate. This one, again, features the man himself. But the actress co-starring with him is none other than Kerri Lawson.

For the first time in my life I find my sister to be speechless.

I speak for her, "Don't be shy, sis. No reason to let little things like dignity and self-respect get in your way now."

"Where did you get this?" she demands.

I turn the video off without responding. Seeing your sister in the act is not something you want to view more than you have to.

After an extended silence, a pained-looking Kerri begins to spill her guts, "Drew and I had a relationship. I was his personal lawyer during the Tony Rivotti investigation, and we spent endless hours together—and things just happened."

"No offense, but you've never struck me as a 'things just happened' type."

She inhales a deep breath and slowly blows it out. "He made me feel like nobody ever had. But he never lied to me or gave me any happily-ever-after illusions that he was going to leave Marissa. He was crazy about her—maybe a little too crazy—and I knew she was the one who would always control his heart. And I was right. He eventually stopped seeing me, but we maintained a professional relationship. Nothing went on during the trial."

I fake wiping tears from my eyes. "Oh, there is more."

I change disks in the DVD player. Having an affair with her client is the least of her worries.

Chapter 78

The screen again displays Drew and Kerri in action. But this time Drew stops and stands in all his glory. He looks off camera, noticing that someone has entered the room. It isn't just someone. It's Laney Bang!

Kerri begins to argue with Drew—she wants no part of what is about to happen. It's pretty clear that she doesn't want to share her Max Q. She then storms out of the room, but before exiting she turns back and shouts at them, "Mark my words, you will regret this!"

"Where is this going, Jack?" she asks tersely. "Or are you just looking to embarrass me more than you already have? I guess it's not enough that you sent an innocent man to prison."

For different reasons, we both have seen enough of the video, and I shut it off.

"So you knew Laney Bang long before July 23?" I stick to the facts and don't let her muddy the waters with her bravado.

"Knew her?" Kerri responds, incredulously. "I *made* her. Do you think it's a coincidence that when she met up with Drew that all of a sudden she went from the queen of the underworld to a mainstream superstar?"

"That doesn't sound very LB&G. Last I checked, Lawsons are lawyers, not porn managers. But then again, I've been out of the loop lately."

Kerri frowns at me. "It was Drew's idea. Back when he was having his financial troubles, he had been looking for new revenue streams. He'd seen Laney in one of her movies and thought with the right management he could make her the biggest star in the world. I acted as his go-between, and eventually became her official representative. Of course it had to be completely behind the scenes, only the top partners at the firm knew—it was not a partnership that would be acceptable. But nobody had a problem when they cashed the checks. Laney Bang was a goldmine."

If what she's telling me is true, that means the Grand Poobahs at LB&G had knowledge of this, which means Ethel likely knew. I recall her words at the racetrack about how women like Laney were ruining society, or something to that effect. But this might work out well for Kerri, as the dirt she has on the firm might provide some job security.

The ironic part is that while Laney was desperately working to get close to Max Q to launch her blackmail plan, including attending that New Year's party in Vegas, Anderson actually came to her, looking to turn her into a star.

I get back on track, "You had dealings with the defendant *and* the victim in the case. At the very least, your behavior is unethical. But this went beyond unethical, didn't it, Kerri?"

"What's that supposed to mean?"

"You gave Laney Bang more success than anyone could imagine and she returned the favor by stealing Drew away from your bed. You were insanely jealous. I saw the look in your eyes when you told them they'd regret it, you were playing for keeps.

"The more I think about it, who had a better opportunity than you? As Laney's manager, you knew that she would be at the estate, and based on your relationship with Drew, you were aware of his regimented schedule. It's also why she let you get close without a fight. Maybe your excuse was another big business deal you needed to talk to her about. And we always assumed that it was Laney on that 911 tape, but now I wonder if it's really you disguising your voice."

She looks incensed. "And I was able to pull this off all by myself? I'm good, but not that good, Jack."

"You didn't, and you're not. Your first helper was someone who wanted to rid the world of Laney Bang as much as you did—James Lansdale. And his helicopter served as the proverbial getaway car. It was his way of shaking the hand of the one who killed Laney."

I hand her the photo that George Herman provided me of the woman getting off Lansdale's helicopter at 8:30 a.m. "You toss on a wig and attach some artificial curves, and he gives you a lift back to Manhattan. You were sitting at your desk at LB&G when your client calls from jail, charged with murder."

Kerri looks like she just bit into a lemon. "That's preposterous!"

I ignore her theatrics and press on, "Who better to play the strings of the trial than the defense lawyer? Your pleas for Drew in court were heart-warming, but I've known you since we were kids. You acted too well. I know Kerri Lawson doesn't have that kind of heart in her."

"You aren't going to have a heart either, Jack—because I'm going to rip it out of your chest!"

"Then it was time for Drew to 'regret it' and you played us all like a puppeteer. As his lawyer, you had access to his film library, so you could provide us the video when it looked like we might not prosecute. Then when our case was looking bleak, you provided the PE Albertson tip, which you learned from Laney while working on her memoir as her manager. But I'm still confused who your tattooed messenger was, Kerri—another one of your boy toys?"

She glares at me. "Get over yourself, Jack. First of all, that isn't me in that helicopter photo. I was in the office by five that morning, check the records. And secondly, that is the dumbest story I have ever heard!"

"I'm not sure I trust anyone from LB&G to back up your story, especially with the ethics issues I just learned of. And Ryan Maxon—your co-star in that great off-Broadway play you acted out in court—didn't think it was the dumbest story he ever heard. His conscience must have gotten the best of him, which is why he gave me the video. But luckily for you, he isn't around to testify to that."

Kerri looks dazed. She then does something that I've never seen in my thirty-one years on this planet. She begins to cry.

When she gets herself under control, she says, "Off the record, my client revealed to me who he believes killed Laney, and it certainly wasn't me."

"That's convenient. So who killed her, sis?"

"I can't tell you the name. Drew's life is already in danger, and if the truth ever gets out, he's as good as dead."

"Is convenineter a word?"

"I could care less what you think. I love him, and I just want him to be safe."

There's that love word again. I look skeptically at her. Her tears do not fool me. Ever since we were kids, she has been the master of faking honest emotion to con her way out of a hole she dug for herself. But this takes it to a whole new level.

She looks tired and drained, but doesn't look like a murderer. I don't know what to think anymore, so I decide I need to go right to the horse's mouth.

"Start driving," I command.

"Where are we going?" she asks, irritated.

"We are going to get your client a new trial."

Chapter 79

We meet Drew Anderson in a private meeting room at the Otsego County Jail. He wears an orange jumpsuit and is handcuffed. He looks weary, but lingering behind his exhaustion is the self-assured presence that has always comforted people, made them believe his words, and inspired them to strive to be like him.

The guards leave—since Kerri is his lawyer, we are granted privacy—and Drew sits down at a table across from us.

I meticulously outline to him the cold hard facts that his lawyer committed a serious act of unethical behavior, and that I'm confident he can get a new trial. I feel relief that there's a way to rectify an egregious error that would send an innocent man to prison, perhaps for the rest of his life. A new trial will be the fair and just resolution.

"I had a fair trial and Kerri did an amazing job under the circumstances," he astounds me with the answer. His voice is unyielding.

"This is your get out of jail free card," I reply, not sure that he understood what I just told him.

"Please, Drew, throw me under the bus if you have to. You must get out of here—it's not safe for you," Kerri pleads.

"I have said what I have to say. I will not put Marissa through another trial. It's important for her to move on with her life. Another trial will just be more years of limbo where she has false hope. That knife with my fingerprints on it isn't going anywhere."

He is in a trance-like state, appearing to be a man who has accepted his destiny, no matter how wretched it is.

"Ryan Maxon is dead," I blurt out.

I hoped to be more tactful, but desperate times call for desperate measures. I inform him that the death was suicide, and the way he took his life would cast suspicion on his past testimony. It's a legal miracle, or at the very least, a second chance for a man facing life in prison.

The news doesn't seem to impress him. "I have made my decision. No appeals. No new trial. Now let's all move on with our lives."

Kerri begs. She is willing to be disbarred. She is willing to give up her inheritance. To be publicly exposed, ridiculed, and possibly tried for murder herself. I am stumped. Is this is the acting job of the century or the truth?

I consider why he won't accept a new trial. Is he protecting someone? Has somebody threatened Marissa? What is the motive behind Kerri's incessant claims that he's not safe in prison?

"Are you the one who chose not to testify in your defense?" I ask him point blank.

"We're done here," he avoids my question and stands.

I look to Kerri, but she looks away, giving me my answer. "Who are you protecting?" I demand.

He looks me square in the eye. "I will not put people through this again. The jury has spoken and they have ruled me to be guilty. I await my sentencing."

"Are you willing to live your life without Marissa?" I play my last card.

His face crumbles. "I think you would know that feeling more than anyone, Jack. Another trial might kill her and I love her more than I love myself. I have no choice."

His voice is calm. He must have ice in his veins.

"You aren't safe!" Kerri cries out, as Drew leaves with guards.

He stops abruptly, turns back, and stares me down. "Jack—why are you so interested in my well-being? You just achieved one of the great legal victories of all-time."

"It was a great legal victory, but not a victory for justice. You didn't kill her and you know it."

The door buzzes open. And by his choice, Drew returns to a prison cell.

Chapter 80

I must convince Drew to accept a new trial and there is only one person I think he'll listen to. I speed the F-41 south down the New York Thruway.

I station myself on 161st Street. Friday afternoon traffic is heavy and honking. It's even more congested than usual due to a playoff game at nearby Yankee Stadium, scheduled for later in the evening.

Marissa steps out of the courthouse. She looks physically similar to when I last saw her descend these steps back in July. But her movements are foreign. It's as if each step is thought out, lacking the confident bounce.

It's only the second day since the verdict. The press swarms her. Marissa looks like she's using every ounce of her fortitude to fight off tears.

I make my move. I rev the engine and speed toward the pack of media sharks that surrounds her. I fishhook the bike, causing a panic-filled evacuation, and leaving only a frightened Marissa.

When I flip up my visor, her face twists with anger. The last person she wants to see is the man who just took her husband away from her. But her choices are limited.

"Get on," I urge.

She takes another look at the media that is moving back in her direction. All of a sudden I don't look so bad.

"Hurry!"

This time she gives in and hops on the back, wrapping her arms tightly around my chest. I speed off to the Anderson's home on 123rd Street in Upper Manhattan.

It is an eight-story building that they converted from apartments into a townhouse. From the outside, it doesn't live up to the Max Q standard. A typical redbrick apartment building with a rusting fire-escape stairwell that scars the exterior. No awning or doorman. And the neighborhood is more grit than paradise.

Without a word, Marissa gets off the bike and walks toward the building. I park and follow. I need to talk to her, whether she wants to talk to me or not.

The interior looks much more like the place I visualize the power-couple residing. I stand in the living room area between an over-sized couch and a simple glass coffee table. My eyes wander to a large decorative fireplace that anchors the room. Above it hangs an enormous painted mural on the twenty-foot high wall. It's a collage made up of multiple images of Drew. As a young boy, as football star at FSU, army hero with a buzzed haircut, and the suave businessman of current day. No mug shots are included.

Marissa wanders into a large country-style kitchen—still not uttering a single word in my direction. It features cherry wood cabinets, a huge wine cabinet, and numerous shiny pots and pans hanging above an island stove. She acts as if I'm not there. The quiet is becoming awkward.

She finally breaks the silence, "You stole my life, you son of a bitch—now I'm going to kill you!"

Before her words register, she reaches for a skillet and hurls it in my direction—it cracks off the glass coffee table. Then a saucepan whizzes by me. When she reaches for a large kitchen knife, I look to duck for cover.

But just before she launches it in my direction, her body slumps and I notice her eyes welling with tears.

"You took my husband away from me," she cries out.

"That's what I'm here to talk to you about—Drew didn't kill her."

She wipes the tears from her face. "You're too late, Jack. You should have figured it out earlier."

"He can get a new trial. I discovered things about Kerri that are totally unethical, but I need you to convince him. He won't listen to me."

"That they slept together? I hope you can do better than that, Jack," she says. The response surprises me.

"Not only did he have an affair with Kerri," I hesitate, uncertain how this next part is going to go over, "but he was intimately intertwined with both Laney and his lawyer. And I have it on video. The same lawyer who refused to put him on the stand in his defense."

Marissa takes a seat on the couch. "This is not news, Jack. I talked to Drew an hour ago, and he told me that he talked to you. He said he refuses to put me through another trial, no matter the consequences. I love him, but he is the most stubborn man on the planet."

I want to comfort her, but it feels wrong.

"It was my fault," she unexpectedly says, tears dripping from her eyes.

I sit beside her, bemused. "What was your fault?"

"I pushed him into the affair with Kerri. Despite popular mythology, Drew isn't perfect. But he was to me and I would do anything to please him. Before we were to be married, I discovered his video-making hobby, addiction, whatever you want to call it. I made it clear that if we got married, he would be out of the video business."

I listen intently. Night has fallen on New York and only lights of neighboring apartment houses shine through the windows.

"The issue never came up again until one day when he came to watch me in court. The guy I was defending was a good-looking nineteen-year-old kid from the Upper East Side who had robbed a couple of homes in the Bronx with his friends. That night, Drew casually brought up that he would love to see me with the man from court, and he wanted to have it filmed.

"At first I thought he was kidding, but when I realized he was serious, I went ballistic—didn't talk to him for weeks. It didn't stop him, and he has this convincing way about him. He would chip away at me, saying things like, 'You said I couldn't make any more films, but you never said anything about yourself,' but I refused. I don't know what eventually made me give in, perhaps because I was always so deathly afraid of losing him, or maybe I was just a sucker for that killer smile, I don't know.

"And I should have trusted my first instinct—it turned into a disaster. Drew became so cold toward me. He no longer looked at me the same way, but he couldn't be outwardly angry, since it was his idea. He bottled it all inside and became more and more distant. It hung over us every moment. That's when the Rivotti investigation began and he started spending most of his time away from home … with Kerri. So basically, I drove him into her arms."

"What about Laney Bang?" I ask, intrigued, and maybe a little bit titillated.

She straightens her head and displays a sardonic look. A more recognizable Marissa. "That wasn't an affair, Jack—that was sex. An affair involves feelings and intimacy."

"But you and Drew seem so in love—you must have worked it out?"

The cold leaves her face and a proud look takes over. "We did—started from square one and built it back up. I can't tell if we fell in love all over again, or that our love just never left, but we ended up stronger than ever. That's what makes all this even harder…

Her voice trails off.

"You didn't mind Kerri representing your husband in his trial?"

"I didn't blame Kerri for loving Drew. Actually, I felt sad for her. I can't even imagine loving someone you can't be with." She swallows hard. "Like I said, it was my fault, and she's a great lawyer. We both wanted the same thing—Drew to be free."

She momentarily pauses, before asking, "Can we discuss something else, like who framed my husband?"

"What was the guy's name again that Drew brought into your marriage?" I try to ask casually. But she makes me nervous and nothing I do flows freely.

I catch a small smile escape from the corner of her mouth. "Once a prosecutor always a prosecutor, huh, Jack? Want to check out my story? His name was Jordan, like the basketball player. Now you know name, age, and time frame of the case. Is that enough information for you, counselor?"

I laugh to myself at how un-smooth I am. I file that tidbit of information in my memory hard drive and change the subject back to the case. "Ryan Maxon didn't kill her."

I expect her to argue, but she doesn't. "I know."

"You know? But you insinuated…"

"I never accused Ryan Maxon of murdering Laney Bang, so please don't put words in my mouth. I was just trying to get you to open your mind and see the whole field. Maxon was an obvious choice, yet you overlooked him. But maybe in retrospect you were smart to avoid the obvious candidate."

"Your husband is afraid of somebody. He might even know who the real killer is. Do you think it's Lansdale?"

A strange look comes over her face, and then a laugh. "Jimmy is a good friend to both Drew and me. He puts on this tough guy front, but he is nothing but a big pussycat. Besides, he only cares about one thing these days and framing my husband would take too much time away from that."

"The smut fighting business?"

"No—Jimmy is in love. Maybe for the first time in his life—he's finally discovered that life is more than a quest for the best toys. Better late than never, I guess. He freaked when you brought up the helicopter flight in his interview—it's all he obsessed over for days. He's very protective of the relationship—it's kind of a sticky situation."

"By sticky situation, you mean that she's married."

"It's more complicated than that. The marriage has either been annulled, or it's in the process of such, something to that effect. The problem is that the husband is a powerful man who still thinks she is his property." She pauses. "I really shouldn't be talking about this—let's get back to my husband's stubbornness."

I file away her words, and move on, "Kerri claims that Drew told her who is setting him up, but won't tell me because Drew's life would be in danger if she did. But I think Drew believes that you're the one in danger, and is protecting you."

She grabs my hand and tingles shoot through me. "Come with me"

Chapter 81

Marissa leads me down a hallway to a small bedroom with pink and blue painted balloons on the wall. She looks despondent.

"We had planned on having a baby." Her voice is filled with defeat, which makes me feel even worse.

She moves a crib, then kneels down and pulls away a small cutout of carpet. It exposes a safe that is built into the floor. She puts in a digital combination and the safe opens.

She reaches in and pulls out a manila envelope. "When we started having our problems, Drew was so distant, and sometimes wouldn't come home for days. My first thought was that he was seeing someone else, so I hired a PI. Not my proudest moment, although that's how I found out about him and your sister. But there was something else, which had me even more concerned … maybe even scared."

She offers me a handful of photos from the envelope. "I overheard him on the phone one night in an intense conversation. And being that I was the jealous wife, I thought it might be Kerri or some other woman, so I picked up the other end. It wasn't her. It was a man's voice—a deep voice—and I only caught the end of the call. But enough to hear him mention Rivotti, and then threaten to kill me. Drew tried to calm the man, suggesting they meet. I jotted down the time and place of the meeting, and passed it along to my PI."

I look at the first photo and my head almost explodes. It's Figliomini with Drew, in what looks like an intense conversation. Suddenly I have a good idea why Drew doesn't want a new trial. The judge is his enemy, which means he has no chance. It also makes sense why Kerri is worried about Drew's safety, as I'm sure Figliomini has many connections within the prison.

"The same guy who ruled admissible the illegal search, the video, PE Albertson's testimony. I could go on," Marissa adds.

I'm about to re-argue the legal points on those subjects, but the second photo captures me. The time printed on the bottom says that it was taken twenty minutes after the photo of Drew and the judge. This photo is of Figliomini and Ryan Maxon.

"The same guy who cemented my husband's fate with the discovery of that knife," she states the obvious.

Marissa puts the photos back in the safe. "You can't tell Kerri that I had Drew followed. She tells him everything, and he would go out of his mind if he knew I'd discovered that he might be in danger."

I nod in agreement, but I have my own reasons not to tell Kerri—that I don't trust her. I think of the photo I just viewed of Figliomini and Maxon. "You just told me that Ryan Maxon wasn't involved."

She looks exasperated. "I said that I believe he didn't kill her, and I never accused him of doing so. And I didn't say anything about whether he was involved or not involved. For all I know, these photos might be an innocent business meeting, unrelated to the case. That's what I need you to figure out."

She pauses, her eyes growing deathly serious. "Jack, I was honest with you when I told you I'll do whatever it takes to free my husband—lie, cheat, you name it. But it's really important that you listen closely when I speak specifically about the facts of this case—because I might be the only one who is speaking the truth to you."

We return to the living room area and I plop on the couch in exhaustion. Marissa sits next to me, tucking her legs underneath her. I notice a framed picture of the two of them in happier times. They are scuba diving in some exotic locale.

Marissa notices my interest in the photo. “That was taken in Jamaica, three years ago. Drew loves to scuba dive. I think it allows him to temporarily leave this world and enter another. He loves his life, but it comes with a lot of pressure and responsibility. Being a national role model is a 24/7 job.”

“If we don’t convince him to pursue a new trial, he is going to permanently leave this world. And enter one where there is no scuba diving.”

Marissa contends that we need to find a different avenue, since Drew will never agree to a new trial. Especially if he believed it put her in danger. It’s a standoff, and the conversation lapses into a quiet malaise. I am out of ideas.

My grumbling stomach breaks the awful silence. Marissa can’t help but to laugh, breaking the tension. “Have you eaten today, Jack?”

Come to think of it, I haven’t.

Marissa gets up and heads toward the kitchen. “I’ll make you something.”

She grabs a pot from above the stove, before turning to the refrigerator. She begins to open it, and then stops. She stands frozen like a statue. Her back is to me, but I can tell she has begun to cry. Then as if a trap door opened beneath her, she drops to the floor.

I hurry into the kitchen. Marissa is curled in a ball on the floor. “Drew is the one who always does the cooking,” she says and angrily tosses the metal pot across the floor, reverberating a clanging sound.

I sit next to her. Marissa’s lip is quivering and I instinctively reach out to touch it. She looks up and our eyes meet. All I can see is Reyanne.

I know I’m too close, but it’s too late. Within seconds our lips meet.

Chapter 82

I awake to the sounds of honking horns, reminding me that I spent the night in the city. It makes me long for my annoying alarm clock.

Marissa is nowhere to be found. I get up and look for her. I find her standing by the hallway window in just a T-shirt, deep in thought and looking utterly despondent.

Without looking at me, she says, "We made a mistake, Jack."

First I convict a guy for a crime he didn't commit and then sleep with his wife. Not my best week. I feel regret pound me in the gut.

I step beside her and push her hair out of the way of her sad eyes. She's right, it was a mistake—and an even worse judgment on my part to think that I could ever fill the void that Reyanne left, even temporarily. But I can still get Marissa back her version of Reyanne. I know I need to do everything in my power to give them a chance.

I must get Drew Anderson out of prison.

The trip back upstate provides time to think. My legal compass had always been impeccable, but it has betrayed me in this case. And I broke my own golden rule—keep an open mind. I lectured Shep about it, but mine was closed throughout the trial, until Marissa re-opened it for me.

I know I'm rationalizing my actions, but I can't shake the thought that feeling so close to Reyanne last night has knocked my compass back into orbit, and I feel that my instincts have returned.

That doesn't mean that I'll be able to bring Laney the justice I promised her, and I will be forced to live with that for the rest of my life. I am resigned to the fact that her killer will likely never be caught. The person or group that manipulated her trial must be a powerful entity, and I've seen firsthand how the powerful can make things disappear when they desire.

The possibilities of who was behind her death seem to grow every day. Kerri, Maxon, Amber, Lansdale, the mysterious woman from the helicopter, and those whose possible involvement I don't even want to contemplate. One of those is Figliomini. I can't get the photo of him and Drew out of my mind, and it would make sense as to why Drew is refusing a new trial, but my legal idealism won't allow me to believe that a sitting judge could be involved in such a thing.

I look up in the sky and I feel Reyanne reaffirming my belief, urging me to block out the past and trust my instincts. And they are now telling me that Drew Anderson didn't murder Laney Bang.

I go straight to the office to begin formulating my plan, expecting it to be empty on the weekend. It's a rainy Saturday afternoon, which matches my mood. I step inside and the quiet is soothing.

An explosive sneeze breaks the silence, causing me to jump. Another sneeze fills the air and I apprehensively call out, "Hello?"

"Jack?" echoes a female voice. It's coming from Shep's office. I find her sitting behind a desk that is piled in paperwork.

"It's Saturday, Shep, what are you doing here?" I ask. My heart rate returns to normal.

"I guess I could ask you the same question," she retorts. She begins examining my clothing, and probably analyzing the smell of perfume.

"I have a lot of cases backing up that I need to get to now that the Anderson case is over," I lie.

"It's not over yet," Shep says, holding up a stack of papers. "The sentencing is less than two weeks away."

Even though I know this, it still startles me when I hear it from her mouth.

I don't know exactly what I am going to do, but one thing I do know is that I must keep Shep out of it at all costs.

"Where have you been, Jack?" she asks me. "I called you last night…I was worried about you."

"I was in the city—had some business to take care of."

Shep's expression changes. I can see her putting pieces of a puzzle together. "It's funny, Jack, I saw some video of Anderson's wife on the news. The reporters were chasing after her like hungry paparazzi and a guy swooped in on a motorcycle and swept her away."

I try to remain calm. "It's terrible how they won't let her alone. What's the funny part?"

"That it looked like the same motorcycle you have. Isn't it a coincidence that you were in the city and..."

Shep gives me the opening I need to begin pushing her as far away from me as possible.

"What are you getting at?" I snap.

She backpedals, not expecting the forceful response. "I'm not getting at anything."

"That's the problem with you—you always have an agenda!"

"Jack, I didn't mean..."

"You got what you wanted, Shep. You're on the fast-track now. So why don't you go do your television shows and write your books. While you keep working on the Trial of Max Q, I have work to do on cases that won't get me on the front page."

Shep looks mystified. "What are you saying, Jack?"

"I'm saying the case is over. You got what you wanted, now stay out of my life!"

She looks like she is going to cry, but the fighter in her won't allow it. "Jack, I don't know what you think I meant, but..."

I walk out of her office in a huff.

"Jack, if this is because I tried to push you into doing those interviews, I'm sorry," she says, searching for reasons for my unforeseen shift in behavior. "I thought we were partners?"

I stop at the nearest desk and pick up a pile of documents and throw them wildly in anger. Shep looks horrified.

"Partners?" I shout derisively. "Partners trust each other—not make accusations about me and the wife of a murderer I put away. Have you always told me the truth?"

"C'mon, Jack, that's not fair."

Marissa's words stick with me. "If I remember correctly, you never mentioned your annulment to a controlling and powerful man. And you're quite mysterious when it comes to your boyfriend."

I march into my office and slam the door, leaving Shep searching for answers.

Chapter 83

I stand paralyzed, looking at my desk. It is piled with newspapers and magazines.

The first thing to catch my eye is a picture of Shep and me on the cover of *Newsweek*. It reads: *Legal Eagles—the story of two young prosecutors and how they slayed Goliath.*

I recognize the *Max Q Guilty!* headline from the *New York Globe* that I had seen earlier in Kerri's car. I sift through more newspapers from the day after the verdict. A sticky-note is lying on top of them. *Thought you'd like to see these. You are the best lawyer on the planet, Jack, and it was an honor to work with you...your partner, Shep.*

It rips at my insides.

I sift through more paraphernalia. The Democrats, Republicans, and Libertarians all have provided information packets and are urging me to run for office.

I can pick my next job. Everybody wants a piece of the brilliant young lawyer who took down Goliath. I wonder if they still would want me if they knew the truth.

I check my voice-mail messages. More offices to run for, requests for interviews, and products to endorse. Then a familiar voice crackles into my ear.

Ethel Lawson is falling all over herself to praise me. She calls my victory, "The greatest moment in two hundred and fifty years of great moments by the Lawson family," and closes with, "We need to talk in the next few weeks to discuss your bright future, Jackson. I think 'youngest partner in the history of the firm' has a nice ring to it." I can't erase the message quick enough.

I clear off my desk with one push and the clutter crashes onto the floor. I sit down with legal pad and pen in hand.

I already took the first step this morning. After leaving Marissa's place, I headed straight to LB&G. Knowing the sweat shop that it is, I was guaranteed a nice-sized audience when I walked past the gold plated doors, even on a Saturday.

It was a priceless moment. I just hope their medical plan covers dropped jaws. On one hand, I'm a traitor who just publicly humiliated them. But I'm also a Lawson, and not just any old Lawson. I am sure the term "youngest partner in history of the firm" has made the rounds. *Do you want to be the person to call security on your future boss?*

I wasn't there to gloat. I had business to attend to. I went directly to Kerri's office, where she was furiously packing boxes. I'm sure the associates could imagine the fight-of-all-fights when we shut the door.

They actually would have witnessed me pleading with Kerri to convince Drew to change his mind.

Kerri's eyes were puffy and she looked like she hadn't slept a wink. "We have to get him out of there—he isn't safe, Jack!"

I pushed hard, but she wouldn't budge when it came to why he wasn't safe, or who she believes the real killer to be, again citing her willingness to protect Drew at any cost. And it's not as if I can sit down with the judge and discuss the situation.

I don't trust Kerri enough to bring up the Figliomini subject. In fact, having to put my trust in Kerri at all is a nightmare scenario—especially when I consider that she still hasn't been ruled out as being the killer, or the one who manipulated the trial. But sometimes you have to make a deal with the devil. She is the only one who can get the kind of access to Drew that I need.

I provided Kerri with the key to a P.O. Box in the Bronx that I rented earlier in the morning. From here on out, it will be our only form of communication.

“We have to get him out of there, Jack,” she pleaded once more as I left.

“Get him to take a new trial,” I bargained back. But something tells me that Drew Anderson has his mind made up. As is mine—I won’t be responsible for taking away an innocent person like those subway bombers took Reyanne away from this world. I made this mess and now I’m going to clean it up. No matter the personal cost.

Chapter 84

Half past midnight, I leave the deafening silence of my office and drive the empty streets of Cooperstown. The only visible sign of life is coming from Touch ’Em All, while the rest of the town has seemingly called it a night. Then as if someone upstairs is trying to warn me, the night sky opens and releases a torrential downpour.

I arrive back at the Cirillos’. I run to my apartment and change out of my soaking wet clothing.

The new venue doesn’t improve my formulation abilities. As I listen to the rain violently pounding on the roof, I’m overtaken by hunger. I remember the cold pizza that I left in the refrigerator a few days back. So much has happened in just a few days. The verdict, Maxon’s suicide, Amber’s death, Marissa…

I shake her image out of my mind and head to the main house, hoping to beat Mac to my leftovers.

I tiptoe into the kitchen, but I’m too late. Mac and Ashley are sitting at the kitchen table, eating my desired pizza and drinking glasses of red wine.

"What are you doing up at this hour, Jack?" Ashley greets me.

Mac doesn't look up from his pizza. Priorities.

"I got a craving. I think I'm pregnant," I attempt to joke.

I drag a heavy wooden chair over the timber floorboards and fall wearily into it.

"What are you two doing up?" I shift the emphasis.

"Had a craving. I think I'm pregnant, too," Ashley touchés with a grin.

Mac finally looks up. "If you want some real wine, Jack, I can open a bottle. This is just cranberry juice—if you haven't heard, my wife is pregnant."

"We can still pretend," Ashley adds, holding up her wine goblet to toast me.

Mac raises his glass to match. "To Jack Lawson—the greatest lawyer in the world! We are honored to be in his company!"

"Here-here," Ashley seconds and they clank glasses.

"We also will be raising his rent," Mac adds with a snicker.

Ashley's face turns serious. "I'm sorry that you had to be there when Ryan Maxon…" her words trail off.

"Me too," I say.

"And I'm also sorry about Amber."

I nod my thanks. But it's hard to mourn a fictional character, which is what Amber Jazz was. The true sorrow should be reserved for Courtney Hamilton, who died the moment she got on that bus headed for fame and fortune, even if she didn't know it at the time.

"Is that what has been troubling you the last few days, Jack?" she asks.

I'm thrown off by the question. "What?"

"The last few days since the verdict, you haven't been yourself. And your trip to New York. That was you I saw on the news, rescuing Drew Anderson's wife like a knight in shining armor, wasn't it?"

I choose not to incriminate myself. I feel like I am on the witness stand and Ashley is cross-examining me in her soft, concerned way.

"You don't think Drew Anderson is guilty, do you?" she gets right to heart of the matter.

Criminology-101 states that if you are about to engage in illegal activity, you should tell as few people as possible. Friends and loved ones are the last people you should confess your plans to. But I come clean with Mac and Ashley. I'd bet my life that they will carry my secret to their respective graves. I also feel the need to inform them, so I am not putting them in harm's way. And most of all, I hope they can talk me out of it. So I go through the entire story, leading up to the insane part.

"Why wouldn't he just go through the legal process?" Mac asks with a quizzical look and mouth full of cheese and pepperoni.

"He believes they will harm his wife if he pursues a new trial, which is why he didn't take the stand in the first place. I think he's dealing with really powerful people who can get to them anytime, anywhere. So even if he wins in the courtroom, he loses. He believes this is the only way to keep Marissa safe."

I leave out the possibility that the judge might be this powerful person.

Silence fills the kitchen, as Mac and Ashley absorb the mind-numbing news. Then Ashley breaks the silence. "I'm in, Jack!"

I'm startled by the response, but probably shouldn't be. "I didn't ask for your help, Ash. The best thing you can do is stay out of the way and forget we ever had this conversation."

I look to Mac for help, but I see that unstoppable look in her eyes.

"Mac's in too," she declares.

I furiously shake my head. "You are the most loyal people in the world and I love you for it. But I have to do what I have to do, and putting either of you in danger is not an option." I try to reason with her and look for backup. "Tell her, Mac."

I see his mind working. I can visualize him thinking of when Ashley told him the story in Florida. A knife to her neck, and a threat that he knows where they live.

"We're in, Jack," he announces.

"How could I explain to our child that a friend needed our help and we were too concerned about our personal safety to help them out," Ashley builds on her argument.

"At least you wouldn't be having that conversation in prison," I say.

I fight them off for another hour. I'm not sure they really understand the magnitude of what I'm about to attempt.

Finally, Mac sits back in his chair and swigs down his cranberry juice. He rubs his scruffy chin and reality seems to dim his initial enthusiasm. And as if I'm unable to figure it out on my own, he informs, "It will be damn near impossible. Almost as impossible as it was for NASA to land a man on the moon."

Ashley glares at him, "Don't even start."

But something hits me. "You really think the moon landing was staged?"

Ashley shakes her head at me. "I really can't believe you're going there."

Mac never has to be asked twice to delve into his moon theory. "How do you explain that we really didn't have the technology to go there in 1969, the pictures transmitted don't include stars, the flag is waving even though there is no breeze on the moon? Not to mention the most compelling evidence: based on the gravitational level of the moon, the astronauts should have been able to jump much higher than they did, six feet easy."

"But how could something like that be kept a secret for all these years?"

"In the short run, involve as few people as possible and create dire consequences if the truth is revealed. But over time the myth takes on a life of its own, so people don't even believe the truth when presented logical evidence." He sends a glance in Ashley's direction.

I've heard this argument from Mac ad nauseam, but this time it holds a different meaning for me. I suddenly have a plan

"Are you going to fill us in on what you're thinking, Jack?" Mac asks. "Being that when I turn state's evidence against you, I want to have my story straight."

I pull a piece of pizza off his plate and chomp a bite out of it. I think better when I'm eating. "Not right now." My mind is in a full sprint, and I ask, "Are you scheduled to have the Ghosts of Baseball Past event this year?"

"Of course," Mac says. "The third annual."

It's his pride and joy. An event he created, held every Halloween at the Hall of Fame.

"The same day as the sentencing," I think out loud.

Mac cringes at what I ask next. But he doesn't blink, and takes me upstairs to a secure room, which was built for his memorabilia collection. He opens the combination lock and pulls it outward like a vault door.

"Take good care of it," he says.

I look for a hesitation when he hands me his prized possession. I don't see any.

"Thank you," I say, looking him directly in the eye. "It might save a man's life."

Chapter 85

Unable to sleep, I sit on my porch in the early hours of Sunday morning, drinking a glass of orange juice and staring out at the still lake. Only an occasional boat bumping over the water breaks the morning calm.

Right on schedule, I observe a 1937 Packard pull up to the front of the Cirillos' house. The door opens and George Herman scoops up the package sitting beside the mailbox. I think he will like what he sees.

Later in the morning, I arrive at the Hall of Fame incognito. I find George in a section of the museum dedicated to the exploits of Ruth. He has the ear of a young couple, explaining that the Baby Ruth candy bar had nothing to do with Babe Ruth, but was named for Teddy Roosevelt's young daughter, Ruth.

When the coast is clear, I approach. He is staring at a large photo of Ruth's last appearance at Yankee Stadium for a 1948 ceremony, celebrating twenty-five years of the stadium that he was responsible for building. Ruth looks gaunt, gravely thin, and leaning on a wooden baseball bat to keep him from toppling to the ground. It would be only months before the once indestructible slugger would succumb to throat cancer.

George gets right to the point, his eyes never leaving the sad photo. "Anderson didn't kill her, did he?"

I nod, as I view a happier photo of Ruth "calling the shot." I remember the dissertation Gifford Brown provided on the subject, which seems like ten lifetimes ago.

I explain the whole story to George in a whisper. It sounds even crazier than when I told it to the Cirillos, if that's possible.

"What can I do to help?" he asks.

George Herman has created the CISA—Celebrity Impersonators Society of America—where aspiring impersonators can get advice and information on what, believe it or not, is a highly competitive profession. From what he's told me, certain groups like Elvis and Bill Clinton impersonators have their own unions, but the industry as a whole is every man and woman for themselves.

"I need someone who wants to get famous," I say.

"That is why most people do what we do. They can't act, sing or write, but they look like someone. It's showbiz, kid."

"How about one who wants to be famous so bad they're willing to go to jail."

"Ever since the trial started, Max Q impersonators are everywhere. I can think of a few that might meet your criteria. It amazes me the lengths people will go to for fame."

George's face turns serious. "Listen, kid, I'll do anything I can to help you, no questions asked. But you are putting yourself in a vulnerable spot, and I think you need to know more than ever that your team is really on your side."

I know where he's going with this. I can't say it hasn't crossed my mind since Marissa mentioned Lansdale's mystery girlfriend. And it has led to nagging questions: why was she late that morning? What did she mean when she spent the weekend on a friend's boat? And like Kerri, who better to control a case than one of the lawyers? But I feel confident that my instincts are back from sabbatical.

"I understand that your cover was blown, and you got sent on that wild goose chase right after I revealed your true identity to her. But I think it's a coincidence. I trust her."

He hands me a photo. It's another security photo from the helipad in Manhattan, featuring the blonde woman who arrived on Lansdale's helicopter—the time reads 8:33. As far as I can see, it's nothing new.

"Check out the woman in the background," George advises.

When I do, I notice a woman dressed neatly in a pinstriped suit, her hair in a bun. It can't be! What is Shep doing there?

"Are you sure?" George asks again.

"I told you—I trust her. And besides, I've pushed her out of the loop … for her own protection," I stand firm.

"Or yours," George adds with a frustrated look. "Just looking out for you, kid. Anything else?

"I need a thorough background check on Figliomini, specifically his business dealings. Anything that might connect him to Anderson."

George looks puzzled by the request, but doesn't pry.

He begins to walk away when I remember something. "One other thing, George."

He nods his large head, indicating for me to go on.

"Look into Marissa Anderson's cases the last three years. Someone she defended named Jordan—stolen cars—all the info you can find."

"Is this business or personal?"

"I'm not sure," I concede.

George glances at his watch. We know we have already spent too much time together. "You should take in a movie, it'll take your mind off things," he offers and wanders away from me, casually disappearing into a sea of tourists.

I take the elevator back to the first floor and enter the Bullpen Theater. Today's movie is *The Natural* starring Robert Redford as mythical baseball legend Roy Hobbs.

My eyes adjust to the dark and I see what looks like a young George Herman, wearing an ill-fitting pinstriped baseball uniform over his portly body.

I ask him if the seat beside him is taken. When I do, his apprehensive look turns to a smile.

Chapter 86

"Jaaack!" Andy Kass bellows as I slip into the seat next to him.

"Shhh!" I greet him with index finger to the mouth.

Andy ignores me. "I knew such a plan of deception had to be the work of Jack Lawson."

I put my hand up to cut him off, and lower my voice to a whisper, "I think we should talk about a plea bargain."

"Plea bargain?" Andy asks. I can sense the disappointment in his voice. His day in court is about to be nixed.

"Listen closely," my tone is serious, "we will meet Monday at my office. You, your lawyer, and myself. I will present a deal to you. You will plead guilty to lesser charges such as reckless endangerment, but the major charges that coincide with the heavy jail time will be dropped."

Andy looks skeptical. "Is that why you had that guy kidnap me from the park this morning? And why would you dress me up in this baseball uniform? I don't know what kind of kinky stuff you are into, Jack, but just because I was living at the YMCA doesn't mean I am into that."

I begin again, but then stop in mid-sentence. Park? YMCA? "The court order specifically says you will lose your bail if you are not with your family twenty-four hours a day, unless you get the court's permission to do otherwise. Didn't you learn your lesson when you attended the trial?"

He snorts a sarcastic laugh. "Be with my family—that's a good one. They couldn't deal with the bad press they got from their psycho kid, so they bailed."

"Bailed?"

"Yeah, sold the house and moved to Canada. Left in the middle of the night. Just a heartfelt note that said I was old enough to screw up my life without them."

"Did you say you are living at the YMCA?"

"I was, until they figured out I was the guy who blew up the school. They threw me out, so I'm living up at Glimmerglass State Park. I found a nice rent-controlled three bedroom loft under a maple tree."

"You're homeless?"

"If by homeless, you mean I don't have a roof over my head—then yes, I am. But I don't think I ever had a home," he states defensively.

This cements my idea to go ahead with the plea bargain. Andy was on the verge of losing his bail anyway; having received a stiff warning after he attended the Max Q trial. With his parents out of the picture, his bail will certainly be revoked. I can't let that happen.

We don't have much time, so I push on, "The first major condition of your plea will be a world record amount of community service working at Otsego County civic buildings and properties. The second will be to contribute substantially to the cost of the reconstruction of Otsego High with all future earnings. But it will also include a hefty, but reasonable down payment."

"And how do you expect me to do that, Jack? Being homeless doesn't pay what it used to."

I remove my backpack and hand it to Andy. He looks in the knapsack and is astounded by the blocks of green bills.

He tries to hand it back to me. "I've seen this movie before. Take it back, Jack—I wanna go to court."

"I don't think you heard me the first time, Andy—you *will* accept the plea. Whether you accept my second offer is up to you, and if you refuse, it won't be held against you. But the plea deal will stand."

"What's the catch? Why would you offer me the deal of the century?"

"What I'm about to tell you is top secret. Can I trust you, Andy? A man's life is on the line."

The words seem to jolt him. "Sure, Jack, you can trust me."

I try to gauge his expression in the darkened theater. I already decided that I was willing to take the risk, but with the stakes so high I need to be sure. The more people involved, the less chance of pulling it off. I am already spreading it thin.

I look at the baseball uniform he wears. A bona fide 1936 Lou Gehrig model that had been the pride and joy of Mac Cirillo. George Herman brought it to Andy this morning, following my instructions.

"The first purpose of the uniform, Andy, was to conceal your identity for our meeting today. Most places, it will make you stand out, but here it helps you to blend. Not only is it important that you are not seen breaking your bail agreement, but it's imperative that we are not recognized being together.

"But it has a second important purpose. I want you to take a bus this week to Plattsburg—near the Canadian border—and mail the uniform to an address in the Bronx, which is written down for you, hidden within your moneybag. I also want you to rent a P.O. Box in Plattsburg. Three days later, you will return and find instructions in your box."

"Instructions for what?"

"Remember when we talked about perfection, Andy? The most beautiful thing you've ever seen?"

"Yeah."

"Well, you are going to get to create your masterpiece."

Chapter 87

He looks like he is going to shoot from his seat with excitement. I need to sober him, and caution him of the heavy cost that will result if he is caught—this time I won't be able to save him from jail. If the mission is successful, he will be forced to change his identity and never be able to return to this area, and possibly the country.

I must give him the option of not going through with it, but it's not a hard decision for him. "I'm in, Jack," he asserts. I explain it one more time, this time I paint an even darker picture, but his enthusiasm again spills over. The part that I was most concerned about—starting over with a new identity—actually seems to be the biggest selling point for him. A new start.

I sit back and silently examine what I just did. I brought into my plan an unstable teenager who blew up his high school.

Underneath Andy's sense of adventure, and his clamor for a new beginning, I detect a sadness. When a journey is coming to an end, we tend to look back on how the whole thing got started. And what led Andy to this moment is not pretty.

He stares at the screen, trying to escape from the painful subject he is thinking about—the first nineteen years of his life. Playing out on the screen is the climactic scene where Roy Hobbs breaks his trusty bat and tells the chubby batboy: "Go pick me out a winner, Bobby." The kid runs off the field in an uncoordinated waddle and I can hear the laughter from the front of the theater.

"They're laughing at the fat kid, " Andy informs me. His tone tells me he is talking from experience.

"I got picked on relentlessly as a child … and that was just by my sister," I try to lighten the moment, but I fail.

"Nothing like being ten years old and called fat-ass or pancake head. They both have such a beautiful ring to them. I once came late for class in the seventh grade and my teacher said I should never be late for class. His reasoning was that I was so fat, I should already be there. But lucky for me, when I lost a few pounds I got acne—it all balances out. Then my name changed to Andy Crater-face, ain't life grand."

I cringe, wanting to prosecute each and every bully he had to deal with to the fullest extent of the law. And not the law that's written in the books.

Andy continues to vent, "My favorite was they took my name and switched it around. Andy Kass became Kandy Ass. Not exactly creative, I know. You would think if you were going to torture someone on a daily basis, the least you could do is show a little creativity. *Kandy Ass is ugly! Kandy Ass is fat! Kandy Ass is stupid!*

"You ever play Little League, Jack?" he asks, his eyes never leaving the baseball scene in the movie.

"Wasn't allowed in my family. Lawyers work on Saturday."

"I wish I was so lucky. They had rules so that every kid gets to play. You know, sportsmanship and such. But my coach had a way around that. He paid my parents to keep me home, and of course they gladly accepted. Think about that for a moment."

"Andy, a lot of people have shitty parents. You can't let that affect the decisions for the rest of your life."

I tap Andy on the shoulder and point to the screen. "This is a good part."

The catcher looks at the blood on Roy Hobbs' abdomen. He tries to use it as an advantage and calls for an inside fastball. Hobbs responds with a dramatic game-winning home run. He hits the ball so hard that it reaches the light-tower, causing a massive Hollywood fireworks display.

Andy perks up. The chubby batboy had made the correct choice. I can tell Andy loves both the underdog and a good explosion. The movie has all the elements for him. So will our plan.

I have one last caution. “Andy, tomorrow at the hearing for your plea deal, it will be the last time we will ever talk. You will only be contacted through the P.O. Box. And when the mission is complete, we must cease all communication.”

He nods eagerly. “You can count on me!”

“There is one more catch,” I say.

“What is it, Jack?” He looks apprehensive—Lucy is always pulling the football away from him, too.

“When you start your new life, you have to promise me that you’ll turn your passion from misguided to good. And playing by the rules is the only way you will be able to change this world. Acting outside the law never results in good.”

“Do as you say, not as you do, right, Jack?”

I can’t argue with him, he has a point.

“Do we have a deal?” I remain steadfast. There is no room for wavering.

Andy surprises me by wrapping me in a hug. I think that’s a yes.

The plan is now careening toward a Halloween showdown.

Chapter 88

Drew Anderson looked out of the window of the heavily guarded police van that was delivering him to the courthouse for his sentencing.

It was sixty-five degrees, which was practically a heat wave for Halloween in upstate New York. The leaves had changed, turning Cooperstown into an exquisite watercolor painting. It crossed his mind that this might be the last time he saw the outside world for a long time, maybe ever. He looked to Kerri for her usual encouragement, but remembered that she was riding in the vehicle directly behind them in the motorcade. It was just him and a group of heavily armed security officers.

The double-locked handcuffs were tight around his wrists. He wore his favorite brown suit. The lucky one. The same one he wore to the Downtown Athletic Club in Manhattan when he collected his Heisman Trophy all those years ago. And more importantly, he wore it on his first date with Marissa.

Judge Figliomini accepted Kerri Lawson's motion for his last public appearance to be done with dignity. Jack Lawson argued vehemently against such. According to Jack's arguments, the van should be pulled to the back of the courthouse with Drew dropped off in one of those Hannibal Lecter masks. The judge ruled that he could walk to the courthouse from the front. His hands would be double-cuffed, but his suit jacket could be placed over the cuffs.

Drew again looked out the window to see the security lock-down in front of the courthouse. His supporters were still present, although not as many as before the verdict. They were roped off behind barricades that were set up across the street from the courthouse. If that wasn't sufficient to discourage disruption, the numerous men wearing military fatigues and carrying AK-47s sure were.

He thought of his father, Cal Anderson, and the memories weren't pleasant. *How do you like me now, Dad?*

Cal Anderson decided that his only child was going to be a professional athlete. More specifically, Drew was going to be the greatest quarterback in the history of the NFL. He didn't make this decision after Drew showed some athletic promise in his formative years. He decided it when he was still in the womb.

There were no dates in high school. Just a regimented schedule of school, practice, weight workouts with Cal, followed by work with his personal throwing coach, and video instruction until midnight. He would be woken the next morning at the crack of dawn for an intense five-mile run, in which Cal followed him in his car.

He was only twelve when the *Sports Illustrated* article came out with the blond haired, blue-eyed Pee Wee quarterback named Drew Anderson donning the cover. His second *SI* cover was during his freshman year at Florida State. The caption read: *Perfection.* But behind the scenes, his life was anything but perfect.

College was when the inevitable rebellion began. I can't have a girlfriend, Dad—take a look at these videos of me with every girl on campus. You bred me to go to the NFL, Dad—I think I'd rather be all I can be in the military.

But none of his achievements could heal the huge hole that Drew had inside of him. That was, until he met Marissa Torres. Their road turned rocky, for which he blamed himself, and his one shot at happiness appeared bleak. But they overcame it, only to fall in love all over, and it made them even stronger. He learned that love really can conquer all, and he believed it would pull them through again today, no matter how the odds seemed stacked against them.

The vehicle slowed, and Drew took the deepest breath possible. He was a man who believed in meticulous preparation, but facing the "game" of his life, he knew his destiny was in the hands of others, and the lack of control left him with an uneasy feeling.

As the courthouse came into view, he found himself thinking of Marissa. Kerri informed him that she couldn't be part of the plan. He understood—despite Kerri's jealousy, he knew she only wanted the best for him. A refreshing change from most people he had met in his life. He never would have agreed to another trial—it would have put Marissa in harm's way once again—but an escape would allow him a chance to get back to her one day, while also being able to protect her from future repercussions. It was ironic that Jack Lawson, his one-time adversary who fought to take his life away, was now his chance to live again.

The van came to a stop. "You ready, Drew?" the friendly but heavily armed guard asked. Just doing his job. Drew received one final pat-down and the jacket was placed over the cuffs.

He stepped out into the spotlight for what most people believed was the last time. With his thoughts still on Marissa, he was able to remain composed. That was how it always worked since the day he met her.

As if his foot touching the pavement was the detonator, the first bomb went off. It boomed like thunder and echoed off the nearby lake. The second explosion shook the ground, shooting debris in all directions. The third blast seemed even louder—a fire hydrant exploded, water shooting into the air like a geyser.

People began running in all directions, screaming with panic. Police were helpless to react. Guns were drawn, but they had no idea who to shoot at, and held their fire.

Another explosion violently shook the ground.

"We are under attack!" hollered a member of the security team.

The last thing on their mind was Max Q.

Chapter 89

Drew immediately dropped to the ground and rolled under the police vehicle, just as Kerri had instructed. Now all he could do was wait. Another explosion rocked the ground and the van bounced. Then he heard what sounded like a machine-gun.

Only thirty seconds had elapsed. It seemed like hours. He wasn't exactly sure what he was waiting for, but then it appeared.

Rolling next to him, wearing the exact same brown suit, was…his twin.

"Hi, you must be Drew Anderson, I'm Drew Anderson," the man said with a nervous laugh. "Actually my name is Shane King, and it's an honor to meet you, Mr. Anderson—you're my hero."

Drew said nothing, placing the handcuffs out for the man to see. Another bomb blast shook the undercarriage of the van.

Shane looked at the handcuffs and his training clicked. He talked himself through the process. "They are professional, police, double hinged cuffs. Made of satin nickel steel. The inner perimeter is somewhere between five and three-quarters inches and eight inches."

Shane struggled to maneuver in the cramped space under the vehicle—they were both large men—but he was eventually able to gain use of a small toolkit. Using two different length hooks and a flat tension wrench, he first removed the double lock. He then used a shim key to free his hands.

Drew felt huge relief as he shook blood back into his hands. He still had a long way to go to reach freedom, but he felt like he once again controlled his destiny. Another loud bang filled the air. Drew looked at his watch and it was still under two minutes.

Shane pulled out his own pair of handcuffs. He handed Drew a small knife, a plastic bag, and a New York Yankees baseball cap. "I was told to give these to you, I assume you will know what to do with them."

He nodded, then did the honors of placing the cuffs on Shane. "Thank you," Drew uttered with sincerity.

"What are you thanking me for? At the end of the day, I'm going to be on the front page of every newspaper in the free world," Shane said with a smile. Drew would have cautioned the man about being careful what you wish for, but time was of the essence.

Shane rolled out from under the vehicle and immediately surrendered himself to the police. "Anderson in custody," shouted out one of the police into the radio.

The real Drew Anderson took the knife and carefully cut off his suit. Underneath, he wore a baseball uniform that Kerri had supplied him when he was getting dressed earlier in the morning. Because of his collectibles business, it didn't even get a curious look from the security guards when he chose to wear it beneath his suit. In fact, the men were impressed by it. Kerri told them it was for luck. The men mumbled that he would need it.

He pulled the Yankees cap as low as he could on his head and shoved the crumpled suit and handcuffs into the plastic bag, leaving the knife behind. He tucked the bag under his uniform shirt, giving him more the belly of Ruth than Gehrig.

He counted to ten and then rolled out from under the van and into the autumn sunlight. It wouldn't be strange for someone to be hiding under a vehicle in the midst of this chaos. And everyone was more concerned about their own safety to notice, anyway.

One final bomb rocked Main Street like an earthquake—it was exactly what he needed. While others took cover, Drew Anderson walked calmly away from the scene. Out of the corner of his eye he could see Shane King in the custody of the police.

When Drew reached Fair Street, he began to trot. He ran all the way to the Lake Front Motel, a quarter mile down the road. Once in the parking lot, he moved toward a station wagon.

Chapter 90

Following orders, he climbed into the backseat. The first thing he noticed was techno-looking special effects panel taking up most of the front seat.

"That's how I controlled the explosions," Andy Kass said with pride, noticing Drew staring at the panel. He turned the key and the car started with an engine cough. "We have to get out of here while the going's still good. Shane's buying you time, but roadblocks will be set up within ten minutes."

"You did all that?" Drew asked with amazement.

"Pretty impressive, huh?"

To say the least. "How the hell did you pull it off?"

"Pretty much all special effects stuff that's used for movies. Was able to control it from here—totally based on radio waves."

They drove down Lake Ave until it became Route-80. Just as predicted, the focus remained at the point of attack, and not on the getaway … for now. They wouldn't be looking for the car that Andy stole from local resident, Matthew Kenner, either. Matt the Drunk, as he was known around town, probably wouldn't realize it was missing until Thanksgiving.

Andy continued detailing his masterpiece. "It's a combination of a lot of material. Flash powder, rifle powder, and black powder. The large explosions are the key—the mortar shots. For those I used iron pots. The mortars are wide at the top, narrowing toward the base. This forces the power generated by the explosion to go up, and not out, so you don't hurt anyone. It's kind of like a balloon bursting. If you hold the balloon by the stem and burst it, the force is equal on all sides. But if you put the balloon in a bowl, and force it upward, it will be safe."

"So nobody got hurt in that?"

"Not from the explosions. I used balsa wood and cork to serve as the debris. That way there is no shrapnel, which is what usually screws people in war and such, more than the actual blast. My only real worry was the fire hydrant."

"What about the gunshots I heard?"

"All electronic detonation. The charge splinters the pieces of wood, providing the illusion that it's being hit with bullets. It's an important aspect of the escape because the threat of gunfire keeps the police from moving freely. Explosions are more targeted where bullets can spray at random."

Drew shook his head in admiration. "How did you set this all up?"

"Unlike yourself, Mr. Anderson, the fat kid can operate under the radar—been doing it my whole life. Plus, part of my community service agreement was to work on town property. I was able to bury many of the small pots in the ground with only a small portion sticking out above ground level. I was able to cover them with the balsa wood and peat moss. The average person wouldn't know what it was if they found it."

The conversation was cut short when they reached the entrance of Glimmerglass State Park. Andy pulled the car to the side of the road. "I have a boat to catch, so this is where we part company. I suggest you go for a walk along the road."

With that, Andy handed Anderson a wig that simulated Lou Gehrig's wavy brown hair, and a pair of sneakers. In return, Drew swapped the plastic bag under his shirt and his dress shoes. "They will soon be on the bottom of the lake," Andy assured him, and was off.

Drew walked about two hundred feet out onto Route-31, feeling both strange and vulnerable in the baseball uniform. That's when the 1937 Packard stopped and a pudgy man in a Babe Ruth uniform uttered, "Get in, kid—I guess it's your lucky day."

Drew smiled. "Today, I consider myself to be the luckiest man on the face of the earth."

Chapter 91

I check my watch for the umpteenth time. Shep looks strangely at me, noticing my agitation. She has grown accustomed to my courtroom confidence.

We sit at the prosecution table, awaiting the guest of honor for his sentencing. It seems like Shep wants to tell me something, but decides to hold back. Our relationship has been as cold as the Arctic Circle for weeks, but that's the way it has to be. We have only spoken when the topic has been the case, and even that has only been brief, calculated responses on my part.

The most frustrating thing in life is to not have control of your destiny. And once I set the plan in motion, my fate was taken from my hands. George Herman was in charge of finding the optimal, overly ambitious Max Q impersonator. Andy took over from there—contacting Shane King, making him an offer he couldn't refuse, and then training him in Handcuffs-101. Using the P.O. Boxes—Bronx and Plattsburg—he provided Kerri with the baseball uniform, while Kerri sent inside information to Andy.

My emotions swirl, just as they have since the jury handed down their guilty verdict. Fear, hope, regret, despondence, and most of all, desperation. I even briefly shifted my anger toward Drew. But I know he's trying to protect Marissa. I would have done the same.

I wipe beads of sweat from my brow, as if I'm the one facing life in prison. If this doesn't work out, there's a good possibility I will be. Shep looks like she's trying to gauge my strange demeanor and I can feel her mind racing.

Without warning, a jarring explosion rocks the courtroom. Then another. The blasts are thunderous and the floor shakes.

Shep tries to get up and stumbles, falling into my arms. Her face registers terror. I begin panicking like everyone else. I remember a documentary I watched on earthquakes—get under something because the shake won't likely kill you, but a flying object might. I pull Shep to the floor and drag her under the prosecution table. Another booming explosion drowns out the screaming that surrounds us. Shep clings tightly to me and I whisper to her that everything will be all right.

Security swiftly moves into action. Since the prosecution has received more death threats than the president since the trial began, we are considered prime targets. We're rushed out of the courtroom, our feet barely touching the floor.

Shep and I are amongst a group of judges and attorneys who are escorted to a bomb shelter that was built below the structure during the Cold War era.

Moments later, Judge Figliomini is brought kicking and screaming into the room. "I won't let terrorists see me weaken. If I acknowledge them then they win!" he shouts at the guard.

"Live to fight another day, Your Honor," the guard replies dispassionately.

Shep looks shaken. "It will be okay," I again try to assure her.

"Thanks," she says and labors a smile, but another round of booming thunder unnerves her once again.

After a few minutes that feel like hours, the eruptions stop. The silence allows me to consider the all-important question—was Anderson able to get away? The logical part of me doubts that it could have worked.

A lengthy half-hour passes before Figliomini approaches Shep and me. “This proceeding will go on today. These terrorists will not stop the American justice system. Drew Anderson was rightfully convicted by my court and he will be sentenced today!”

We say nothing. Shep is out of sorts, and I have too many questions on my mind. If everything went as planned, the real Drew Anderson has already made his way to Glimmerglass State Park, while Andy Kass was headed to his connecting flight. Shane King is hopefully in custody. If he sings, then the only person they can connect him to is Andy—George Herman only set up Shane King with a customer, and Kerri and I had no contact with him.

“I just talked to the guard. The building is secure. I guess it was some sort of prank,” Figliomini rambles in fiery style. “Initial reports indicate that it was all Hollywood special effects stuff. They have cleared us to resume court in fifteen minutes and I want you two ready to proceed in sixteen.”

It doesn’t get past me how keen he seems to start the clock on Anderson’s prison sentence.

Exactly sixteen minutes later, Shep and I are back in the courtroom. I scan the room and notice most of the gallery has left, giving it a quarantined feel. But it doesn’t keep Marissa away. She looks as anxious as I do. I have not made contact with her since the night we spent together, as I made the choice not to include her in the escape. She is too emotionally tied to Drew, and vice versa, which could cause errors. She is also too much of a control freak who would want to run the show. Shep notices my glance and I wonder what her thoughts are.

Kerri enters and takes her place at the defense table. She looks shaken, which is understandable since she was riding in one of the vehicles that made up the caravan. She doesn’t provide me any clues one way or another.

Seconds later, two bailiffs escort a blond man in a brown suit to the defense table. Hal Metzer gives him a supportive pat on the back and Kerri puts her arm around him for comfort.

I know right away that it isn’t Anderson. To the untrained eye, he appears to be an exact replica, but his mannerisms aren’t the same. I can tell by the awkward way he greeted Kerri like this was the first time they’d met, which it is. The stiff coolness of Drew Anderson has been replaced by Shane King's nervous energy. Shep's antenna is up. Her expression says that she notices something different about him, but just can't place it.

"All rise for the Honorable Judge Antonio Figliomini."

Figliomini takes his position. He first gives everybody in the court the same rah-rah speech he gave Shep and me in the bomb shelter. "Now let's proceed—we are here for the sentencing of Andrew Christian Anderson, convicted of one count of murder in the first degree. I understand, Ms. Lawson, that Mr. Anderson has a statement he would like to read to the court."

All eyes in the court go to the man in the brown suit. He isn't sure what to do, so Hal Metzer urges him to stand.

The man stands and looks around. This is his big moment. Anybody who would have two ribs removed and a chin implant to look more like Drew Anderson, is serious about seeking fame.

The silence annoys Figliomini. "Mr. Anderson, do you want to address the court?"

He smiles, showing off bright, capped teeth. "I guess I'd like to wish everybody a Happy Halloween." The voice lacks the confident cadence of Drew Anderson.

Figliomini looks curiously at him. "A lovely sentiment, Mr. Anderson. Would you like to expand on it?"

"I'd like to add that my name is not Drew Anderson. It's Shane King, I live in Manhattan, the West Village."

Murmurs fill the courtroom. Maybe Anderson is flipping out—having a mental breakdown.

"If you don't believe me, maybe you'll believe the hair," he says and pulls off his blond wig, tearing the glue from his scalp, revealing a bald head.

The murmurs change to chaotic shouts. Figliomini bangs the gavel. "Ms. Lawson, what is going on here!?"

Kerri looks aghast. "Your Honor…um…I'm not sure."

Shep's mouth is hanging open, but nothing comes out. She searches for similar astonishment in my look, and I hope she sees it.

Figliomini bangs his gavel and I think the bench almost cracks. "My chambers now!"

Chapter 92

I go right on the offensive. "This is outrageous!"

Shep jumps in, "I don't want to state the obvious here—but where is Drew Anderson?"

Figliomini takes back control. "Sit down, both of you. The only person I am interested in hearing from is you, Mr. King. And I have one question for you—why the hell are you in my courtroom?"

"I am here because your policemen grabbed me and told me to get my hands up or they were going to shoot. I don't do well with pain or scarring, and I'm sure bullets cause both. I tried to tell them that I was only a Max Q impersonator, just trying to do my job, but they kept telling me to shut up. No human being should be treated like that!"

"I was just informed that you surrendered to the police, claiming to be Anderson," Figliomini barks in an accusatory tone.

"I was only kidding," he says with a dismissive wave of the hand. "It's part of the act—I'm a method actor."

Figliomini boils over. "Kidding? I promise that you won't find prison so amusing."

I jump into the fray, addressing Shane, "Why were you wearing handcuffs?"

Figliomini raises a hand to inform me that I've overstepped my bounds. He then sends a death stare in Shane's direction to indicate he wants an answer to my question.

"It was Max Q's sentencing, so I figured I should wear a suit and a pair of handcuffs to indicate I'm going to jail. My fans expect me to be authentic."

"I'll tell you what, Mr. King. Because I'm in character, I'm thinking about giving you an authentic prison-issued jumpsuit and putting you in an authentic jail cell."

"It would have been simple for the police to identify the cuffs as amateur," Shane fights back.

He's playing this splendidly so far, sticking to the script. He will get what he wants—a pile of money, and he'll be on the front page of every newspaper tomorrow—and he isn't stupid enough to discuss what he did. Not only could that end him up in that jail cell that Figliomini speaks of, but he is aware that only powerful people could pull off what he witnessed today—the type of people that can make you disappear without a trace. The price of fame.

Figliomini picks up the ringing phone and barks into it, "A goddam impersonator, if you can believe that. It's been almost an hour, the man's a pilot, he could be somewhere over the Atlantic right now!"

He slams down the phone and again peers at Shane King. "Until Drew Anderson is found, I am holding you personally responsible!"

I look directly at Figliomini and point an accusatory finger in his direction. "You were the one who accepted the defense's pleas to lower the level of security for PR sake. If you remember, I wanted him taken through the back entrance, away from the public. I am holding *you* directly responsible until he is found."

"Jack!" Shep blurts out, unnerved.

The judge looks at me like he'd like to shoot me and mount my head over his fireplace. "You want to get in a pissing match with me, Mr. Lawson? I can assure you that you don't."

Undeterred, I turn to Kerri and Hal. "I am also holding you responsible. Are you behind this!?"

Kerri shoots me a look to kill. We've had so much practice at the hatred thing that it's second nature. "Get over yourself, Jack. It's those idiot cops in this one-horse town that screwed things up to start with, and now they let Drew get away. You think this helps us?"

"Let me see—life in prison or a free man? Come to think of it, it does help you!"

"Spare me, Jack. I would kill you on appeal. The video being allowed. The illegal police tape admitted. I would have had this turned around in a second. And now Drew is out there in danger of taking a bullet in the back from these morons who let him go in the first place."

No judge likes to discuss his decision being overturned on appeal. "Enough, Ms. Lawson!"

She quiets, but I'm not done. "Lose the sob story, Kerri. This has the work of Lansdale's cult all over it. You know—the moral and ethical ones. And if I find that you are involved, you're going to be sharing a cell with them!"

Kerri stares back at me with faux anger.

Figliomini again picks up the phone and begins indiscriminately yelling at people.

I sit with the look of defeat and run my fingers through my hair in disgust.

Deep down, I feel anything but defeated. The first part of the plan somehow worked. The blastoff. Now it's time for Drew Anderson to land on the moon.

Chapter 93

Approximately an hour after the explosions ceased, Mac Cirillo, flanked by two police officers, marched out of the front entrance of the Baseball Hall of Fame.

His heart felt like it was going to jump out of his chest and flop like a fish on the brick-lined sidewalk in front of the museum. His skin had turned ashen and a lake of sweat had stained his shirt.

They headed toward a trio of men who stood under a flagpole, in which a large American flag rippled in the autumn wind. The men had ominous looks on their faces. Mac tried to take a deep breath, but his lungs weren't fully functioning.

Mac recognized the scholarly-looking museum president, Peter

Connolly. He was both his boss, and the man he hoped to replace one day, but right now Mac's biggest career goal was to stay out of prison. He looked up to Connolly, who was a refined man with a passion for baseball, which he viewed as the romantic and magical game that has played an epic role in American history. There wasn't a fact or anecdote about the game that Connolly couldn't eloquently recite.

The other two men standing with Connolly were Otsego County Sheriff Roddy Opp and Special Agent Hawkins of the FBI. They didn't appear to be happy. Mac wiped a trail of sweat from his brow and rubbed it on the pant leg of his khakis.

Out of the Hall entrance came two more uniformed police with bomb sniffing dogs on sturdy leashes. "The building is clear," announced one officer.

Both Opp and Hawkins nodded, each trying to act like they're the one in charge.

"Just trying to be safe, Peter," Opp informed Connolly. "We feel the target of the explosions was the courthouse. I don't believe the Hall of Fame was ever in danger."

Connolly nodded somberly. "Better safe than sorry, officer."

"Our initial tests on the explosions were that they were similar to special effects used on a movie set. Just some pranksters trying to make a name for themselves. If there was any intent to stop or delay the proceedings, they failed. Drew Anderson is being sentenced as we speak.

Mac felt sick. *He wasn't able to escape!*

Connolly took his eyes off the authorities, noticing Mac for the first time. "Macauley—you look tepid. Are you well?"

Mac wiped some more sweat and fought an urge to vomit on the spot. "I'm just a little shaken up. I'm not used to bombs going off. Just give me a moment and I'll be fine."

Connolly returned his focus to Opp and Hawkins. "I will leave any decision to continue tonight's festivities up to you good officers. The Ghosts of Baseball Past has been a great invention by Macauley here." He patted

Mac on his sweaty back. "Children don't connect to baseball like they once did. In my day, fathers handed down the revered history of the game to their children, and their children to their children. Now the father is working sixty hours a week and the son is addicted to video games. Our Halloween event does its small part to reconfigure this grand tradition."

Opp began to speak, but Hawkins overpowered him. "President Connolly, like I said, we believe this was nothing more than a hoax. I see no reason that you can't have your event."

Connolly appeared inspired, his faith restored. "Baseball has been a rock for this country in its most turbulent times—it kept going during World War II and provided a welcome diversion after the tragedy of 9/11. And now at this low moment, we shall proceed as planned!"

Out of the blue, two large men approached the group—both were wearing pinstriped Yankees baseball uniforms.

For the first time since the bombs began bursting in air, Connolly smiled. He was back in his element. "Ah, the great Babe Ruth has joined us tonight, and I see he has brought a friend—a very famous friend!"

George Herman trotted right past the array of law enforcement officials to greet his longtime friend, his booming voice echoing, "Good to see you, Mr. President."

"As you, George. I heard rumors that the great Babe Ruth might not be able to make it to Ghosts of Baseball Past this year. It wouldn't have been the same without you, and the kids would have missed you greatly."

"I have a previously scheduled event—a cruise sponsored by a Yankees fan club that leaves for the Bahamas—but I pushed our flight back until after tonight's event."

"The Bahamas? We all should be so fortunate to have your life, George," Connolly said with a gracious smile.

"Well, I've had a better year than you, Mr. President." George replied with a smile. Connolly didn't take offense—George was reciting one of Babe Ruth's famous quotes, from when he was asked about making more money than the president of the United States, which was a big controversy at the time.

After sharing another laugh with George, Connolly's eyes moved to the strapping Lou Gehrig impersonator. He wasn't an exact match, but Mac thought that there was enough of a resemblance to pull it off. He was an impersonator, not a doppelganger. And he smartly had pulled his cap down close to his eyes.

Mac recognized his collectible wool uniform, and now understood why Jack wanted it. He was at first relieved that the escape worked, but then a terrifying reality socked him between the eyes. *Max Q is standing two feet away from Roddy Opp and a special agent of the FBI!*

George energetically introduced Lou Gehrig, staying in character. Drew Anderson responded with round of handshakes, including the police. Mac almost dropped his grip, his hand sweating so profusely.

Connolly was in his element. "You do know, George, that the real Babe Ruth and Lou Gehrig would never arrive together. They weren't exactly fast friends. Despite being yin and yang on the field, they were mostly oil and water off of it."

George boomed a laugh. "You got us, Mr. President—we are nothing but imposters!"

Connolly studied the Gehrig impersonator, a little too closely for Mac's blood pressure. "He's much like the real Gehrig," Connolly mused. "The strong silent type. Gehrig was a man of few words who let his bat do the talking for him. He was also one of the more popular players of his day, and since I've already seen six Gehrig impersonators inside for tonight's event, I see that popularity continues to flourish. Would you agree, Macauley?"

Mac felt a huge lump in his throat as he began to talk. His mouth moved, but no words came out. He felt he was going to pass out.

But nobody noticed. They were focused on the crackling radio on Opp's waistband.

A voice called out, "Sheriff—I have Judge Figliomini on the line and he says it's urgent."

Chapter 94

The FBI man barked orders into his cell. When he ended the call, he turned to Roddy Opp.

"Sheriff, I want all potential routes out of this area cut off. I want every car, plane, and boat checked. He's got an hour on us, but he will need a week-long head start to escape the FBI."

Opp returned a look of annoyance, but had to follow the orders. The FBI took precedence in this situation.

Mac stood between Connolly and Drew Anderson. His heart almost exploded when the FBI man began walking in their direction. But he wasn't coming to slap the cuffs on him, or Max Q—he was moving toward Connolly.

"President Connolly, now more than ever it's important for you to hold your event. The last thing we need during a dangerous manhunt are groups of trick-or-treaters on the streets. The Hall of Fame will serve as a safe haven for the children."

Connolly again appeared inspired, turning to Mac. "Why don't you take Mr. Ruth and Mr. Gehrig inside and allow them to set up. I will work on putting out the word about the importance of tonight's event."

Arm-in-arm with George Herman and Drew Anderson, Mac nervously entered the museum. Impersonators were everywhere, mingling amongst early-bird arrivals, mostly young children who were accompanied by their parents.

Mac felt a small sense of relief upon entering the Plaque Gallery, the cathedral-like centerpiece of the Hall. He felt a certain confidence in here, kind of like Jack feels in the courtroom. But not enough to dim the fact that he was walking with the most wanted man in America. *Who I am helping escape!*

The gallery served as both the starting and ending points of The Ghosts of Baseball Past experience. A maze had been set up within the museum that was decorated with baseball memorabilia, and dramatized with the use of fluorescent lights and sound effects. At specific stations, a "ghost of baseball past" impersonator performed a skit that helped bring their legend to life. A journey through the maze told the chronological story of baseball from the nineteenth century to the present.

The impersonators without skit responsibilities worked the crowds within the museum and throughout the grounds, handing out candy and taking photos with children. George Herman and Drew Anderson would be in that group.

Moving to the second floor, Mac couldn't take his eyes off Anderson. He focused on his Lou Gehrig uniform with the number '4' embroidered on the back. Gehrig once wore this uniform in the World Series, but now it had been reduced to assisting the escape of a fugitive. Mac couldn't believe he was risking everything—Ashley, the baby, and this prized treasure—for a man he didn't even particularly like.

Mac did take some solace in that Anderson didn't have the same confident stride that he did when he last saw him at the racetrack. He might escape, but his downfall has already happened—the old Max Q was nothing more than a "ghost from the past."

Chapter 95

When the clock struck 6:30, the lights were turned down, music was cued (Take Me Out to the Ballgame), and the journey through baseball history had begun.

By 7:30, "The Ghosts of Baseball Past Halloween Celebration" had its biggest attendance ever, helped out by the local authorities urging people to do so on the six-o'clock local news.

At 8:15, Drew Anderson slipped into a bathroom on the second floor of the museum and locked the door behind him. He went to the mirror and removed his cap and wig. In his back pocket was a pair of scissors he had found in Mac Cirillo's office. He began clipping his blond locks. He looked up into the mirror and admired his work.

The short cut to the scalp reminded him of his military days, which seemed so long ago. And like those days, he had a mission to accomplish. The goal this time was to protect Marissa. He would do anything for her. Take any risk. Make any sacrifice.

He re-applied his wig and took one last look in the mirror. Staring back at him was a man who was prepared to face his latest, and most dangerous mission.

A tick after 8:30, George Herman rounded up the group that would be joining him on the cruise. The rest of the group was made up of a Joe DiMaggio clone, who was accompanied by a Marilyn Monroe, DiMaggio's wife in real life. She wore a cheap knockoff of Marilyn's famous white dress from the *Seven Year Itch,* and looked like she had applied the trademark mole with a Sharpie pen. The last member was a good-looking, muscular man with an Oklahoma drawl, impersonating Mickey Mantle.

They said their goodbyes to Mac and Connolly, and then loaded into George's Packard. Despite the cool temperatures, they drove with the top down. The Gehrig impersonator sat in the front and didn't say a word. In contrast, the drunken DiMaggio wouldn't shut up. Marilyn sat between Joe and Mickey in the backseat, and seemed to like Mickey better, flirting with him and running her hand up the inner-thigh of his wool baseball pants.

On the outskirts of town, George spotted the lights of a police car. All vehicles were being stopped and searched. George drove confidently to the checkpoint.

"Where ya headed, George?" Roger Beneke asked, shining a flashlight into the car.

"Oneonta Air Field—flight to the Bahamas. We're working a cruise."

George showed Beneke the itinerary, which had been booked months in advance.

Beneke shined the light into Gehrig's face in the passenger seat. "We are on the lookout for Drew Anderson," he stated the obvious.

"All I got in here is DiMaggio, Monroe, Mantle, and Gehrig," George replied with a nervous chuckle.

Beneke turned his attention to the backseat, taking particular interest in Marilyn. "I'm going to need you all to step out of the car. We are looking for a fugitive and if I let a group pass by, who are wearing disguises and holding airline tickets, they'll crucify me. Just doing my job, folks."

He patted down the men, and shined his flashlight in each impersonator's eyes. When he arrived at Gehrig, he seemed to hold the look longer. "Do I know you from somewhere?"

The man shrugged. "I doubt it, I'm from New York City. Don't get up here that much. Except when I was elected to the Hall of Fame back in 1939."

Beneke held his stare on Gehrig for a few tense seconds, but moved on.

All supplied their passports to the officer for identification. He returned to his squad car and officially called them in. Beneke then made George open the trunk, which was empty. But just when it looked like they were home free, the flirty Marilyn cooed, "Aren't you gonna frisk me, officer?"

She didn't have to ask him twice. She theatrically oo'd and ah'd in a sultry voice, seemingly enjoying it as much as Beneke, who made sure to brush by all the strategic spots. He was completely distracted.

When Beneke's fun and games were over, he allowed the Packard to pass through the security check.

George drove to Oneonta Air Field, where they boarded the small plane he had chartered for the trip. Shortly thereafter, they took off into the dark night.

George looked at the pilot and smiled.

Ashley Cirillo smiled back at him.

Chapter 96

The first pictures of Drew Anderson hit television this morning. I view them closely.

He is sporting his newly short-cropped hairstyle, as he parties in an upscale bar in the Bahamas. A bunch of tanned tourists surround him, drinking margaritas and he appears oblivious to the fact that he is a hunted man.

GNZ interviewed a couple on their honeymoon, who took the photos. They confirmed that Drew Anderson looked and acted like a man celebrating his release from prison. They had never met him, having only seen him on TV, but their "expert" opinion concluded that it was truly him, not a doubt in their mind. If it's good enough for the news media, then it's good enough for me. *Max Q is in the Bahamas!*

Ironically, his escape has done what a guilty jury verdict couldn't do—shifting people's beliefs about his guilt. When I was sure of his guilt, I couldn't make the public believe it. Now that I'm convinced he's innocent, he's been convicted in the court of public opinion. Seems like I'm practicing Murphy's Law these days.

Law enforcement has descended upon the Bahamas. But Drew isn't there. It is like those Grisham novels I've read where scheming lawyers are transferring money to off-shore accounts. It's important to let it be seen—as Drew was last night—then move it again. Soon the trail will be lost forever.

I ride my bike to the office on a leaf-filled Route-80. November has begun with a cold rain. When I arrive, I perform my daily ritual of walking past the wall of media without giving a comment.

I walk straight to my office and shut the door. I sit silently at my desk. I mentally review the whole case once more. As usual, I drive myself to madness, contemplating where I went so wrong.

A knock on my door returns me to reality. Shep enters and tosses a newspaper on my desk, in case I hadn't seen the photo of Drew in that bar in the Bahamas.

She swallows some pride—not the easiest thing for her—and says, "I know we've had our issues lately, Jack, but I just want to say I'm sorry how this all went down. You are a great lawyer who did an unbelievable job, and I hope people remember that—you had nothing to do with this fiasco."

I nod lifelessly, and then return to my brooding stare.

"Do you think they'll ever find him?" Shep asks.

I sure hope not. "I don't know."

She is hovering around my desk, and I can feel her studying me. It makes me uncomfortable. "Is there something on your mind?"

"I don't know, I just feel like there is something you're not telling me."

I shrug. "Like what?"

She's becoming skeptical of my wall of negativity. And knowing Shep, she will keep pounding away until she knocks the wall down. So I change tactics—I will now let her in to keep her at arms length.

With a heavy sigh, I act as if I give in. "I think Andy Kass is behind this explosion. I know his calling card from the school demolition, and this one has Andy written all over it."

I can tell the thought hadn't crossed her mind. "Do you think he did this on his own? I don't see what his motivation was, unless Lansdale's people got to him."

"I went to find him last night and it seems as if he has disappeared. His parents moved to Canada without him, and from what I found out, he was living homeless up at Glimmerglass State Park. But when I went to find him, he was gone."

Shep appears to be contemplating what this means.

"The bottom line, is that when they connect Andy to the explosion, they're going to come looking for me, and I don't want you near me. Guilt by association."

Not to mention his connection to Shane King and the impersonators, which I choose to keep to myself.

"C'mon, Jack, nobody in their right mind would believe you had something to do with what Andy Kass might have done."

I remain serious. "My concern is that I will come under heavy criticism for the soft deal I offered him—I thought I was helping a kid get his life together. I don't want you near the fray. I will take sole responsibility."

Shep's face tightens with resolve. "Last I checked, we're still partners, and partners have each other's back."

"I appreciate the support, but this isn't a negotiation, Shep."

Something holds me back from embracing the moment—that picture. What was she doing at the helipad that morning? My tone firms, "Anything else?"

"Yeah, Jack—I came to tell you that your sister and Anderson's wife are holding a press conference. I thought it might interest you."

Chapter 97

The office staff is huddled around a television in the conference room. NBC has just pulled away from its live coverage from the Bahamas to carry Kerri and Marissa's press conference at Anderson Estate.

A teary-eyed Marissa stands behind a conglomerate of microphones. She is dressed casually in a sweater and jeans, and is visibly shaking. The cold rain could be the culprit, but I think it has to do with the emotional toll this has taken on her. Drew is still in danger, which must be weighing heavily on her. I recognize the older man holding the large golfing umbrella over her—Lansdale.

She wipes away tears, before looking into the camera. "Drew, I don't know if you are watching this, but if you are, please listen to me, baby. Please give yourself up immediately. As long as you are out there, you are in danger. Come back and fight these false charges in court. Everybody knows you couldn't have killed anyone. You couldn't even bring yourself to kill that mouse in our kitchen." She pauses for a moment, seemingly overwhelmed, before making one final plea. "Please come home, baby. I need you."

She takes a step back. Flashbulbs go off, looking like lightning bugs.

Kerri steps to the microphones to assume the role of the unemotional lawyer. "Drew Anderson is my client and I take full responsibility for him not being here. We are fully cooperating with the authorities to bring him back home to us safe and sound. As you can see, Drew, there are so many people that love you. Please turn yourself in. It's the only way this can have a happy ending."

Shep looks at me with an envious "she's good" look. I agree, but for different reasons.

Kerri steps away from the microphone and puts her arm around Marissa. They walk under the columns of Anderson Estate and disappear through the front door. With my current understanding of their relationship, this last part might be one of the great acting jobs of all time.

The rapid-fire coverage moves back to the anchor, who hot-potatoes it to the Bahamas. A split screen shows both the rain-soaked Anderson Estate and the swaying palm trees of the sunny Caribbean. Too bad Drew Anderson is in neither place.

Before we leave for the weekend, Gifford Brown demands my presence in his office. I take a seat before his desk and can tell it's been a two-pack day, which means I might be in trouble. *Could they already know about Andy Kass?*

He moves to the door and calls out, "Shepherdson—get in here now."

She races in and takes a seat beside me.

I brace for the worst, but Gifford surprises, "You two are excellent prosecutors. You did your job and I'm proud of you."

I see no reason to interrupt him while he's on a roll.

"Law enforcement has been screwing us over in this case from day one. I just want you two to know that none of this nonsense going on now is your fault."

He then orders us to "get the hell out of here" and to have a good weekend.

On Saturday morning, I watch a special news report from my apartment. Drew Anderson has just released a video he recorded in front of the Eiffel Tower. He is fully clothed in this one.

Onscreen, a man with a short-cropped military style haircut, claiming to be Drew Anderson, makes a short statement.

He looks into the camera like a pro. "I am innocent of the charges against me. The decision to take this course of action in the face of this injustice was mine, and mine alone. I want to thank all those who supported me during my trial, and promise that I will not let you down."

A reporter appears with *Live from Paris* written below her on the screen, her hair blowing wildly in a stiff Parisian wind. "This tape is now in the hands of the FBI. My sources tell me that there are those within The Bureau who believe the tape is real, while other camps believe it to be a fake. It has been sent back to Washington for more testing, but as of now, it is inconclusive as to whether the man on the tape is Drew Anderson."

An anchor appears on the screen and states, "The office of the French President has released a statement that it will use the full force of the French Judicial Power to help bring Anderson to justice."

It will be a waste of time—Drew Anderson is not in France.

On Sunday, a similar tape surfaces with Drew Anderson speaking in front of the Colosseum in Rome. GNZ reports that numerous eyewitnesses spotted him there.

I expect police sirens to dash toward my residence at any second, but nothing but silence fills my room.

So far so good.

Chapter 98

I stroll into the office on Monday morning with mountain-bike in hand. It instantly doesn't feel right. Everything appears normal, but something is wrong.

I see Shep coming out of the conference room with a man in a sharp suit. They shake hands like they just closed a sales deal, but I can tell from Shep's expression that something's up. She walks past me without saying a word.

The man approaches me with an extended hand. "Jack Lawson—I'm Special Agent Scott Hawkins from the FBI. I was wondering if I could have a few words with you in the conference room?"

I can tell I don't really have a choice in the situation. I put my bike down and follow him. We sit on opposite sides of the conference table, intently gauging each other. From the many Lawson functions I've attended over the years, I can sense a power-hungry, pompous ass with a sense of entitlement from a mile away.

"I would like to congratulate you on your work in the Anderson trial. You are a fine litigator. What impresses me most is that it seemed you had the deck stacked against you, yet were still able to pull it off."

I distrust his tone. I knew I would be questioned at some point, but I wasn't expecting it to be this morning.

"We had some help," I reply humbly.

"Yes you did."

I remind myself that normal behavior would dictate that I'm a little upset that after all my time and effort, the man I convicted won a free European vacation. So I choose to go on the offensive, "Are you here to tell me you captured Anderson, or is he still backpacking through Spain?"

Hawkins smiles strangely at me. "You go to the movies a lot, Jack?"

"If you want to make a film about my life, take a number—already got over fifty offers."

He doesn't even twitch. "You see, the thing I've always found fascinating about movies, is that they always make sense in the end—resolution in a neat package. But things don't always make sense in real life."

"I'll take that as you haven't found him yet. Do you at least know where he'll be appearing today—London? Moscow?"

Hawkins' look is frosted with smug confidence, which concerns me.

"Have you ever heard of the term 'where there's smoke, there's fire,' Jack?"

"I'm a prosecutor. I'm only concerned if I can prove to a jury that a connection exists between the smoke and fire."

"Then maybe you're the right guy to talk to. Because ever since I started investigating Drew Anderson's escape, I've come across a lot of smoke. And I have been wondering how it ties to the fire."

I remain silent, letting Hawkins carry on with his orchestration.

"I keep coming across this one name. A meeting between Kerri Lawson and Drew Anderson took place the day after his conviction. And strangely, the prosecuting attorney, *Jack Lawson,* was also there. I viewed pictures of Anderson from a bathroom security camera at the Hall of Fame the night of his escape, during an event put on by Mac Cirillo, who happens to be a close friend of *Jack Lawson.*"

My mouth is a cotton field. I need a glass of water, but there's none in sight. I will take complete blame for this straight to the electric chair before I allow Mac, Ashley, or George to go down with me.

"A police officer reported that a group leaving the Hall of Fame left on a charter to the Bahamas. Coincidentally, the same destination where Anderson had been spotted that night. Armstrong Airlines chartered the plane, and what do you know, the pilot, Ashley Cirillo lives at the same residence as, you guessed it, *Jack Lawson.* Do you see the pattern, Jack?"

"The only pattern I see is a consistent failure of law enforcement, who keep trying to cover their asses by attempting to blame others, and tossing wild accusations against the wall." I surprise myself with the strength of my words.

Hawkins still looks like he is holding a winning lottery ticket.

"We've done a lot of talking with Shane King in the last few days."

"Please let me know when you're finished, because the Otsego County District Attorney's Office would like to have a few words with Mr. King."

Hawkins ignores me, plowing ahead, "From our discussions, along with witnesses at Glimmerglass State Park, and the Cooperstown Public Library—where he left a trail on the public-access computers—the FBI has enough evidence to conclude that Andy Kass was the one responsible for the explosions. And to stick with our theme, Andy Kass had charges against him conveniently dropped just a week prior by none other than *Jack Lawson.*"

My arms have gone completely numb. I want to reach to wipe the beads of sweat from my forehead, but I don't think I physically can. My one salvation is that the Andy Kass accusation is the one I've been prepared to answer since the escape. The connection was inevitable.

"We didn't release Andy Kass, or drop charges. We agreed to a plea bargain with Andy and his lawyer that was approved by the judge in the case. Our budget wasn't exactly prepared for another high-profile trial after Anderson. And last I checked, Andy was out on bail awaiting his trial, anyway. If he wanted to cause this explosion, then there was nothing the DA's Office could have done to stop it."

The key to the plea deal was getting him that community service in which he could plant the explosives. I keep that part to myself.

Hawkins looks at his notes. "That's an interesting point. I also find it interesting that your colleague, Jessica Shepherdson, told me that you wanted to prosecute Kass to the fullest extent, but she was the one who pushed for the plea."

I try to hide my surprise. *Shep lied for me.*

"If you're so sure, why don't you go arrest Andy? You don't need my permission—seems like nobody consults the DA's Office before making arrests in these parts."

"Andy Kass is missing."

"Who isn't? It seems to be an epidemic," I say with a shrug. "Andy was about helping the downtrodden. He's a misguided modern day Robin Hood. He fought for those who couldn't fight for themselves. The last person in the world he would help is someone with a sense of entitlement like Drew Anderson."

"Maybe he thought Anderson was being railroaded. There was something shady going on during that trial, and maybe Robin Hood was fighting against such injustice. Or who knows, everybody has their price, maybe Andy Kass was hired to do a job for a lot less romantic ideals and a lot more dollars."

"I'm hearing a lot of maybes. I shouldn't have to explain to someone in your position that law enforcement is based on facts, not maybes."

"The one thing I am sure of is that you know more than you are telling me, Jack. And that's a fact."

"Are you accusing me of conspiring to help the man I convicted on murder charges? What possible motivation would I have to do something like that?"

"You know, Jack, I've been asking myself the same question." He reaches into a folder and takes out glossy 8x10 photos. He slides them across the table for my viewing pleasure.

One is of Marissa and me entering her apartment. Another of yours truly leaving the next morning. On the bottom left hand corner of the photos is the time and date. The third photo is a close up of Marissa getting on my motorcycle.

I'm fuming. "Are you following me?"

"Actually, we were following Marissa Anderson. You are just the guest star. Should we have been following you?"

I choose not to say anything. I wonder if Shep would represent me at my trial.

Hawkins is in all his glory. "I couldn't figure out what your motivation would be. Then I remembered that throughout history, man is motivated by three things—power, money, and a beautiful woman. I think what we have here is door number three, Jack."

My head is spinning, but I fight to think clearly. Hawkins is tossing a lot of damning coincidences my way, but he still has nothing concrete. He's not even sure what he's fishing for. I'm still in control.

"So let me get this straight, Agent Hawkins. I conspired to work with Andy Kass to help Drew Anderson escape, all because I fell under the spell of Marissa Anderson? If I was handed that scenario as a prosecutor, the first thing I would wonder is, if Jack is so smitten with her, then wouldn't it have been in his best interest to have her husband locked up for life?

"I would also look at the other side of the coin—perhaps she was trading favors with Jack in exchange for freeing her husband. But the big problem there, is that it would make more sense for Jack to free Anderson by fixing the trial in the first place. So I'd have to inform you that despite the high entertainment value of your theory, you are low on motive and evidence, not to mention logic. I'd then send you back to do more investigating, to save you from making a haphazard arrest, in which I would be forced to drop the charges for lack of evidence."

After my performance, I stand and begin to walk out.

"Where do you think you're going?" Hawkins barks.

I turn toward him, oozing adrenaline. "I'm going fishing. Since this little charade is nothing but a fishing expedition, I figure I'll go where the fish actually bite. The only lead you have is Andy Kass. You are unable to connect him to any legitimate suspects like Lansdale and his group. The only person you can connect him to is me, due to my involvement in his plea agreement and a couple stalker-shots you have of Anderson's wife and me. And I'm sure your boss is up your ass about making an arrest. So you come down here hassling me, all while Anderson remains on his world tour. Stop wasting my time, Agent Hawkins!"

I march to my office and slam the door. I fall into the chair behind my desk and slump down. I knew that Andy would be fingered for the bombing, and eventually his trail would lead to me. So the meeting with Hawkins wasn't unexpected, but he hit a little closer to home than I thought he would—the way he connected the dots between me and the escape, and even incorporated Marissa into his theory. I wonder how long he's been tracking me. I sit in my chair, paralyzed, my hands trembling.

About a half-hour later, Shep enters. "Are you okay, Jack?"

I try to smile, but my shaky hands tell a different story. "I will be, this whole thing is a little overwhelming."

"They have no idea where Anderson is, do they?"

"Not a clue," I answer. "And Shep, you don't have to lie for me. I don't want you to get yourself in trouble."

I can tell her mind is on something else. "Is the stuff Agent Hawkins said in there true?" she asks hesitantly.

"Like I told you before, they're going to try to attach the explosions to Andy Kass, and then they will try to draw a connection to my generous plea agreement. He was basically fishing."

"That's not what I meant—I was talking about the pictures of you and Marissa Anderson."

I swallow hard. "She reminded me of the past, but I now understand that it's the future I should be concerned with."

I suspect my words confirm what she already believed. I sense disappointment, but not judgment. I can tell she has many more questions, but she doesn't push it, before leaving.

I have just as many questions about Shep. From my desk drawer I take out the folded photo of her at the helipad, and stare at it.

The Trial of Max Q has been nothing but questions, with few answers. And the conclusions I've drawn have either been wrong or manipulated. But as I sit alone in my office, over three months after the murder, I am confident of two things that I'd be willing to bet my life on. One, is that Drew Anderson didn't kill Laney Bang.

The other is that Shep is on my side.

I rip the photo up into tiny pieces and toss the confetti into the garbage can. All I can do now is wait for the final move.

Chapter 99

After a painstakingly slow movement of the calendar, the day has arrived for the final move of the plan. It is a day when most people are with their families, eating turkey and watching bad football games—Thanksgiving.

I sit deathly still in my guide boat, surrounded by nothing but darkness and the frigid waters of Otsego Lake. I supposedly left for a day of fishing at noon, and now ten hours later, ice fishing might be a more appropriate description. My body is numb from the plunging temperature. Cooperstown had its first light snowfall this past Tuesday.

Mac Cirillo has always theorized that the best time to commit crimes in America is the night of Thanksgiving, because everyone is suffering the affects of the sleeping agent Tryptophan that is in turkey. I laugh to myself at the absurdity of the "Great Escape," and my likely prison term, hinging on a theory of Macademia.

I hear a loud splashing sound. Even in the darkness, I can detect a human head sticking out of the water, wearing a scuba mask. A gloved hand reaches up and grabs the side of the boat, which goes into a treacherous rocking motion.

I lean over and help the diver over the rail, gripping the scuba tank. The diver falls into the bobbing boat and immediately removes their mask. Her dark curly hair falls to her wet shoulders.

Marissa sits on the floor of my boat, gasping for breath. I wrap her in multiple towels, and can feel her shivering.

"Nice night for a swim?" I ask.

"Had to work off all the turkey and stuffing," she attempts to joke, still breathing heavy.

I convinced everyone involved, including Marissa, that any plan to free Drew wouldn't include her. It was just too dangerous. Once free, they can risk contact if they desire, it will be out of my hands at that point. But all along I knew she'd have to play a big role.

We have no time to lose, so I toss her a paddle. She looks strangely at it. "Just follow my lead," I instruct.

Marissa drops her air tank and mask to the bottom of the lake and we head toward the lone light in the distance.

When not traveling to exotic locales around the world, James Lansdale's yacht is normally anchored at the north end of Otsego Lake, and has become a Cooperstown landmark. It is two hundred and fifty feet long, and is the sixth largest yacht in North America. Always the competitor, Lansdale is probably disappointed that it isn't the largest.

We paddle the Adirondack to the rear end of the yacht and a rope ladder is thrown down from three decks above. I look up I see Lansdale peering down at us. I am now completely convinced that I've sold my soul to the devil, but I feel like I had no choice but to include him.

Marissa climbs first. I follow, unable to avoid noticing how her wetsuit hugs her body. My mind backtracks to the night we spent together.

We ascend the ladder until we reach a landing area at the rear of the ship, where a small seaplane rests. Marissa instantly rushes to Lansdale and embraces him. I settle for a firm handshake. Every instinct in my body told me to not include him, but Drew and Marissa both believe in his loyalty, and they are the ones who have the most to lose if this doesn't work.

There is no time to waste. We hurry across the deck, which is devoid of lighting, and enter the yacht's interior through magnificent French doors. The first room is a reception room that looks like a Parisian café, full of glass tables and wicker chairs. A window the size of a movie screen provides a brilliant view of the lake. I visualize Lansdale and his cronies in here, sipping drinks and plotting the fate of the universe, while rays of a beautiful Cooperstown sunset fill the room.

My heart is thumping. Ever since my meeting with the FBI I've been looking over my shoulder, and expect a sting operation to swing into action and pounce on us.

We climb a staircase to the next deck. Lansdale transforms into a tour guide, proudly showing off the yacht's movie theater, master stateroom, and racquetball court. I'm not listening, and I get the feeling that neither is Marissa.

We pass through a piano bar with a dramatic domed ceiling, leading us to the dining room. Expensive woodcarvings and oil paintings line the walls. An enormous oak table sits beside a crackling fireplace, and appears to be prepared for a Thanksgiving feast. Lansdale tells us that he modeled the room after the first class smoking room on the Titanic. Outside of hoping this trip has a better ending, I am not interested.

I am preoccupied with the sight before me. If I had to describe it in one word it would be…perfect.

Chapter 100

Marissa runs straight for the arms of her husband. He picks her up and twirls her around and they kiss passionately. It's like a scene from a movie.

My feelings are mixed, but the overriding feeling is that of good. I smile for the first time in a long time.

Drew never left the country on that flight to the Bahamas. The man who left with George Herman on Ashley's plane was a legit Lou Gehrig impersonator who went on the cruise and performed his strange craft without incident, fanfare, or any knowledge of what was taking place. Similar to making the world believe that man went to the moon, yet he'd never really left the planet. Hopefully, Hawkins and the other authorities are too busy following the false trail to discover that Max Q has been right under their nose the whole time.

Besides Shane King, three other impersonators were anonymously recruited by George, and hired by Andy Kass. As much as the spotlight motivated Shane, the others were desperate for money.

Andy approached the men using an alias, and made them an offer they couldn't refuse. And after all three leaped at the winning lottery ticket, he took charge of their preparation. He kept his identity hidden, and made it clear he worked for a ruthless and powerful man who could make them disappear if they ever spoke on the subject.

This is where Lansdale came in, and why he was a necessary evil. He could easily transfer a few hundred grand apiece into offshore accounts, without denting his billions or arousing suspicion. Andy provided the men a partial payment, using the money I supplied him, along with the plane tickets to their assigned destination, whether it was the Bahamas, Paris, or Rome. Andy's training included everything from rehearsals of their speeches, to providing them with inside information such as Anderson was planning a newly close-cropped haircut.

They were sent to their locales a week prior to sentencing. When the time came, they played out their roles. It was the easiest work they had ever done. A week later, they returned to the US with a lot more money and a dark secret.

Marissa and Drew can't stop kissing and caressing. I look at my watch—I hate to be the wet blanket, but we still have to move fast.

Lansdale has other ideas. "Everyone please take a seat—Thanksgiving feast is about to be served."

This isn't part of the plan. My distrust of Lansdale rises to the surface. *A stall tactic to hold out for the FBI?* I visualize Shep marching in with an army of FBI behind her to arrest us, and then she kisses Lansdale, her secret boyfriend. I shake the thought out of my head.

Lansdale adds, "I think we all have a lot to be thankful for tonight."

Marissa and Drew smile their agreement, never taking their eyes off each other. They sit together on one side of the long table. I hesitantly take a seat across from them. A smiling Lansdale sits at the head of the table.

"My assistant will be out in a moment with the food," he declares.

I look at Lansdale with disbelief. Nobody else is supposed to be here! "I thought we agreed…

Before I can finish, a pudgy teenager in an apron comes in, carrying a large roast turkey.

"Jaaack!" Andy Kass says and a big smile appears on his face.

I guess he isn't as long gone as I thought. I'm not pleased.

He places the turkey down, understanding that this change of plans could use some explanation. "Mr. Lansdale had Drew and myself sealed under the hardwood floor of the racquetball court. It was like a tomb, with only a small opening to breathe, and so he could send food and water to us. I know it went against the plan, but there was a lot of heat out there, and Mr. Lansdale thought it was best to go into lock-down mode."

There's nothing I can do about it now, so I grudgingly nod my blessing. Lansdale was supposed to pick Andy up after the explosions and hide him out for a few days, then use his influence to get him out of the country with a new identity. At that point, Andy would be on his own. The lack of control I feel is driving my nerves more than anything.

Andy makes a couple more trips to the galley to add to the feast, returning with cranberries, stuffing, mashed potatoes, and wine. Andy and Lansdale seem to have forged a strange bond. It's sort of like Robin Hood and the Sheriff of Nottingham breaking bread together. A little weird.

Lansdale pours the wine and we all raise chalices. "To love," he toasts.

When I look around the table, I want to feel like justice was served, but all I really see is loyalty amongst thieves. However, it doesn't diminish the good feeling I get when I see Drew and Marissa together.

Following a rushed meal, we head to the deck. It's the moment of truth. A cold wind shoots through me. We walk to the rear of the boat where the seaplane is latched.

Final goodbyes are a blur. Drew shakes my hand. "Thank you for saving my life," he says in the most heartfelt way.

I never asked who killed Laney Bang, and framed him for it—I doubt he would tell me, anyway—but Kerri promised me full disclosure after he is safely off. I plan to take her up on that offer. But it's more out of curiosity than anything. I'm a prosecutor, not a cop, it's not my role to solve crimes.

My job is to make sure that justice is served in the end, and I have regained confidence in my compass, which is telling me that Drew Anderson didn't kill Laney Bang. So tonight I am dropping all charges against him. Happy Thanksgiving.

I take a final look at Marissa. I see a rare fragility, but also joy. She hugs me. "I will never forget this, Jack," she whispers in my ear. I struggle to let her go.

Andy Kass understands that this will really be the last time he ever sees me. He again wraps me in a hug, which is starting to become a trend.

"Remember what you promised," I say.

"I know, I know. I won't ever mention this again."

"Not that, Andy. I'm talking about the part where you will use your passion to help the downtrodden by legal means. That is the only way to accomplish it in the end."

"I promise," he says and pulls from the hug, this time refraining from mentioning what a hypocrite I sound like. "You're different, Jack."

I smile. "I'm not much different from you, Andy."

When Lansdale finishes his corporate goodbyes, Drew, Marissa, and Andy climb into the seaplane. Drew sits in the pilot seat, just as he once did during his heroic military career. The plane is lowered mechanically into the cold lake.

I have no idea where they are going, and don't want to know.

Chapter 101

I feel relief each time my paddle hits the water. If the FBI is waiting for me with guns blazing, then so be it. Drew Anderson is long gone and reunited with Marissa. I couldn't have lived with myself if I was the one responsible for them being apart. We didn't take the easiest route, to say the least, but Reyanne taught me that the journey of life can be much more gratifying when you have to fight against all odds to get to the finish line. I think she'd be proud.

I use the light from the Cirillos' house as a guide to shore, which I find symbolic. I drag the Adirondack onto dry land, bracing for guns pointing in my direction and a loud shout of "Freeze, Lawson!" But all I hear is the crunching of leaves under my feet.

Then suddenly I feel a sharp pain in my left knee. I tumble to the ground, crashing hard on my side. Another sharp blast to my abdominal region is followed by one to my ribs—I am under attack.

I regain my bearings enough to grasp that the weapon used against me is a foot—the sharp end of a boot. Just as I recover, another swing heads violently toward my ribs. Direct hit. "Ugh!"

My eyes adjust to the dark. I see Shep is standing over me, shaking with anger.

"What are you doing?"

"What am *I* doing?" she asks incredulously. The frigid air makes her angry breaths appear like smoke. "I think the question is what the hell are *you* doing, Jack!?"

"I …I was…"

"You were what?"

"Fishing," I say, feebly.

Wrong answer—kick. "Ugh!"

"Does conspiring to help Drew Anderson and his wife escape, ring a bell, Jack?"

I have envisioned scenarios in which I'm caught. The visions always feature Agent Hawkins falling over himself taking credit, Roddy Opp smiling smugly at me, and Gifford Brown joyfully prosecuting me. Not Shep kicking me in the ribs. We never die the way we think we will.

"How did you know..."

"Because instead of having a nice Thanksgiving dinner like most normal people, I was freezing my ass off in a kayak on Otsego Lake, watching Jack Lawson break the law through a pair of binoculars. I saw you with Lansdale, helping Drew and Marissa take off in that plane with my old buddy Andy Kass."

"Why were you spying on me?"

"This isn't about me, Jack. Why did you do it?"

Writhing in pain, I shout out, "Anderson didn't kill her! We put the wrong guy in prison. He refused another trial because he was protecting his wife; he got messed up with powerful people who were threatening her. I couldn't live with myself if I put an innocent man away for life."

I brace for another kick, but it never comes. She doesn't look as surprised as she should.

"Then who did it, Jack?"

"Whoever was pulling the strings in the trial. I don't know who it was, but I'm sure it wasn't Anderson."

Shep begins to pace. "I can't believe I fell for this partners BS. That whole nonsense about keeping me out of it because you didn't want me to be connected to Andy Kass, and how worried you were about my future."

"I understand you have to turn me in, Shep. I'm okay with it. In fact, I don't think you have a choice. I couldn't put an innocent man away—they are gone now and I am willing to pay the consequences."

She stops pacing and glares at me. "I'm not going to turn you in."

I look up at her, unsure.

"I think Lansdale is the one behind it. He's the puppeteer," she blurts.

"So you were spying on Lansdale, and not me?"

"I wasn't spying on anyone."

"Then what were you doing?"

"I was following up a lead. I got a call today from George Herman, who provided some interesting information. Like an investigation he did on me over the last few weeks that included tapping my phone and bugging my car. Said he grew suspicions of me after he was sent on that wild goose chase, and began to wonder if I was Lansdale's mystery girlfriend. Then after he found a photo of me at a helipad in Manhattan the morning of the murder, he started wondering much worse stuff. Does any of this ring a bell, Jack?"

I play it safe by saying nothing.

"I'm sure you'll be relieved to know that George found that I am a boring workaholic who has nothing better to do on Thanksgiving. And not only am I not dating James Lansdale, I don't have a boyfriend at all—I made him up to impress a guy, but he turned out to be a felon with trust issues. Not a real man like George, who had the guts to call me up on a holiday to apologize for his actions."

As much pain as I'm in, the part about the boyfriend almost makes me smile. "You still didn't answer my question—what led you to do surveillance on Lansdale tonight?"

"George had another reason for calling. Turns out Lansdale had a motive to take down Anderson. But since you were off pursuing a life of crime, he couldn't find you. So he trusted me with the information."

"Lansdale just helped Drew escape—you saw it with your own eyes."

"When Anderson's business hit those major financial problems a few years back, he entered into a secretive agreement with Lansdale. It injected capital into Max-Q-Collectibles, and for his trouble, Lansdale received a stake in the company."

I remain quietly lying on the wet ground. So far, it sounds like two businessmen doing business. I nod for her to go on.

"But it wasn't just a business deal—it was a bet. Winner take all. If Anderson won the governorship, then he got back complete control of the company. But if he either didn't run or didn't win, Lansdale got controlling interest. So by getting rid of Anderson prior to the election, he would acquire the company. And by using Laney Bang to set him up, he also got rid of his arch-enemy in the process. He killed two birds with one stone, so to speak."

I'm skeptical. "Lansdale and his group would have profited much more by Anderson becoming governor. That's why he made the bet in the first place—he wanted Anderson in Albany. And I'm not sure he really wanted to get rid of Laney Bang. He needed her. Every great revolutionary needs a worthy opponent to validate their quest."

"Regardless, since Lansdale is now a prime suspect in Anderson's escape, I'm going to have a talk with him," Shep says, holding a determined look at the yacht in the distance.

As if on cue, a helicopter lifts into the air and roars over the dark trees that surround the lake.

"He's heading back to his ranch. Maybe you can catch up with him there. I've gotten Drew and Marissa to safety, so I've done my part. I'm done with this case," I contend.

"I don't think you're in a position to be making declarations."

"It's a waste of time. Lansdale couldn't be the one who set him up."

"I'm not saying he killed Laney. My only point was that we need to have an open mind."

The conversation is starting to sound familiar. We are right back where we started, except for a surprising role reversal.

She lifts me to my feet. She then takes off the winter cap that is snuggled over her hair and tosses it to me. "You take it, you'd have a lot more to lose from a head injury."

I smile through my pain as I follow her out of the woods.

Chapter 102

As dawn breaks, we ride up the long driveway of Lansdale's Saratoga ranch. I'm tired, beaten, and skeptical, but Shep appears to have found her second wind.

"So why aren't you going to turn me in?" I muster the energy to ask.

"George said you refused to approve his investigation of me. You insisted to him that you trusted me and wouldn't waver … so consider this to be me returning the favor."

"Then why did you get all Bruce Lee on me?"

"Because in the end, you didn't trust me. I don't need a guy looking out for my safety like I'm some little girl. I might not have revealed personal stuff like my marital situation to you, but when it came to the case I was completely honest. I trusted in everything you preached to me about the law and justice, and then you go behind my back and betray every principle you claim to believe in."

I can't argue—she's right. "Next time I help a convicted murderer escape, you will be the first person I call."

I actually get a slight smile out of her. But then something hits her. "Oh, Jack, I almost forgot. George provided me some other information for you. Something about a scouting report on a judge that came up clean—told me you'd know what he means."

He's telling me that Figliomini isn't the one who manipulated the trial. Score one for my legal idealism. But reopens the question—if not him, then who is Drew afraid of?

She continues, "He also researched Jordans who stole cars in the Bronx, as you requested. He has your profile narrowed down to two possibilities. He'll have something solid for you by Monday. Do you know what he is talking about?"

I think of Drew and Marissa happily flying away to a new beginning. "Thanks, but it doesn't matter anymore."

The first thing I notice about the ranch is how empty it is. It's the crack of dawn, but having been around the Lawson stables during my childhood, I know that this time of morning is usually filled with great bustle and energy. It's strange not to see even one thoroughbred out for a morning gallop.

As we get closer, I ask with trepidation, "What are you going to ask him?"

"Don't worry, Jack, I'm not going to blow your cover. If he thinks I know what you did last night, then I'll never get any answers out of him. Just follow my lead."

When we arrive at the ranch house, I notice that the helipad is empty. He should have beaten us here. His cars are also missing, but maybe he moves them into a garage this time of year. A knock on the front door gets no response, so we decide to walk the grounds, searching for signs of life. After spending endless hours in my small boat the night before, it feels good to stretch my legs. My bruised ribs, courtesy of Shep's boot, are another story.

We walk into the stables, greeted by the smell of horseshit. But while their aroma remains, no horses are present.

We turn the corner and spot human life. A stable boy is standing outside the stall of a lone thoroughbred. The horse is sticking its head through an opening, and the man is rubbing its snout in an affectionate way. As far as I can see, it's the only horse remaining in the stable.

"Hello," Shep calls out.

We move closer.

The man continues to caress the horse's face, oblivious to our presence.

"Hey—we're talking to you," she follows up with authority.

He slowly turns his head in our direction. He doesn't look surprised. Actually, he looks sad.

"Can I help you?" he finally replies in a calm voice.

I realize that he is the same guy that Shep found so attractive on our last visit.

"We are looking for James Lansdale."

"He's gone," the man says dismissively, his concentration on the horse.

"We'll wait," Shep remains diligent.

The man turns back toward her and his peaceful demeanor washes away. "Get it through your thick skull, woman. He's gone! He's with *her* now. He has no need for this place anymore, so he sold it."

Shep and I both see it at the same time. On his left arm, staring us straight in the face. A tattoo. Cross in the middle, a 'J' on one side of the cross, and an 'M' on the other.

Chapter 103

As I stare at him, Shep shows her pragmatic side. She pulls out a 9mm pistol and points it at the stable boy. "Freeze!" *Shep packs a gun?*

The man remains disturbingly calm. It's as if he is completely detached from this world, sort of like Maxon at the end. He gives no indication that he'll flee, gun or no gun.

"So we meet again, Jessica," he says.

Shep says nothing, gun locked and loaded.

He smirks at me. "I'm disappointed you didn't recognize me, Jack. Perhaps you only remember my fist against your face."

It makes no sense that he'd be the one who ran us off the road. The attacks on George and Ashley helped our case, but our "accident" was a warning to back off. Our attacker had a long sleeve shirt on that night, so I can't identify him by the tattoo, but the voice matches.

Shep's gaze remains locked on the man. "If Lansdale sold this place, what are you doing here? We saw you here on our first visit—you work for him."

The man turns to pet the snout. The horse is beginning to get protective of his stable friend, turning rambunctious.

"Keep your hands where I can see them!" Shep screams, her gun is still pointed at his pretty face.

The man completely ignores her demands. He still appears more concerned with the horse, whom he calms with a few loving strokes.

"His name is Common Decency. The new owners came by earlier this morning, and as you can tell by the empty stalls, all his compatriots were shipped off like royalty to the highest bidders after the sale. Nobody wanted CD, so I bought him myself—plan to take him back with me to New Zealand."

The man looks at Shep. "If you want to arrest me, knock yourself out. It doesn't matter anymore."

"Stop covering for him. You work for James Lansdale and you know where he is."

A creepy smile replaces his melancholy facade.

"What's so funny?" Shep demands, gun still pointed directly at him. If she's bluffing she sure is doing a good acting job.

He mocks her with a laugh, before dropping a bombshell, "I don't work for James Lansdale. I'm his son."

Shep takes a step back, jolted by the words.

My mind overloads. "You're a Lansdale?"

"I chose to change it to my mother's surname of Kelly. Thought it would give me a fresh start. Does that sound familiar, Jessica?"

"Stop playing games with us!" she shouts. But I get the feeling he isn't.

"You might remember Kirstie Kelly, the New Zealand model from back in the day. Had an affair with James Lansdale, which got her knocked up. My loving father's wife at the time tried to convince my mum to get an abortion, but she disagreed. I'm not saying it was an act of nobility, as I'm sure she was more interested in the mighty Lansdalian child-support payments.

"Life was good growing up in New Zealand, before my mum decided she wanted to make a comeback in the modeling world, and moved me to New York when I was sixteen. The only good part was that I might get to see my father, who was always too busy doing business in New York to come visit me in New Zealand. But never saw the bastard once. Then, in the irony of ironies, when I got in trouble with the law, he went to court to get custody of me and enslave me up here. And now he stole *her*! He always gets his way."

Shep holds the gun on him with her right hand, while punching numbers into her cell with her free hand. "We'll see about that," she announces, then speaks into the phone, "George, it's Shep—sorry to bother you so early, but I need some information, and it's urgent."

I take the good cop approach. "Did your father order you to give us that evidence against Anderson … the video? The tickets?"

"I wouldn't do anything for that deadbeat. I did it for *her!* She said we could be together again."

*S*omething clicks. "I have a photo of a woman getting off your father's helicopter the morning of Laney Bang's murder. He claims it was his girlfriend. Is that who *her* is? Is that who he ran off with?"

"Girlfriend? If that's what you want to call her, mate," he responds. He looks at the horse for comfort. "The sad thing is that if she showed up here right now, I'd take her back. She's my addiction."

Shep ends her phone call with George. "James Lansdale and Kirstie Kelly had one child, a son named Jordan."

"In the flesh," he directs toward her. "Would you like to check my driver's license? Luckily it didn't get revoked when I ran some dumb bitch off the road."

Shep does a slow burn, her gun firmly locked on Jordan Kelly.

"Any of that trouble you got in with the law happen in the Bronx?" I ask.

Jordan flashes me a smile. "Life was real boring in our stuffy Upper East Side neighborhood. So my boys and I used to go up to the Bronx and rob cars. Borrow cars, actually. We would return them a few days later with a heartfelt note about how we needed the car for an emergency and had no choice. For their trouble, we left a couple Broadway show or Knicks tickets on the front seat. The night they would attend, we would rob their house." He laughs.

"Let me guess, your lawyer was named Marissa?"

"I had to use the public defender because my billionaire father wouldn't reach into his pocket to help me out. But it turned out to be the best money he never spent. I told you it always works out for him."

"That's how you came across Drew Anderson and he made you a movie star."

Jordan laughs again. "Drew didn't make me into anything. His wife was the aggressor, and it killed him to know that for all his supposed perfection, the one thing that mattered to him preferred some punk kid over him. And the funny thing was, I think she got off on the fact that it made him want her more."

"Whatever the circumstance, she eventually dropped you to go back to her husband. Is that why you provided us that evidence against him?"

"One thing Drew and I have in common is that neither of us ended up with her."

"They are together now," I challenge.

"Marissa is only together with one man and it's not Drew, or myself. Marissa ran off with my father!"

Chapter 104

"It can't be," I say to myself. I go into prosecutor mode with Jordan. "She was there that morning, wasn't she?"

He shrugs. "All I did was sneak her on that helicopter at West 30th, and pick her up when she returned the next morning. What happened in between is your job to figure out."

Marissa's words fill my mind: *Someone is trying to frame my husband for murder. If someone is going to such great lengths, his life will be in danger when he's acquitted.*

It was Marissa who went to such lengths, and in the next breath she told me that I was the only chance to catch that person before they did further harm to him. I know now that she was right … and I'm too late. The puzzle has all come together for me and I feel sick.

Overcome by dizziness, I sit down on the straw-filled floor of the stable.

Sheplock Holmes has also put the pieces together. "Gifford Brown is right. It's not about the money, it's about the amount of money. After the bet, Lansdale has the company, so she devised a way to align herself with the winner."

"I don't think it's about the company, or money."

"Then why?"

"It's about perfection. Marissa's idea of perfection is security—knowing that something can't be taken away from her. She had wealth with Drew, but the deep fear of abandonment never went away. At some point, she realized that Drew still held her destiny in his hands and she was powerless. Both Drew and Lansdale had plenty of money, but Lansdale represents certainty."

"You call it perfection, I call it trading up—it's all semantics. Marissa framed him for Laney Bang's murder so she could be with Lansdale, and I'm guessing a more reasonable pre-nup."

"Drew knew that Marissa was the one who really killed Laney. He wasn't protecting her from Figliomini or some ruthless business partners, he was protecting her from an investigation that would reveal the truth about what she did. And she was counting on this type of response from him."

My husband's only fault is loyalty.

She was true to her word—she lied about Drew pushing the affair with Jordan, as part of her strategy to do or say anything to "free my husband," but when it came to the facts of the case, she did tell the truth. She showed me the pictures of Figliomini, but went out of her way not to accuse him of anything, same with Maxon. What she did was open my mind and let me do the work for her to free her husband.

Marissa's words smack me in the face once more: *Why would I want him in jail? With my pre-nup I would be better off with him dead*?

"She never wanted him to spend life in prison, and until Ryan Maxon came along, he would have gotten off. Maxon accidentally threw a wrench into their plan."

"I still don't get it," Shep says with a confused look. "If she didn't want him to go to jail, why would she have Jordan give us that video in the first place? He would have walked without a trial."

"For her plan to work, he needed to go through the process, and who would know that better than a lawyer of Marissa's caliber? It had to look like Drew really was the killer, but that the jury let him walk due to some combination of his influence, celebrity, and the best attorneys money could buy. She wanted him to win legally, but lose in the court of public opinion. That way all investigations cease. I seriously doubt that anyone is spending any time or money looking for the 'real killers' in the OJ Simpson case, even though he was acquitted."

I've been wrong numerous times on this case, but my instincts have returned, and I know I'm right this time. And thanks to me he never looked guiltier.

"But why would Drew go along with this?"

"To protect her. As Jordan said: she was the one thing that mattered to him. She was his symbol of perfection, his mechanical rabbit. He wanted to get off, but his first priority was to protect his prize possession—Marissa. So when Maxon hit him too close to home, he decided to sacrifice himself. That knife Maxon buried wasn't the murder weapon—I'm guessing the real one was buried at sea—it was his insurance policy in case things started pointing in his wife's direction. He didn't want to face me on the stand or give me the benefit of a second trial to figure it out. He was going to fall on the sword to protect Marissa."

"Which means that escaping was the only way he could be with her. It also made him look guiltier than sin, which protected her from any future scrutiny. But he really was just playing into her plan."

I nod. Luckily they had a crazed prosecutor to help them out.

"Now I understand his motivation, but I'm still not clear as to why she was willing to risk it all on an escape. After Maxon's testimony, she was in the clear from future scrutiny, just as she planned. And with Drew in jail, she and Lansdale could have run off together. It seems her objectives were already met," Shep says.

"Drew spending life in prison was going to be an obstacle to her new life. If she stopped being the supportive wife or sought a divorce, he might stop being the protective husband. Her goal is security, and the only way to achieve it is to control your destiny. He would still have control over her from prison."

The way I see it, shortly after his release, "depressed" over his sullied reputation and fall from grace, Drew would have taken his own life. At least Marissa would have made it look that way.

The grieving widow would run to the arms of James Lansdale for comfort. Drew and Lansdale symbolized the men who tore down her father's store—the gatekeepers to the kingdom of perfection. Only when Drew and Lansdale are out of the way, will the kingdom be hers. Then nobody will be able to take it away from her, and destiny will finally be in her hands.

"But after Maxon foiled the plan, she needed to find a new way to get rid of him. She's going to kill Drew, and if I'm Lansdale, I'm not making any long term plans," Shep adds.

I can't summon any sadness for Lansdale. His quest to acquire the best toys at any cost led him to Marissa, but this trophy will likely be very costly. The big game hunter was now the hunted, and was likely too blind and arrogant to see it.

"And we can't do a damn thing about it. Laney Bang's murderer will be recorded in the history books as Drew Anderson, a fugitive who will never be seen again. But the reason he will be able to avoid the authorities for the next half century, is not due to his savvy, it's because he is dead."

"The only persons left who witnessed tonight's escape are you and me, and if we ever voice the truth, either nobody will believe us, or we'll be the ones who end up in jail," Shep bemoans.

I remain on the damp straw of the stable floor. I try to come to grips with the fact that I just sent a man to his death. And Shep's right—who was I going to tell? I turned Drew Anderson into a fugitive from the law, and played right into the hands of the killer.

I begin to tremble, remembering that Andy Kass was baggage on the getaway flight. I begin to dry-heave.

Kerri knew that Drew was taking the fall for his wife—she was trying to protect him from her. She likely wanted to have her fried for the murder, but her stubborn client wouldn't allow it. That is why she desperately pushed me to keep Marissa out of the escape plan. I thought it was because she was jealous. She thinks I was saving him from Marissa last night, when I actually led him right to his demise.

Marissa's words fill my head again. *What I would do to just feel that sense of safety for one day, Jack. That feeling that things can't be ripped away from me.*

Shep puts her gun away. She kneels down and wraps her arms around me, trying to console the inconsolable.

"I killed him."

She pulls me tighter.

Jordan Kelly continues stroking the snout of his beloved horse, oblivious to the scene before him.

Chapter 105

The day following Thanksgiving is referred to as Black Friday. Never has the term been so appropriate. Reality has begun to sink in—I sentenced an innocent man to death and there is no appeal process.

I have made my way to Manhattan. The city is bursting at the seams with hordes of shoppers on what is the biggest shopping day of the year in the United States.

Shep and I grilled Jordan Kelly for another hour earlier this morning. We learned nothing of note. He was positive that Lansdale would meet up with Drew and Marissa, but had no idea where or when. I had left the safety route up to Drew—I thought it would be best for them if I had no knowledge of it. It turned out to be best for Marissa. And like everything else in this case, I doubt it was a coincidence.

We did learn that Jordan's tattoo of the 'J' and 'M' next to the cross stood for Jordan and Marissa. The cross represented his belief that she was his savior. We also learned that the strange passive/aggressive behavior of threatening us, yet also providing us valuable evidence, was because Marissa drilled him over and over about keeping people off balance. Which is why they hit us from both sides—providing us evidence against Drew, but also running us off the road in support of him. It was a tactic she was a master at. As she was with the use of the knife, taught to her by her former Special Forces husband, for self-defense purposes.

In the end, arresting Jordan Kelly would accomplish nothing. Even if we gave him immunity, Marissa is long gone, so the only person he would put away would be yours truly. His story also lacks credibility, due to his intense anger toward his father. We eventually left Jordan, who only seemed interested in his horse, so I'm not sure he noticed that we'd gone. He's probably still clinging to some delusional idea that Marissa will return to him.

I walk into Nellie's, a sports bar on the Upper West Side. It's the place I first met Reyanne. I need all the help I can get today.

Crowds are gathered around assorted television sets, watching college football rivalry games that are traditionally played during the extended Thanksgiving weekend. The biggest crowd is viewing the game between Notre Dame and USC.

I arrive at a table in the back and sit down across from Kerri. She looks different, dressed in a baseball cap, jeans, and a light blue Columbia University sweatshirt that she wears over a white turtleneck. Her expression is also different. I've always wanted to wipe the smug expression off her face, but it looks as if somebody has beaten me to it.

"How are you?" I ask.

I expect a sharp reply about wasting her valuable time, dragging her to some bar when she could be billing some client a couple grand an hour. But I get the opposite.

"What are you going to do now?" I ask.

"I'm going to take a leave of absence from LB&G. I need some time to think. Re-evaluate things."

"Be careful about those leave of absences, they can become permanent," I reply and try to smile.

"I'm not going to move to Sticksville and become a prosecutor, Jack, if that's what you are getting at."

A much more Kerri-like answer, which gives the conversation a sense of normalcy.

"Is he gone?" she asks.

"Yes," I reply, but leave out the sordid details.

A sense of relief comes over Kerri's face. "Thank God."

"I did my part, Kerri, now it's your turn. We talked to Jordan Kelly this morning, so I have a pretty good idea of what happened, but I still need a few blanks to be filled in."

"Jordan Kelly," she says, and takes a sip of water. "That's a good place to start, because it's where this whole mess began."

Chapter 106

"When Marissa pursued a relationship with Jordan Kelly, it set her plan in motion, whether she knew it or not at the time," Kerri begins.

"Marissa told me that it was Drew who pushed her into the relationship with Jordan," I interrupt, knowing now that I was completely manipulated.

It might just be coincidence that Jordan Kelly also happened to be the son of James Lansdale, who would become such an intricate part of the Anderson's life. But I've learned that Marissa leaves nothing to chance. I can picture her "innocently" trading cases with a co-worker to be able to defend Lansdale's son.

Kerri looks like she wants to reach across the table and slap some sense into me. "A little charisma and a lot of skin—it works for her with a jury, and with slobbering men like you, Jack. If you haven't figured it out by now, she tends to sway from the truth when it benefits her. Not only did Drew not push the relationship with Jordan, he was devastated by it."

Just like when I first witnessed her in court, her nature was to take control, and this situation was no different.

That's not to say that I think Marissa entered her union with Drew to have extramarital affairs and plot murders. Just the opposite. I think she was searching for a utopian existence in which the things she loved couldn't be taken from her, and thought she had been rescued by her prince. And her refusal to sign any pre-nup was based on idealism, not calculation. But she found out that Drew was the gatekeeper of her dream, and could take it away at any moment. She was just as vulnerable as when they took away her father's store.

She made a pledge to fight for those who fought against such machines—the ones that could steal away people's safe lives—and she found herself to be one of those she vowed to protect. By bringing Jordan Kelly into their lives, she showed Drew that she was now the one who could take away his perfect life.

Kerri continues, "He would never leave her, and she knew that. But he feared that she might leave him, especially when the financial problems began to pile up."

"He brought in Tony Rivotti, the forger, and made the gamble with James Lansdale for control of the business—a deal that seems like a win-win for Jimmy."

She nods. "Drew was desperate. His life was on the line—company, image, and most importantly to him, Marissa. Lansdale is always there to lend a helping hand when it benefits him."

My insides wrench, remembering how Marissa convinced me to bring Lansdale into the escape plan, going against my instincts. "It sounds like you were also there to lend Drew a hand, among other things, during his time of need."

"I'm not ashamed to say that I fell in love with him, but like I told you, I had no illusions that he felt the same about me. I provided him warmth and comfort when all he was getting from her was rejection."

"Was he going for warmth and comfort with Laney Bang? I sensed in the video that other needs were being met in that relationship."

"Laney was his drug—the one that temporarily made the pain go away. I warned him against her, but he was too addicted at that point."

"So I guess if you can't beat them, join them."

"I hope you're referring to our business arrangement and not other things, because that never happened."

"Of course. I would never think such a thing. But I do think that his affair with Laney changed the dynamics with Marissa."

"What it did for Drew was regain the control he lost after the Jordan Kelly affair. At one point, he even had me draw up divorce papers. Like I said, he wasn't thinking straight—the drug was in control of him. But Marissa opened her arms to him again and he came running like the obsessed, lovesick kid he was. He broke it off with both Laney and myself, and he and Marissa seemed to be in as much love as ever—spending every waking minute together and planning a family. If you're keeping score, the control had tilted back in her direction."

Which brings me to the night of July 23.

Chapter 107

I think I've figured out how the night unfolded, but I need to hear it from Kerri.

"No matter how coldly he ended things with me, I still loved Drew. And I don't think I've ever been as excited as the day I got the text from him last spring that said he had made a mistake going back to Marissa, and that he wanted me to meet him in Cooperstown."

"But it wasn't from him, was it?"

"When I arrived I was met by Marissa. But I wasn't alone. Laney was also there, having received the same message. Marissa was angry and accusing us of sleeping with her husband."

"Wasn't the affair with Laney what drove Drew and her back together? She knew about the relationship."

"Of course she did, but you have to remember that things I mentioned to you earlier were based on hindsight. Drew and I went to great lengths to keep our relationship secret. And because I was her business manager, I read the manuscript of Laney's memoir—Drew was practically the only member of the male race that she didn't name in there. So I assumed Marissa didn't know at that point, and was just a pissed off wife who wanted to give her husband a little payback."

"Okay, she's got you there. Now what happens?"

"There was a lot of shouting and name calling at first. But when the dust cleared, the one thing that stood out was that Drew had hurt each of us. Marissa appeared to be the victim of infidelity, and I had been kicked to the curb after being used as a crying shoulder. But most surprising to me was the vitriol that Laney showed toward him."

"Her anger was not an act. It actually went back to her earlier life when she was Darby, and that incident in college. She had been waiting for the right opportunity, and Marissa provided her the platform for revenge."

"I was unaware of that at the time. But her mindset now makes more sense. Laney was the one who suggested we join forces to get revenge on Drew, and was the driving force behind the strategy to do so. Little did she know that she was doing Marissa's dirty work for her, and unwittingly plotting her own murder."

"So how did Laney plan to take down Mr. Perfect after all these years?"

"Even though Drew had gone cold turkey from the Laney drug at the time, she knew if they crossed paths again it would be like a recovering alcoholic walking into a bar. With Maxon's help, we were able to set up the meeting."

"Was Maxon involved?"

"No, but he'd do anything for Laney and she took advantage. She convinced him that she and Drew had mutual business interests, and he moved heaven and earth to make it happen."

"I assume Drew succumbed to his addiction."

"It was like child's play for Laney. Once the others left the meeting, and it was just the two of them, the deal was sealed. She could also push his buttons and get him to threaten her on film, which was a big part of the plan."

I finally had the answer to who the third person was—the one who filmed it without Drew's knowledge. "It was a Marissa production, wasn't it?"

"Having Anderson Estate as the meeting place that night was key. Marissa knew the place inside and out, and didn't need to force entry. And if her prints were lifted, it's her house, of course they were. Plus, she had knowledge of how Drew and Maxon had made their films over the years. Using a hole in the wall, she could remain undetected"

A loud cheer arises from the other side of the bar, as Notre Dame has scored in the midst of a furious comeback, momentarily interrupting us.

When the cheering dies down, I pick up, "The next step is when he leaves for his usual run the next morning. The way I see it, Laney calls 911, so that the police will be waiting for Drew upon his return."

"When they arrived, she would accuse him of assault. And she would look the part—it was Laney's idea for Marissa to beat up her face for authenticity."

"That's why there was no resistance."

"It's also why the threats on the tape were so important. Laney figured that the police would never believe her word against Drew, even with the bruises. She could have embarrassed him with the video, but she had grander plans."

"When the police witnessed the threats, combined with the bruises, they would have no choice but to make an arrest."

She somberly nods her head.

I now know everybody's role in this, but one. "I'm still not sure what your job was, Kerri."

Her expression fills with regret. "As his lawyer, I was going to use the system to make sure he got his public flogging in court, but ensure that he got off in the end. I was supposed to control the trial."

She learned the lesson we've all learned the hard way—the only one controlling the strings was Marissa. She was the true puppeteer. "But things didn't go as planned, did they?"

"It was going fine up until that point—Laney had made the 911 call and it was time for Marissa to approach her and apply the bruising and abrasions to her face. But instead of bruises, Marissa stabbed her to death."

Just like that. Kerri looks devastated, which makes me think. "How do you know this? You weren't there, were you?"

"I got it from an eyewitness."

"There was an eyewitness?"

Chapter 108

"The witness was Drew himself. He unexpectedly returned early from his jog. And what he saw was his beloved wife stabbing to death his mistress. He believed it was a crime of passion, resulting from their affair."

He did change his routine that morning.

Kerri shakes her head like she still couldn't grasp what happened. "It was typical Drew. A combination of chivalry, naïve loyalty, and self-flattery. He actually blamed himself for Marissa killing Laney. He refused to even consider any other possibility."

"She can be quite convincing."

"Oh, she was. She lied to him that she was willing to take responsibility and turn herself into the police. He actually bought her act, and sent her to safety on one of his motorboats. On her way, she dropped the murder weapon to the bottom of Otsego Lake."

"Then Drew does what he always does when he gets himself in to trouble over the years—he calls Maxon."

"Correct. He arrives by boat shortly thereafter, and Drew makes up that hard-to-believe story about a jealous lover showing up and attacking Laney, in which he was forced to stab the woman in self-defense. It wasn't a total lie—he really did believe that his jealous wife arrived to confront Laney. But the reality was that nobody was there to save her."

"Marissa still wasn't completely in the clear. He needed to ensure her protection."

"Drew took another knife from the kitchen and dipped it into Laney's blood, which there was no shortage of. He wanted the second knife hidden, so that if the story about Marissa came to the surface, he would be able to use it to protect her by framing himself for the murder. That's the knife he gave Maxon, with instructions to hide it at the construction site for the new high school. He was willing to go to jail to save her!"

I swell with anger. "You could have gone to the authorities, Kerri—you're an officer of the court. You would have taken a hit for being involved in a conspiracy that got a woman killed, but you could have stopped this." And Drew would still be alive!

"My goal was to protect Drew. He wouldn't believe the truth when I came clean about the plan, and the more I went against Marissa, the more headstrong he got. When I told him my suspicions that she was having an affair with Lansdale, he accused me of trying to come between them out of jealousy. I had to back down—he threatened to fire me—and whether I liked it or not, I was his best chance to survive. I was convinced that I was going to get him off, and once he was free, I could blow the whistle on Marissa. But I first had to get Drew to safety."

"That was until Maxon decided to fight back."

"Maxon was convinced he was going to be the fall guy. That's why he reacted so aggressively when I interrogated him on the stand. All I was doing is what you accused me of in court. What did you call that again?"

"Semi-plausible OJ smorgasbord strategy."

She looks like she wants to roll her eyes at me, but can't summon the energy. "Obviously he felt backed into a corner and came out fighting. Drew had informed me that he had hid a knife as insurance to protect Marissa, but I had no idea that Maxon was the one who knew where it was. I guess his loyalty to Drew was conditional."

I understand her frustration. The worst type of client a lawyer can have is one that doesn't tell you everything.

"Why do you think he gave me that video of you and Drew?"

"We weren't conspiring, or putting on an off-Broadway play, as you put it. Quite the opposite. I think Maxon detected that something seedy was going on, and believed that I was at the center of it, which I can't deny. He must have thought that you were the one who could get to the bottom of it. Since he had access to Drew's video library, and likely was the one responsible for filming us—I had no idea the video even existed until you showed it to me—he was able to gather any incriminating material to protect himself."

My thoughts return to the getaway. "So as Maxon headed across the lake toward Anderson Estate after the 6:19 call, Marissa was already heading toward Lansdale's yacht. A helicopter was waiting to bring her to Manhattan, just in time to for her first case. That was her in that security footage with a blonde wig—Lansdale didn't lie, it was his girlfriend. And it didn't seem out of the ordinary—the Lansdale Shuttle to Manhattan was a normal occurrence."

"She arrived home from the party the night before, made a scene outside her building, appearing to be fall-down drunk for her neighbors to see—then took the predictable call from Drew just after 11:30. The minute she hung up, she was out the fire escape, undetected."

I fill in the blanks, "Jordan Kelly was waiting for her in a car. Since he worked as his father's assistant, he often loaded luggage onto the helicopter.

But this time the luggage in an oversized duffel bag was Marissa, and she stowed away. When they arrived at Anderson Estate to pick up Lansdale, Marissa got off and hid in the mansion. They passed like two ships in the night."

"I couldn't reveal any of this during the trial. Whenever Drew felt that a suspicious eye might look toward Marissa, he threatened to plead guilty, and we both know he wasn't bluffing. When evidence began randomly falling into your lap, it fueled his paranoia that someone was onto them."

"And it turned out that 'someone' was his own wife. And she was skilled at keeping people off balance."

"I talked him down off that ledge numerous times, but after his insurance policy was revealed by Maxon, he made the decision to fall on the sword by refusing to take the stand."

"That is why he wouldn't pursue a new trial." Not a dirty judge. "And also the reason you feared for his safety in jail."

"He was an eyewitness to a coldblooded, premeditated murder. The killer was a lawyer, and a good one, so she knew that the only witnesses that don't talk are dead ones. And she'd come across many unsavory characters through her job that had connections in prison to take him out," Kerri's voice trails off, still not seeing how it was always more advantageous to Marissa to have him out of jail.

I lean back in my chair and take a deep breath. "The man was willing to go to jail for the rest of his life to protect someone who was plotting his own murder," I utter in disbelief.

Kerri begins to tear up. I try to comfort her. This really is new territory for us.

"He is such a fool, but I still love him. You have to believe me, Jack, that I would never have intentionally hurt him. I just wanted to scare him a little bit, that's why I went along with it."

I do believe her. That doesn't change the fact that her behavior was reckless, abhorrent, and illegal. But I'm not in any position to be judging the actions of others.

The Notre Dame game is down to the final play and the bar is bubbling over with excitement.

"Thank God, Jack, that you got him out of here and away from her. She was planning to kill him, I just know it."

I just look blankly at her.

She reads my look. "What are you saying?"

I continue staring straight ahead, avoiding eye contact.

"No, Jack. We agreed that…"

I say nothing.

"Tell me that she is nowhere near him. Tell me, Jack! Tell me!"

A sudden burst of cheers fills Nellie's. Notre Dame has just scored the game-winning touchdown. Kerri and I stare straight at each other like we're on our own little island. My silence speaks volumes.

"Tell me!" she screams out at the top of her lungs. The crowd noise swallows up her scream and only I can hear the terror in her voice.

Chapter 109 (Epilogue)

The ferry chops over the crystal clear waters of the Hauraki Gulf. The wind whips my hair as I look out at the battalion of sailboats. I overhear a middle-aged couple mention that Auckland, New Zealand has the highest per capita boat ownership in the world.

I return to my copy of today's *Auckland Herald* that has turned damp in the mist. The wind makes it difficult for me to steady the paper. I look at the rippling front page and notice that I am once again front-page news, despite being halfway around the world. Fortunately, my eight months without a haircut helps conceal my identity from those around me.

It's July 24, the anniversary of the Laney Bang murder. To me it's just *Day 366.*

The article is a retrospective. A detailed analysis of the Trial of Max Q and its cataclysmic aftermath, including Anderson's now mythical escape, in which he has beaten great odds to elude a worldwide manhunt.

I don't need a newspaper to tell me the outcome. I lived every gory detail. My conclusion is that there were no winners, just degrees of losing. What all the pundits, prognosticators, and historians have missed, is that the trial was about Max Q and not about Drew Anderson. Perfection was on trial.

The verdict is that there is no perfect beginning, middle, or ending in this life. Life's not a destination, but a continuous roller coaster ride in which glimmers of hope are replaced by feelings of doom, and then if you're lucky, an angel shows up to revive the hope.

All we can do is just hang on to the people we love as long and hard as we can and LLF. By doing so, we open our hearts to their most vulnerable position, which is the only way that we can find a sense of peace and fulfillment when the ride is over. On the other hand, the cost of a ticket to ride the train of perfection is expensive. Your soul becomes an empty vessel going from port to port with no home.

There are no such philosophical musings in the *Auckland Herald*, so I discard it on the wet ground. I begin my own reflection. Sometimes when you near the end it's important to look back to see how it all began.

Following the Thanksgiving getaway, I shifted to autopilot. I was becoming more distant and numb by the day, but I continued to win cases with ease. I was able to hide it from most people, but not Ashley. My excuses of post holiday blues, or inability to adjust to such a mundane life following the adrenaline-filled trial, just didn't hold up with her. But she didn't push it.

I did no interviews and made no public comments on the case. The only time it came up was when I would get an impromptu visit from Agent Hawkins. He would imply that I knew more than I was letting on—if only he knew.

Then on a cold February day in Cooperstown, Agent Hawkins and

Sheriff Opp held a joint press conference. They had concluded the investigation, and their verdict was that Andy Kass was the "lone gunman" behind the Halloween explosions. According to Hawkins, Andy's motive was to make a name for himself at the expense of the system that tried to send him to prison, just as he had taken revenge on the school. So basically, they concluded that Drew Anderson just got really lucky and took advantage of the chaos and confusion from the explosions to escape. Hawkins was just as lucky, in that he didn't have to try to sell that cockamamie to a jury like a prosecutor would have to.

I'm convinced that Hawkins didn't believe it either, and likely succumbed to the pressure to bring resolution to the case. Yet he stood before the world and called the conclusion a "no brainer," and released handwritten notes by Andy Kass—confirmed by the FBI handwriting specialists—in which Andy confessed to the crime. This juror wasn't buying it, and would want to bring in an independent handwriting specialist to look at those letters.

Gifford Brown thought "no brainer" was a fitting description of both Opp and Hawkins, but he also doubted that the case against Andy Kass was. Gifford always likes to say, "The shoo-in doesn't always fit." Hawkins ended his press conference by guaranteeing the capture of Kass and Anderson for their separate crimes. I could have saved them the time and money. I knew his chances of finding them alive was less than zero percent. The only question that remained was—were they on the bottom of the Atlantic or the Pacific?

After the FBI announcement about Andy Kass, my once adoring fans turned on me. They now looked upon me as if I paroled Manson, for what the "experts" called the "gift plea deal" I gave Andy. I attempted to use it as an excuse to leave my position, but Gifford Brown refused my resignation.

Then on the first week of March, George Herman requested my presence at the Bullpen Theater. I thought it was about another case that I was prosecuting at the time, but he surprised me by handing me a folder relating to the Trial of Max Q.

"It's a John Doe they found in the East River, kid," George boomed in the empty theater. I viewed the contents within the folder. Staring at me was an autopsy photo of a boy who matched the helicopter license photo of Anthony Forge. The missing helicopter pilot who transported Marissa to and from the crime scene.

The photo inspired me to bring some semblance of resolution to the case. I returned home, searching for a connection. In the purgatory between late night and early morning, I grew hungry, and moved my operation to the Cirillos' kitchen table, seeking some leftover pizza. As I tossed another crumpled piece of yellow paper toward the garbage, my adrenaline rush ran out. I put my head down on the table, for what I told myself would only be a minute. The next thing I remember was a very pregnant Ashley tapping me on the shoulder the next morning.

"I didn't mean to look at your stuff, Jack, but I know that guy," she said, pointing to the before and after shots of Anthony Forge that were lying on the table.

"You do?"

"Yeah, a couple years ago I gave him flying lessons. I remember him because I couldn't believe how young he looked. He was really interested to learn how to fly a helicopter, so I sent him to someone I know who could help him."

Mac appeared behind Ashley. He reached his hands around his wife's pregnant waist and gave her a good morning kiss. Then he caught a glimpse of the photos. "I guess he finally pissed off the wrong people," he stated, matter of fact.

"You know him, too?"

"Any collector in the area knows of him. That's Tony Rivotti."

I stared sadly at the photo. They were the same guy.

Drew met Lansdale when his wife defended Lansdale's son, and they became close. So when Drew had financial troubles, his new friend Lansdale sent Rivotti. This allowed him to infiltrate his business. But I now understood that it wasn't the first business deal in which Drew was indebted to him. Lansdale had provided him the important service of removing Jordan

Kelly from Marissa's life, by taking custody of his son after the arrest, and banishing him to Saratoga.

This was still a better fate than the one Rivotti/Forge received. When Lansdale needed a pilot to escort Marissa to and from the scene of the crime, he once again called on the kid to do his dirty work. But as soon as Rivotti/Forge ceased to be useful, he was sent up the river. I saddened, thinking of Andy Kass.

My newfound inspiration led me to resign my position, and this time Gifford couldn't talk me out of it. Resolution was not to be found in Cooperstown.

Before leaving, I checked my mail one last time. Following the trial, it arrived in large bins instead of the traditional mailbox. They were usually filled with a combination of offers that ranged from the bizarre to the sublime, hate mail, and mug shots of Max Q that the mailer requested me to autograph—you can't make that stuff up. But this time I was drawn to a letter postmarked from Sierra Leone, Africa with no name or return address.

Jaaack!

And you thought we'd never speak again. I read that I am now the number one suspect. Remember to never believe anything you hear and only half of what you see. I'm already caught.

Your friend, Max, and his wife were so grateful for my help that they booted me out of the plane when we arrived at the first stop at some lake outside of Nova Scotia. Now some advice—if you are ever a suspect in a worldwide manhunt, don't try to cross the border without any identification. But luckily for me, it seems that the CIA was quite impressed with certain skills I demonstrated while creating my masterpiece, and overruled the FBI, who wanted to interrogate me and have me spill the beans on others involved in exchange for a shorter prison sentence. That is what the fabricated press conference was about with that fake confession they made me write. Everybody got what they wanted. Kind of a plea bargain between the FBI and CIA—who says they can't work with each other?

They had no clue who was really behind the escape. One day KL, the next day JL, sometimes it was you and Max's wife conspiring together. But I kept my promise, I didn't say a word to anybody. You can trust me. I'm playing for the good guys now. Well, I'm not sure the CIA is really the good guys, but you get my point. I'm not sure spy is what you had in mind, but I think I kept my promise.

Your friendly neighborhood CIA explosives expert,
KANDY ASS

PS. This note will self-destruct in five seconds. But just in case it doesn't, I would put it through a shredder.

Chapter 110 (Epilogue)

The news of Andy's demise being greatly exaggerated filled me with relief as I headed on my journey toward resolution. A journey that first took me where I always go when I need answers—Reyanne.

It was late March and spring had arrived early in Louisiana. I walked through the muddy cemetery under sharp early morning rays of sunshine. As I approached Reyanne's headstone, I noticed a woman. Her hair was a little grayer than the last time I saw her, but outside of that she seemed to be her normal quirky self. It was Reyanne's mother.

"Jack!" she called out. We embraced and I could tell she thought she'd never see me again.

She held a dark green garbage bag and had been unloading objects and mementos onto Reyanne's headstone like gifts under a Christmas tree.

"I try to surround her with the things she always loved. I put them in storage in the winter and then bring them out in the spring. And I also want to let her know about anything new going on." She holds up a picture of a small infant. "Reyanne's an aunt. Her sister Jocelyn had a baby girl the day after Christmas."

I smiled with mixed emotions, barely able to force out a choked-up, "Congratulations." I couldn't get the vision out of my head of Aunt Reyanne and Uncle Jack getting off a plane from New York, carrying more gifts than Santa could cram into his sleigh for their beloved niece. Instead, I was standing at Reyanne's grave, watching her mother decorate her headstone with memories she'd never get to have. Forget perfection, some days I'd settle for life being less cruel.

With another reach, her mother pulled out the *Newsweek* magazine that followed the trial last fall, featuring Shep and me on the cover. She stared long and hard at Shep, then proclaimed, "I know that Reyanne would approve."

I got the message as if Reyanne delivered it herself. Maybe she did.

"So you're really leaving," were Shep's words, as I packed boxes in my office last March, about to embark on my journey.

I looked up from the boxes and it hit me how much I missed her. Keeping with my vow to shield her from any possible fallout, I had put up the equivalent of the Great Wall of China between us. And since she had gained direct knowledge of what I did, I thought it was important to keep my distance during the winter. It's a painful penance, but I was not fooled by the FBI press conference; I know that a watchful eye is still cast in my direction.

"I heard you got an offer from EKG. Congratulations—it's your dream job."

"Thanks, but I am not taking it. I decided to take the position as Chief Assistant District Attorney of Otsego County instead," she stated proudly. "The job just opened up."

"I knew you always wanted my job," I replied with a surprised smile.

"Oh please, Jack—if I wanted your job I would have taken it a year ago."

"Maybe your dream was really to get EKG to offer you a job, so you could turn it down."

"It did feel good, I can't deny it."

"I'm sure you did great in the interview. Most people do better in their second interview."

She looked confused. "There was only one interview, Jack. Last week in the city."

I shrugged. "I must have been mistaken."

I couldn't figure out why Shep had traveled to New York that morning of the murder, via a helicopter. And she invoked her personal life amendment rights when I asked. I had recently learned that EKG had flown her in for a job interview under an assumed name, in order to not tip off her current employer. I'm sure glad she stayed—I wouldn't have survived the trial without her.

An awkward silence hung over the moment. Until I broke it, "When we were in Florida and you said a person came into your life and saved you, did you mean me?"

"Could you be any more narcissistic? If anything, I was *your* person."

"I thought you meant Reyanne was that person for me?"

"She was the love of your life, Jack. But I think you were the one who brought joy to her last days on the planet. I think you saved her, not the other way around."

Those were the last significant words said between us. Our final act was a brief hug and a moment that went by too fast.

But if things work out today, I should see her next week for the christening of Mac and Ashley's newborn son. Mac wanted to name him Derek Jeter Cirillo, after the famous baseball player, but Ashley outranked him. She named him Donovan Jackson Cirillo, but they call him DJ as a compromise.

I am to be the godfather, while Shep conveniently will be the godmother. I have only seen photos, but it doesn't get past me that every picture Ashley sends me has Shep in it, smiling. It's a great smile. She should do it more often.

Following my pilgrimage to visit Reyanne, my next stop was another cemetery, one state to the east. For some reason I expected a circus to be revolving around Laney Bang's gravesite, much like Jim Morrison's at Père Lachaise Cemetery in France. But as usual, Laney surprised me, and this time saddened me. She was buried in a small, unmarked grave hidden beneath overgrown grass on the outskirts of Pensacola, Florida.

I don't know what to make of Laney's life. She was a riddle of contradictions.

What I do know is that whatever angel was supposed to help her didn't get there in time. Her life reminded me of something I read once about the murder of John Lennon: *He beat the rock n' roll life. Beat the drugs. Beat the fame. He was the only guy to beat it all. That was the victory that was taken from a man who had an abundance of what everyone wants and wanted only what so many others take for granted. A home and a family—some still center of love —and one minute more.*

I never cast judgment on her like so many others did, and always kept an open mind, but in the end I failed to deliver the justice I promised. All I could do was sit before her headstone and apologize.

I had one more stop in Florida. I don't know why I had to see the dorm room where the whole thing began. Ironically, another golden boy quarterback—a limping Doug Leach—now occupied the room. I didn't find any resolution, just an attractive young woman in a towel, which made wonder if a pattern was repeating itself.

I ate lunch that day at the local Chili's where Shep and I had interviewed PE Albertson. While munching on a bacon cheeseburger, I saw it. *Wife of Former Seminole QB Re-marries*. It didn't make the front page, just a blurb buried toward the back of the newspaper.

Marissa Torres, the wife of former Seminole, Drew Anderson, married billionaire James Lansdale in a small ceremony on his yacht off the coast of Monaco. Ms. Torres was recently granted an annulment with the help of the

US Justice Department, citing her husband being a fugitive from justice as grounds. The couple plans to sail the world.

Chapter 111 (Epilogue)

The ferry arrives at Kawau Bay, the east-facing bay of Kawau Island. The trip was about an hour through the Hauraki Gulf. I had picked up the ferry at Sandpit Wharf, which was about a half-hour drive from the capital city of Auckland, where I flew in yesterday. The temperature is in the mid-fifties. The wind off the water is brisk, but the sky is a sharp aqua color, littered with white fluffy clouds.

There are no cars on the island, so I approach a teenager on what they call a motorized bicycle. Much like a Moped. Wadded cash is the international language.

"I need to go to Lansdale Estate," I tell him.

Kawau is a small island of only five thousand acres and a hundred permanent residents, so it wouldn't be a long trip.

"That was terrible news about Mr. Lansdale," my driver says.

"Yes, it was tragic. I'm going to pay my respects."

When I read in the Tallahassee paper of the nuptials, I began trying to track down the Lansdales, port to port. I thought I had them in my sights three weeks ago in Brazil, but that is when I received the news.

Traveling up the coast of South America from Brazil to Venezuela, and docked for the night, James Lansdale's yacht was boarded by pirates armed with automatic weapons. They killed James Lansdale, stole millions in jewels, but *luckily* Marissa was spared.

My driver drops me at the outskirts of Lansdale's property and I face a fierce-looking jungle he refers to as New Zealand bush. I adventure through the rugged terrain, which is full of exotic tree ferns and wildlife like wallabies, kookaburras, and peacocks.

I arrive at a jagged cliff, which Lansdale's mansion hangs over like it's suspended in air. The property extends back from the cliffside—flat ground that seems to go on for miles, scattered with horse barns. A large helicopter sits on a helipad.

I reach the edge of the cliff and look down to see a splendid beach that touches a calm body of water known as Lansdale Bay. I cautiously work my way down the rocks. When I hit the beach, I look out and see a dock that extends out into the bay.

I put my hand up to shade my eyes from the sun, which allows me to view the dark curls of her hair dancing in the cool wind.

She appears wonderstruck when I approach her. Somehow I doubt she is.

"Jack, I haven't seen you since…"

"Thanksgiving," I respond coldly.

She looks at me blankly, as if it has been washed from her memory bank—ironically, her last words to me that night were that she would "never forget this."

"Did you come with good news—have you been able to locate Drew?" she asks.

"What did you do to him, Marissa?"

She looks out at the endless sea. "I thought about Drew a lot when Jimmy and I were sailing around the world. I was sad that he chose to run away from the law. I thought he should stay and fight the charges like a man. We tried to find him, but I remember when I looked out at that mind-boggling huge ocean and thought that he could be anywhere, and nobody would ever find him."

I get the message. Drew's body will never be found. Max Q-gitive will be nothing more than a myth with occasional inaccurate sightings in a tabloid. Some people still claim to see Amelia Earhart.

"I forgot to offer my condolences for the death of your latest husband."

"It was a tragedy. But I cherish every minute that I got to spend with Jimmy in the winter of his life. He helped me through some hard times after my husband ran off."

I view the large estate—it's breathtaking. The stunning cliffs, the mansion on the hill, and a bay filled with sailboats. It's paradise on earth. "You seem to have landed on your feet."

"Jack, I don't think two people who know each other as intimately as we do, should beat around the bush. I have always been honest with you—I told you I would do anything within my powers to get my husband off, and I did. I told you I was the only one telling you the truth when it came to the facts of the case, and I was."

I hand her an enlarged copy of one of the helicopter security photos that features Marissa in a blonde wig. When we blew it up, you couldn't miss those green eyes. It wouldn't hold up in court, but I just want her to know this will never be over. If her perfection is security, then I don't want her to ever feel secure. "I thought you might want this to remember Jimmy by."

She barely looks at it before tossing it into the bay.

I let her know that not only am I aware of what she did, but I know what she plans to do.

She flashes a cocky smile. "I'm glad that you are beginning to see the whole field, Jack, but I'm afraid what you're seeing isn't adding up. If you check the pre-nup that I *forced* Jimmy to sign before we got married, you'll find that his fortune goes to his son, Jordan." She lets out laughter that echoes off the bay. "I guess Jimmy's accident would have looked bad if I didn't make him sign that. I would have had a lot of suspicious fingers pointing in my direction."

Suddenly I hear a voice coming from shore. I look to see Jordan Kelly, sitting on a magnificent horse and shouting, "Are you coming, baby?"

I can tell he doesn't recognize me from the distance, but he's probably jealous of any male near his beloved Marissa.

There is one more step for her to gain control of the palace. *Call me an optimist, Jack, but I really think perfection is possible.* Just like Drew,

Lansdale, and myself—Jordan Kelly has played into her hands again like a lovesick junkie. My guess is, when she marries Jordan there will be no strings attached. If he seeks one, she probably has proof that he was behind his father's death, or something along those lines. Then there will be no more things being taken from her. She'll be in control of her destiny.

"Just give me a few minutes, Jordan," she yells in his direction.

She gazes at him as he gallops down the beach on his horse. "I worry about that boy. He's always riding horses and sailing. It's so dangerous, I worry myself sick that he might have an accident one day."

Marissa looks at me, as if to say: *It doesn't matter what you know, Jack. There's nothing you can do about it, and you certainly can't prove it.*

She holds the look for a long moment, and then stares out into the boundless water. "Look at it, Jack—isn't it just perfect?"

Acknowledgments

Max Q is my second book published. The reason there is a second book is because of the great support of my first book Painless. Especially those readers in the beginning who shouted about it to anyone and everyone, when the only people reading it were my family members. I'm so very grateful to you!

Publishing a book is a team sport, and I am lucky to work with a great team. Charlotte Brown is the first line of defense on editing and helped turn a 300k word monstrosity into a page-turning thriller. I can't imagine working with someone who is more thorough, brutally honest, and cares about the book as much as I do. And her sense of humor kept me sane throughout the process.

I thank Carl Graves for a great cover that captures the essence of the story. Christina Wickson took my handwritten scribbles and turned them into a typed page. Curt Ciccone is the technology guru who does great work on formatting, website, and all things that are over my head. I'm also very appreciative of the proofing and insights of Jenny Carey.

And a special thanks to attorney Nicole Ludwig, who provided her legal expertise to help make the legal and trial scenes as real as fiction will allow.

Cooperstown is a great place and I hope I did it justice. I apologize for the bad cell phone service and obnoxious yachts anchored in the lake, but they were needed for the story! Anyone who hasn't been there should plan a trip (preferably in the summer), and if you're a baseball fan it's even better. I spent a "research weekend" in Cooperstown and surrounding areas with my two brothers that will always be the first thing I think of when I think of The Trials of Max Q.

Also want to send out a thank you to my star saleswomen (and my grandmothers) Harriet and Margaret, who made sure every person on the east coast read Painless. And of course, every book I'll ever write is dedicated to my parents – who always encouraged their children to pursue their dreams, and continue to do so.

Excerpt from The Truant Officer

Chapter One

Jorge DeRosa was half watching the monotonous security feed when she pulled up to the pump.

He observed the woman step out of the pricey SUV, unable to take his eyes off the black mini-dress that hugged every curve of her toned body. All of a sudden his job didn't seem so bad.

As the dark-haired beauty began to fill the tank, her body language suddenly turned flustered, and she headed in Jorge's direction.

She entered the food mart, her heeled shoes clicking loudly on the linoleum floor. He recognized her as Mexican, like himself, but she sure didn't look like she came from the same South Phoenix neighborhood as he did.

She approached the register. "My card didn't work in the pump. A message said to see the attendant—is that what you people are calling yourselves these days?"

When Jorge looked closer, he noticed something that surprised him. She *did* come from the same neighborhood as him. He hadn't seen her in at least ten years, but despite the fancy clothes and uppity tone, he was sure it was her. "Liliana?"

His words snapped her out of distraction. "Excuse me?"

"I'm Jorge DeRosa. Our families lived in the same apartment complex on South 40th Street. You went to school with my brother, Estaban."

She smiled at the remembrance, but it seemed fake. It was obvious to

Jorge that she wanted to leave her old life behind. He knew the feeling—the gang-infested section of South Phoenix was a hard place to escape, and once you got out there was no looking back. Jorge got as far as this night manager job in suburban Chandler, but by the looks of things, Liliana had gotten much further away.

As if reading his mind, she mentioned, "It's been a long time since someone called me Liliana."

She handed him her Visa card. He ran his fingers over the plastic as if he were reading Braille. The name had changed to *Lilly McLaughlin.*

She began impatiently tapping her manicured nails on the counter. People like Lilly McLaughlin always seemed to be in a hurry—perhaps by never stopping, they would never be forced to look back. Jorge didn't bother to ask her about her mother Rosie, or her six brothers. The youngest, Manuel, was killed in the crossfire of a gang war. The thought reminded Jorge of the dangers of present day.

He held up the credit card. "I'll run it in here. I'll watch you on the monitor."

Her eyes narrowed with suspicion, but his intentions were honorable. He pointed at the stack of Sunday editions of the *Arizona Republic* that were wedged between bags of Doritos and other assorted chips on the overstocked shelves. The headline screamed at them: *Abducted!*

It was the Valley's third such abduction in the last month, and the source was familiar to Jorge and Lilly. It was an initiation ritual in which a prospective gang member would travel to suburbia with the intent of kidnapping a woman from a public place. The first victim was an Arizona State University student who was doing some late night grocery shopping at a Safeway in Tempe. A forty-one-year-old mother of three was next, taken from a park while walking her dog, right here in Chandler. Then just yesterday, a thirty-year-old real estate agent was snatched from outside a home in Scottsdale. The good news was that the first two women were found alive. The bad news was that they were beaten and raped—their lives never to be the same—and were either unable or unwilling to identify their attackers.

The headline seemed to soften Lilly. By removing her shield of aloofness, she now more resembled the girl that Jorge remembered. The one who wore hand-me-down clothes and tirelessly helped teach English to the many immigrants in their neighborhood.

She smiled at him. This time it wasn't fake. It was a tough smile from the old neighborhood. The one where you never showed a hint of weakness. "That stuff doesn't faze us, does it, Jorge?

He smiled back at her, noticing that she dusted off the accent for his benefit. He was now talking to Liliana. "Because we're from South Phoenix?"

Her smile turned into a chuckle. "South Phoenix wasn't so tough. I teach high school English. Teenagers—now those monsters scare me."

She sauntered toward the door.

Jorge turned his attention back to the security feed, watching Liliana return to her vehicle. When she finished filling the SUV with gas, she took out her phone and appeared to be snapping a photo of herself. Jorge looked on curiously—whatever she was doing, she seemed to be enjoying herself. Now that they were homies once again, he would feel comfortable asking her about her theatrics when she returned to retrieve her credit card.

But the picture quickly changed. It happened so fast he couldn't respond. All he could do was watch in horror.

A dark figure in a ski mask rolled from underneath the car with knife in hand. By the shape and size, Jorge assumed it was a male. Lilly's scream pierced the night.

Even without the knife, the man looked like he could tear apart the petite woman, limb by limb. In a matter of seconds, he grabbed her by the neck, opened the back door of the vehicle, and threw her in like a piece of luggage. He ripped the nozzle from the tank. He then climbed behind the wheel.

The SUV tore out of the gas station as Jorge looked on in horror.

www.ingramcontent.com/pod-product-compliance
Lightning Source LLC
LaVergne TN
LVHW050922080826
845145LV00001B/170

* 9 7 8 0 9 8 5 4 2 8 7 0 9 *